KATE
CANTERBARY
USA TODAY BESTSELLING AUTHOR

This is a work of fiction. Names, characters, places, and incidents are the product of the author's imagination or are used fictitiously, and any resemblance to actual persons, living or dead, business establishments, events, or locales is entirely coincidental.

No part of this book was created, edited, or designed using AI.

Editing provided by Julia Ganis of Julia Edits.
Editing provided by Erica Russikoff of Erica Edits.
Proofreading provided by Marla Esposito of Proofing Style.
Proofreading provided by Isabella Bauer of Como la Flor.
Cover art and design created by Qamber Designs.

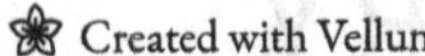

For the oldest sisters who are never, ever wrong about anything. Ever.

About Change of Heart

***Grey's Anatomy* meets a gender-swapped *Wedding Crashers* in this spicy rom-com about a one-night stand with The One, walking the tightrope of love and workplace ethics, and knowing which rules are worth breaking.**

Every summer, superstar surgeon Whitney Aldritch crashes weddings with her best friend. The first one was an accident though after a decade of dropping in uninvited, they're masters of their craft. They keep the rules simple and they never go to bed alone.

Then there's Henry Hazlette, best man and the best one-night stand of Whit's summer. She never imagined she'd see him again but now he's one of her new surgical residents—and *completely* off-limits.

Whitney has staked her reputation on leading the hospital's new ethics initiative. While Henry is under her supervision, they have to keep it professional. But it doesn't help that she can't turn around without running face-first into his offensively broad chest or rubbing up against him in crammed elevators. Also not helping:

the way he smiles at her like he can hear her every not-safe-for-work thought.

All they have to do is survive this residency—and the accidental tarot card readings that hit too close to home, a few uninvited houseguests, and the hospital's hyperactive rumor mill—but only if they're prepared to bend some rules as the feelings go from *just for tonight* to *get it out of our systems* to *mine*.

Content Notes: Parental estrangement and abandonment; parental divorce; chronic illness (secondary character); brief mention of suicide (in the past, not detailed, not a central character); mention of infidelity (secondary characters); frequent medical, hospital, and surgical discussion (no blood, no gore); discussion of donor organ retrieval and organ transplant surgeries (no blood, no gore); brief discussion of mountain rescue situations (not detailed); discussion of workplace bullying (off-page).

One
Whitney

The Good Girl's Guide to Crashing Weddings,
Rule Number Six:
The bridal party is always off-limits.

June

I PAUSED, THE EYELINER POISED OVER MY LID, AND blinked at my reflection in the mirror. "I don't think I know who I am anymore."

I took in the loose waves, subtle makeup, and flowy dress. It was all mine yet I didn't recognize any of it.

"You're 'Olivia Whitney.'" The shout came from the adjoining room before Meri Mercer appeared in the doorway, her attention fixed on clasping her bracelet. "I'm 'Emma Meriweather.' Remember? We nailed down the backstory this morning."

I gave myself an up-and-down glance in the mirror. This

morning was a faint, foggy memory thanks to last night's tequila shots and dancing until two a.m. My body still hadn't fully recovered from any part of that.

Hello, thirty-five. You're not a lot of fun.

"We talked about this. We're teachers." Meri dropped her hands to her hips. "Because no one ever asks a teacher to diagnose the rash on their ass in the middle of cocktail hour."

I glanced down at the eyeliner pen. "That is true."

"The only time I want to see someone drop their pants in front of me tonight is right before they rail me with their giant dong. Speaking of which, I went downstairs and did some reconnaissance while you were daydreaming in the shower, and I'm confident saying that tonight we will be having our beefcake and eating it too. I think we missed the turn for the wedding and ended up at a sausage convention, but I'm not mad about it."

I turned back to the mirror to finish my lids. "Okay, great."

She cocked her head. "Are you good?"

I caught her eye in the mirror. "What? Me? Yeah. Of course. Great. Very pleased to hear about both the beefcake and sausage."

I'd never admit it to Meri though I was exhausted. We were seventeen days, nine different hotels, and seven crashed weddings into our three-week summer getaway, a tradition we'd started back in med school. Our annual girls' trip had survived residencies and fellowships on opposite sides of the country, insane schedules where we could barely pull together a long weekend, and the golden shackles of intern poverty.

For the past decade, these vacations had been the best parts of my year and I knew it was the same for Meri.

It was the one time when there were no rules and we didn't have to be all the things we'd built ourselves into. We didn't have to be professional or mature or anything like the women we were the rest of the year. We could let go of our entire worlds and be anyone from anywhere.

And we could spend the night with whoever we wanted.

Which we did. *A lot*.

As was often the case with the best things, crashing the first wedding had been an accident. We'd agonized over it after the fact. Then we sent a gift from the registry and did it again. The ethics were absolutely questionable though we went to great pains to ensure we did no harm. If anything, the weddings we crashed were better because we'd been there. Whether it was waking up a sleepy table or defusing a bridesmaid fight in the bathroom, Heimliching and EpiPenning whenever the moment called for it or talking someone's misguided boyfriend out of proposing in the middle of the toasts, we were a force of good. Chaotic good, but that had to count for something. And we gave the best—albeit anonymous—gifts. The professional food processors and the stand mixers, the high-end vacuums and the trendy luggage.

But make no mistake about it, peak summer season wedding crashing was not for the faint of heart. I had several blisters in various states of awful from dancing my ass off in ridiculous shoes, my throat was sore, and I'd burned the back of my ear on the curling iron. On top of that, I'd been mildly—or more than mildly—hungover for so long that wearing sunglasses indoors was part of my personality now.

And I couldn't keep track of my backstory.

"Are you sure you're okay for this? The Belwood-Ballicanta wedding is the Super Bowl of our summer. It's the big one. I need you solid. Solid for all this sausage." Meri was a one-woman hype squad on a normal day, but she turned into a Texas high school football coach one score away from clinching a spot at the state finals when it came to crashing weddings. She traveled with enough medical supplies to pop out my appendix in the morning and march me onto the dance floor the same evening. "By my estimation, we'll be literally drowning in dick so you're going to need your wits about you."

I frowned at her in the mirror. "Do I really want to *drown* in dick?"

"I do." Meri smoothed a hand down the length of her dress and shrugged. "I just want to lie there while the beefcake buffet comes to me. Or have them wheeled over on a cart like dim sum."

"You're going to need to ice your vagine again if you do, and it's your turn to drive tomorrow."

"I can do that and drive at the same time!" She fluttered her hands like I was testing her patience. "If anyone needs dim sum dick, it's you. All you did was dance last night."

I tossed the eyeliner back into my makeup bag. "You say that like there's a moral failure in not bringing a guy back to my room. I had fun last night."

"Yes, I heard you snoring through the walls."

"Are you sure that wasn't the echo of your headboard?"

She belted out a laugh and shook her head. "You know how it goes. The shorter ones always have something to prove"—she pounded a fist against her palm—"and they don't stop until they prove it three or four times."

I swallowed a laugh. "How are you able to walk today?"

"NSAIDs and benzocaine spray. Why? Do you need some?"

"I'm good." I motioned to her floor-length navy blue gown. "I thought you said you weren't bringing the strikeout dress this year."

"We are not calling it the strikeout dress." She shifted to face herself in the mirror and futzed with her ribbon-tied shoulder straps. "I've only worn it three times. That's hardly an adequate sample size to draw conclusions."

"Last summer, you said that dress was a clam-jamming chastity belt and you swore you were selling it to someone who deserved that kind of curse."

"Well, I have a new bra and I think it's safe to say it's working miracles." She cupped her breasts and gave them a jiggle. "These are no longer basic boobs. These are cautionary-tale tits."

Not for the first time in our friendship, I gave her cleavage a meaningful glance. Meri was beautiful. Short, curvy, redheaded, and she had a personality that could always find its light. She could suck the oxygen from a room with one smile. "Here's a cautionary tale for you. If you start bouncing around on the dance floor, one of those things is going to bust out and break your nose."

She circled me, eyeing my dress. "And what about you, Miss Olivia Sexyskirts? Where did this thing come from and why did it make you forget the number one rule of wedding crashing—never outshine the bride or her maids?"

"I am not outshining the bride." I glanced down at my peachy-pink dress. It had been a splurge, and a misguided one at that seeing as it had required tailoring and weapons-grade shapewear to fit my size fourteen ass. I'd justified it all by telling myself I had tons of places to wear a flowy gown with a hand-ruched sweetheart neckline and the most gorgeous chiffon flowers climbing over my shoulders and trailing down my back like a vine of pale morning glories. What workaholic surgeon living in the ever so temperate climate of Boston, Massachusetts didn't need that exact thing in her closet?

"Let's hope not." Meri headed toward the balcony doors, saying, "We're friends of the bride's family on her father's side. He's one of those guys who knows the entire world and hasn't been stingy with the invites. I overheard someone in the elevator saying he invited everyone who works for him and loads of business associates. He's the reason this shindig is rounding out at nearly six hundred guests. Apparently they reserved rooms on three whole floors of this place."

I joined her on the balcony, watching while the hotel crew put the finishing touches on the outdoor ceremony space. Hundreds of white chairs fanned out around a raised platform with the shimmering summer blue of Lake Tahoe and majestic ponderosa pines as the backdrop. When it was time for the bride to walk down the aisle at five thirty this evening, the sun was going to hit her like a halo.

Brilliant planning, I had to admit.

"We live in the Bay Area. I teach middle school science and the kids are a nightmare, but I love them," she continued. "If we get stuck for any reason, talk about University of Nevada, Reno football. It seems like both families have a lot of alums and the father of the bride is a big fan of the Wolf Pack. He has high hopes that they slaughter Boise State this year."

"Love that for him."

Meri looped her arm around my shoulders. "Are you sure you're good? We can swaddle up in robes, eat room service, and then diagnose injuries in action movies if you want. That's always an option, Whit."

My best friend was *the* best friend in the world. There was no one better, of that I was certain. "We look too good to miss this. Seriously, it would be a disservice to this wedding for us to sit it out. We're going to dance until we kill the nerves in our feet and we're going to drink like we're twenty-five, and we're going to have the best time of anyone at this wedding. Plus, I'm dying to see the bride's dress and I'm sure the food is going to be insane." I motioned between us. "Most importantly, we need to break the curse on this dress."

With a nod, she said, "We saved the best for last this year. This is going to be a good one. I can feel it."

"Yeah," I said, blowing out a breath. "Me too."

As a rule, we only crashed big weddings. It was easier to blend in when there were at least three hundred guests in attendance. We'd added that to our rule book several years ago after an awkward situation in South Carolina that nearly ended in us being escorted off the property.

This wedding wasn't big. It was *massive*. Hell, it wasn't even a wedding, it was a festival with the bride and groom headlining the main stage. Sixteen attendants on each side, seven flower girls, five ring bearers, a four-minute solo from the harp player, and—so far—three dramatic recitations of love poems, songs, and movie monologues from various friends and family.

We were forty-five minutes in and we hadn't even gotten to the vows yet.

"What's happening next?" Meri flipped through her program. "I honestly don't think there are any other sonnets to read at this point."

"'A special blessing from Luisa Ballicanta,'" I read. "The groom's aunt."

Meri wiggled in her seat. "I cannot wait to hear this," she whispered as an older woman wearing a long silver dress that was more than a little witchy stepped up to the microphone. It was the sort of frock sold only in museum shop catalogs. "I love when they let the wacky aunts talk. This will either be straight-up sex advice, astrology, or a soup recipe that starts out as a metaphor but—surprise—is legit soup."

I squeezed her forearm. "Or all three."

Aunt Luisa opened a thick journal—a spell book, probably—and adjusted her glasses. "When Mason and Florrie announced their betrothal, I knew I had to conduct a study of their star charts—"

Meri pressed her fingers to her mouth, whispering, "Oh my god, I want her to adopt me."

"Serious question," I said as Aunt Luisa jumped into the couple's rising signs, "do you think she'd study my star chart?"

"Keep the gin flowing and she'll be your fairy godmother."

"Too mainstream. I'm guessing sambuca or—" My gaze settled on the best man as he turned his back, a fist pressed to his lips as his shoulders heaved. "Please tell me he's not going to vomit."

"As if we needed more proof that grooms shouldn't give flasks of whiskey as gifts to their guys," Meri said under her breath. "Let's pray he excuses himself instead of interrupting this precious woman's astrological analysis. I need to hear this. Or climb into her pocket and stay there forever, either one."

He steadied himself on the shoulder of the groomsman beside him and returned his attention to Aunt Luisa. He pulled a sober expression and clasped his hands in front of him like nothing had happened.

"As a slow and sensual Taurus, Mason always knows what he wants," Aunt Luisa continued. "Where we see Florrie's sun sextiling his Venus, it's clear she shares his desires. They have a deep, luscious well of sexual compatibility that will hydrate them for years to come."

"Did you hear that?" Meri asked, leaning into my shoulder. "The well is deep and *luscious.*"

"It doesn't matter how deep it is if it isn't luscious," I murmured. "And hydrating."

"Florrie's Pisces energy brings dreamy magic and passionate emotion to this union," Aunt Luisa went on. "There will be fireworks, especially where her Venus trines his Chiron, but the key is to express your love without inhibition. Be unafraid to stand before each other, stripped of material goods and mindset blocks, and speak the honest words of love."

The best man snorted. I was certain it was a snort because I was guilty of making the exact sound in the most inappropriate moments and I knew it couldn't be explained away as a cough or a hiccup or anything less offensive than a laugh birthed from my nose.

"What's going on with that one?" Meri asked.

"I don't think," I started, blinking in disbelief as he violently rolled his eyes when Aunt Luisa moved on to Florrie's sun opposing Mason's Uranus, "he's a believer."

He clapped a hand over his mouth and pounded a fist against his chest like he had a tickle in his throat, but I knew better. The other six hundred people here knew it too.

"Sorry." He pointed at the ponderosas when Luisa glanced in his direction. "Allergies. So sorry. Please continue."

"This might be a first," Meri said.

I hummed in agreement and turned my attention back to Aunt Luisa, but the second she said the words "a quincunx of Florrie's Mars and Mason's Neptune," my eyes were on the best man. He had an arm banded around his torso and a hand over his mouth like that level of physical restraint was necessary to keep him from dissolving into a fit of giggles.

"When I finished reviewing Florrie and Mason's charts, I decided to pull three tarot cards for them." She held up one card, saying, "The first card that presented itself to me was The Five of Pentacles." She wagged it at the happy couple. "Pay attention to each other. Don't let things slip through the cracks. Next, The Ten of Coins. This tells me you're going in the right direction, but the path won't be a straight one. Focus on this day and the road ahead of you. Don't fixate on the end."

Aunt Luisa shuffled through her pages and cards for a moment and I found myself swinging a glance between her and the best man. He swayed from side to side, though it was slight. I wouldn't have noticed if I hadn't been observing him closely—and if all the other guys weren't standing ramrod like this was some kind of military presentation.

"The cards have a way of sneaking up and surprising me, and this final card did exactly that," Aunt Luisa said. "I had to sit with this card for a long time to understand what it was saying to me."

Despite the best man's efforts at containing himself, a loud, infectious laugh barked out of him and a low rumble of amusement worked its way through the guests. The groomsman beside him dropped both hands to his mountain range shoulders and gave him a hard shake. It was the kind of bro-ish gesture that looked friendly enough and probably hurt like hell.

To her credit, Aunt Luisa didn't seem to give a fuck. I *loved* her. "The Five of Swords usually speaks of conflict and defeat. It speaks of loss, failure, walking away. But I don't think that's what it's saying to Mason and Florrie. I think it's telling them to surrender their need for control on this altar and embrace the wild, unpredictable path ahead. Don't get lost in the maps you've drawn for yourselves. Don't cling so hard to your idea of the path that you wring the life out of it—and each other."

"Well," Meri said, "that took a spicy turn."

"There are many ways to read the stars and cards. But the way I see it," Aunt Luisa said, "there will be obstacles and challenges aplenty, but their bond is strong and their passion burns white-hot. Florrie and Mason are uniquely aligned for a union of love and good fortune."

I rolled my eyes at the last part.

I adored weddings. I wanted to soak in all the weird, wonderful bits of tradition and custom that came along with them until my fingers were pruned and pale. But there was always a moment when the soapy, iridescent glee of it all burst, and reality—the ugly truth of it all—wedged itself between my ribs until I couldn't breathe without acknowledging that love wasn't real. Not the stars-aligned, now-and-forever, soul-recognition kind of love that we tried to glimpse at weddings.

Even if romantic love did exist, it didn't last. No one could convince me otherwise.

I tucked my hair over my ear and forced a neutral expression as I returned my gaze to the altar only to find the best man staring at me.

Of course he wasn't looking at *me*. There were literally hundreds of people here. He was probably looking at any of the fifty people in my general vicinity. Since I enjoyed being right and liked to prove my own points, I hooked a glance over my shoulder as subtly as I could manage. The gentleman behind me was holding his phone sideways and watching something on the screen. Two other men nearby leaned forward to join the viewing party. Beside me, Meri was busy studying the program. In front of us, a string of twentysomething women passed a small bottle of Fireball down the row while picking apart the bridesmaids' dresses. Over my other shoulder, a woman with a hat that seemed to feature a bird's nest was conked out and snoring softly while the man with her yanked at his bow tie.

I glanced back to the best man and shook my head because no, there was no way that look had anything to do with me. He'd been focused on any one of these curious cases. Not me.

But then he shot a glance toward Aunt Luisa and gave a subtle eye roll.

Shit. Okay, then. Maybe he had noticed me.

He arched a brow and the corner of his mouth quirked up, and it felt like we were all alone here with the gently setting sun, the towering trees, the clear June sky.

I glanced away and brushed a hand over the chiffon flowers on my shoulder. When I returned my gaze to the altar, he'd shifted his attention toward the lake.

Aunt Luisa offered some final remarks, and when she returned to her seat the relieved exhale that shook out of the best man had me holding back a giggle of my own.

The officiant stepped up to the microphone, saying, "Florrie and Mason chose to write their own vows."

"This is going to be epic," Meri said, leaning forward. "Which one is going to cry first? I'm calling groom. He looks like a teddy bear."

Florrie glanced down at her notecards before beaming up at her groom. "Mason, I—"

She choked out a pretty sob.

"And there we have it," I said.

"Mason, I knew the minute I met you that you'd be my forever," she said through tears.

Mason knuckled a tear from his cheek and Meri nudged me with her elbow. "Like I said."

There was a comment on the tip of my tongue, but the best

man stole my attention once again. He looked like he was in real danger of choking to death on his own tongue this time.

"Okay, what is his story?" Meri asked. "Run-of-the-mill jackass or—"

"Conscientious objector," I said. "He's here for his buddy, but hates everything so hard that he's slaphappy about it."

"I don't want the real answer," she whined. "I want to believe he's the mastermind behind some prank to release fifty piglets down the aisle right before they say 'I do' or he accidentally ate an entire bag of shrooms for lunch."

I watched as he sucked in a breath and stared up at the sky for a moment, like he required the aid of divine forces to survive this ceremony. The sunlight smiled on him, setting fire to the gold and auburn highlights in his dark chestnut hair.

He was on the tall side and broad in a way that suggested he did something that risked life and limb in his spare time, like playing rugby or competing in lumberjack games. I'd bet he wore a lot of flannel and had a favorite pair of boots. His shoulders were like the ridgeline of the Rocky Mountains, but I was guessing his thighs were where the real trouble started. They had to be thick and powerful, the kind that would pin you to the bed and not let up until he was good and done.

I cleared my throat. "That tux does nice things for him."

"Don't," Meri replied quickly. "Rule number six. The bridal party is off-limits."

"Do not quote the rules to me, Meriweather. I was there when they were written."

"Especially a best man," she said. "No good could come of that."

"He's fun to look at," I said. "It's a nice tux. That's all."

"I can agree with you on those points and still remind you that noticing the way the tux fits is too close to the danger zone for my comfort. The last thing I want is to be perp-walked out of this place because you threw out the rule book for a dude who can't keep his shit together for ten consecutive minutes. This dress and this bra are working too hard for it to end that way."

I nodded as Mason started in on his vows, but I didn't listen because the best man was staring in this direction again and I had no doubt whether his attention was on me.

Two

Whitney

Rule Number Twenty-One:
Play the whole field.

The cocktail hour featured three signature drinks, a mile of cheese and charcuterie, and an alt-rock tribute band that was not at all bad. We lingered on the stone patio, hammering out our game plan for the evening while the wedding party gathered for photos near the lake. I loved this part. I loved seeing all the poses and pairings and the way the families meshed.

Or didn't.

There was always an in-law who looked like they had a mouth full of mayonnaise and couldn't possibly stop to listen to the photographer's instructions. There was always one bridesmaid deeply committed to fluffing the train or holding the veil at the perfect angle to get that windswept look and there was always a groomsman playing catch with a pinecone.

I wished those moments made it into the photo album. I liked them so much more than the stiff lineup of family and friends.

Meri had a few gentlemen on her watch list tonight, as was her usual approach. I didn't share her ability to eagle-eye and rank prospects. My preference was to withhold judgment until the dancing started. There was something about dance floors at weddings that revealed everything you'd ever need to know about physical chemistry. Plus everyone was properly liquor-lubricated at that point and I'd met my daily cake requirement, which made everything better.

We waited until the last minute to select seats. This made it easier to spot the tables with openings and reassess our plans if needed. Over the years, we'd determined that all weddings had between two and five percent absenteeism. We'd yet to drop in on a wedding with fewer than six empty seats.

Yes, we were also data wonks. Brains, beauty, the balls to crash weddings—we had it all.

This wedding, however, was enormous even by *Titanic* standards and there were at least twenty-five place cards waiting to be collected when we finally entered the opulent tent.

We chose a table toward the back corner with a bunch of mismatched people who didn't appear to know each other—the strays and leftovers. Every party had them. Usually good, fun people who were at least a little surprised that they were invited and never asked too many questions of their tablemates.

Best seat in the whole house.

"Not a penny spared," Meri said, nudging my arm as she tipped her chin toward the stage. The entire ten-piece band was decked out in purple velvet suits to match the thousands of plum-throated calla lilies spilling from the centerpieces and hanging from floral chandeliers around the tent. "Not a single one."

"What would it take for you to spend this kind of money on a party?"

"Let's start with some student loan forgiveness," she said. "Add in some parents with a couple hundred grand they want to blow on one day. Oh, and a man I tolerate and trust for more than a night. That might do it."

The bandleader kicked off "About Damn Time" as the bridal party arrived, dancing into the tent in pairs. It was clear they'd choreographed and thoroughly rehearsed this though it was also clear that rhythm had not been equally distributed, which made this even more sensational. There was nothing better than a groomsman with the grace of a pickle jar while the bridesmaid with him had clearly dedicated a decade of her life to ballet.

My gaze immediately snagged on the best man, who—I had to bite my bottom lip to hold back a grin as I realized this—knew *exactly* how to move that tall, broad body. The most surprising part was that he was having fun doing it. He wasn't rolling his eyes or going through the motions. He was into it *and* compensating his ass off as the maid of honor was at least seven months pregnant and looked like she'd commit some light treason to get out of those heels and that mermaid-style dress.

I tapped my glass against Meri's. "What are the odds you deliver that baby tonight? What would you say? Twenty-nine? Thirty weeks? You can eyeball these things better than I can. She's carrying *low*."

"Bite your fucking tongue." She gave a rueful shake of her head. "Sit down, sister," she muttered toward the maid of honor. "Get those feet up. Drink some water. Hold that kid in until tomorrow. I beg of you." She knocked back the rest of her lavender lemon drop. "I'm really hoping there's another couple of docs in this house."

I raised my glass. "Let us pray."

The bride and groom entered from opposite ends of the tent as the band kicked off an extra-peppy rendition of "Marry You."

"She changed," Meri said, her gaze on Florrie. "I knew she would."

The new dress was very fun and very sexy with a skirt made for twirling. I wanted one for myself. Just to wear around the house. I loved a good twirl. "Completely gorgeous."

"This is adorable," Meri said as the happy couple danced through the tables toward each other. "God. They are so damn cute. I hope these two make it."

I nodded as Florrie and Mason launched into choreography that must've required months of prep. They really were cute. I could almost delude myself into believing they could be the real deal. The one in a million that didn't end up broken and miserable and irrevocably damaged from letting themselves believe they could ever truly trust anyone.

They danced another two songs before ending in a dramatic dip that spoke volumes about Florrie's flexibility. The crowd erupted into cheers and applause when Mason pulled her up into his arms and kissed her.

"Get it, girl," Meri hollered. To me, she added, "I like these kids. I'm happy we're here to celebrate with them."

Meri would sooner fight me than admit it, but she was as hopeless as any romantic could ever be. She loved love in all its beastly and beautiful shapes, even if she'd long since amputated the part of her that could receive such things. The wound had never quite healed, but she wouldn't admit to that either. It was like she preferred the scar tissue and phantom limb pain to the risk of losing herself again.

"Me too," I said. "And I'm happy I'm here with you."

As a fleet of servers fanned out with the first course, Florrie's father crossed the dance floor to hug his daughter and shake his son-in-law's hand. He was a cartoonishly big guy, his booming voice almost enough to reach every corner of this tent without a microphone.

In his toast, he spoke of his daughter's vivacious spirit and her many achievements, and not a single word about Mason. "Please raise your glasses," he said, "to my daughter's happiness. May it fill all of her days."

Meri and I exchanged a glance as we drank. "Fathers of the bride," I said. "Surprisingly fluent in the language of passive-aggressiva."

As we dug into the first dish, Meri bonded with the guy beside her over a shared distaste for pomegranate seeds. They'd picked a small mountain of them out of their salads and were now bemoaning apple cider vinegar, or something like that.

Since they were busy hating things, and the couple on my other side had their hands full itemizing all the ways *their* daughter's wedding was better, I occupied myself with people-watching. It wasn't my intent to immediately catch sight of the best man as he stood at the head of a long table near the dance floor, one knee dropped onto a seat and his huge hands flying as he told a story.

He was expressive in a way that engulfed his whole body. Energy and emotion rolled off him in waves, and even from here I could tell he had the entire table hanging on his every word. I was half convinced I could walk right up to him and wring enough of that charisma out of his bow tie to fill a champagne flute. It was just that thick.

"Have you heard about the dead bodies in the lake?"

I whirled around to blink at the man beside Meri. "I'm sorry. *What* are we talking about now?"

Meri waved me off, saying, "No. Tell me everything."

His brown eyes twinkled behind wire-rimmed glasses. "The water is very cold and very deep, and anyone who goes missing out there—for whatever reason—is often extremely well-preserved," he said, and I had some big questions about the enthusiasm in his tone. "But the crazy part is that these bodies don't usually sink to the bottom like you'd expect. Atmospheric pressure competes with the pressure of the water's depth to keep these bodies suspended in a band around three to four hundred feet below the surface. They call it the Tahoe Dance Floor."

As I said, "*Oh my god*," Meri said, "That's the most bizarrely morbid story I've ever heard at a wedding."

The guy gave a goofy little wiggle of his shoulders like he was tickled by this fact. That was when I realized he was not Meri's usual type. Though he was dressed in a dark suit that was mostly well-tailored, he had an academic scruffiness to him that brought to mind tweed blazers and khaki pants forever dotted with ink stains. His hair was floppy-curly and his short beard would've appreciated a more aggressive approach to its maintenance. He was the kind of guy who, at first glance, seemed a good ten or fifteen years older than us, but upon closer inspection probably landed closer to forty. He seemed kind, if not a bit odd, and the gaze he leveled at Meri was much too fond for anything he'd get in return.

If she'd noticed this, she didn't care because she shifted closer to him, asking, "So, are we talking accidents or is there an organized crime element here?"

He leaned in, his elbow sliding against her forearm and his eyes bright. I could almost hear his heart rate kick up at her interest. "There are stories about both that will blow your mind."

I tried to give her the kind of look that would ask *what the hell are you doing to this sweet, nerdy, inevitably clingy guy?* but she was already too entranced to notice.

She was determined to break the curse of that dress.

Right after the second course dishes were cleared, the best man stepped onto the dance floor, microphone in hand. I leaned back in my chair, crossed my legs. I knew this was going to amuse the hell out of me.

"Hello, everyone," he started, that sunshine-in-the-morning smile beaming across the tent. "I'm Henry. I'm the best man though I'll argue that title should go to Mason because he's the best of all of us. I'm just lucky he lets me tag along."

"It's not that easy to get rid of you," Mason shouted, giving rise to a chorus of chuckles from the crowd.

"Is that why you're always leaving me on the side of the road all these years?" Henry ran a hand through his dark hair as he blew out a breath. "I thought you were teaching me some kind of advanced survival skills. Hide-and-seek on steroids. Wow. I'm reevaluating everything now."

"You're supposed to be the smart one," Mason teased. "I assumed you knew."

Henry scratched the back of his neck. "Right, and I'm supposed to say nice things about you now. Awesome. Thanks for the heads up, man."

My cheek twitched and I was stunned to realize I was smiling.

"Personal revelations about my alleged best friend aside, we are here tonight at this"—he gestured to the flowers hanging from the tent and the velvet-swaddled band—"cosplay carnival of conspicuous consumption to celebrate Florrie and Mason."

A few of the bridesmaids glanced to each other, their brows furrowed and their faces pulled into taut smiles as if they couldn't decide whether to laugh. I wasn't one hundred percent certain, but it seemed like the father of the bride was cracking his knuckles.

"And what a beautiful day to celebrate these crazy kids," Henry went on as he strolled across the dance floor. "It doesn't get much better than this. I mean, look at all of this. This is...it's really something."

He waved a hand at the seven-tier cake and the accompanying groom's cake in the shape of some kind of dog. I loved cake and I especially loved the whimsy of groom's cakes, but I always had mixed feelings about eating a slice of the family pet. It didn't land quite right for me. Even worse when it was red velvet.

"It's important to remember the good times," Henry continued, his knuckles scraping over his closely trimmed beard. "Nights like this, they're special."

"Please tell me you don't intend to wing this entire speech," I whispered.

That was exactly what he did. He meandered through an assortment of his favorite memories with Mason, all of which started with "Remember the time we almost got arrested?" or "How about that time we got drunk and lost in the woods?" before hitting a punch line or landing on a sentimental note.

But as someone who'd heard a whole bunch of best man speeches in the past few weeks plus the past ten years, it was clear he hadn't thought out this toast or had any particular throughline in mind. He rambled, dropping platitudes and saying nothing, but he was so damn magnetic while doing it that no one seemed to mind. And he couldn't seem to keep his hands out of that thick, wavy hair.

Until he said, "And you know, nothing lasts forever so you really need to squeeze all the juice out of this while you can. Who knows? The next go-round probably won't have all these bells and whistles."

Six hundred people fell silent at once and that sound sliced like a long, brutal paper cut. Florrie's father shot to his feet while Mason sighed up at the flower chandeliers. One of the grandmothers asked, "What did he say? What's happening? A merry-go-round? Here, at the wedding?" Florrie laughed, loud and fake, while squeezing her husband's hand. A beat passed before the maid of honor shuffled across the dance floor, her shoes long discarded and an arm cradling her pregnant belly.

"Someone get her a chair," I said under my breath.

"Can someone get a chair for Miah?" Henry bent down, speaking directly to her belly, "I'm warning you that we have a strict policy against wedding crashers."

A wry laugh rattled in my throat.

She wrenched the microphone away from him. "Henry's right, nothing lasts forever, but it's enough to be here tonight, seeing the love shared by my little sister and her precious new husband, to make me believe in eternity. I'm so happy we get to shower you in all our love and affection and hope for your future." She slapped Henry's arm for him to raise his glass. "Congrats, you two. We can't wait to see the forever you create together and I know that you'll build the most amazing life for all your years to come. To all your bells and whistles."

"Oh, she's smooth," I said, shifting toward Meri. "But that has to be one of the top five worst best man speeches I've ever heard."

Meri's seat was empty. The nerdy guy's too.

A small hum shook out of me. *Good for her.* I wanted her to have fun tonight, even if the "let's talk about lake corpses" guy wasn't who I would've bet on from the start.

I'd hear all about it tomorrow.

I always did.

There were a few more speeches before the father-daughter dance, which was another one of my favorite wedding rituals. There was something beautiful and foreign about it to me. Like watching a film in another language. I could appreciate it and admire it, but I'd never understand.

Once the groom and his mother started their turn around the dance floor, I excused myself to the dessert buffet. I didn't even think about dancing until after I'd assessed the entire dessert situation and sampled enough of everything to make me deeply regret shoehorning myself into shapewear.

Fortunately for me, the buffet was as excessive as everything else at this wedding. I'd nearly filled a plate when I heard a familiar voice ask, "What do you recommend?"

I glanced up to find the best man on the other side of the table, his bow tie loose and his hands in his pockets.

I allowed myself a moment to take in all the great and wonderful burliness of him. The guy definitely worked with wood. Lumberjack, forest service, artisanal furniture. Something like that. He was probably pine-scented too. It would just figure.

I licked a bit of frosting from my thumb. "What do you like?"

His gaze stayed on my face, but I could feel him taking in all of me, swallowing me up whole. "Everything."

"Oh, really?" I selected a mini cupcake from a three-tiered tray and ate it while I studied the table. Cookie dough in the middle. Fantastic. "Affogato? Tres leches? Fruit flan?" I motioned to the shot glasses and espresso cups containing each confection. "Or am I right in thinking you're a little more simple? Basic, perhaps? Eclairs, cheesecake, lemon meringue?"

He laughed. "I'm gonna pretend you didn't just call me basic." Tipping his chin toward my plate, he asked, "What do you have?"

If Meri was here, she'd fake an emergency and yank me away from him. She took the rules *that* seriously. She was going to murder me tomorrow. I'd let her.

And yet I couldn't stop myself from saying, "Everything."

His face broke into the most glorious smile, like that was the exact response he'd secretly wanted and now he could die happy. "Then you've chosen well."

"That toast was a train wreck," I said, grabbing another cupcake. This one had chocolate ganache. Never made it to my plate. I ate it in two bites.

He ran a finger along the inside of his collar. It was open at the throat. The muscles there were a whole damn delight. I was overcome with an absurd desire to lick him. With a quick shake of his head, he said, "Yeah. It was. Clearly, it's been a tough night for me. Am I going to have to fight you for a cupcake on top of everything else I've been through?"

I reached for a red velvet. "Probably not."

"Are you sure? You seem a little protective of them."

"If I'm going to protect anything, it's going to be the mini cupcakes."

"And why is that?" He didn't so much say the words as he smiled them and I couldn't help smiling back.

"First of all, variety. No need to limit yourself when one regular cupcake is roughly equivalent to thirty-five mini cupcakes."

"Is that the conversion? Really?" The laugh that boomed out of him was so rich, so warm. There was no resisting. Meri would be on the floor, faking anaphylaxis by now. "I'm gonna need a minute to sit with that math."

I chose another cupcake. Spice cake, maybe chai, with cream cheese frosting. Lovely, even if spice wasn't my first choice for cake.

Henry cocked his head, that smile still lighting up his face. "Do you want to dance?"

"Hmm." I studied the table for a long moment like I had some serious reservations. He could sweat for a minute. He'd survive. "There's a lot of good things going on here. I should stick around. Explore my options."

As I said this, he reached over, taking my plate and setting it down. "You're coming with me," he said, holding out his hand.

I glanced down at his wide palm. He looked like he split firewood with his bare hands. Like he wrestled bears and waded into rivers just to grab a salmon out of the water. Like he came home from his rugby matches with blood running down his face and a few dislocated fingers, and the only treatment he required was a cold beer. Probably the furthest thing from a surgeon as I could find tonight, which was a relief. The more distance I could put between the real me and the person I played at weddings, the better.

"One dance," I said, taking his hand.

He slapped his free hand to his chest like I'd wounded him. "I'm going to need a lot more than one."

"Sorry. Can't help you. There are at least five other cupcake flavors I haven't tried."

He led me away from the buffet, his fingers slipping between mine. His thumb swept over my knuckles. Goose bumps rippled down my arms, which was ridiculous. I did not goose bump. Certainly not from a mere thumb on my knuckles.

"I have about twelve hours until I have to be on a flight out of here, eleven if we count the drive down to Reno," he said, looping an arm around my waist as we stepped onto the dance floor. "I could play this game with you. I could go on telling you that you're heart-stoppingly beautiful while you ignore me for a cupcake. But

I'm short on time and I've wanted to talk to you since you rolled your eyes at me during the ceremony."

"Bold of you to assume I was rolling my eyes at *you*," I said as we started moving with the music. His hand was warm on the small of my back, his fingers sliding over my dress in lazy circles that sent another wave of goose bumps down my arms, my legs, my chest.

Goddamn goose bumps.

"Right, so the part you want to focus on is the subject of the eye roll?" he asked. "Not the heart-stoppingly beautiful thing? I was really hoping you'd give me a chance to lean into that."

"Trust me, your heart has not stopped." His shoulders were a craggy mountain range under my hands and—because of course he did—he smelled clean and woodsy. A small laugh slipped over my lips at that discovery.

He peered down at me, a quirk pulling at his mouth. His full-blast smile could light up this whole tent, but that slow, scrunchy half smile? It lit up everything inside me.

"My moves aren't that bad," he said.

"No." I shook my head. His moves were amazing. "It's —nothing."

He dragged his hand up my spine, settling between my shoulder blades. His palm was so steady and certain against my bare skin. "Somehow I doubt that's the truth."

"And that's what you want for the next eleven hours? The truth?"

He stared at me then, his dark gaze dropping to my lips. "I should probably know your name before I answer that."

Olivia was on the tip of my tongue. That's who I was tonight. That's who I was to this guy. Nothing more. And I needed to remember that. "Not sure that's necessary."

"I could guess," he said after a pause.

"Seems unwise."

"Yeah, but I should tell you a secret about me." He held me tight and leaned in close, his beard scruff rasping against the shell of my ear. "I run headfirst into challenges. The harder, the better."

"I hope you're wearing a helmet while you do that. If you don't break your neck, you'll get a helluva concussion."

He pulled back just enough for me to catch his grin. "Safety first, right?"

"Nothing you've done here tonight suggests that's your first priority."

"First? No. Is it in the top ten? Yeah, probably." We swayed for a moment before he added, "You know, some people aren't good at public speaking. It's not easy to get up in front of all these people."

"I don't think that's your excuse."

I felt his laugh against my cheek. "Yeah. It's not."

Another song ended but we didn't stop swaying. It wasn't even a question and we both knew it.

The band kicked off the opening chords of Van Morrison's "Into the Mystic" and I hummed in pleasure.

"What was that for?" Henry asked.

I thought about giving him some kind of nonanswer or busting his balls again about that terrible toast, but I said, "I love when they play this song at weddings. It's always perfect."

He blinked at me like he didn't completely buy that response, but then he said, "All right."

He held me close, moving more deliberately with the music now, and when the bridge hit, he spun me away and back. I couldn't have held in the surprised laugh even if I'd wanted to. "That was unexpected."

He banded both arms around my waist. It felt like I was

enclosed in steel. "If you love it, you should let yourself love every second of it. No reason to hold back."

"Kind of like how you love a star chart reading?"

He dropped his head to my shoulder with a groan that felt glorious against my neck. "My god. I didn't think I was going to make it out of there alive."

"Is it weddings in general? You're just not a fan? Or is it *this* wedding?"

A snarly sound rumbled up from his chest. "That's a story for another day."

He spun me away again and then we sang along as the song ended, and though the next one was a faster Taylor Swift song that had everyone mobbing the dance floor, we went on swaying.

He asked, "What's your name?"

"That's a story for another day."

He tossed back his head with a laugh. "I might not have many days here, but I'll work with what I have. Let's go."

He pulled me into the bouncing crush of Swifties, yell-singing along to "Cruel Summer" with them. And make no mistake about it, he knew *all* the words. He kept those huge hands on my waist or my hips the whole time, holding me so tight against him that I could feel his shirt studs pressing into my skin and his beard scraping my neck.

I did not mind.

One song bled into another, and then another, and so many more. The band transitioned into all the loud, fun wedding songs, the kind that had the guys rolling up their shirtsleeves and the gals kicking off their heels. This was when receptions turned into parties, all concern for the precision and pretense forgotten because it was time to celebrate. It was when everyone was a little tipsy and a lot silly, and nothing else really mattered.

We were hot now, the air inside the tent warm and close as the band kept everyone hopping for hours. My skin was flushed and humid, and the back of Henry's shirt was damp when I circled my arms around his waist. It was too loud for talking but the language of touch and movement filled in all the gaps.

His hands on my hips, his fingers sliding over my belly, up my ribs, along the side of my breasts. My palms on his chest, his shoulders, the back of his neck. The press of his torso against my back, his arm locked around my waist as I rocked against him. The burn of his beard on the slope of my shoulder. The vibration that hummed inside him when I raked my fingers through his hair.

As the song ended, I pushed up onto my toes to speak into his ear. "What do you think about—"

"The food trucks are here!"

We turned our attention to the stage where Mason and Florrie stood at the microphone. The music cut out, but we were still swaying, his hands clasped low on my back. It was like we'd started moving together and now we didn't know how to stop.

Mason said, "We've been waiting for this part all night."

"I've been waiting longer," Florrie added.

"Okay, babe." Mason laughed. "We've got tacos, In-N-Out, hot donuts, Chicago-style dogs, churros, ice cream—"

Henry leaned down, his lips on my neck. "Please tell me you're not nearly as obsessed with ice cream as you are with cupcakes."

"I don't eat ice cream," I breathed. That wasn't fully accurate but I wasn't going to see this guy again after tonight and he didn't need to know the details of my dessert hierarchy.

"Yeah, that's not true for a second, but we don't have the time, my little heart-stopper, to get to the bottom of anything more than your name and whether you want to leave with me right now."

Again, I was *this* close to telling him my name was Olivia, but I held back. "Yeah. I do."

The words had barely passed over my lips before Henry grabbed my hand and pulled me through the crowd. "Come on," he yelled as we cut around the swarm of people headed for the trucks. The crisp mountain air bit at my skin when we stepped out of the tent. "If you don't keep up, I'm going to throw you over my shoulder. I'm just warning you now."

"I am wearing heels," I yelled back, my shoes clacking against the stone patio. "And you have at least six inches on me."

"More than that, honey," he said under his breath.

"Is that how it's gonna be? Don't make promises you can't keep."

"That's not a promise you have to worry about me keeping."

We burst into the hotel, laughing, stumbling into each other and completely oblivious to the world around us. The elevator opened the second Henry pressed the call button and he roped his arm around my waist as he ushered me inside.

He backed me up against the wall, his arm braced above me and his hand splayed on my hip. I reached inside his jacket, running my palm up his side. He was granite under my touch, solid and unyielding in the best ways. I wanted to rip his shirt off and map the bend of those muscles with my mouth. But I wouldn't stop with the shirt. Rip it all off, explore all of him. Take everything.

He leaned in, his lips on my neck, my jaw. I pulled him closer, tipping my chin up to meet him. A low growl sounded in the back of his throat as our lips met. We were slow at first, almost studious, but then a switch flipped, as if we'd both remembered that the night might be long though our time together was short.

My hands were in his hair. He flattened me to the wall. He was hard against my belly and his beard was rough where it rasped against my chin but I didn't care. He kissed like he wanted to see if he could get me off from that alone, and I wasn't against that kind of research.

"Hold the door! I'll be right there! Hold that door for me, please!"

I heard those words though I didn't process them. They were distant and muffled, like a phone lost in the bottom of a backpack while playing an audiobook.

But then someone bustled into the elevator and I realized we hadn't even left the lobby yet. A stunned laugh stuttered out of me as Henry held me close to his chest.

"Don't mind me, don't mind me. I'm just hitching a ride. I didn't see a single thing, Henry. Oh, biscuits! I've dropped everything."

I peeked around Henry's shoulder to find Aunt Luisa, in all of her witchy glory, shaking her head at the overturned purse on the elevator floor.

"Let me help you with that, Lulu," Henry said as the doors closed.

He stared at me while he adjusted himself, a big, devious grin stretched across his face that said *Look what you've done here*, and I had to fold my lips together to keep from laughing.

"Oh, would you look at that," she murmured.

Henry shifted away from me and I spotted a few tarot cards on the floor beside a flask definitely filled with liquor and a leather pouch definitely filled with crystals. "I'll get it," he said.

Luisa was quick to wave him off, saying, "Don't you dare." She picked up one card and stared at it for a long moment. "The World." She tapped a finger against the mostly naked woman on the card. "The World reminds us that we only get this one sensational life and we better not waste a single second of it."

"Right," Henry drawled, settling an arm over my shoulders.

She held up another card, this one with a naked jester on it. "The Fool is tarot's way of saying the universe wants you to bet on yourself and bet high. Leap, even if you don't know where you're going to fall."

"Yeah." He nodded, his tone gentle. I appreciated that. We couldn't have another snorting situation on our hands. Not in this proximity. "I hear that."

"I'm sure you do, Henry." She arched a brow at the last card, also adorned with naked people, and gave us a knowing smile. "The Lovers. I can see this one doesn't require much explanation, but when it appears in this position with The Fool, it tells us of powerful new beginnings." She gathered the cards and tucked them back into her bag. "And soul mates."

A laugh barked out of me as Henry said, "Wow, so you're really doing this."

"Mmm." She twisted open the flask and drank deeply. "It could be that we're on a path to find a soul mate. Or it's tarot's way of kicking us in the ass and telling us to stop obsessing about finding that person, and just open our eyes because they're right in front of us." The elevator came to a stop and Luisa stepped out. "You two have fun tonight."

"Thanks for the reading, Lulu," Henry said.

"Use protection," she called over her shoulder.

"Oh my god." A strange, fizzy laugh shook my shoulders. "What just happened?"

The doors closed and Henry jabbed the button for his floor again. "Nothing. Just Mason's aunt telling us what she thinks we want to hear. I know for a fact that she makes this stuff up as she goes along."

I blinked up at him. "Really?"

"I've known her my entire life. I consider her family, so when I say she's full of shit, I say it with love." He backed me against the wall again and traced the line of my dress where it hugged my breasts. "She was trying to be my wingwoman."

"Because you need the assist?"

He dipped his head down and kissed his way across my clavicle. "Because I'm married to my job. I have no life outside of my work and it will be another five or six years until I have time for one."

"So, that's your way of telling me you don't usually do this?"

The doors opened. We stepped out of the elevator and walked down the hall, stopping in front of a door I presumed to be his. He pressed a lazy kiss to my lips that seemed to wrap around me like a vine, twisting and gathering until my skin was enclosed in heat and need so great it swept everything from my mind.

"I *never* do this," he whispered against the corner of my mouth. "You probably won't believe that because it's the kind of thing a lot of guys say, but you know I don't have a lot of time. I'm not going to waste it lying to you."

"Whitney," I said, out of absolutely nowhere. "My name. It's Whitney."

A slow smile brightened his face as he opened the door. "Whitney, I'd like to spend the next nine hours doing unspeakably rude things to you. I know it's a lot to ask but—"

I grabbed him by the lapels and sealed my lips to his. We walked backward into the room and the door closed behind us with a heavy slam that seemed to spur both of us into action. My dress was bunched up around my waist. His shirt and jacket went flying while his trousers fell to his knees. I tossed him a condom from my clutch while I peeled down the shapewear as gracefully as possible. A second later, he hooked an arm under my thighs and boosted me up against the wall.

Our eyes locked as he pushed into me. He was thick and *huge*, and it was a damn good thing we'd spent the past few hours groping and grinding all over each other because this would've hurt without all that buildup.

His lips parted on a quiet groan. "Whit," he cried. "Fuck, honey. You really are going to stop my heart."

"Probably not." I shoved my fingers into his hair and kissed him. It was the only thing I could do as I felt myself fraying at the seams. We were ravenous, too starved to care about the mess we were making, the steps we were skipping. This was more urgent than the urgency of most one-night stands. It was almost primitive, like we'd been waiting ages for this and now—finally, *now*—we could let go.

He slipped a hand into my bodice, teasing a finger around my nipple as he hammered me into the wall. "Why are you so fucking perfect?" he asked, his voice impossibly deep and rumbly.

I loved it. I wanted to suck it from a spoon.

"It's one of my many gifts," I said.

"Your gifts are going to fucking kill me, Whit."

He pulled the bodice back and dragged his tongue over my nipple and I was more than a little shocked by the breathy wail that shot out of me in response. He brought his teeth down, biting just enough to have me clenching around him hard.

"Fuck, what did you just do to me?" He groaned into my breast. "Dying, honey. I'm *dying* here."

"You can't die on me now." I tightened my grip on his hair. "We have nine more hours."

He bit down on my nipple as he slammed into me, and I broke like a mirror that never saw the fist coming for it. Everything was unbelievably hot and sensitive and loose, and all I could do was cling to him as he broke too.

Three
Whitney

Rule Number Five:
One night only. No overtime.

Henry slept like a bear.

He was a solid, immovable slab of man all the way from the rock-hard arm locked around my waist to the erection nudging my hip. Yet there was something precious about the way his thick lashes fanned over his cheeks and his lips gathered in a pout. The need to run my index finger over those lips and cheeks swelled inside me until I closed my eyes and reminded myself of the exit strategy.

I didn't have time for another round. Even if I wanted one, Meri was waiting for me. More importantly, I was convinced my vagina would go into lockdown if Henry so much as glanced in that direction.

It took some careful maneuvering but I wiggled my way out of Henry's grasp and managed to tuck and roll off the mattress without waking him. I could handle the awkward morning-after convo though I really didn't want to. I wanted this night to go down in the wedding crashing memory book as the best of the summer and I didn't want anything to haze over the perfection of it. I wanted to think about this night when I was seven months deep into another round of work-induced celibacy and I wanted to remember Henry as the guy who'd said, "Hold on tight, honey," when he bent me over the desk and fucked me like it was his job.

I did not want to deal with stilted offers to exchange numbers and I didn't want to know what his voice sounded like when he tried to let me down gently. I didn't need either of those things and I didn't want to leave with that bitter taste on my tongue.

Because he was one of the good ones, at some point in the night, he'd draped my dress over the back of a chair and set the shapewear that Meri had named Girdle McHurdle for the lunge-and-shimmy required to get into it on the seat with my clutch, which now held eight fewer condoms than it did yesterday. My shoes sat beside the chair.

As I slipped the dress over my head, I shot one last look at his long, rugged form. His dark hair shone in the morning sunlight. A tattoo of trees and mountains wrapped around one bicep. Woodsy to the core, this one. The bedsheets rode low on his hips, showing off a delicious pair of dimples below his waist. A small pile of damp washcloths sat on the floor beside the bed, one for all the times he'd put me back together after breaking me apart.

He really was one of the good ones.

Meri was waiting for me in the lobby. Her red hair was tied back in a low ponytail and she had a baseball cap shielding her eyes. She was halfway through a huge bottle of water and she was pushing her luggage back and forth like it was a baby carriage. She only tipped her chin up when she spotted me and I nodded in response as I stopped at the front desk.

I had to schedule a wake-up call for Henry. I didn't want him to miss his flight.

With that handled, I trudged toward Meri, sore and exhausted and a little dazed. We walked toward our rental car in silence. It wasn't unusual for us to go an hour or two without talking, especially after a late night. Especially after two weeks of late nights.

We didn't say much until agreeing to stop in Sacramento for coffee.

On the way out of the café, I said, "I'm surprised you're not limping."

She gave me an *if you only knew* shake of her head and handed me the keys. "Wake me up when it's time for my mud bath."

The drive to the middle of nowhere spa we'd selected for the last few days of our vacation took another hour. We were quiet all the way to our casita.

"Pool?" she asked, yanking off her cap. "Or food?"

My need for discipline and order drowned out my exhaustion and I started unpacking. I knew I'd feel better when everything was in its place. "What about poolside food?" I asked. "That has to be an option. At the very minimum, we can ask about making it an option."

Meri flopped face-first onto the bed while I hung up my clothes. "I like that," she said into the linens. "Almost as much as I like this bed."

"Good news. There's an identical bed on the other side of the casita all for you."

She rolled over, watching as I organized the drawers. "Remember when we were poor med students and we always shared a bed?"

"How could I forget?" I grinned at her. "I'm the one who diagnosed your bruxism. Speaking of which, have you been wearing your mouth guard?"

"Yes, it's extremely sexy. All the boys love it when I talk dirty with it in." She pushed off the bed with a grunt. "Okay. I'll leave you alone with your compulsions. Be ready for the pool in fifteen." Stopping in the doorway, she asked, "Was there a taco truck for the after party? Or donuts?"

"All of the above," I said. "A whole bunch of food trucks."

"Should've seen that coming," she mused. "How was it?"

"I don't know." I folded my panties into crisp, clean squares. "I didn't stay."

Meri thunked her head back against the door. "Had something more interesting to do?"

I lifted a shoulder, still focused on my undies. "You could say that."

A hissy growl sounded in the back of my throat as I glared at my phone.

"Put that thing away." Meri slapped my arm. "We agreed we wouldn't touch our work emails until we were back in Boston because they result in feral noises like the one you just made." She adjusted the brim of her ultra-wide hat and futzed with her caftan again. "Don't make me wrestle it away from you. You know I'll win. I am small but scrappy."

"It started with my sister."

"Of course it did. She's the origin of all your tension headaches."

"She sent a text telling me to check my email because she sent me something last week and I hadn't replied."

"Is that something a heartfelt thank-you for being her continual safety net? Or repeatedly picking up her life and putting it back together at no cost to her? Better yet, your ongoing management of her medical care? Tolerating the way she bounces in and out of your life like a goddamn ping-pong ball? Anything along those lines?"

I rubbed my forehead. I *was* getting a tension headache. "She's coming to stay with me."

"Delightful." Meri turned to the mezze platter on a table between our lounge chairs. She scooped an outrageous amount of hummus onto a cucumber. "Let me guess how it went down. She didn't ask if it was okay, she didn't indicate how long she'd be staying, and she offered no explanation as to why she's leaving D.C."

My relationship with my sister was complicated. *All* my relationships were complicated. Aside from Meri, I didn't have a single personal relationship that functioned normally. Everything was always one sudden move away from disaster and Brie was no different. If anything, Brie was my most complicated relationship because she was the only real family I had left.

So, I put up with her chaos. I didn't have much choice.

"I give it six weeks," I said. "She'll remember that she doesn't like me enough to live with me."

"If it goes a day past six weeks, I reserve the right to show up at your place and make passive-aggressive comments until she blows her top."

"That will only punish me," I said with a laugh.

"For a minute, yeah, but then she'll invent a spiffy new reason to get the fuck out." She pointed to my phone, adding, "What else is going on? You look like you're chewing on a lump of coal over there."

"Cossapino wrote me a dissertation-length email about the *time-honored traditions* of surgical resident training. He endured it and therefore they should be able to endure it too. Apparently there's no reason to alter a system that's served us so well for generations."

"He was emotionally abused as a resident and therefore it's not only his right but his duty to abuse every resident who passes through his service. Sounds like a rock-solid system."

"He goes on to say that, according to him, *lowering the bar* will lead to negative patient outcomes and therefore he will not be implementing my committee's new professional standards. Despite the very clear messaging that it's not optional."

"Constapino is full of shit and he will fall in line the second the chief blinks hard in his direction," Meri replied. "Don't let yourself get worked up about that gasbag."

"Okay, sure, but I have Pecklewithe telling me that he's not about to alter his method of teaching to accommodate the new generation of surgeons and their *thin, woke skin*. If they cannot tolerate his mentoring, they won't complete his rotation."

"It's funny how Peckerwithe is so sensitive," she murmured. "It's almost like he's too fragile to adapt to new situations. I wonder if there's any way to help him with that." She tapped her chin. "Probably not. Best to see if he'll sink or swim."

"Then we have Bass yelling—literally, the whole email is

written in all caps—that anyone entering the medical profession knows they'll be subject to difficult, directive feedback and we're only doing a disservice to the program by watering it down by centering residents' feelings."

"Big Mouth Bass? He's an all-caps rageaholic."

"Yeah, but also, we're just asking attendings to acknowledge that it's unnecessary and unproductive to engage in *any* abusive conduct. Is that really too much to ask? Perhaps the issue and the solution speak for themselves?"

She rolled her green eyes. "You're assuming a lot of these guys. Most of whom still believe that mental illness is all in your head and gynecology is to blame for every issue women present with."

"Maybe I am expecting too much, but I also have Sadiskowski bitching about—"

"What does the Sadist have to say now? I cannot wait to hear this."

"He's pissed that we're mandating implicit bias training. He claims that his teaching is equitable for all residents and his delivery of care is equitable for all patients, and he can't possibly give up OR time for a training he doesn't need."

"That man calls every scrub nurse Blondie. He could do with a minute of reeducation."

"It kills me how so many of these people are exceptional physicians and surgeons, and they're also incapable of considering the possibility that they have anything to learn where it comes to training residents and generally not being toxic dickheads."

Meri nodded for a moment as she poked at the olives and peppers. "I understand why you put yourself in the line of fire by chairing this committee and I understand that it's personal to you, but I don't understand why you're letting the sausage brigade get to you. We've never given a single fuck what they have to say so why are we doing it now?"

"Because I need this to work," I said. I'd dedicated the past year to leading a committee to develop and implement professional standards of conduct. I'd thrown myself into this project, dedicating every spare second I had to gaining the support of the board of directors, hospital leadership, the school of medicine, and all the department heads. And I'd sworn that it would only take another year to get it off the ground. "All of my credibility is on the line here. I'm the face of this thing, and if it goes up in flames, I'll have to start looking for the emergency exit."

"You're not going anywhere," Meri said. "Everything will work itself out. It always does. Your sister will kick up another one of her chaos tornadoes and the wieners at the hospital will huff and puff and make themselves look like tools. We're not going to worry about them, especially not when Chief Hartshorn is squarely on your side."

"I know, but—"

"Nope," she snapped. "Don't even start. We are on vacation for five more days and we've already granted too much of our precious time to the wieners. Put the phone away or I'll make good on that promise to wrestle you for it."

I made a show of dropping the device into my tote bag.

"Good girl," she said with a wide grin. "Now, hand mama some SPF. This sun is going to turn me into redheaded jerky."

After Meri applied another thick layer of sunscreen, I said, "So, the *bodies in the lake* guy."

She grunted around a wedge of pita but didn't meet my eyes. "What about him?"

"Did you crush his entire spirit? Or just part of it?"

For a long moment, she didn't respond. Her lips pulled tight into a line as she picked at a chunk of grilled artichoke. "He's fine." She cleared her throat. "So, the best man."

I plucked a green olive off the tray. "How'd you know?"

"Call it an educated guess," she said. "Also, you have bruises and hickeys all over your chest."

I glanced down. "I do not."

She jabbed a finger into the side of my boob. "Yes. You do. Also, your legs look like you've been manhandled. You'd tell me if these weren't enthusiastically consensual, correct?"

I groaned when I shifted my cover-up and spotted all the tiny bite marks on my breasts. "Oh my god."

"Did he laugh inappropriately the whole time? Just giggled his sweet little rocks off?"

"He did not." I gazed at the fingertip bruises up and down my thighs. I wanted to tell her about the tarot cards and washcloths and all the condoms we went through. But I also wanted to lock it away. "Did lake guy talk about corpses the whole time?"

"Yeah, but I was into it. New kink unlocked. Very sexy."

I tossed an almond at her. It landed on the brim of her hat. "I guess we can say that dress has what it takes."

"I'm crediting the bra," she said. "Tits for the win."

"Another successful season, then?"

She grabbed the almond and popped it in her mouth. "Any more successful and a few days at the spa wouldn't be nearly enough recuperation. I'd need a ten-day course of antibiotics and some pelvic floor physical therapy to recover."

I held up my sparkling water and she did the same. "To weddings," I said.

She tapped her glass to mine. "May they continue to provide us the mischief—and mindless sex—we lack in our everyday lives."

We drank and lapsed into a drowsy silence. The hills in the

distance were the color of toast and I had the distinct sense they'd feel like it too. We were only a couple of hours from Tahoe, but everything was different. No shimmering blue, no pine trees reaching up to touch the sky.

"Do you think we have it wrong?" Meri shifted to face me, her gauzy caftan bunching and tangling around her legs. "Have we been doing it wrong all this time?"

I watched as she dragged her teeth over her lower lip. Whatever she was thinking, it was big. I could think of only a handful of times when I'd seen Meri unsure of anything. "Doing what wrong?"

"Everything? Nothing? I don't know." She jerked a shoulder up. "But what if there's a point when we have to stop having mindless sex? What if we're actually supposed to put energy into connecting with people and building relationships rather than banging random dudes at other people's weddings? I just have this prickly sense that we made a mistake along the way and we're so far down this road now that we don't even realize we're lost." Pressing a hand to her chest, she added solemnly, "Maybe it's just acid reflux."

"I don't think we're the ones who have it wrong. All the focus is put on finding someone, getting married, starting a family—and prioritizing that relationship above everything else. As if this one person could be everything you could possibly need for the rest of your life. We know that's not how it works. We know that guys are fun, but true friends are forever." I reached over, gave her hand a good squeeze. "And it's also acid reflux. Please tell me you're taking something for that and not singeing your esophagus."

She laughed, saying, "You're right. I know you're right. I'm just"—she flopped onto her back, her profusely freckled arms hanging limply off the lounge chair—"I'm thinking too hard. That's all."

"Are you sure?" I wanted her to say yes. I wanted her to tell me she was in a mood—probably because spooky lake guy hadn't been up for all of her bedroom adventures—and that she was all right. I wanted to know that she wasn't sliding back into that dark place, just like the one she'd been in all those years ago when I'd dragged her off for a vacation and accidentally crashed a wedding. Selfishly, I wanted to know that she wasn't looking at our long-standing resolution against dating and the hunt for Mr. Right with fresh, critical eyes. "Thinking about downloading some apps? Interested in giving the talking phase another chance?"

"Are you kidding me? No way." She held up her glass again. "Single ladies for life."

I breathed a low sigh of relief and tapped my glass to hers. "Single ladies for life."

Four
Henry

Transplant Surgery Rotation:
Day 1, Week 1

September

I JUMPED INTO A PAIR OF TROUSERS IN THE DARK. Questionably clean, but it didn't matter that much. I'd be in scrubs before noon. It wasn't like anyone was going to call me out for wrinkled pants during rounds. I could turn on the lights and dress myself like a grown-ass adult, but that would force me to admit I wasn't still in bed, and I was a big fan of lying to myself. I enjoyed nothing more than pretending I was asleep when it was four thirty in the morning and I was already late for work.

"Yeah, it was an epic climb." Mason's voice came through the speakerphone, fracturing the fragile détente between me and my lies. "Definitely one of my favorite expeditions of the year. Such a good group. The kind of people I would've hiked with even if they weren't paying me to get them up and back again. I hope the group I'm leading on Wednesday has the same vibes. You would've loved it, man."

"I'm sure of it." I pinned the phone between my fingers as I buttoned my shirt on the short walk into the kitchen. "Hey, so, what's up with the other photos I asked you about?"

"Oh, yeah," he murmured. "I still don't get what you're talking about."

I chugged a protein shake instead of verbally wringing my best friend's neck. "The wedding photographer," I started, "took a lot of photos. Right?"

"I'm with you so far."

"But not all of those photos made it into the album. Right? They took more photos than just the ones in the online gallery."

"I think so? I don't really know how it all works. I could ask Flor, if you want. I bet she'd know."

I went back to the shake instead of sighing because we'd had this conversation approximately fifty-seven times. Then I caught sight of the time on the microwave and groaned out loud. I was *so fucking late* that I could already feel the chief resident's rubber clog up my ass.

This was the downside of having a ten-minute commute on foot, seven if I sprinted like a bear was chasing me down Charles Street. It seduced me into believing my entire day wouldn't suffer because I stole a few extra minutes of sleep or stood still while eating.

"I love you, man, but you said you'd stop dying every time my wife's name comes up in conversation."

"I'm late, that's all," I said, scrambling to get myself into shoes while grabbing my fleece zip-up and messenger bag. "It's not Florrie."

Even if that woman was going to destroy my best friend's life.

"How can you be late? It's almost five in the morning out there."

"The same way it's the middle of the night out there and you're driving home from an expedition now." I jogged down two flights of stairs and out into the periwinkle light of morning, the phone trapped between my shoulder and chin. "About those photos—"

"Why do you want them? What's the deal with you and the wedding photos?"

I'd dodged this question all summer. We all knew I couldn't feign any desire to memorialize the event, and I knew I couldn't tell Mason the truth. Especially since I'd reached the point where I was more than a little convinced that I'd dreamed the whole thing into existence and there was a very good chance I'd experience a quick mental breakdown if I didn't make some tangible progress soon.

"Is this about that woman you talked to?" he asked. "What was her name again?"

An ambulance screeched past me, lights and sirens slicing through the predawn stillness. I crossed the street and headed for the side entrance of the ER. "Sorry. I gotta go. We'll pick this up after your expedition later this week. Take care, man. Be safe on the mountain."

We parted with a promise to reconnect over the weekend which wasn't a promise I had any business making since I didn't know what to expect from this new rotation. If the cohort ahead of mine could be trusted, we were in for eight nonstop weeks.

I hit the stairwell and sprinted up five flights to the resident team room. The chances were slim to none that the fifth-year resident supervising my cohort during this rotation would also be running late this morning, but foolish optimism was at least half of my personality. The rest was sandwiches and the variety of stubbornness that thrived on proving people wrong.

As I burst into the room, winded, sweating, and dangerously close to tasting that protein shake again, I heard, "Dr. Hazlette, I presume? You're late."

"Yes," I wheezed, holding out my hand to the tall Black woman with a glare that could grind bone. "My apologies. Won't happen again."

"Unless you want to spend the next two months parked in the clinic, I should hope not." She shook my hand and then motioned for me to join the other three members of my cohort. "In the future, I expect to find the entire team present and prepared at five on the dot for pre-rounds. Anyone who elects to be even a minute late will not see the inside of an OR that day. Understood?"

Cami Cortes-Dixon nodded vigorously. "Yes, Dr. Copeland. Of course." She adjusted her headband and then smoothed a hand over the lapels of her white coat. Not a wrinkle to be found. My white coat, on the other hand, was probably balled up in my bag. "We are very excited for this rotation and we're going to do whatever it takes to meet your expectations."

Cami was our *pleasure to have in class*. She was wound tighter than a spring-loaded bear trap.

Dr. Copeland grimaced like she was trying to identify the source of a foul smell. Then, "You're very...exuberant. I'm going to need you to channel that into something more productive than kissing my ass."

"Oh, yes, well, I am fluent in three languages: Spanish, Portuguese, and Cantonese. I picked up enough Haitian Creole during a semester-long clinical internship to communicate with patients and—"

I cleared my throat. "CCD. You're good."

Beside me, Tori Tran ran a hand down her face, doing nothing to hide her laugh. On my other side, Reza Ansari pressed a finger to the bridge of his glasses. He wasn't one for big reactions. Or small reactions. Any reactions, really. Over the past three months, I'd checked his pulse a few times to confirm that he was alive and not an exceptionally realistic robot.

Funny thing though, he and Tori were deep into a complex bow tie pact that I still didn't understand. They both wore bow ties every day. The same bow ties. Different shirts and trousers, but... matching bow ties.

Dr. Copeland spared Tori an impatient glance before frowning down at her tablet. "Hazlette's time management issues have put us behind. We'll walk and talk," she said, elbowing open the door and stepping into the hall. "Pre-rounds in the transplant unit is going to look a little different than what you saw on your last rotation in general surgery."

"Get your shit together," Cami hissed with a jab to my arm. From the feel of it, her wedding rings were going to leave a mark. "You can't be late on the first day! Do you want the resident to hate us? What's wrong with you?"

I dug through my bag, handing her my notebook, stethoscope, and the laminated cheat sheets she'd distributed during last weekend's prep session. "Didn't sleep well," I muttered. There was no point in mentioning that I hadn't slept well in months. That I wasn't sure I'd ever sleep well again.

"Sleeping is not part of the curriculum here," she snapped. "Come on! We're missing everything!"

We caught up to the others while I pulled myself together. Since the start of residency in July—and trauma-bonding our way through a hellish rotation in burn surgery—our cohort had turned into a peculiar little family. There was no way around it when you spent sixteen hours a day together for three months straight.

"Transplant surgery is among the most interdisciplinary programs you'll encounter. You will work with more providers on this rotation than any other in the entirety of your training," Copeland continued. "It's also one of the most unpredictable programs. There will be days that start out with an empty surgical schedule and end with every OR in use. That's simply the nature of a specialty dependent upon donated organs. Prepare yourself for ambiguity now."

"That means less sleep," Cami whispered.

"I got the subtext, thanks."

I went back to shuffling my notes and cheat sheets as Copeland went over her expectations for pre-round preparations. Compared to the actual drill sergeant we'd had down in the burn unit and then the power-tripping prick in general surgery, Copeland was like a field of daisies. The type of daisies that gave off a *take no shit* vibe and glared laser beams, of course.

"Dr. Aldritch is the attending surgeon for this rotation," Copeland went on. "However, you'll often be assigned to work with other attendings in this practice to gain exposure to as many transplant procedures as possible"—she narrowed her gaze on me—"assuming you're on time."

"Never living that one down," Tori said under her breath.

"Engrave it on my tombstone now," I replied.

For the next hour, Copeland led us through the hallways, talking as fast as she walked and tossing out orders we had limited hope of understanding on the first try.

Once we'd stopped by the rooms of all the transplant patients, she wagged a pen at us, saying, "I need to grab Dr. Aldritch for a few minutes before the start of rounds." She swept a gaze over the group. "Use this time to get yourselves ready. We will move through cases very quickly and you will be asked questions that you should be able to answer. Dr. Aldritch is looking for you to be prepared and competent."

The second Copeland walked away, we circled up to rapid-fire through every question we could imagine coming our way about these patients and their surgeries. This was where Reza shined. He had a way of knowing that we'd be asked to discuss the signs of some rare reaction or a triad of symptoms required for a certain diagnosis versus a pentad of symptoms for another. That computer brain of his was amazing.

As I was jotting down some notes, I caught a low burst of laughter from somewhere down the hall. It landed in my stomach, a sudden, fizzy wave of heat that commanded me to find the source of that sound.

Even as my head jerked up, I knew there was no point. That sound was an echo of a memory, one I barely trusted to be real anymore.

I scanned the corridor and was immediately disappointed with myself for wasting this time when the only people around were a few techs buzzing in and out of rooms and Dr. Copeland down near the nurses' station. She was talking to someone, but that end of the hall bent to the right, obscuring the other side of that conversation from view.

Not that it mattered. That sound lived in my head and perhaps only there. I shook off the fog of those memories and went back to my notes as my team bounced through various signs of organ rejection.

And then I heard it again.

More than hearing it, I *felt* it.

My heart rate stuttered as that sound slipped up my spine and warmed the back of my neck. I blinked at my notebook, willing myself to write down the words swirling around my head.

I dared a glance up and my entire world turned upside down.

No more than twenty feet away stood the woman I'd nearly convinced myself was a dream. The one who'd disappeared without a trace. The one with the hazel eyes that saw through everything and golden brown hair that almost brushed her shoulders. The one with the secretive smile and the laugh I'd know anywhere. The one I fit inside of like I'd been made for her.

There you are.

Then she started walking in this direction and all at once I registered her white coat, the badge reading *SURGEON*, and that she was speaking with Copeland. My head filled with static.

"Fuck" croaked out of me and I dropped everything. Notebook, pen, cheat sheets. Even my stethoscope clattered to the floor. *"Fuck."*

"I specifically told you to get your shit together," Cami added.

"Did you fall out of bed and hit your head or something, Hazlette?" Tori whispered.

As I knelt on the floor, suffocatingly aware that the space between us was narrowing with each sharp click of her heels, all I could manage was a roughly panted "Fuck."

Reza crouched down, gathering the laminated cards and shuffling them into an order he found acceptable while I shoved the stethoscope into my pocket. He didn't say anything as he handed them over, though the slight quirk in his brow seemed to ask *Is everything all right?*

How could I begin to answer that? After a long slide into near insanity, I'd finally found Whitney, the woman who hadn't been on the guest list or in a single one of the hundreds of wedding photos *—and she was my new boss.*

I pushed to my feet as they stopped in front of us though I kept my head down. I needed another minute to figure out how the fuck I was going to handle this. It wasn't as if I could throw her over my shoulder and charge toward the nearest empty room to ask why the hell she'd found it necessary to vanish on me. Was I even allowed to acknowledge that we knew each other?

And yes, I knew her. I'd drunk whiskey from her belly button. I could draw her nipples from memory. The soft, contented sighs she made as she drifted off to sleep were carved into my bones.

There were plenty of blanks to fill in, that was more than obvious, but I *knew* her.

"Welcome to transplant surgery," she said, and her voice unbraided the tension in my shoulders. "I'm Whitney Aldritch. I'll be your attending for this rotation. As I'm sure Jenelle—Dr. Copeland—has discussed, you'll see a full range of major organ transplant cases over the next eight weeks."

I edged behind Reza as I opened my notebook while Whitney continued previewing the rotation. The guy was tall and reed-thin, but he was the only shelter I had in this storm. By my math, I could hide behind him for a handful of minutes before we started on rounds, but then I'd have to look Whitney in the eye and answer her questions.

I held my pen like I was jotting down everything, but I was busy drinking her in. She looked different here than she had in Tahoe. More serious, more composed. Everyone was more serious in a hospital though there was a calm confidence that radiated from her. It would've knocked me back a step if I hadn't known how completely unhinged she could be on the dance floor.

She wore a creamy white shirt—something that probably qualified as a *blouse*—with soft trousers the same color as the whiskey I sucked from her skin. Made me want to drop to my knees and rub my face against the thick of her thighs. Shiny black heels peeked out from the hem of her trousers, adding a couple of inches to her frame. A few ultra-thin gold chains circled her neck. I was jealous of them.

She held a cup of hot coffee from a nearby café in one hand, a tablet tucked under her opposite arm. No cupcakes in sight.

"Before we begin, I'd like to take a moment to hear a bit about what brought you to medicine," Whitney said. "Tell me why you're here. I know you want to be the best—you wouldn't have made it this far and into a surgical program as competitive as this one if you didn't. What I want to know is what started you down the road to medicine in the first place. For some, it's loss. Losing a family member, a friend. Feeling powerless at a young age stamps itself on us and drives us to right that wrong."

Down the hall, a large laundry cart squeaked by while someone was paged to the ER.

After a pause, Whitney continued, "For others, it's the desire to care. To make things better, to solve the problems." She glanced at Cami, who responded with another vigorous nod. Copeland sighed. "And there are others who are marched into medicine, *fait accompli*, and they find their own reasons along the way." With a shrug, she added, "Some will confess their god complexes and others will make noise about money, though I have yet to meet a single surgeon for whom those are the *only* true reasons. There has to be something more than a desire to be the best." She motioned to us with her coffee cup. "Who are you and why are you here?"

Surprising no one at all, Cami went first. "Good morning, Dr. Aldritch. So good to meet you and very excited to learn from you. I'm Camilla Cortes-Dixon and I'm a caretaker," she said, a hint of self-deprecation in her tone. "Also, I lost my abuela to an extremely aggressive cancer when I was a teenager. It was only three weeks between the diagnosis and when she passed. And you're right, it is stamped on me."

Reza lifted a hand, saying, "I'm Reza Ansari. Hello. I hail from a long line of physicians though I've always been drawn to working out problems and finding solutions after everyone else has already given up. Thank you."

I felt Whitney's gaze pause on me as she listened to Reza though I didn't look up from my notebook. If she recognized me, she didn't show it, but time was ticking down here. I needed Tori to go next even though she liked getting the last word in. Just another minute to figure out how I'd get both hands around this situation, that was all I needed.

After a heavy pause, my teammate jumped in, saying, "Thuy Tran, call me Tori. I'm a competitor. For me, the only desire is to be the best. It wakes me up in the middle of the night. But it's not simply a matter of being number one. It's about zeroing in on the most pervasive issues affecting the most underserved populations, and making them my bitch."

A noise belonging to the laugh family huffed out of Copeland while Whitney gave Tori a slow nod. For no good reason at all, I hated the sterile neutrality of that nod. I wanted to shake Whit until she belted out a belly laugh over Tori's dramatics. I wanted to see one of her bright, wide smiles and I wanted her to criticize my wrinkled pants.

Whitney lifted her chin in my direction. "And that just leaves—"

I stepped out from behind Reza as my heart hammered its way up my throat. In so many ways, I was balanced on the edge of a cliff with miles of air beneath me, and the rest of my life depended on this moment. "Henry Hazlette," I said, meeting her gaze for the first time in too damn long.

Her lips parted and her eyes widened, and she wobbled on those heels like the ground couldn't be trusted. I was pretty sure I heard her stomach drop to the floor. But then she fixed a stiff smile on her face, swallowed thickly, and said, "Dr. Hazlette. Why are you here?"

The multitude of answers to that question. If she only knew. "You could say I'm a fixer. Always have been. And I have a tendency to run headfirst into challenges." I waited a moment for her to take that bait, but she went on watching me with the same cool equanimity she'd offered my peers. "I don't always wear a helmet, even though I've heard I could end up with one helluva concussion."

"What the fuck," Tori coughed while Cami stared at me like I'd grown an extra eyeball. Copeland just shook her head and muttered something about being too old for this shit and Reza blinked in my direction which was the most aggressive censure I could receive from the man.

Whitney arched a single brow as she stared at me and I didn't know if I'd fucked it all up or did this exactly right. And I wouldn't know, not until I could get her alone. Which was the next impossible thing for me to figure out.

"Thank you all for sharing. Push yourself to keep those reasons in mind as you make your way through residency. It's all too easy to forget why we chose this in the first place when we're competing for procedures and hearing pagers in our sleep." Whitney glanced at the smartwatch on her wrist and drew in a wavering breath. No one else noticed it, I was sure of that. But I did, and I knew she was on the edge of that cliff with me. "We're due to begin rounds. Dr. Copeland, why don't you get us started?"

Every minute of the next hour was a study in Whitney Aldritch.

She was different here in ways I'd only begun to catalog. There was a rigidity in the way she carried herself, the way she spoke, and I would've fixated on that if I hadn't been so busy being charmed at how fucking good she was at her job. She asked tough questions and pushed us hard, and I'd learned more from her in an hour than some other attendings in a whole month.

But it was nearly impossible to stay focused on the cases, and my team noticed. By the end, I was on the receiving end of a steady stream of pointed stares and barely concealed sighs. Even Copeland was giving me side-eye glances every time I was a few seconds late in responding to a question or asked for information to be repeated.

"Y'all are due downstairs for adrenal conference," Copeland said, her gaze locked on her tablet. "Once that wraps up, you'll meet me back in the clinic. We're seeing a lot of post-op patients today so you'll be busy. Get your bedside manner on."

"Do you know where we're going, CCD?" Tori asked when Copeland had disappeared down the hall.

"Of course I do," Cami replied.

I glanced back to where Whitney leaned against the nurses' station, her arms folded on the countertop. Two women behind the desk had her attention as they spoke with their hands. She dragged the toe of her shoe up the back of her leg and my mouth went dry.

I didn't know much, but I knew I couldn't let her out of my sight until we'd had a private conversation. I didn't care what it took.

"I'll catch up to you guys," I said, forcing my gaze away from Whitney. "Save me a seat."

"Please tell me you're going to slap yourself across the face seventeen times or try out some light waterboarding," Tori said. "You're off your game today and we need you to straighten that shit out."

I gave her a crisp salute. "Will do."

As the group filed into the stairwell, I headed toward the staff lounge but then turned in the opposite direction when I heard the door close behind them. The last thing I needed was those three—or anyone in this building, actually—turning an observant eye on me right now. First, because this situation was a special kind of fucked, but also because my improv skills left a lot to be desired. My attempt at absentmindedly strolling down the hall while paging through my notebook like I was on the edge of my seat with these post-op orders was not high art.

But as I walked past the nurses' station, I heard, "Dr. Hazlette. A word, please."

Thank god.

"Certainly, Dr. Aldritch."

I turned on my heel and followed Whitney into a small meeting room. She settled against the table, her arms folded over her torso. She drummed her fingers against her elbows as she stared at the floor. There was a dainty gold ring with a pale blue stone on her index finger. There were a million things I wanted to say, but I held back. I had the sense that I had to let her lead this even if I bit straight through my tongue in the process.

I could see all the questions and conflict scrawled across her face. They were the same ones on repeat in my head.

After a long, gut-twisting silence, she asked, "Is this going to be a problem?"

Somehow, I hadn't been prepared for that question. "What?" I asked. "No. No, of course not."

She looked up, taking me in with a steady, steely gaze that very nearly sliced me in half. "I would understand if you're uncomfortable having me as your supervisor given our"—she paused and I could see her cutting and shaping the word in her mind—"history."

"No." I sliced my hand through the air. "Not at all."

"I wouldn't take offense if you were."

"Maybe *I'd* take offense," I said. My heart was back to thumping its way into my esophagus. "You're nothing like that. I know you wouldn't leverage our history against me."

She gave a tight shake of her head like that was a ridiculous thing for me to say. "You've been here all of two hours and you know how I run my practice?"

"I have a pretty good idea and—"

"Comments like that suggest this *is* going to be a problem." She curled her fingers around the edge of the table. Her knuckles turned white. "There's an empty spot on the other cohort. I can move you there—"

"No." My hands settled on my hips so I didn't reach for her. At this point, I'd be content to take a few steps closer and simply breathe her in. I just wanted to remember what it was like to feel her head nestled under my chin, to inhale the warm scent of her skin. To remind myself that it had been real. "That's unnecessary. I want to stay in this cohort. As far as I'm concerned, everything that happened in Tahoe is between us, and the last thing I'd do is discuss it with anyone here. I won't have any issues with you as my supervisor."

Her shoulders dropped and the line of her jaw softened, but she continued holding on to the table. "I'm relieved to hear that though I have to be clear that any personal relationship we had is over. I'm responsible for training you and I take that responsibility very seriously."

There it was, the empty air over the edge of the cliff. I knew it was there and I knew I'd fall, but I hadn't expected the journey down to feel like a kick in the ribs. "I can see that you do."

A series of vibrations sounded from her phone, but she went on staring at me and made no move to acknowledge it. Eventually, she narrowed her eyes, asking, "Did you know? That I worked here? Have you known since the start of your residency and waited to spring it on me today?"

"No, Whit, that's not—"

"I am not *Whit* to you anymore." She pushed her hands through her honeyed hair and stared up at the ceiling. "You don't get to do that here. Do you understand? Either I'm Dr. Aldritch to you and nothing more or I find a seat for you on a cohort that's already rotated through transplants. Tell me now which one it's going to be."

"Yeah. I get it." I shoved my fists into my pockets. I had to get myself together. The last thing I wanted was to be separated from my cohort. Reza, Tori, Cami—they were my family now. "We started at the burn unit and then moved on to community general surgery at the Wellesley campus. This is the first time we've been in the surgical wing aside from a tour during orientation." I let myself stare at her now, just as I'd wanted to stare all morning. She was beautiful in a way that made me press a hand to my chest just to keep my heart from throwing itself at her. "I had no idea what I was walking into today. If I'd known I was going to see you again, I would've found a way to do it without blindsiding you."

Her phone buzzed again. She ignored it. "I appreciate that." When the next series of vibrations started, she blew out a breath and pushed away from the table. "Thank you for discussing this with me. I hope we've come to an understanding."

As she headed to the door, I couldn't stop myself from asking, "Can I see you? Take you out for coffee or something? When this rotation is over?"

She glanced in my direction, but let her gaze settle south of my eyes, on the name embroidered on the breast of my white coat. Her lips moved as if she meant to respond though the words wouldn't take shape. After a moment, she said, "I don't know. We'll have to see what happens and—and you have to swear you have no intention of specializing in transplant surgery and won't be back on my side of the surgical wing in two years."

She left the room before I could respond, but I stayed there, listening as the click of her heels dissolved down the hall. I brought a hand to my chest, rubbing hard at my sternum. "I swear."

Five

Whitney

Rule Number Fourteen:
Establish exit strategies and distress signals in advance.

I was exceptionally good at three things.

First off, surgery—specifically, heart transplant surgery.

Next, applying a winged eyeliner. While they probably didn't seem interchangeable on first glance, my capability with number two had a lot to do with number one.

Finally, intimidating the shit out of people without saying a word.

Three things sat on the opposite end of this spectrum.

One: boundaries—with everything, everyone, everywhere.

Two: balance. I had no doubt there was another circular relationship between one and two at play here.

Three: catastrophizing. I could drown myself in a downward spiral of intrusive thoughts the second I was hit with a problem with no apparent solution.

It was easier this way, distilling myself down to bits and pieces. Lists with clear, discernible items. These aggregate parts were manageable.

Until today, an otherwise uneventful September day when the trapdoor I'd never noticed beneath my feet gave way and everything was raining down around me as I fell.

I scrambled up the stairs, my heels snapping against the concrete and my hair flying into my face. As a rule, I did not run, definitely not on stairs and never in heels. But there was no other option at the moment. The inside of my head sounded like a screeching heart monitor crossed with Henry singing along to "Cruel Summer" while the Chief of Surgery formally reprimanded me.

I slammed into the door on the sixth floor and then bolted down the hall. Terrible, terrible decision in these shoes though it seemed many of my decisions were terrible these days.

When I blew through the doors into the surgical wing, I headed toward the charge nurse. "Where's Dr. Mercer this morning?"

She eyed me for a second before glancing down at her tablet. "Thirty-five," she replied. "You good, Dr. Aldritch?"

I didn't even have to imagine what kind of mess I looked like right now. I knew my face was beet red, the boob that was slightly larger than the other was very close to flopping out of my bra, and I'd probably sweated through my blouse and into my white coat. I blew some hair out of my mouth as I turned in the direction of Operating Room Thirty-Five, saying, "Never better."

I scrubbed and masked before entering the OR. As a nurse stepped up to get me into a gown and gloves, I asked Meri, "How much longer do you have here? I need to talk to you. Right away."

She looked up from the preemie on her table. Couldn't be more than a few days old. "What did your sister do now?"

"It's not about Brie," I said, although she was still a holy terror. "It's about Lake Tahoe and it's very urgent."

Meri gave me the same up-and-down glance I'd received from the charge nurse. Everyone else in the OR did the same. The tea was going to be hot on the surgical wing today. "Did the hotel call about those earrings you'd lost?"

"Not quite." I motioned to the patient. "Seriously, how long?"

"Five minutes to close and then another five with the family," Meri said. "I'll meet you in my office."

Twenty-seven minutes and several journeys through worst-case scenarios later, Meri arrived. I'd worn a ditch into the floor with my pacing and gnawed my thumbnail ragged in that time.

She shut the door behind her, saying, "What's happened?"

I continued pacing, my thumb still snared between my teeth. "He's *here*," I managed.

"Who is here, sweet cheeks?" She dropped into one of the chairs in front of her desk, her legs dangling over the arm. "I can't help if you don't use your words."

"The best man." I turned, shoving my fingers into my hair. "He's one of my new residents."

Meri was silent for a long moment. Then she dissolved into a fit of deep belly laughs. "Are you fucking kidding me? The best man from that huge wedding in Tahoe is a surgical resident at *this* hospital and he's on *your* service?"

"How can you laugh at a time like this?" I gazed at her, my mouth open in shock, hands still fisted in my hair. "What about this do you find funny?"

"The entire thing," she said. "Every drop of it, starting with you breaking all the rules at that wedding and—"

"How long have you been waiting to bring that up?"

"—ending with you paying for that crime in the most painful and hilarious way possible."

"Do you honestly think I have the capacity to deal with the fact that I've had a one-night stand with a resident? And I have to see him every day for the next two months? I have to teach him?"

Meri shrugged. "If there's anyone who can, it's you."

"Shall I remind you that my sister is still living with me? And that she's strangling every last inch of order and peace I have with her craft projects and all-night binge-watching and the laundry that she compulsively fluffs and never takes out of the dryer? Or that I am still spoon-feeding the basic tenets of professional standards to our colleagues? Do I really need the added bonus of a wedding hookup on my service to round out my life? *Really*?"

She gave me a monstrously tart grin that sent me in search of objects to throw at her. A heart-shaped pillow from her sofa embroidered with *The best gifts come in the tiniest packages* was my first choice. She caught it and tucked it against her chest. "It could be worse."

"How could it be worse?" I roared.

"I don't know." She rolled her eyes to the ceiling. "He could be married. Is he married?"

"He asked if he could buy me coffee sometime, so I'm going to assume that he's not."

She winged the pillow back at me, nailing me on the side of my face. "Why didn't you lead with that? Here I am, thinking he's playing it off like he doesn't know you and pretending it didn't happen, when in reality he wants another bite."

I pressed both palms to my face. "Don't say that! There will be no biting. Nothing like that. He's a first-year resident."

"Wait a second. How is the best man a *first-year*? He's way older than all the fresh-faced twentysomething baby surgeons running around here. He's at least thirty-two, thirty-three. I'd bet money on it."

"I don't know that either." I tossed the pillow back to the sofa. "I just told him that whatever happened at the wedding happened and we had to keep it professional now."

"And his response to that was to ask you on a coffee date?"

I shrugged. I couldn't tell her the rest. I couldn't process those details yet. This was very much a *run from the saber-tooth tiger and sort out the shit later* situation. "Yeah, pretty much."

"Whit, he *likes* you!" She kicked her feet up and cackled. "It's going to be so much fun to watch you sweat and squirm for two whole months."

"He does not like me. Even if he did, it doesn't matter. It *can't* matter." I resumed my pacing and went back to whittling away my thumb. "I've tethered my entire career to implementing this professional standards initiative and giving everyone some goddamn ethics. The absolute last thing I can do right now is start a relationship with my resident. That's even worse than being verbally abusive. There's a significant power imbalance. I'd get fired if anyone found out—"

"In no world would you get fired for hooking up with a resident *before* he was your resident and without you knowing that he would be your resident," she interrupted. "We are crazy about a lot of things around here, but we're not *that* crazy."

"What about the part where I hooked up with him while attending a wedding I wasn't invited to?"

Meri snagged her lower lip between her teeth. "I will admit that's less than ideal."

"I don't get to fuck up, Meri. I don't get to have less than ideal situations on my hands. Cossapino, Pecklewithe, Sadiskowski—

they're all just waiting for the moment when I snap at a tech or yell at some residents. If they found out about any of this, it's over and all my work will go down in flames with me." I met her gaze. "I can't let that happen. I cannot have that girl's death on my hands *and* throw away the only hope I have at making it right."

Meri ran the pad of her thumb over her nails. "Her death isn't on your hands. You know that as well as I do."

The logical, intellectual part of my mind agreed with Meri. That part knew it was absurd to shoulder the blame. Yet there was a small, steadfast corner clinging tight to that blame because *someone* had to be responsible. Someone had to *do* something.

"I know that I've put too much into this initiative to throw it away for coffee with a resident who made excellent use of eight condoms in one night."

"Eight?"

I gave a slow nod. "Eight."

With a sigh, Meri swung her legs over the chair and pushed to her feet. "Then we'll come up with a plan to keep him as far away from you as possible until it's time for him to bounce on over to a new rotation." I started to interrupt, but Meri cut me off, saying, "Before you tell me that you're duty-bound to teach him everything you know about heart transplants, I'll remind you that your chief resident and your fellows carry most of the instructional load when it comes to first-years. Unless you want to hand-select this boy to scrub in on your procedures, you'll primarily see him during rounds. Do you think you can keep your hands off each other for an hour or two each week? Or will you need eight condoms for that too?"

"He's going to know I'm avoiding him," I said.

She threw her arms out at her sides. "So what? He's just a guy. Let him suffer for a couple of months."

All the panic inside me suddenly gathered into a throb of exhaustion. I dropped to the sofa, my elbows on my knees and my face in my hands. "I can't believe this happened. I know surgeons and he didn't seem like a surgeon. He said he'd be married to his job for the next five years, but I didn't think that meant he was a resident. And he kept making stupid comments about me stopping his heart."

"What do you mean?"

I pressed my fingertips to my eyes. "He said"—I pushed air through my lips—"he said I was heart-stoppingly beautiful. No one with even a basic understanding of cardiac function would ever say anything like that."

She laughed through my misery. "He must've been so confused when he realized your name isn't Olivia."

I kept my eyes closed. I didn't need to watch her process this admission. "I didn't give him Olivia. Back in California. I gave him Whitney. But that was it. Nothing else."

Meri was quiet for a moment. "You like him, don't you?"

I dropped my hands. "No, and it doesn't matter."

"It could," she said gently. "If you wanted it to matter."

"I don't." I stood and went to the mirror near the door to check out the state of my face. Fortunately, only some of my makeup had melted off in my wild dash across the building. My eyeliner, as always, was flawless. "That's how it has to be."

Six

Whitney

Rule Number Twenty:
Cool girls don't let anything bother them.

I STEPPED OUT OF MY BEDROOM AND INTO CHAOS.

It was no different from the chaos that had greeted me every morning for the past few months and yet somehow I still managed to be shocked by it. Today, every article of clothing my sister owned—along with all the ones she'd *borrowed* from roommates past—had exploded across my living room. Piles upon piles of t-shirts and leggings, cut-off jeans and baggy sweatshirts covered the furniture and floor. An old-fashioned dressmaker's form I'd never seen before stood in one corner. A clothesline bearing bras and underwear stretched down the hall, anchored to doorknobs.

I knew I'd been bleary when I returned home late last night after a long surgery, but I would've remembered limbo-ing under a clothesline to get to my room. That meant Brie had gone on this anti-organizing spree after I went to bed and I'd slept through the whole thing. Maybe that wouldn't startle anyone else, but my place was small—which made it downright enormous by Boston standards—and I'd spent yet another night being chased around my dreams by the worst possible results of allowing my one-night stand to stay on my service for the next two months. I should've heard a clothesline being constructed a few steps from my bed.

But that was how Brie operated. She slept the morning away, worked remotely throughout the afternoon and early evening, and came to life after dark. Some nights she went out with friends, hopping from bars to clubs to house parties until the sun came up. Brie had friends in every city and she picked up more the minute she arrived. Other nights, she dumped a shoebox of sequins on the coffee table and settled in with the glue gun and some Hallmark holiday movies. There was no predicting which way she'd go and I knew better than to ask.

One of the most unforgivable sins in the world was asking my sister about her plans. It was second only to letting on that I had a hard time supporting some of her choices. That was at least part of the reason I continued to bite my tongue about her prolonged stay. It was easier to have my home be turned inside out for a little while than have her angrily pack up and leave while I was at work because I was too loose with the questions. She'd hold that against me for months.

I preferred to eat breakfast at home while I read through my schedule for the day, but there were dresses hanging from every cabinet in the kitchen and skirts all over the table. A handwritten inventory had been abandoned on the countertop along with price ranges, and I realized she was selling her clothes again. She did this a couple times each year. It usually signaled the start of something new, which could be anything from cutting her hair to picking out a different career. I just had to wait and see.

Rather than fighting my way through any of it and disrupting the system she had in place, I grabbed my things and once again headed to my favorite coffee shop.

I'd always put in long hours, but around the time Brie's *short visit* marched into its second month, I'd taken to spending a bigger chunk of my day at the hospital. This meant I was often the first in line when the doors opened at Coffee Exchange and they usually had a latte and muffin waiting for me. They were angels like that, even though they nudged me almost every day to give the yogurt and granola bowls they were known for a chance.

I'd made that mistake once and spent the entirety of a six-hour surgery trying to work a flaxseed out from between my teeth. If I couldn't have my usual morning routine at home, I was sticking with unfrosted breakfast cupcakes.

When I made my way down Beacon Hill to the coffee shop on Charles Street, there were already a few people in line ahead of me. It would've been a fine time to review my schedule or dig through some emails, but my attention snagged on the person at the front of the line. He wore a pair of dark blue trousers and wingtips with a gray hoodie which I usually considered an unnecessary quirk of modern man-boys, but I couldn't force myself to look away.

I knew for a fact that I'd never before been captivated by the simple act of someone reaching into their back pocket and retrieving a wallet. I wasn't sure that I'd ever stopped to carefully observe the mechanics of that move or how it quietly screamed everything about that person's command of their body.

Right around then was when I realized I was staring at this guy's ass, and honestly, it was a great ass. Round and firm, like someone had not skimped on the squats. And those trousers were doing god's work with a straight cut that was slim enough to highlight the goods yet not so much as to give an anatomy lesson. I enjoyed everything about this.

After another moment of open appraisal, I was ready to chastise myself for objectifying strangers while I was too groggy from a shitty night of sleep to do it without any subtlety. Before I could do any of that, he turned away from the counter.

And I died a little bit because that ass belonged to none other than Henry Hazlette.

His gaze landed on mine and his whole face brightened. He smiled and that was all it took to burn off the fog of my bad-sleep bleariness. I was wide awake now and right back to the breathless shock I'd experienced since seeing him again two days ago.

For my part, I dropped my phone to the floor and it wasn't until two whole blinks later that I realized what I'd done. In that time, he'd closed the distance between us, grabbed my phone, and started polishing the screen on the fleecy interior of his hoodie.

I drew a panicked breath through my nose. He couldn't be here. He just could not. This was my neighborhood, my coffee shop, my town—and it was my hospital too. I didn't know how to exist in my world anymore if I had to do it with him right there, watching it all.

Last night's dreams had been a hazy collection of moments just like this one where everything seemed fine, but then I'd do something crazy like turning to Henry during rounds and asking him to discuss the sexual position where he had the most stamina. Or we'd be in the OR surrounded by staff and residents, and I'd give him instructions, only for him to respond with, "No problem, baby girl." I didn't think he'd ever called me that and I couldn't actually imagine him saying it with a straight face, but none of that mattered as much as the inevitability of my relationship with him coming to light.

He held the phone out to me. "I think this is yours."

"Thanks." I tried to pluck it from his hand without touching him at all though I failed miserably, instead dragging my fingertips over his palm and sliding them between his long fingers as I pulled away. It was impressive how hard I fumbled around this guy. No chill, no finesse.

He motioned to the cozy interior of the shop. "Do you live around here?"

I glanced at my phone before sliding it into my pocket. I couldn't turn around and stroll out of the shop now, not at this point, but the thought crossed my mind. "I don't think we should—"

"Oh. Right." He rocked back on his heels. "I didn't mean to cross any lines."

"No, I know that." We shuffled forward. "Anyway. I'm sure I'll see you later."

Henry nodded. "Yeah, I—"

"It's not a good morning until Whitney walks in," the barista sang, his Boston accent thick like chowder. "Same as always, sweetheart? Or you need a little somethin' extra today?"

"Extra sounds about right," I said with a laugh.

"I could tell. I could see it the minute you walked in. Late night at the hospital?" I nodded because it was true enough. "I got you, hon. Don't you worry about nothin'." He winked over the hood of the espresso machine. "You want me to toast your muffin for you too?"

I laughed as I swiped my card. "No, not today. They're saying it's going to be a warm one."

"Who knows what's happenin' with the weather anymore. Global warming, you know?" He gave me a wry smile. "All right, you give me a minute and I'll getcha taken care of."

As I moved to the opposite end of the counter, I glanced over to find Henry studying the barista, his bearded jaw set and his midnight eyes narrowed. I'd watched many expressions cross over Henry's face though I wasn't sure I'd ever seen so much intensity from him outside the bedroom.

It was fascinating. I had to force myself to stop looking at him. And thinking about him in the bedroom. *God.* I wasn't helping myself here.

He stood beside me, silent for a long moment as we stared blankly at the menu board. When the bellow of espresso machines and milk frothers died down, he glanced over at me. "You must come here a lot. They know your order." Henry tipped his head toward the barista. "And your name."

His tone was even but the edges were sharp, a pointed reminder that I'd withheld my name from him until the last moment.

"It's on my way to the hospital," I said, "and it's always the same people working at this hour. It's really just a matter of routine at this point."

"Then if I come here every day, will they want to warm my muffins too?"

"I don't see why not."

He made a noise that sounded like polite disagreement. "You really believe that?"

I turned my head in his direction but didn't meet his eyes. "I do."

He laughed and I could taste the salt in that sound. "Right. Of course."

I wish I could say that simply being near him didn't loosen every one of the mental laces holding me together or that his deep voice at this close distance didn't envelop me like warm bathwater. I wish I could pretend that I didn't feel the seams of my professional responsibility as his teacher marking my skin or that I didn't want to press them a little harder just to see what happened.

The barista called my name. I grabbed my coffee and muffin, and marched out the door.

I really was terrible at boundaries.

It wasn't as simple as walking away from Henry and I should've known that.

I *did* know it, but I didn't expect to be confronted with that truth just a handful of hours later when I stepped into the elevator. Henry leaned against the back wall, his ankles crossed while he frowned at his notebook. His legs were a full mile long. He was in dark blue scrubs and running shoes now, a pen tucked over his ear. His forearms were bare and that was a national emergency.

He glanced up, surprise registering in his eyes when he caught me staring.

The doors started to close at my back. Since I'd already pulled one disappearing act today, and running out of the elevator seemed like a level of drama I wasn't ready to embrace for myself, I gave him a quick nod and devoted all my attention to pressing the button for my floor.

I stayed there, staring at the panel like I'd incinerate if I allowed my gaze to wander anywhere else, until the doors opened on the next level and a flood of people boarded. An entire resident cohort or two, some med students, and one of the many attendings who really liked the sound of his own voice. He was deep into recounting a story and paid me no attention.

I tucked myself into the side wall, my arms crossed and my gaze on the floor to minimize any chance of accidental eye contact. When the doors opened on the next level, several more people crowded in. A pair of nurses edged in front of me, sending me back a few steps until I felt the heat of the person behind me.

"Easy there," Henry whispered.

He closed one hand around my elbow as the other landed on my hip, his fingers sliding just inside my pocket. I hoped against all things that he didn't notice the shaky breath I sucked in. The attending was still going on with his story and the nurses in front of me were comparing notes on who had the worst staffing situation today. No one was paying attention to us.

I made an attempt at shuffling forward to put a wisp of distance between us, but the nurses in front of me turned to face each other, forcing me flush against the hard slab of Henry's chest, my head under his chin. His hands flexed, holding me tight for a moment before I felt a rough exhale on my neck.

It took nothing at all to remember the feel of him behind me like this, the low, growly sounds he made and the way he held me like he'd never let go.

And it took everything to remember that we weren't those people anymore.

My shoulders hitched up as I pulled in another wobbly breath. "Dr. Hazlette—"

"I know," he said on a sigh. *"I know."*

The elevator stopped again and a few people exited, but neither of us moved. His hand stayed on my arm and I didn't step out of his orbit. I'd long forgotten which floor I was heading to and why I was due there. I'd tuned out the incessant buzz of my phone. Everything save for the press of his fingers into my skin and the solid heat of his chest on my back ceased to matter.

The resident cohort with the talky attending got off on the

next level, and just as the doors came together I realized we were alone. The elevator jolted as it rose and that was enough to snap me back to reality. I bolted to the other side of the car in two long strides and glanced over at Henry while I straightened my sleeves.

"That can't happen again," I said.

He crossed his arms over his chest. As if I needed to watch those forearm muscles rippling in real time. "I am aware."

I ran a hand down my arm, desperate to smooth the wrinkles at my elbow. "I'm sorry if I gave you the impression that I was interested— That I wanted—"

"Believe me," he said, his voice low and quiet, "I know what you want."

"And yet we continue to find ourselves in situations where you seem determined to test that theory." I couldn't stop touching my sleeve. *Out, damned spot.* "It can't happen again."

The doors opened once more, and for the second time today, I walked away from Henry as if that would solve anything.

SEVEN

HENRY

Transplant Surgery Rotation:
Day 4, Week 1

IT WAS FREEZING IN THE AUDITORIUM. IF I DIDN'T KNOW better, I'd assume I made a wrong turn and stumbled into the morgue. They never could find a consistent temperature for this place, which was irritating since I was down here every other day.

It was a good thing that my little sister-slash-adoptive mother Cami had insisted I run halfway across the hospital complex to grab my fleece zip-up for this week's morbidity and mortality conference. Not that I was going to tell her that. Cami was amazing, sister-mother for life, but she was right about everything all the time and I was legally obligated to keep her humble by any means necessary.

I spotted Tori in one of the back rows, kneeling on her seat. "We couldn't find anything together," she called. "Reza went down front and Cami's somewhere on the right side."

"No worries. We'll regroup back in the clinic."

"Watch out for yourself in here," she replied with a pointed look at the residents seated beside her. "Everyone's a little feral this morning."

I dropped my hands to my hips. I had at least a hundred pounds on Tori plus enough height to make a difference, and my background could be loosely described as *medical MacGyver shit*. "I think I'll be okay."

She tossed up her hands. "Don't say I didn't warn you."

It took a couple of minutes, but I found an empty seat on the left side of the auditorium that wasn't being aggressively held by a med student or stab-happy resident. *Feral* was the right word for it and it was exhausting.

On most days, I didn't feel almost a decade older than many of my first-year peers. That was largely due to the fact I didn't care, but also, the averages didn't speak accurately to the whole. My man Reza went off and grabbed a whole other chemistry degree before starting med school. Mama Cami had taken two gap years to work in Central American clinics. Tori was the only one in our cohort who'd done the straight shot of college, med school, and residency. None of us could say we'd taken the path that was right for everyone, but we knew it had been the right one for us.

Days like today, however, when I had to fight my way through a sea of twentysomethings who hadn't yet realized their career didn't hinge on sitting near the doc they idolized or coming up with a clever question to ask the presenter, I felt my age. I wanted to tell everyone to calm the fuck down and be quiet.

Fortunately, the lights dimmed and the conference started, and I didn't have to yell at anyone to get off my lawn. Especially since the guy next to me tucked his arms into the body of his fleece jacket and promptly fell asleep.

If I had to choose which of the twenty or so conferences, multidisciplinary meetings, and other convenings we had each week to sleep through, I'd probably go with inflammatory bowel disease conference over morbidity and mortality, but everyone's priorities were different.

Halfway through the first presentation—a necrotizing fasciitis case with a good patient outcome though a loud and clear reminder that minutes mattered with that shit—the person on my other side, not the snoozer, received a page and headed for the door. With that seat vacant, I unpacked myself a bit, spreading my knees and elbows until I no longer felt like I was crammed into a tin of sardines. I used that space to rest my head on my palm while I took down the important highlights of this presentation, my notebook balanced on my thigh.

I didn't notice someone shuffling along the row until they plopped down beside me. There was a second when I assumed it was the person who'd left, but then I breathed in the warm fruity-flowery scent that had followed me everywhere since June and I immediately turned to the left.

And there she was.

It was always like that with Whitney. She just...appeared. At the wedding and here at the hospital, in the coffee shop and then in the elevator. Like a hummingbird, stopping only long enough to fuck me up.

Her hazel gaze collided with mine for a moment that boiled over as we blinked at each other. As if I didn't know what she was doing, she swept a quick, furtive glance around the auditorium. There were no other seats, and though I didn't doubt she'd stand in the back because she didn't care if her moral high ground was comfortable, I was curious whether she'd get tired of running away from me.

I was trying to do this right, to follow her lead, but that elevator killed all my best intentions. I'd always been good at lying to myself though it was dense of me to think I'd be able to lie about how much I wanted her. How much the feel of her hip had made my fucking day. How I'd only reached for her to prevent her from backing into me, and then realized that her objectively terrifying *don't fuck with me* stare was a serious turn-on for me.

"Dr. Hazlette," she managed.

I stared at her for longer than could be considered polite before nodding. "Dr. Aldritch."

She tipped her chin toward the stage, a firm reminder of where my attention belonged. Fine. I could get through this. Just another seventy-five minutes of my brain carrying on a debate as to whether her scent was peaches or plums, and if I even knew what plums smelled like, or perhaps it was a flower, and did I have any idea which flower? This led, predictably, to thinking about the way she tasted, which was far better than any scent. She tasted like sex and summer and all the things that made me really fucking happy, and she was *right here* and I couldn't even look at her the way I wanted to without her closing in on herself.

What was another seventy-five minutes when I'd already survived three months? When I had at least another two months to go? Or longer, assuming I even had a chance here. I didn't know. I didn't know if things would change when I wasn't reporting to Whit anymore, if she'd ever be able to see past our respective roles. If she wanted to see past those roles.

I could've deluded myself into believing it was nothing at all, but I wasn't so good at lying to myself when it came to Whit. I didn't know what that said about me and I sure as shit didn't know what it said about her, but I was smart enough to avoid making eye contact with any of the possible answers.

From the corner of my eye, I noticed Whit patting her pockets and then rustling in each of them. She made sweet little frustrated sighs when she didn't find what she was looking for. She leaned back and drummed her fingers on a small leather-bound notebook.

I plucked a pen from my pocket and handed it to her without taking my focus away from the stage. The pause between my offering and her accepting was ridiculous, but eventually she did, whispering, "Thank you."

I murmured in acknowledgment and assigned myself the task of copying down everything on the presenter's slides just so I didn't do anything stupid like press my face to her neck or ask why she left the way she did after the wedding.

She clicked the pen and I heard, "Oooh."

I watched as she examined the pen like it was the most marvelous thing she'd ever seen. Her shoulders bounced and her lips curled into the first real smile I'd seen from her in this city as she tested it out. If she knew I was drinking in every ounce of her joy *over a pen*, she didn't let on.

I flipped to the last page in my notebook and wrote *pens*. I added *cupcakes* on the next line.

The next case presentation started, this one focused on post-operative infection rates for patients with gunshot wounds, and I listened closely. The assumption had always been that I'd pursue trauma surgery. I didn't come here believing that I already knew everything there was about trauma, but I'd lost track of the number of compound fractures I'd managed on mountainsides while blizzards whipped around me. I knew more than most. Being here for the past few months, however, had dimmed the brightness of that assumption. Some of the best trauma surgeons in the world worked here and I'd heard great things about the fellowship program, and I knew I'd do well there but it was no longer my only option.

Dr. O'Rourke was deep into discussion of a data set when Whit's elbow connected with my arm and all I could do was slow-blink in her direction.

"Sorry," she whispered.

I refused to let my gaze drop to the spot where her elbow still nudged my arm. If I did, she'd move, and I was a floundering, helpless fool who'd live off these tiny interactions indefinitely. "No problem."

She scrolled through an NIH journal article on her phone while she tapped the pen to her notebook. I had the sense she was listening and reading at the same time, which only reinforced the fact that she was gifted in many insane ways. Some I knew all too well.

As I shifted to get a better view of O'Rourke's slides, my knee pressed against Whit's thigh. We both stared at the spot where my navy blue scrubs seemed to dissolve into her black pants. It took a minute for me to stop thinking about her soft, thick thighs and get the manspreading under control.

"My bad," I murmured.

"You're fine," she replied, though the tightness in her tone suggested otherwise.

A solid seven or eight minutes passed without incident. We didn't touch each other. I didn't dump the contents of my pockets in her lap just to see if any of it impressed her as much as the pen. I didn't beg her to tell me if it was plum or peach or some other thing I didn't even know about.

She laughed under her breath a few times while O'Rourke fielded questions and roasted his colleagues in response. He was a low-affect, brick wall kind of guy. He glared down at the audience like we were wasting his damn time, asking, "Is that really what you want to ask *me*, McCurty? Not your Intro to Gross Anatomy professor, somewhere around thirty years ago?"

Whit brought a hand to her mouth as a laugh shook her shoulders. Her elbow was on my arm again and I shifted toward her by millimeters. I wasn't sure if I'd invented this in my head, but it seemed like she shifted toward me too.

"Is he always like this?" I asked.

"Mmm. Yeah." She shrugged and there was not a single chance in hell that she wasn't fully aware that we were pressed together from the armrest on up. "Not the most conventional style, I'll admit."

I went back to that last page, adding *Coffee Exchange* and *muffins—hot?* to my list.

The Q&A ended and the next presenter took the stage. This one was about recent outcomes of minimally invasive surgical interventions for adolescents with chronic heart failure, and Whit put her phone away. She'd probably come specifically for these cases.

One of the many things about Whitney that amused me to no end was how she telegraphed every thought and feeling—when her guard was down. The rest of the time, she was a wall of cool, unyielding granite, and that made these rare flashes of her personality even more amazing. Right now, her face was a kaleidoscope of reactions. Interest, doubt, disagreement, excitement—it was all there, shifting by the second while she jotted down notes.

I wanted to hear every thought crossing her mind.

While processing the complete *what the fuck* of this situation over the past few days, I'd let myself wonder what would've happened if either of us had been upfront about our careers at the wedding. Would we have run through our histories, comparing notes on who we knew and where we'd been? Would we have fallen into bed the way we did? Would it have mattered after the hours we'd spent on the dance floor? I didn't know, and chances were good I'd never know, but playing *what if* was simpler than trying to figure out how to play *no one has to know.*

Whit's elbow jolted me again, though when I glanced over this time I found her dragging her palms up and down her arms. A small shiver sent her burrowing into herself, which had the complicated effect of drawing my attention to her lips and then her chest. Specifically, the nipples stabbing their way out of her blouse.

My god.

And fuck me, I remembered exactly how her breasts felt in my palms. The perfect handful. I swallowed hard and tucked my pen over my ear while I shrugged out of my fleece, careful not to wake the snoozer. "Here." I motioned for her to lean forward so I could drape it over her shoulders. She didn't move. "Have mine."

She waved me off, saying, "No. Thank you, Dr. Hazlette, but no. I'm fine."

I leaned in close so that only she could hear me. "If you don't take this, Dr. Aldritch"—I drew a pointed glance down to her shirt—"I will put it on you myself."

Her stare turned as hard as her nipples and there was a second where it seemed like she wanted to press her luck with that ultimatum. Which was fantastic because there was nothing better than getting a real reaction out of her. It was a big improvement over her walking away from me.

But another shiver moved through her and she snatched up the fleece, settling it over her lap like a blanket. She folded her arms beneath it, officially removing her elbow from my bicep.

"Thank you," she said, though it sounded a lot like *fuck you.*

I arched a brow but didn't say anything. We turned our attention back to the presentation, her nodding along and murmuring to herself as the fellow spoke and me scribbling down everything that seemed relevant—which was most of it. This was the sort of material I remembered Whit bringing up during rounds and I'd bet anything she'd reference these cases next week.

When the fellow started winding down the presentation, I felt Whit's gaze on me. She tapped her pen to one of the notes I'd written. I glanced over. She nodded enthusiastically, saying, "That's a smart point."

"Thought you'd like that."

She huffed out an impatient breath. "It's not that I *like* it, it's that it's a meaningful observation."

"You're welcome to cling to that difference as long as you can see it."

Another huff. "I'm not clinging to anything."

I held her gaze as I shifted my knee toward her again. I saw it the minute she felt me against her thigh and I saw the rapid-fire debate occurring behind her hazel eyes. For all that debate, she didn't seem to come to any quick conclusions because we went right on staring at each other through the remainder of the Q&A portion. Somewhere in there, she'd edged her elbow out from under my jacket and returned it to my arm.

I couldn't say with any accuracy what she was thinking. I didn't know anything other than the fact we were pushing and pulling at each other. And yet it felt like we were saying something. Like we were swearing that we remembered that night, *everything* about that night, and we couldn't stop thinking about it. That we'd tried and failed and we were here now, in this unbelievable situation where everything was difficult. That we missed each other.

Like I said, I didn't know what was happening behind those eyes. But I felt something.

The guy beside me startled himself awake, springing out of his seat and shaking himself like a wet dog when the conference ended. "Good talk, good talk," he muttered. He shoved his arms back through his sleeves and rubbed his eyes before jogging down the row.

I had to leave. My schedule had no breathing room and my cohort would be waiting for me. But I stayed, scribbling notes I didn't need while the room cleared out.

Whit's phone buzzed and she had to displace both her elbow and the jacket to fish it from her pocket. She glanced down at the screen, muttering, "Dammit."

I closed my notebook. "Important?"

"It's all important." She pushed to her feet and I did the same. "Thank you." She held out my jacket. "For this."

"Keep it," I said, backing down the row.

She thrust it toward me. "No. That's unnecessary."

"It's always cold in here. You'll need it for next time." I motioned to the nearly empty room. "Unless you're planning on sitting next to me again."

"I'm not planning on it."

I held out my hands, let them fall. "Maybe you should."

Eight

Whitney

Rule Number Fifteen:
Don't overshare, even when the conversation flatlines.

"And in general, I do agree with you," Dr. Jurgen said. "Just because we were trained a certain way doesn't mean that's the only way to train new surgeons."

Since I knew from experience that he was going to continue speaking regardless of whether I agreed, argued, or shape-shifted into a dolphin, I glanced over his shoulder to where Jenelle had a few resident cohorts circled up down the hall. She liked to run through highs and lows for the week and used that time to get a pulse on everyone. She was good about getting people extra help when they needed it and doing it without making them feel small.

I mean, she was one of the toughest fifth-years in the building and she didn't let anyone get away with anything on her watch, but she never dropped the hammer unless it was fair and warranted.

If only surgeons fifteen years her senior could master the same skill.

Hell, at this point, I'd take surgeons who could acknowledge that it was a skill worth having.

For all his gifts and talents, it did not seem that Dr. Jurgen was one of them.

"As you're well aware, we don't always have time for niceties," he went on. "I can't stop to make sure everyone feels loved and appreciated while my patient is bleeding out on the table."

A laugh rippled through Jenelle's group and my gaze landed on Henry. I glanced back to Dr. Jurgen before Henry noticed. We didn't need another accidental encounter.

"If there was one thing for your committee to reevaluate—"

"As I know *you're* well aware, it's not *my* committee," I interrupted. "It's a committee co-chaired by the Chief of Surgery and the hospital president, on an order from the Board. That I've taken on a leadership role in developing and disseminating this code of professional standards does not mean it isn't the product of collaborative work."

"Then I'll take my issues to the board."

"By all means. I'm sure they'd love the feedback. There was an extensive feedback period last spring when these standards were originally presented, but I'm sure they'd be thrilled to hear your thoughts now." Since this week had drained me of all my better judgment, I added, "You should know that the board, the chief, the hospital president—they all know that we don't always have time for niceties. That's not new information. They also know that there is a difference between being tough and demanding and having high expectations, and toxic, abusive behavior. It's pretty easy to see and it's always surprising when otherwise smart, talented people don't notice that difference." I glanced down at my watch. "You'll have to excuse me."

He raked an irritable glance over my scrubs and clogs. "Then I take it you're perfect at all of this."

I took a minute to gather up the patience I required to explain that treating others with decency wouldn't cost him anything before responding. "No, of course I'm not perfect. No one is. Not me, not you, not anyone else. But you're good at vascular surgery, Jurgen, and from what I've heard over the years, you're a good teacher too. So, what's the real problem here?"

"I just think it's unnecessary to take it all this far," he said.

I nodded. I'd heard variations on that so many times. *One resident kills herself and we have to change everything?* As if she was the first resident to end her life. As if other outcomes—substance abuse, self-harm, and untreated depression and anxiety, not to mention throwing away years of medical training—weren't also cause for action.

"Maybe for you it is unnecessary," I said, though this conversation gave me some doubts. "Great. It isn't for all of our colleagues. And without formal guidance, it's a lot tougher to weed out the issues." When his shoulders slumped in very reluctant agreement, I gave him a tolerant smile. "Now, you really must excuse me."

Since I didn't want to wait for an elevator while Jurgen lingered nearby, I headed down the hall toward Jenelle. I didn't need another excessively intimate moment with Henry on hospital grounds, but I figured there were too many people around for that to happen.

Then what the hell happened in the auditorium?

The less I thought about that, the better. I still had his pen in my pocket, but in my defense, it was a really nice pen. I'd smuggled his jacket out of here last night like I'd started trading in blood diamonds, glancing over my shoulder every few steps and clutching my bag to my side the whole time. I figured it was safer at my place than in my office, even while I rationalized that *no one* would care about a stray jacket, much less demand an accounting of how it came to be in there.

As I approached the group, the third-year cohort peeled off, leaving behind the first-years. Residents didn't rotate to transplant surgery after the first year unless they chose it. I had Jenelle because she'd chosen transplant as an elective. I was hoping I could convince the residency director to trim down some of her other rotations and let me keep her a little longer.

"I have to say," I started, "I'm impressed to see that you're all still standing after getting called in at three in the morning and a nonstop day of surgery." I dropped a hand to Jenelle's shoulder. "How many kidneys did we transplant today?"

She held up a hand, wiggling her fingers. "Five. It was raining kidneys around here." She motioned to the first-years. "Everyone here scrubbed in at least once."

"Yeah, I saw Dr. Ansari when I assisted Dr. Hirano this afternoon. Nicely done."

He nodded in acknowledgment. I had a soft spot for the quiet ones.

"It was insane." Tori ran her hands through her short cropped hair. "Can we do it again tomorrow?"

"I'll page you at three a.m.," Jenelle said. "See if you're still interested."

Tori bounced from foot to foot. "I already know I'll be down for it."

Cami stepped forward, saying, "We were just talking about going out to celebrate the end of our first week in transplant surgery. It's a little tradition we started during our first rotation and it would be great if you'd join us." When I didn't respond immediately, she added, "Copeland is in and the pediatric surgery group is going to be there too."

"I heard from a few people that Dr. Acevedo will be there," Tori said. "Rumor has it he's buying the first round. Can we put you down for the second?" When she saw me biting back a laugh, she added, "Game recognizes game."

I had to respect how hard Tori went with everything, even if I'd sooner donate my own kidney to avoid this shindig. "I appreciate the offer though I'll have to pass tonight. Be sure to ask Dr. Acevedo about his time with Doctors Without Borders. He has some amazing stories."

"Is there anything we can do to convince you to come along?" Cami asked. "Help me out here, Hazlette." She gave him a conspiratorial grin. "You're the one who always gets everyone together."

I met Henry's gaze and instantly knew it was a bad idea. Part of the problem was that he looked at me like he knew me, like he could read my thoughts the same as words on a page. The other part, perhaps the most dangerous of all, was that I wanted—secretly, desperately, loudly—to be known.

After a pause, he said, "You should stop by."

Meri and Brie and everyone else would say I was strong and fearless, but that wasn't always how it sounded in my head, and right now I wasn't sure I was strong enough to hold off a man who seemed determined to know me.

"I'll see what I can do," I said, forcing a smile.

"I NEED YOU TO COME TO A BAR TONIGHT AND physically restrain me," I said into my phone as I climbed the stairs of my Temple Street brownstone. I lived on the third floor, which made for a lot of time on these stairs.

"Who is this?" Meri teased. "I'm sorry, but you have the wrong number unless you're paying fifteen hundred an hour for my services."

I laughed. "Is that all?"

"Yes, darling, I'm giving you my friends and family rate."

"Because you're a gem," I said. "So, listen. The best man and my first-year residents kind of cornered me into showing up at their happy hour tonight. That would be fine if I didn't keep making supremely bad decisions every time I get within ten feet of him so I need you to be the *oh hell no* friend. Can you meet me there? Please?"

She blew out a long breath. "I wish I could, but I have a thing."

"What's the thing? How is it that I didn't know about a thing?"

I stepped into my apartment and found Brie sitting on the floor in the living room, her laptop on the coffee table and a giant to-go cup of iced coffee in her hand. I glanced between her and the coffee with *are you seriously drinking that?* eyes. She pursed her lips and turned back to her screen as if the flare-up all that caffeine would cause didn't bother her.

Today Brie was never concerned with Tomorrow Brie's problems. I was the only one concerned with all the problems, all the time.

"It's nothing," Meri said in my ear. "It's just a thing."

"It's a thing you don't want to tell me about?"

"It's really not a big deal and it's been such a crazy week that I didn't even remember to mention it," she said, and her glib tone made it clear that she knew none of this made sense. "But maybe I can swing by this happy hour thing on my way home? Text me the location. Hey, should I call you at a certain time with some kind of fake emergency so you can leave? Anything to keep your virtue intact, young lady."

"My virtue is long gone, but I'd love to keep some of my sanity and all of my job." I headed toward my bedroom and closed the door behind me. I didn't know what was going on with Meri and why she was so oddly evasive, but I'd get to the bottom of that some other time. "Should I change? I'm wearing those gray pants, the ones with the superfine windowpane print and that barely pink button-down that you always threaten to steal."

"I know you're not trying to give him the trouser tingles, but I'd only stick with that if you want him to think you don't have a life."

"I have a life!"

"Trust me, I know," she replied evenly. "Might as well make sure the best man knows too."

I choked out a laugh as I returned my shoes to their spot in the closet. "I cannot see why that's our goal."

"I want you to let him think you have a lot going on—*a lot* as in fun and sexy things that have you hopping from one place to another on a Friday night. There's a very good chance that he won't read anything into you wearing your regular workday look, but if he sees you all dolled up and hears that you have other stops to make tonight, he'll get the message that he's not the only sausage on your plate."

"My god, Meri. I didn't need that visual. And he's not on my plate."

"Put your fine ass in some jeans," she said. "Throw on a spiffy top with a hint of cleavage that says you're effortlessly chic and definitely not trying too hard, which should be easy since that's everything you own. Get your hair out of those French braids and go bold with the lip color. Got it?"

We talked for a few more minutes while I dug through my closet. I still didn't know where she was going and why she wouldn't just tell me what was up, but I trusted her to tell me when she was ready. I never had to worry about where I stood with her.

Once I was changed and my hair was loose around my shoulders, I left my room. Brie was still on the floor. She was watching a makeup tutorial while editing a slide deck.

"I'm going out for a bit," I said, slipping earrings into place as I headed toward the door. "Meeting some people for drinks."

"Okay, cool." She paused the video. "I talked to Dad today."

Everything inside me froze and flipped like I'd missed a step and now I was falling to my clumsy death. "I'm sorry. What?"

"He's coming to Boston sometime before the end of the year," she said. "I was thinking we should try to get together with him. Maybe meet up for dinner."

Cold sweat ran down my back as my stomach churned. If I didn't know better, I'd think it was a sudden wave of food poisoning. But I did, I knew better, and I knew this was how my body reacted to the idea of seeing my father.

I sucked in a few deep breaths before saying, "I don't know that I care to do that."

"You should at least try."

This was always Brie's position. That we should *try*. That we only had one father in this life and we should put in the work to build a relationship with him. I didn't see a reason to chase down a man who'd made clear *over and over* that he had no interest in our existence only for him to prove to my face that he didn't give a damn about us. Was there a good reason to incinerate my self-worth and mental health like that? I didn't think so.

I headed for the door. "I'll be back later."

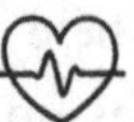

I STEWED ABOUT BRIE AND OUR FATHER THE ENTIRE RIDE to the Seaport neighborhood of Boston. She always did this. She always put me in impossible positions where I had to choose between tanking my relationship with her or harming myself, and then acted like *I* was the outrageous one for not putting a smile on my face and going along with it.

Maybe it would be different if we'd just now found our father after living all these years in the dark. But his identity had never been a mystery. There were no secrets, only choices. He'd chosen to exclude himself from our lives, first when I was born and then again when Brie came along. I couldn't pretend that hadn't happened.

My sister didn't see it that way.

I didn't want to spend the whole night feeling messy and lonely because I couldn't even count on my sister to be on my side, but the weight of it all settled on my shoulders like a dark, sad cape. I knew I could shove it off and trudge on like everything was fine, like I always did, but I really wanted to climb into bed and watch something that would give me an excuse to cry.

Stepping out of the car at the beer garden, a thick wall of late summer humidity hit me hard. Even an hour past sunset, it was still warm. I made my way through the outside seating area and focused on looking for familiar faces, preferably Acevedo or Jenelle. They were both on the tall side, making them easy to locate in crowds.

And neither of them was Henry Hazlette, the last person I needed to lock eyes with right now.

"You're here!" Tori appeared beside me, a loaded tray in her hands. "Come on. We grabbed a few tables in the back. You just missed the peds crew. They bailed to go bowling."

In the minute it took us to weave through the crowd, I mentally ran through all the ways to exit this situation without making it obvious that I couldn't be anywhere near Henry. Meri was available to swoop in with an emergency, there were the fictional *dinner plans downtown*, and in a pinch, I could always fake a call from the hospital. Or I could be a grown-ass adult and leave without explanation or apology when I was ready.

"We need to plan a day-trip to Salem for spooky season," I heard Cami saying as we approached. "I really want a witch to read my cards and I know y'all would love it."

She sat beside Jenelle, their backs turned to us. Ansari was on the end and Henry was on the other side of the table, staring down at his phone. He hadn't noticed me yet, giving me one rare moment to study him without the overwhelming awareness that always came with his gaze. He'd changed into jeans and a t-shirt with *Heavenly Lake Tahoe* scrawled across the faded front. As if I required the reminder.

Jenelle leaned her head against her upturned palm. "How does that work in your mind? The witch stuff and the science stuff? Because I don't understand how anyone can practice medicine and believe in witches and card readings."

"It's no different than religion," Cami replied.

"Well, it's good you brought it up because I have a lot of questions about that too," Jenelle said.

"We're not debating faith and science again," Tori said as she set the tray down. "Put that away for tonight. Aldritch just got here. Hazlette, get off the dating apps and grab another chair, would you?"

Everything inside me sank. It was a fully unnecessary reaction and I resented everything about it, especially since I expected Henry to be dating. Why wouldn't he? He was young and in a new town and...single. He was single. He should be getting out there. No reason not to.

He jerked his head up and stared at me, frozen for a moment before gaining his feet. "I'm not on any dating apps." He said this to Tori while keeping his eyes on me. "You know that."

I refused to do anything with that comment. Anything at all.

"Yeah, but maybe you should be," Cami said. "Might help with that sleep issue you've been having, if you know what I mean."

I couldn't help but glance his way as he plucked a chair from an empty table. He rolled those dark eyes with those thick, dark lashes and shook his head, saying, "Everyone knows what you mean, CCD, but I'm fine."

I forced a quick smile and glanced around the table as everyone shuffled to accommodate another seat. "I can't stay too long, but I wanted to pop in and congratulate you on a great start to this rotation."

As I settled between Jenelle and Ansari, Tori started distributing drinks from her tray. "I ordered everything that sounded good, so we have loads of extras." She rattled off the names and detailed descriptions of all the remaining beers and glanced at me. "What would you like?"

I pointed to the pale golden beer because she'd mentioned that one first and all the others had blended together in a blur of terminology that meant very little to me. "You know your way around beers, I take it?"

"No, I just remember things," she replied.

Jenelle leaned in, whispering, "Her recall is ridiculous. Basically, if she's read it, she doesn't forget it. It's been driving me crazy all week."

I nodded as I took a sip. "How is it that you've made it all the way to your fifth year without realizing you're not the only smartest person in the room?"

She scoffed. "My year is full of idiots."

"Right." I gave her a sympathetic nod though they were far from idiots. Jenelle was both exceptionally bright and talented, which was a combination few could truly claim. Instinct and being quick on your feet usually filled in the gaps where others fell short.

Cami held up her glass of dark brown beer. "Hazlette, it's your turn to make the toast."

He paused for a long second before reaching for his glass. He seemed to consider it for another second, blinking slowly. Then, "Here's to one week down." His gaze circled the group, eventually stopping on me. "Only seven to go."

As we clinked our glasses together, I found myself coming out of my seat to reach Henry's. When we finally connected, we stayed there, staring at each other while everyone toasted around us. Eventually, he said, "Fifty-one days."

I pulled back like I'd been startled, beer sloshing over the rim and onto my fingers. I turned my attention to Ansari, who seemed to be drinking soda, and tapped my glass to his.

He responded with, "Yes. Thank you."

I devoted all my attention to the next sip. By my math, I was over the legal limit for heavy glances shared with Henry and now it was time to go. If I stayed much longer, I'd slip up again. I knew I would. And it didn't matter that we had a table between us and all these people watching. We'd had an auditorium around us the other day and that hadn't stopped a damn thing. All I had to do was stand up and—

"Dr. Aldritch, have you been to Salem? Can you give us any insider info?" Cami rubbed her palms together. "My family takes spooky season very seriously. I know it's different around here than where I'm from but I'm hoping it will treat some of my homesickness."

Okay, so I wasn't leaving just yet. Five more minutes wouldn't kill me if I focused only on Cami. "Where are you from?"

"I grew up in Houston, though my mom's family is from the Rio Grande Valley, near Brownsville. We love a good Día de los Muertos season."

"I did a fellowship at Baylor," I said.

"I went to Baylor! For med school! You know my city?" she cried, her dark brown eyes wide and shining like she might burst into tears at any second.

"I was only there a short time, but yeah, it was great," I said. "I spent a lot of time at an ice house on Alabama. And the food was incredible. There's nothing quite like it around here."

"I'll cook for you," she said, nearly bouncing out of her seat. "I always make too much anyway because my husband's residency is in New York and I haven't figured out how to cook for one. I give these guys all the extras. I'll bring you some too."

Before I could decline because I didn't need anyone thinking I made my residents fetch my lunch, Tori said, "True story. She's feeding most of the surgical ICU nurses too."

"This is the first time in years that I'm living alone," Cami replied with a shrug. "I don't know another way."

"So, you want to go to Salem?" I asked.

"Right, yes, my spooky season goals. Here's my plan."

I leaned forward as I listened to her and this had the unfortunate effect of putting Henry right in my line of sight. Even while I looked at Cami, I couldn't help but track every move he made. "I'm afraid I don't know much about Salem though I've always heard it's overrun with tourists in October."

Cami let out a sigh as her shoulders slumped. "I was worried about that."

"We can still go," Tori said. "I don't believe that you should only go places when they're not busy. We just need to be prepared for it."

I found myself swept into an intense conversation with Cami and Tori about local destinations although I was getting the impression that *intense* was the only speed these two operated at. It was like looking back in time at me and Meri.

Before I knew it, I'd finished one drink and Tori was pressing another into my hand while Cami went through all the ways her husband's residency program in New York was different from hers, but mostly how grueling it was to spend their first married year apart after being together through college and med school. It was a wonderful distraction from my own interpersonal issues. Entire minutes went by without being aware of the tender spot where Brie's announcement had landed.

Henry, Ansari, and Jenelle were talking about some preprint research that had everyone up in arms as there seemed to be a lot of issues with the methodology. I knew Henry wasn't as deeply invested in the conversation as Jenelle or Ansari, and I knew he shot a glimpse toward me every few minutes. He'd caught me glancing at him over the rim of my beer and responded with a slight quirk of his lips before shifting his attention to Jenelle's position on the lack of gender and racial diversity in too many medical research studies.

I lost twenty minutes to wondering about that smirk.

Ansari was the first to leave. He had to get home to his cats, he'd said. Jenelle followed him, making some noises about being maxed out on hospital people for the week. This would've been a fine time for me to make my exit. All I had to do was stand up and say goodbye yet I couldn't pull myself out of this chair. It was like all those covert looks had gathered into an impossible weight anchoring me in place and I couldn't move. Not yet.

When Cami and Tori drifted toward the other side of the patio area to meet some dogs, I dug through my bag to keep myself from acknowledging that Henry and I were alone. Again. "I should get going." I tossed a glance in his direction before grabbing my phone and responding to a few texts. I ignored Meri's question about whether I was in need of emergency evacuation.

"Yeah, probably." His gaze was far away. "Or you could stay and tell me what's wrong."

I put my phone down. "Nothing's wrong."

He leaned in, dropping his forearm to the table as he peered at me. He lifted his hand and tucked some hair over my ear. "That's not what it looks like to me."

It took everything inside me to keep from tilting toward him, which was how I ended up blurting out, "Why are you a first-year resident and not at the end of a fellowship?"

He studied me for a second before curling his hands around his glass. "We skipped over those details, huh?"

I grabbed my phone and purse, and pushed to my feet. "Forget it. I shouldn't have asked and I really need to go—"

Henry grabbed my wrist and tugged me back into the chair. His thumb pressed to my pulse point and we both knew how hard my heart was beating. "Sit down. Stay a minute. Please?"

"Just a few minutes."

"That's all I need."

He drew lazy circles on the inside of my wrist. I thought about pulling my hand away, and maybe I should've, but I didn't want to be sad anymore. I didn't want to be lonely.

"I started as a paramedic," he said, "and worked near Lake Tahoe. An opening on a mountain rescue unit in the Sierra Nevadas came up and I was in. It was everything I'd ever wanted. Mostly catastrophic injuries. Broken bones, serious wounds, major head and spinal stuff. Every call was an epic survival quest. I mean, rappelling down from a helicopter to secure a hiker with a brain bleed into a basket at nine thousand feet in mudslide conditions and then keeping them stable all the way to UC San Francisco? That kind of survival quest." He took a sip, drawing a slow gaze down the neckline of my shirt and over my bare arms. "I won't say I got tired of it because that doesn't happen when every day is unpredictable, but I decided I was up for a bigger challenge and went to med school. At thirty."

"A bigger challenge." Instead of laughing, a snort honked out of me. There was no disguising it, no pretending that I'd coughed or fumbled my way through a giggle. I slapped a hand over my eyes. "I can't believe that just happened."

"That was adorable," Henry said through a laugh. He squeezed my wrist. "Do it again. Please."

"First of all, over my dead body, and second, I have no control over these things." I peeked at him between my fingers. "We'll never speak of this again. There will be no resident rumors about the time I did my best impression of a clown horn."

"Your secrets are safe with me, Whit." He dragged his fingers up the inside of my arm and back down, and nothing had ever turned me on so fast as this. "All of them."

I dropped the hand from my face. It would've been so easy to slide my fingers between his and pick up right where we'd left off at the lake. So easy. And it would be *good*. There was no reason to pretend otherwise. But then I'd wake up and find myself in the middle of a homegrown disaster far worse than my summer souvenir disaster, and I couldn't jeopardize all my work for that. I *wouldn't* jeopardize my work just because I was low and needy tonight.

"You can't call me that anymore," I whispered.

He circled my wrist again. "I know."

I gulped my beer. It wasn't cold anymore and I wasn't sure I liked the flavor, but it gave me something to do while I pulled myself together. "I take it you're here for Stremmel and O'Rourke. They're attracting a lot of interest in trauma surgery these days."

"Maybe." He shrugged. "It's possible I'll end up in trauma, if I'm being real, but I want to get a good look at my options first." His gaze slipped from my eyes down to my lips as I chased a stray drop of beer. "Except transplant. That's not an option."

"You've determined that after one week? Didn't you like seeing that new kidney pink up today? That usually sells it."

"The kidney was fucking incredible, but I plan on staying as far away from your service as I can once this rotation is over. Assuming that's still the condition for me taking you out," he added.

"Oh. *Oh.*" I closed my free hand around the armrest to steady myself. It was either hold on tight or fling myself at him, and I'd already established that I wouldn't be doing one of those things anymore. "I don't know if—"

"Fifty-one days, remember?"

"Right." I nodded. "Listen, I should—"

"Why'd you go to med school?" he asked. "What's your story, Whit?"

I hooked a glance over my shoulder to locate Tori and Cami. They were seated on the ground, dogs climbing into their laps and licking their faces. It looked like we had a few minutes, which was fantastic since I wasn't ready to leave. "My grandmother lived in northern New Mexico and, most of the time, we stayed with her. There were a few years when we were in Colorado, but mostly in Rio Arriba County with my grandmother. She was great but there was hardly any healthcare to speak of in that area back then. If you were sick or injured or having a baby, you had a drive ahead of you. Forget about managing chronic illnesses. Even as a kid, it annoyed the hell out of me."

He belted out a deep laugh. "Of course it did."

"To answer your question, I went to med school because I grew up watching people struggle and suffer as a result of not having reliable access to healthcare. But I realized pretty soon that community medicine wasn't the direction for me. I...am not a generalist. I'm better at surgery and I'm much better when I can specialize. I wouldn't have lasted long in family practice."

"That's a damn good reason," he said. "Probably better than mine."

My sister and her jug of coffee flashed through my mind. "There was a time when I would've agreed with you, but I'm not so sure about that anymore. It only matters if the reason is good enough to keep you going."

Nodding, Henry leaned closer to me. His knee pressed into my thigh as his thumb stroked my wrist. We stared at each other like we were the only people in the world. Pressure banded around my chest and I sucked in a ragged breath.

"Fifty-one days," he said.

It sounded like he was offering me a deal, one I'd be crazy to turn down so long as I could ignore all the warnings about the whole thing blowing up in my face.

After a while, though, warnings like that lost their teeth.

"Hello, hello." An arm wrapped around my shoulder and

yanked me back in my seat, effectively cutting me off from all points of contact with Henry. I shifted as much as I could with Meri balanced on the armrest and digging her fingers into my upper arm. She glared at me with *what the fuck* eyes for a second before holding out her hand to Henry. "Hi. We haven't officially met. I'm Meri Mercer. Associate chief of fetal-neonatal surgery."

"Henry Hazlette," he replied. "First-year resident."

"I bet you're pumping Dr. Aldritch for pro tips on how to make the most of your residency and finding *appropriate* mentors," she said, saccharine dripping from her words. "But I'm gonna have to steal her away now. We're going to miss our reservation if we don't skedaddle." She hooked her elbow with mine and pulled me to my feet, grabbing my phone and shoving my bag under my arm. "Do you need to pick up the tab for these kids or are we good to go?"

"Yeah, I should—"

"No. It's covered." Henry stood, sliding his hands into his pockets. "Thank you again for your insight, Dr. Aldritch. We appreciate you joining us tonight."

Meri led me away from the table, saying, "Yep! Have a good night now!"

I glanced back at Henry. He held up a hand, and though I couldn't hear him and I was terrible at reading lips, I was certain he said, "Fifty-one days."

We reached the sidewalk and Meri yelled, "What the fuck was that, Whitney?" She shoved her hands through her auburn hair and stomped for an entire block. When I caught up to her, she continued. "What the literal fuck?"

"That's why I asked you to come with me," I cried.

"I expected to find you sharing awkward glances," she said. "Not eye-fucking each other hard enough to make me wonder if you have an exhibitionist side I didn't know about." She stopped and looked around. "Where are we going?"

"You're the one who said we had reservations."

"Because of the eye-fucking visible from twenty feet away!" She rubbed her temples and blew out a breath. "What's going on, Whit? What is this all about?"

I leaned against a storefront window, my hands propped on my knees. I stared at my shoes for a minute or two. I didn't know what to tell her because I didn't know what was happening. I didn't have the language to explain this. Even if I did, I wasn't sure I could make myself say the words.

"It's nothing," I said eventually. Because that was the only answer available to me. It didn't matter how bitter it tasted on my tongue. It was the truth. It had to be. "It's just been a weird, stressful week. I haven't recovered from the shock of it all. I still can't believe the guy from that wedding is here and he's my resident. On top of that, Brie is—"

"One of these days, you should let me talk to her. She'll find some sense when I'm done with her."

"We might be past the point of no return with that. She's trying to convince me to see the sperm donor again."

Meri clenched her hands into fists. "I want to know what that child says to her therapist because none of it can be true. If any of it was based in reality, she would be a different person. Perhaps someone less self-absorbed. You can't convince me otherwise." She took my elbow again. "Come on. We'll figure this out. We'll get you through it. I just need some food first."

I let Meri lead me to a small restaurant away from the gleaming newness of the Seaport. We grabbed seats at the bar and I nodded along while she ordered a little bit of everything. Once she had a glass of wine in hand, she turned to me, a brow arched.

"Tell me you're not going to have a fling with your resident," she said.

It was cold in here, the air conditioning cranked all the way up. I rubbed my palms over my arms. I could still feel all the places where Henry had touched me. I let those goose bumps stay. They were the only things that could. "Of course I'm not."

She watched me as she took a sip. After a moment of consideration, she patted my leg, saying, "Good. Now, help me eat these apps. You'll have to roll me out of here if you leave me alone with them all."

Nine

Henry

Transplant Surgery Rotation:
Day 1, Week 2

"Before I get to assignments and procedures for the day," Copeland started, wagging a finger at the cohort in the early hours of Monday morning, "there's an important matter for us to discuss."

"There's nothing more important than procedures," Tori said under her breath.

"I can hear you, Tran," Copeland snapped.

I swallowed a laugh and crossed my arms over my chest. I didn't care what Copeland had on her list for us this morning. I just wanted to get out there for rounds and get my eyes on Whit. I'd waited all weekend for this. Every single minute since her friend had arrived at the beer garden.

I wanted to talk to her—alone, without worrying about anyone crashing the conversation. I wanted to know why she'd been so upset last Friday night and what I could do to fix it. I wanted to find out whether she really had plans or if she'd called in Dr. Mercer for backup. I wanted to ask if the way I traced a finger over her pulse reminded her of the way I traced her clit. And I wanted to know if that night we shared in June was the only thing she saw when she closed her eyes.

Once she'd left, I realized I didn't have any way of contacting her aside from her hospital email address, though that didn't seem like a wise path to take. Even if I wrote the most professional, unimpeachable message, I knew it would light up Whit in all the wrong ways. She didn't want to cross any lines and a small part of me respected that.

The rest of me just didn't give a fuck about the lines or the limits.

How much could any of it matter? We were consenting adults, and yeah, the next handful of weeks would be dicey until I rotated to a new service, but I didn't see a reason why we couldn't *talk*. There couldn't be any rules against that. And more to the point, there was no swinging a stethoscope in this place without hitting people involved in an under-the-radar relationship of some sort.

I knew there were guidelines and all, but I couldn't convince myself to care. Not after spending the whole damn summer trying to find Whit only to discover her here, right under my nose. Yet I had to hold my breath and wait to see her at rounds or conferences —or whichever social event we cornered her into joining.

"In other news," Copeland said, "the hospital softball league starts up again this week. This is billed as a fun, recreational event for collegial play within the resident and fellow community. An opportunity to see the sun while it's up and breathe fresh air, which I'm told some people enjoy. Dr. O'Rourke and I take it a bit more seriously. We want to wipe the floor with the medicine team.

I'm hoping that, between the four of you, we can come up with a bit of athletic ability because the other cohorts are a dismal blend of cross-country runners and people who lack the kind of cutthroat competitive spirit we're looking for. Those fools just want to have *fun.*"

Tori strutted forward. "I was a three-time national junior champion on the U.S. tennis tour and I would've turned pro at sixteen if I hadn't burned myself all the way out."

Copeland clutched a hand to her chest and studied Tori with fresh eyes. "Holy shit, Tran. Can you be my power hitter?"

Tori flexed her bicep. "In my sleep."

Copeland shook her head in awe. "I might've manifested a little too close to the sun."

Not to be outdone, Cami stepped up. "I played four years of field hockey in high school."

Copeland snapped her fingers, a grin pulling at her otherwise neutral expression. "Ah, so that's where the killer instinct comes from. Love that for us." She glanced between me and Reza. "What about you two? Anything?"

"I've never found enjoyment in sports," Reza said.

"But can you hit a ball with a bat?" she asked.

He lifted a shoulder. "I'd rather pitch, if there's an option."

"Good to know," she replied. "Come on, Hazlette. You have varsity football stamped on your forehead. Come through for me."

"I've played some baseball," I said.

"There's hope for us yet," Copeland said. "Expect an email about jerseys this afternoon. Don't make me chase you down for your answers. Assuming we don't get pulled into the OR on Friday evening, we're playing ball and we're playing to win. Understood?"

"If there's a different reason to play, I don't know it," Tori said.

Copeland gave a gleeful giggle that sounded entirely foreign coming from her before clapping her hands together. "Cortes-Dixon, Ansari, Tran. You're with me this morning. I'll need one of you to scrub in"—three hands shot into the air—"to retrieve a donor lobe, and another for the transplant. Then, you'll be in the clinic with Dr. Aldritch this afternoon. Put your damn hands down. I'll decide after rounds. Hazlette." She flipped through a notebook before glancing down at her tablet. "You're reporting to Dr. Salas this week. I hope you've done your reading on lung transplants."

"Dr. Salas," I repeated. *What the fuck?* I glanced at my team, but they were busy squabbling over the liver transplant procedures.

Still focused on the tablet, Copeland asked, "Is there a problem with your assignment?"

"No," I was quick to say. "But—"

She pushed her clear frames up her nose and leveled me with a stare that cut me off at the knees. "Then I'd suggest you pay extra close attention to Dr. Salas's patients on rounds this morning because she'll expect a full update."

I moved closer to Copeland, asking, "And I'll be on Dr. Salas's cases all week? Every day? Monday through Friday?"

Again, she eyed me like my existence was a real nuisance. "What part of 'you're reporting to Dr. Salas this week' was unclear to you?"

Shit. "No, I was just wondering if there was a reason why—"

She tucked the tablet and notebook under her arm and leaned in. "Since we're talking, Hazlette, allow me to clarify a few things for you. First, assignments are based on need. That's it. Your entire purpose here is about meeting patient needs and you're going to be sent where your skills can be of most use. Second, just because we hung out on Friday night doesn't mean you have any ground to come in here today and question me like we're friends. We are not.

Get that straight in your head right now. And finally, Salas is one of the most brilliant surgeons in this building. Why you aren't thanking me for the privilege of being assigned to her cases and certain to scrub in on all of her procedures is a mystery I'd like you to solve."

Since I couldn't give her any bit of the truth, I offered a contrite nod. Better that than getting on Copeland's bad side this early on. "It just came as a surprise. Thank you. I'm looking forward to it."

"That's more like it." She turned an impatient stare toward the battle raging between the rest of my team. It was mostly Cami and Tori arguing over who should be on the retrieval versus the transplant while Reza interrupted to tell them they were both wrong. "None of y'all listen," she muttered to herself as she held the door open. "Rounds. Now. Let's move, people. Dr. Hirano will start without us."

What the actual fuck?

"What do you mean, Dr. Hirano? Isn't Dr. Aldritch leading rounds?" I asked as everyone else filed past me.

Copeland squared her shoulders as she shifted to face me, her hand still closed around the edge of the door. She was tall enough that she didn't have to tip her chin up to meet my eyes. "I'm repeating myself an awful lot this morning, don't you think?"

I shoved my hands deep into my pockets. "Just another surprise," I managed. "I got the impression last week that Dr. Aldritch always led rounds on this rotation. Must've misunderstood."

Copeland glared at me for a moment before heaving out a sigh and glancing down the hall. "Usually she does, but we're spicing things up around here this week. Don't ask me to explain because no one explained it to me. Now, get going. We're late."

And all over again, I was fucked.

I thought I'd see Whit at the coffee shop this morning, though I'd brushed that off as the timing being wrong. But she wasn't coming to rounds *and* I wasn't getting anywhere near her cases—and by extension, her—for the whole week? *Fuck.* I knew resident assignments were unpredictable, but this added up to more than bad timing.

I thought we'd come to an understanding on Friday night though now I was wondering whether we left understanding different things. Even though it'd all seemed so clear. I should've known better.

Swallowing a curse, I marched down the hall to meet my team.

COPELAND WAS RIGHT.

Dr. Salas was brilliant. Easily one of the best surgeons I'd ever observed.

She was also in the third trimester of her pregnancy and my primary purpose seemed to be following her around all day, carrying her water bottle and handing her snacks. Or standing in a corner of the operating room, holding a milkshake or cheese sticks for when she was hungry. Not that I had any problem with that. Watching the procedure on the monitors and listening while she transplanted new lungs was worth every minute.

When I'd proven that she could rely on me to not ruin her day, as she put it, she let me hold a retractor for eight hours. Later, she taught me a few stitches. When I kept up the streak of not ruining her day, she upgraded me to holding a clamp. By the end of the week, I'd participated in more procedures than the rest of my cohort. Even better, all that time talking to Dr. Salas was like an expert-level crash course in pulmonology. Whenever I pulled a bag of chocolate-covered almonds from my coat pocket, she'd give me a thoughtful look, point at me, and say something like, "Here's what no one tells you about post-op embolisms."

I had not, however, caught more than a glimpse or two of Whit. It was like she'd disappeared all over again though this time was worse because I knew she was here and I knew she was keeping me at a distance. There was no question about it.

The benefit of all that time spent on milkshake duty was that I could take apart this problem and examine it from every angle. Not that I made any headway in the first part of the week. No, I was too busy being bitter. Just fucking bitter as hell that I was living through the most unlikely coincidence of all time, and the most important part of that coincidence was doing everything in her power to avoid me.

I didn't stop being bitter until I saw her laughing with a surgical tech in the halls on Wednesday. I'd recognized the laugh first. It sparked something warm and electric in my chest, and that pressure only expanded when I traced the shape of her in scrubs, the bottoms cuffed a few times above her emerald green clogs. Her light brown hair was in two braids that came together at the nape of her neck and fine golden wisps haloed out around her face.

She met my gaze for all of a second before the laughter died on her lips and her light expression faded into something chilly—and pained.

That was when I realized this wasn't a matter of pushing me away, not when it hurt her too. I hadn't imagined her leaning into me during that conference last week, just as I hadn't imagined our connection at the wedding or the way it roared to life when we started talking on Friday.

I stared at Whit, silently willing her to know that we could figure this out if she let us.

As Dr. Salas exited the bathroom and wanted the lab coat that she tasked me with holding during these breaks, Whit walked in the opposite direction.

I hadn't been able to find an answer in her eyes, but I knew what I had to do.

IN THE END, IT HADN'T TAKEN MORE THAN A FEW WELL-placed comments.

I'd started with Dr. Shapiro, one of the attendings from our burn surgery rotation. As expected, she had no interest in playing softball, but she promised that her friend Dr. Emmerling would jump at the opportunity to "run around in the dirt and antagonize residents."

From there, I made a point of talking about the upcoming game with the pediatric surgery cohort while Dr. Acevedo was nearby. They were pumped about this in a puzzled, happy way that told me they'd have a lot of fun in the outfield. More importantly, I could tell Dr. Acevedo was the kind of guy who liked a good ball game.

It wasn't long before attendings were stopping Copeland in the hall for the details about this game and asking if it was too late to order a jersey.

So I was hardly surprised when the Chief of Surgery showed up pushing a double stroller on Friday evening, or that his wife and Whit were a few steps behind him. This was the beauty of working with people who drank their coffee with an extra shot of competition every morning. We did not like to look around and realize we weren't doing as much—if not more—than our peers.

It was almost comical to see all these people blindly diving into a resident softball league on the basis of rumors about "everyone" showing up for the first game. The real humor was in how easy it had been to get the wheels turning.

Cami and Tori interrupted their intense warm-up routine when they spotted Whit and jogged toward her. Even from the opposite side of the field, I knew they were hard-selling her on getting in the game.

Just as I'd hoped they would.

I glanced beside me at Reza as he palmed a softball. He wore a McGill School of Medicine t-shirt and hummed a song I didn't recognize.

"How much are you hating this?" I asked.

He thought it over for a moment and gave a slight shrug. "'Hate' is an oversized word for this situation. This is not my preference, though I don't hate it."

I nodded. "Fair enough."

"It's your preference." He shot me a sidelong glance. "You find enjoyment in these social events."

The thing about Reza was that he didn't say much. Even when a surgeon put him on the spot during rounds or in the OR, there was an economy in his language. He only said exactly what was necessary. Which was why I was stunned silent now.

"Yeah, I guess you could say that." I glanced around the infield and at the crowd congregated in the stands. Whit and the chief—Dr. Hartshorn—were deep in conversation, seemingly immune to Copeland and O'Rourke frantically revising their starting lineup right in front of them. "We work damn hard all day—and sometimes all night—and it's good to have some fun when we have a minute off. But I understand that not everyone recharges the same way."

After a drawn-out moment, Reza said, "Should I expect events after the game? Will we relocate to a bar or restaurant?"

"Some will." I said this while watching Hartshorn ticking something off on his fingers while Whit nodded along. She was wearing jeans and a button-down shirt knotted at her waist, and her hair was tied in a little ponytail. She looked good enough to eat. Gulping down the finer details of that thought, I added, "Cami's leaving afterward to catch a train to New York to visit her husband, and a bunch of these people are holding pagers so they won't be going far. You'll be able to duck out if you want to skip that part."

Reza didn't respond and that was for the best because then O'Rourke dug a jersey out of his duffel bag and handed it to Whit —who proceeded to pop the buttons on her shirt and shrug out of it, leaving her in a black tank top. I wasn't sure I was able to speak. She pulled the jersey over her head and—*fucking kill me already*— opened her arms to him for a hug. Which he enthusiastically accepted.

I had to force myself to look away. Hadn't planned on seeing that when I'd constructed this house of cards.

The game got underway with the senior surgeons packing the starting lineup while I leaned against the fence with Cami, Reza, and Tori, who kept muttering, "This is bullshit."

Hartshorn had a solid swing and Emmerling had a real talent for hurling insults while she rounded bases, but the truly astonishing part was how bad Whit was at softball. I wasn't talking about a few strikeouts. No, the girl had no stance, no swing, and no sense of how to coordinate her body to play this game. Even when they slowed the pitch down to kindergarten T-ball levels, she almost knocked herself flat on her ass with that shitshow of a swing.

It took everything in me to stay on that fence and keep my mouth shut.

When they finally sent her to first—because there were no rules here—she tripped over the base for no good reason at all. She tumbled to the ground, a cloud of dust floating up with her laughter. I was pretty sure I heard a snort too, but I was a little busy with my heart stopping for a second to be sure. Emmerling jogged over and helped her up, and they laughed as they brushed dirt off her jeans.

I couldn't help it. I laughed too. How could this woman, this profoundly talented, sophisticated woman, be so fucking bad at softball? Everything about surgery demanded more focus than what she put into that swing. Walking around in those heels of hers required more coordination than jogging to first. She wielded a greater amount of competence in the first five minutes of her day than anything she could ever bring to a softball game.

And I knew she had moves. They'd been burned into my skin's memory the night of Mason's wedding. But this...*this* was something else.

"What am I seeing right now?" Cami asked under her breath. "Is this for real?"

Within seconds, my eyes watered and my shoulders shook as I struggled to contain myself.

"I don't know what the hell is happening out there, but Hazlette's losing it," Tori replied.

"Almost admire it," Cami said. "She knows she's bad and she doesn't give a damn."

"Yeah, but then I'm going to have to get out there and play cleanup," Tori said.

"You say that as if you don't love everything about the idea," Copeland muttered from behind us.

"It's my goddess complex and I do love it," Tori admitted with a preening smile. "Thank you for noticing."

The inning continued with Whit missing all the cues to run to the next base and then cutting straight across to third as if that made a damn bit of sense. Emmerling directed her to second, and in that chaos the ball came back from the outfield and nailed Whit in the thigh.

We all groaned at the hit. It *had* to hurt.

She waved away everyone's concern and insisted it had barely grazed her, but I watched as she absently rubbed that spot the rest of the night.

Right then, I mentally incinerated the remainder of my plan. These games couldn't be the means to my ends.

Most of the attendings bowed out to join the cheering section after that inning, much to Copeland's relief, and the next few flew by. We handily won the game.

As the teams gathered before dispersing, Whit gradually wandered in my direction. She stopped along the way to talk to people, often laughing off her moments on the field and jovially blaming her residents for dragging her into the game. She turned down one invite for drinks or dinner after another, including a very impassioned one from O'Rourke, while I put a tremendous amount of energy into dusting off the balls and dropping them back in the gear bag.

I caught her eye when she approached. She gave a slight smile and I went back to the balls, swallowing her up in quick glances as I worked. It took me a minute to settle on the right thing to say since I couldn't demand that she come with me right now so I could ice that leg or search the rest of her body for so much as a scratch.

With a rough laugh, I asked, "Have you ever swung a bat before?"

She brought a hand to her forehead. "Would you believe me if I said yes?"

"Probably not, no."

She studied the crowd, a curious gleam in her hazel eyes and her hands tucked into her back pockets. Eventually, she said, "Why do I have the feeling you had something to do with all of this?"

"All of what?"

She tipped her chin toward the group of senior staff making their way out of the park. "Everyone coming out for this. It's usually just residents and fellows, but for some reason the entire surgical wing was talking about this game. Five different people told me I had to be here tonight and I'm not even including Copeland in that count. Hartshorn's *wife* texted me to ask about it."

I gave the most convincing shrug in my arsenal. "I have no idea."

"I'm not sure I should believe that."

I yanked the drawstring on the bag and sanded my hands together. "What would you rather believe? That I had no part in the surge of interest around this event? Or that I orchestrated a huge turnout tonight because I knew you'd come if everyone else did and I really needed to see you?"

She stared down at the ground as she sawed her teeth over her plump bottom lip. "You can't do that anymore."

Rather than responding to that, I asked, "How's your leg?"

She waved a hand like she'd already moved on from that. "It's fine."

I shifted to face the field. Anything to get my eyes off that bottom lip. "You could let me take a look at it."

"I think I can handle a bruise on my own."

"I didn't ask whether you can handle it," I said. "I know you can. I'd like you to let me do it for you."

She gave a single shake of her head. "That's not something we can do."

"Not now?" I glanced at her, hoping to read some truth in her eyes before I heard the deflection in her words. "Or not ever?"

She held my gaze for a long moment. Long enough that it surprised me she wasn't looking over her shoulder to make sure no one noticed. "I don't know."

"Then I'll wait," I said. "Until you figure it out."

Ten

Whitney

Transplant Surgery Rotation:
Rule Number Seven: Keep it classy.

I threaded my fingers through his dark hair as I pressed the side of my face into the pillow. I couldn't watch. I was so close and we'd just started. I needed this to last.

"Slow down." My grip on his hair tightened. "Too much."

"You can take it." His words rumbled over my clit.

"I can't." My entire body pulled tight as I arched into the pressure of his fingers, his tongue. "I can't, Henry, it's too much."

"It's not even nearly enough." He pressed his teeth to my inner thigh, nipping just enough to make everything inside me twist and coil. "It will never be enough, Whit."

I blinked and I was on my knees. Henry's arm was banded around my torso, flattening me to his broad chest as he pounded into me. His free hand moved between my legs, circling me in a lazy rhythm that didn't match the merciless way he fucked me and only served to make me shake with need.

He kissed a path from the ball of my shoulder up to the tender spot behind my ear. "Come here," he growled, turning my face to him. "I'll never get enough of you."

Our lips met in an urgent, imperfect kiss and a great ripple of energy moved through me, like I was taking my first real breath after being held underwater. It was a gracious kind of hurt, rolling through me and spilling everywhere, all around me, until I couldn't draw a line between the before and after. I was the energy, the ache, the goodness that swelled until my mind gave up on making sense of it all.

"Never," he whispered to my lips. "Don't you dare forget it."

I reached back, wanting to fill my hands with his skin. To tell him in the only way I knew how that I wouldn't forget—and though it scared the shit out of me, I didn't think I'd be able to get enough of him either.

All I could find was a sweat-damped pillow wedged between my legs and the most hysterical need to orgasm I'd ever experienced. Blindly fumbling in my nightstand, I settled on the first toy I could find. I didn't care. I just needed to relieve this overwhelming pain immediately.

But I couldn't.

The minutes ticked by as I tried to get myself back to the point in my dream where I fell apart while Henry kissed me, but I couldn't seem to reach it. I couldn't reach anything beyond a slight flutter that left me feeling like I was braced on a precipice, my whole body fighting to hold on when all I wanted was to let go.

I tried other toys. My fingers. Even the pillow, god help me.

I ended up in the shower and nearly power-washed my clit off. I found some relief though it came mostly from the freezing cold water shocking my nervous system so hard that it forgot about getting me off for a second.

The apartment was quiet and relatively clean when I headed into the kitchen. Nice change of pace from Brie's usual calamity. I started some toast and skimmed through my emails in an attempt to ignore the throb between my legs.

I was also ignoring Henry's role in that throb.

It wasn't like I needed a reminder about the night we'd spent together. Every time I looked at him, a highlight reel played in my head. But dreaming about him—about *us*—was brutally unfair. I knew we couldn't go there again. I didn't need such vivid reminders of what I was missing.

Since I was too edgy to answer emails, I put my phone down and ate my toast at the sink.

I knew it was rather feral to eat over the sink, but I liked looking out this window in the morning. There was something about the way the sun slanted in over the brownstones that I found beautiful. And I couldn't risk running into Henry at my coffee shop again.

A spider had been spinning a web for months and now it stretched from the far end of the balcony railing to the neighboring building. I wasn't sure I had the kind of faith to create something that fragile. I didn't know if I could keep going, day after day, knowing everything I'd worked for could be lost in a storm. That I could try as hard as I wanted but that didn't mean the things I'd built would last. That I'd always find myself between immovable objects, filling the gaps as best I could to hold it all together.

I glanced through social media as I brushed the crumbs from my blouse. I only followed friends, mostly from med school and residency, and bakeries. I wanted to see everyone's babies with their toothless grins and I wanted to hear about the advancements in cake. There was nothing else I needed from socials.

But today—which was already on the rocks—the first thing I saw was a post from my sister. And she was in New York City with a dozen friends.

Or, she'd been in New York City sometime after midnight. God only knew where she was now.

Immediately, I dropped everything to search for a note, a train receipt, even a riddle written in sequins. Any sign that my sister had made an attempt to notify me of these plans. That, if not for that photo, I still would've had some idea where my only sibling and temporary roommate had run off to now.

I found nothing.

For a minute, I debated leaving a comment on her post or sending her a direct message saying something mild like "Looks fun!" and hoping she took that opportunity to fill me in on the details.

Maybe it was that every inch of my skin was oversensitized or that my brain couldn't see past the pulsing need for release, but I closed the app and shoved my phone into my back pocket. I didn't have the energy for this today.

I SLOGGED MY WAY THROUGH SEVERAL HOURS OF transplant team meetings, constantly crossing and uncrossing my legs in a futile attempt to feel a little less like a faulty grenade. At one point, the nurse coordinator sitting to my left gave me a curious glance that seemed to say *you good?*

I rubbed the bridge of my nose and shrugged. She seemed to accept that.

Once those meetings wrapped, I left the hospital to meet Meri for lunch. We couldn't always make it work, but most Wednesdays we met at a café on Charles Street that had some of the most incredible patisserie I'd ever seen. Aside from the day and location, the only requirement was that we didn't talk about work. No medicine, no surgery, no colleagues. We pretended we were normal people who didn't use extremely dark humor to cope and wouldn't have to sprint back to work if a baby was born with half their intestines outside their body.

Since we weren't actually normal people and our schedules had a lot in common with cats who'd stare you in the eye while knocking things over, I didn't think much of it when I didn't find Meri waiting for me. I ordered, sat outside to soak up the late summer sun, and absently scrolled through my phone. She'd get here eventually, and when she did I'd find a way to skirt the craggy borderlands of *no work talk* and *having sex dreams about my resident-slash-one-night-stand*.

It wasn't until I'd finished eating that I realized she still hadn't arrived—and I didn't have a message telling me she'd been called away. I wasn't concerned because things always came up, but as I walked back to the hospital, I knew I wouldn't survive much more of this frustration. It didn't matter the source. I was irritable and overtired, and worst of all, I'd forgotten to grab dessert on the way out.

As I stabbed the elevator call button several times, I heard the squeak of running shoes coming around the corner.

"There you are," Meri cried, her scrub cap clutched in one hand as she held her lanyard to her chest. "I'm so sorry. I totally spaced on the day, and when I realized, it was already too late." I turned away from the elevator doors as she looked me over. "Did you bring me anything?"

"Yeah, I brought you my best wishes and warmest regards," I replied. "Why didn't you have your circulator text me?"

She pushed some auburn strands of hair over her ear and paused before saying, "I left my phone in my office."

"What? Why?"

Meri yanked the drawstring on her scrubs and busied herself with retying it. "Just a mistake. I really am spacey today. I'm sorry. Lunch is sacred to me, as you know, and I'd never intentionally blow you off. Which you also know."

I peered at her. She looked tired, although she'd been on call earlier this week and she had a spotless record of having to come in for cases every time. "Are you okay?"

She laughed, but it was hollow. Fake. "What? Of course. Why wouldn't I be?"

Super cute way to deflect.

Obviously, there was something going on with Meri. There'd been too many little moments like this one over the past month or two. I didn't know what it was or where it was coming from, but it was clear she wasn't ready to talk about it. More than that, I wasn't in the most helpful or receptive mood right now.

"It happens. I get it," I said. "I could've used your advice though. I'm having some issues with my ongoing situation and"—I zigzagged my hands over my torso as if that was the universal sign for failure to reach orgasm—"related things."

She arched a brow as the elevator dinged. "What does *that* mean? Has something changed with the situation? Do you need me to swab you or something?" She arrowed her hands toward her crotch. "Is it like that? In the lady business? Is it an itch or a burn? Or are we speaking about your metaphorical lady business?"

"We're not speaking at all," I said with a laugh. "Not here."

"I'll take you to lunch tomorrow or Friday," she said. "Somewhere nice where they don't scream at you from a counter when your order is ready. Will that make up for me ghosting you today?"

"You don't have to make up for ghosting me," I said, walking backward toward the elevator, "although I am blaming you for the fact I left the café without any fancy pastry treats."

"Fair," she called as I stepped onto the elevator. "We'll talk later."

"You better believe it." She didn't know it but I was getting to the bottom of her weirdness. I didn't care if I had to dig it out of her.

The doors closed and I found myself staring at Henry. How much of that conversation had he heard?

He leaned back against the wall, those impossibly beefy arms folded over his chest and his ankles crossed in front of him. A small smile warmed the corners of his mouth as he watched me. I blinked several times to clear away any doubt as to whether he was real and not just a product of my horny imagination.

"What's the situation?" he asked.

I pressed the button for my floor and stood as close to the door as I could without mashing my cheek up against it. "Inside joke," I said over my shoulder.

He made a rumbly noise that only tightened the strings holding me together. "Yeah. Sounded like it."

I could feel his dark gaze on my back, my neck, everywhere. I stared at the doors.

"How's that bruise doing?"

"My bruises are not your concern," I said, and I was so proud of my cool, unfussed tone even as my fingers twitched at my side, eager to touch the welt on my thigh. It was a fun shade of plum, the shape of Australia, and large enough that my whole hand couldn't cover it. But it was just a bruise.

"Yeah, Whit, they are."

I didn't know why that was my undoing, but it was. It pulled me apart at the seams until everything fell away, all the layers and structures and weight. I could almost see the shape of it before me, like I was a paper doll, pointless without the pieces swapped in and out to make me into something that mattered. I forced a ragged breath over my lips. My shoulders fell and my neck softened. I wasn't a broken grenade right now, but I was so damn tired. Tired and empty and alone.

"I'm more than capable on my own." I wanted to take a step backward. Just one. There'd still be plenty of space between us. More than enough, really. A respectable, professional amount of space. Though I didn't. I dropped my gaze to my shoes and kept it there. "As I told you last week."

"Both of us said things last week, Whit."

"You can't call me that."

"You've said that before. That I can't. I shouldn't. But you've never said you don't want me to call you that. There is a difference, you know."

"Not to everyone else," I cried, waving a hand at the empty car.

I heard the rustle of his clothes as he pushed off the wall and then I felt a puff of warm air on my neck. He didn't come any closer, didn't touch me, but the heat of him wrapped all around me. We stood there, silent and breathing the same air until the elevator jostled to a stop.

His forehead touched my shoulder. "There's a difference, Whit, and you know it."

Henry stepped around me and exited the elevator without a backward glance.

As much as I wanted to stay in this elevator and obsess over everything that had happened in the past two minutes, I had to get off at this floor. I ran a hand through my hair and marched down the hall while sending out a few pleas to the universe to save me from another tense moment with Henry.

The universe, sadly, wasn't on my side today as I rounded a corner and ran right into the first-year residents. From the sounds of it, they were comparing stories from this morning's liver transplant.

I powered ahead, not slowing down to acknowledge this gathering. I had appointments to get to and I hated starting late because it always snowballed.

But I'd barely passed by when I heard, "Dr. Aldritch! Are you coming to the softball game this week?"

Slowing down—but not quite stopping—I forced a smile for Cami Cortes-Dixon. "Not sure. I have a few things going on."

"We won't make you play," Tori Tran said. Her bow tie was covered in those yellow cartoon characters. Minions. Perfect thing to focus on when I was busy blocking out Henry's entire existence. "Unless you want to. You can do whatever you want. Obviously."

That earned a real smile. "I made a splash last week. I'm not going to top that."

"Okay, well, you know we'd love to see you," Cami said.

Just as I'd fully passed the residents, Jenelle fell in step with me. "Any chance you have a few minutes for me?"

"Of course. You have access to my calendar. Schedule yourself whenever works best."

She gave a slow nod and shoved her hands in her coat pockets. "So, not right now?"

"I'm due in the clinic." I glanced at my watch with a sigh. "And

I'm already cutting it close." When the slow nods continued, I asked, "Is everything okay?"

Her lips parted though it seemed like she was struggling to get the words out. "Yeah," she said after a pause. "Just some personal things I'm trying to figure out. I'll find time in your calendar."

I stopped at a set of double doors. "Is it the social media stuff again?"

Jenelle ran a pseudonymous account where she discussed matters of race in healthcare, particularly issues in appropriately diagnosing and treating Black patients when their symptoms didn't add up neatly. All the cases she referenced protected patient privacy, of course, but there'd been occasions when she'd asked for my opinion on certain content before posting. As far as I knew, I was one of the few who knew the true identity of @ThatHenriettaLacks.

She ran a hand over her hair. "Not this time, no. Not really. But it's fine. I'll catch you later. Thanks."

I watched her turn and walk down the hall, and I couldn't shake the sense that I was missing something. Maybe it was me. Maybe I was the one being strange while Meri and Jenelle were cruising along, good and golden.

But it wasn't just with Meri or Jenelle.

I was missing something too and I didn't know how much longer I could ignore him.

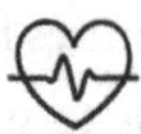

AFTER SEEING PATIENTS IN THE CLINIC, I DRAGGED myself to a meeting of the resident wellness council. We'd made a lot of progress on making the surgical residency program sustainable and creating better systems to support folks through it all, and I was extremely pleased with that work, even if it had turned my personal life into a sexually frustrated hell.

I hated when my colleagues balked at these initiatives by suggesting we'd survived just fine without all this coddling. The thing was, we hadn't survived just fine. The "It was good enough for us" arguments missed the fact that too many people were exited from highly competitive residencies such as this because the ethos—one we were damn proud of—was sink or swim. There was no mechanism for supporting surgeons who were pregnant or had families. There were no mental health resources for those who were overwhelmed by the exhaustion of this work and the enormity of teaching yourself to disconnect from human emotions. There were few, if any, truly functional structures in place for handling bigotry, harassment, or abuse. And no one gave a fuck about whether these folks had any amount of balance in their lives.

However, that these meetings were always held in the evening and consistently went over the scheduled time really called into question whether we were missing the whole point. We sure as hell weren't modeling any amount of balance. I was hoping the next generation could run with that ball.

It was almost nine when I made it back to my office. As I hung up my lab coat, I noticed a box on my desk. It was small with a metallic sticker that caught the light. I recognized that logo.

When I reached for the box, I noticed a folded piece of paper tucked beneath it. I dropped into my desk chair and dedicated an entire minute to debating which item to open first. In the end, I put down the box.

The note was written in a clear, blocky print and my heart was pounding too hard for me to comprehend the words on the first read.

. . .

This might not solve your situation, but it has to make up for missing dessert.

Call me anytime.

NO SIGNATURE, JUST A PHONE NUMBER WITH A 530 AREA code.

But I knew.

I ran my fingers over the words, feeling the indentations in the paper. A shudder moved through me, a great twisting spasm that pulled at my shoulders and spiraled down until my knees shook under the desk. I pressed the note to my chest as my body curled inward with need—but not a sexual one. After a day spent in a state of perpetual arousal, I could recognize the difference.

And that difference hurt. It ripped me open and made no move to clean up the mess.

I could've survived if it was only sex. I could've muddled my way through if it was just about getting him out of my system. I could've pretended none of it mattered.

I allowed myself a moment for this wave of emotion to rush over me. To grieve the distance I had to put between us. To rage against the outrageous unfairness of it all. To stitch my own battered soul back together again because I was always the one who had to make the impossible choices.

I pried open the box. A gorgeous cupcake from one of my favorite bakeries sat inside. The swirl of whipped cream piped on top of the chocolate ganache told me it was Boston cream because I knew my cupcakes as well as I knew my cardiac anatomy.

On my walk home, I kept a hand in my pocket, pressing his note to my palm. I wanted to know when he'd found the time to run all the way to the Newbury Street bakery and back, and I wanted to know why he'd chosen Boston cream. Had I told him I had a soft spot for all cupcakes with filling in the middle? Had we gotten into that over the buffet at his friend's wedding? Or was it a wild guess?

I recited his phone number in my head as I climbed the stairs to my floor. The lights were off and there was no sign of Brie, which bothered me much less than it had this morning. My heart rate seemed to thump to the rhythm of *Call me anytime*.

I wanted to call, if for no other reason than to ask why he'd chosen that flavor. And also because I didn't have it in me to hold him off much longer. Not when he could make me ache with a few words or unravel me with a cupcake.

I wanted to call just to ask him what the hell he expected me to do about this. How was I supposed to juggle my responsibilities, my reputation, with his desire to look after me and my bruises?

And I wanted to know if he could be patient. If he could wait. If he'd still be there in a month or two. In a year. What if it was longer? Would he get tired of it? Get tired of *me*? Would he walk away like everyone else did and leave me to find out about it on social media?

In the end, I stood in my kitchen and devoured the cupcake.

I'd intended to nibble my way through it while watching something mindless, but I cut it into quarters and ate one segment after another as I stared at the note. I heard the words forty different ways in my head and imagined him writing them with all the confidence in the world.

I didn't call.

Eleven
Whitney

Rule Number Four:
Never crash in your backyard.

I didn't know how Henry was pulling it off.

First it was the cupcake and that was fine. Understandable. But then I came into my office Monday morning to find a dozen pens gathered together like a bouquet with a peachy-pink ribbon on my desk. Good pens too. My favorite brand *and* style, which he had no way of knowing. And then, on a day that'd started with a page in the middle of the night and ended with a complicated prognosis for my patient, there was a warm muffin and fresh coffee—my order exactly right—waiting for me.

I couldn't figure it out. I knew Jenelle had him bouncing between Hirano and Salas this week, and neither of them were known for having much downtime in their schedules. Most residents didn't get a chance to eat lunch, forget about running across Beacon Hill for coffee and muffins the minute I left the OR.

What was Henry Hazlette's secret? That was what I wanted to know.

I glanced at the drink he'd handed me while delivering coffee and donuts to the surgical ICU nurses before grand rounds. It was from my neighborhood coffee shop, not the donut place. Which meant he'd made two stops. At four thirty in the morning. In the middle of his first year of residency.

All he'd said was, "This one's all yours, Dr. Aldritch," before pointing out the gluten-free and vegan donuts to the night crew who could not have loved him more this morning.

And I'd walked away with wobbly knees and a goofy smile on my face.

Over a cup of coffee.

I couldn't even believe myself. It was like I'd tripped and fallen into an alternate universe where *coffee* knocked me off course and I allowed myself to wonder about an off-limits man for more than zero seconds.

What was there to wonder about? Aside from all the reasons Henry was not for me, I wasn't for Henry. I wasn't for anyone.

I could count my past relationships on one hand. Didn't even need all my fingers. All of those experiences tucked under the umbrella of friends who turned into a little more before deciding we were better off friends, and I wasn't mad about it. I'd never felt like I was missing out on anything and I didn't love the idea of changing my life to make room for someone else.

I loved my home. I loved that I'd picked out everything and made it exactly the way I wanted. For once in my life, I knew it was all mine for as long as I wanted. I was finished bopping around from med school to residency to fellowships. I wasn't waiting for my mother to deploy again or for her depression to creep back in again until it was so bad that I had no choice but to call Grammy and tell her we needed help.

It was *my* place, the only one I'd ever had, and I couldn't imagine liking someone enough to compromise on any of it for them. I didn't see much of a reason why I'd want to compromise. I liked making decisions without consulting anyone else and I liked sleeping without someone stealing the blankets or breathing in my face. I liked the life I'd built for myself. It was full with friendship and travel and a career that I adored even when it ran me ragged. I didn't want to change any part of my life for a man who would, in the best case, disappoint me and, in the worst case, destroy me the way men had destroyed Meri and my mother.

But that wasn't the whole story.

Even if everything between me and Henry was different, nothing would change with Meri. If I sat her down and explained that I wanted to see what might happen with me and Henry, she'd be happy for me. *Thrilled.* She'd make some bawdy comments and she'd smile, and she'd swear up and down that she loved this development. That she wanted this for me. And then she'd drift away.

Meri could handle love and relationships at a distance, but she couldn't watch them up close.

It'd been years since that awful breakup and she'd put herself back together brick by broken brick, but she'd left the worst of the wounds exposed and poked at them so often she hardly noticed the pain anymore.

She'd notice it if I loosened my grip on our singlehood solidarity and it would kill her. She'd have to take several very large steps back, regardless of how much she wanted the best for me. She'd do it not to punish me but to protect herself, and there was no way I'd let that happen.

Meri was the sister I'd chosen. She was my person and I was

hers, and there was nothing more important to me than that relationship. We'd picked each other up from our worst moments and we'd cheered each other during our best, and our lives were so deeply intertwined we could comfortably impersonate each other. We were there for each other, rain or shine, and thirty years down the road when we lived in side-by-side cottages, we'd still be there for each other.

I didn't need a man to make me happy or complete, but I did need my best friend. She was my family—the kind that stuck around no matter what.

For as much as this coffee had made me giddy, it wasn't worth breaking Meri's heart. Even if everything was different, Henry couldn't give me anything that would be worth losing her.

"Let's crash a wedding this weekend."

I froze with a forkful of salad in front of my mouth. I blinked at Meri before asking, "Excuse me?"

She spent a minute rearranging her panini, rattling the ice in her cup, and checking her phone. It was enough of a pause that I started thinking I'd misheard. Then, "I want to crash a wedding. Think about it. We never go to autumn weddings, Whit. We are missing out on an entire aesthetic. I found several huge soirées around town and—"

"I'm sorry but what?" I put my fork down. I needed both hands to hear this. "You want to crash a wedding *here*? Have you lost your pretty little mind?"

She eyed me like I was the one being crazy and *that* was crazy because Meri was even more cautious than me when it came to choosing weddings we weren't invited to. I'd wanted to go to the Outer Banks of North Carolina one summer because I was obsessed with the area after reading a book set there, but she'd vetoed that idea on the basis of it being too close to Duke University Medical Center where she'd completed her residency. A distance of two hundred and fifty miles plus years since finishing residency was too close, but weddings *here in Boston* where we presently lived and worked were okay?

"I think we can pull it off," she said.

I reached over and pressed my hand to her forehead. "No fever," I murmured. "Do you remember bumping your head at any point? Falling down? Waking up and not remembering how you got there? Eating candy or baked goods of questionable origin?"

"Kindly shut up." She took a bite of her sandwich and stared out the café window at the gridlock on Charles Street. "I think we can get away with it."

I leaned back in my seat and crossed my legs. "Why would we want to risk that?"

"Because we never celebrate Cocktoberfest," she replied simply.

"Cock...toberfest?"

"It's a beloved tradition, Whitney."

"Is it now?"

"Yes! Wear a sweater, drink some beer, get railed within an inch of your life. Everyone's doing it."

I nodded slowly, salad forgotten. "Are you all right?"

She pushed her plate away, keeping her gaze low. "I need to do something fun this weekend and I'd really love it if they could be someone who treats me like an object. I want some good old-fashioned disrespect with that dick."

"Does this have anything to do with your recent weirdness?"

She pulled a face as she asked, "Can you describe this weirdness? I am unfamiliar." That lasted all of ten seconds while I stared at her. "Okay, okay, yes, I've been weird. I know and I'm sorry."

I rolled a hand in her direction. "This would be a great time to explain the weirdness."

She laced her fingers together and pulled them apart again. If I hadn't known her as well as I did, I wouldn't think much of the gesture, but Meri didn't fidget. She was one of those steady, composed people who didn't need a physical outlet for their stress. She didn't have to roll a ball of lint around in her pocket as she organized her words or shift from foot to foot to find an equilibrium. Whatever she had to tell me meant something, and it meant something big.

"There's not a lot to explain," she said.

"I'm a hundred percent certain that is inaccurate."

"Not a lot to explain anymore," she said.

"But there was something to explain at one point." I reached for my iced tea to smother some of my surprise. All my theories had followed the line of Meri getting recruited to a different hospital in the land of far, far away or her family making her life hectic again. "You know I'll judge you, but in a loving, supportive way."

"I do know that and I appreciate it," she said with a laugh. "And I've wanted to tell you. So many times. But there wasn't anything to actually say, so I didn't know where to start. It was a thing that wasn't really a thing."

"A thing like when you had me lance that ingrown hair on your—"

"We've agreed you wouldn't bring that up anymore." She rubbed a hand over her brow, sighing like she really couldn't believe that she had to put up with me. It was precious. "It was *one* time and if *you* asked *me* to check out your undercarriage, I'd find a way to be discreet about it. Okay?"

"Then what kind of thing was it? If it's not an ingrown hair, what are we dealing with here? Are you gambling on those F1 races you're obsessed with? Did you join a cult? Did one of the guys you hooked up with this summer appear in your OR one day?"

She rubbed her eyes. "No, thank god, none of the above. Nothing like that."

I couldn't believe I was asking this, but— "Did you meet someone?"

She let out a brittle laugh that sounded like she'd crack if the air around her shifted just a little too quickly. "No, not like that. I didn't meet anyone of significance. But I've remembered why my interest in men expires after one night."

I sagged as I processed her words. "Who was it? And when? When did it start?"

"I could tell you, but it would make me feel stupid and I've already done quite a bit of that to myself. Besides, it's not like I want to go down that road again or talk to him if he ever—" She glanced over my shoulder and the shadows in her green eyes immediately cleared. "Did you invite the best man to lunch? To *our* lunch? My god, Whit, is nothing sacred anymore?"

"Did I what?"

I twisted in my seat to find Henry holding the door open for someone as they juggled four cups of coffee. There was a fraction of a second, not even an eye blink, when the memory of his scruffy chin on my neck flooded my mind and all I could feel was my heart thumping against my ribs.

Henry's dark gaze landed on mine, smiling at first like he'd expected to find me here and then glancing between me and Meri, slow and just as startled as I was.

"Dr. Hazlette." Meri waved him over like we weren't in the middle of a serious conversation, the topic of which I wanted many more details. "What kind of residency are we running here if you have time to go off-campus for lunch?"

"The kind of residency that prioritizes Dr. Salas's need for eight to ten meals per day," he replied easily.

That was exactly how Henry was all the time. *Easy.* Like he was exactly where he was supposed to be at all times and he never doubted anything about that. He knew who he was and he didn't need to fuck around.

That was how he was in bed too. Not that I needed any reminders about the way he moved in between the sheets. That had been on heavy rotation in my head since the minute I escaped that hotel room.

"Seems like an important learning opportunity," Meri said. "Honestly, how many times in your career do you think you'll have a chance to attend to a hobbit?"

Henry pressed a fist to his mouth as his lips curled into a glowing smile. He had the best smiles. It was like he actually meant it. "I cannot laugh at that because Dr. Salas will know and I'd really love it if I don't have to stand in the corner of the OR holding her water bottle this afternoon."

"Understandable," she replied. "But she's a great teacher. You'd probably learn a ton in that corner."

"Oh, I have." He laughed and dropped a hand to the back of my chair. Meri's brow arched all the way up. "It's the best corner of any rotation so far."

He rubbed his thumb across the back of my shoulder, and even though she couldn't see what he was doing, she knew. She blinked like she didn't know what to do with any of this. Maybe now she understood what I was dealing with here.

"Have you been in Dr. Aldritch's corner?" Meri asked.

"I, uh—" Henry glanced down at me, a smile crinkling his dark eyes. Between that smile and the thumb on my shoulder, I was turning into a marshmallow. Just sugar, air, and chemistry. There was nothing else holding me together. "I haven't had that opportunity, no."

"Maybe the right case will come along." She crossed her arms over her torso. "Well. Always fun to see you, Hazlette."

As he started to respond, someone near the counter screamed. We all turned in that direction to find a woman doubled over, her hand slamming down on a table as she cried out again. Henry took a step toward her as the staff rushed forward.

"Please let it be an appendix," Meri whispered, her palms pressed together in prayer. "Appendix, kidney stone, bleeding ulcer. Anything but—"

As I pushed to my feet, the woman said, "Oh my god. I think my water broke."

Meri hung her head for a second, muttering, "Goddammit." She stood and crossed to the woman in a few steps, gently shoving everyone out of the way as she went. "Hi. My name's Meri Mercer and I'm a baby doctor. Can you tell me your name and how far along you are?"

"Carina and tomorrow's my due date," she wailed. "There's a lot—I don't know, like a lot of pressure?"

Meri hooked a glance over her shoulder at me. "Ambulance. Now." She eased Carina into a chair, asking, "When did the contractions start?"

"I don't know. Last night, maybe? I thought"—she stopped speaking to scream again—"it was just Braxton Hicks."

"Hazlette," Meri called as I waited for emergency services to answer. "You're here, so you'll be useful. Get these people away from my laboring mother, please, while I wash my hands. She doesn't need an audience."

I stepped toward the kitchen as I relayed the information to the dispatcher. When I was finished with that, I asked the café manager for some clean tablecloths, an apron, and the sharpest knife he had. While he ran the knife under boiling water for a few minutes, I returned to Meri's side as Carina cried out again.

"Ten minutes," I said into Meri's ear.

"Fuck," she breathed. "Are they coming in from New Hampshire or something? We could bike to the hospital in less than ten minutes."

"Okay, so you'd like me to put your patient on a bike?"

She rolled her eyes. "You know that I don't, but thanks for the reminder of how much I love it when you assist me."

"I feel like I need to—" Carina bent forward and I dug in my pockets for a spare pair of gloves. "I think I need to push," she sobbed.

"This baby really wants to meet you," Meri said, rolling up her sleeves and pocketing her jewelry.

"But I'm not ready," she said, "and my husband isn't here and this isn't my birth plan!"

"I know, my friend, I know. This isn't how I want it to go for you either, but you have me, my friend Dr. Aldritch, and her friend Dr. Hazlette all here to help you." Meri turned to Henry when another contraction hit, asking, "Have you delivered a baby before?"

"Not really, no," he replied. "I've seen one."

"That's perfect because we abide by a policy of see one, do one, teach one around here and I really don't want to get this sweater dirty," Meri said. "Glove up, Hazlette."

He glanced at me with just enough panic in his eyes to make me laugh. I handed him my gloves and hand sanitizer. "Didn't you learn this as a paramedic?"

"Yeah, I did," he said as he rubbed the sanitizer up his forearms. "And then I spent all my time treating people with busted eye sockets and shattered hips. Not many pregnant people climbing Lassen."

I patted his shoulder as I circled around behind Carina. "Who can I call for you?" I asked her.

"My-my-my husband," she roared.

I placed a quick call to a very alarmed father-to-be and then accepted the freshly sterilized knife from the manager. With any luck, the paramedics would make it here early and we wouldn't need kitchen tools to cut the umbilical cord, but this whole situation screamed *better safe than sorry*.

"That's the head," Henry said, almost like he didn't believe it.

"Yep. She's crowning," Meri said to him. "This baby is in a big ol' rush to meet us. Okay, guide the head. Steady. Gentle pressure there. Check the neck. Good. Get ready to catch this baby."

"What?" he yelped.

"Just catch the baby. That's all you have to do." Meri dropped her hand to Carina's knee, saying, "You're doing great. One more push and we're there."

Within a minute, a cry filled the small café. Henry held the baby in a tablecloth while Meri talked him through an Apgar score.

"Congratulations," I said to Carina as I monitored her vital signs. "It's a boy—and he has quite a set of lungs."

Sirens blared outside as the ambulance pulled up. Handing off Carina and the new baby took only a few minutes and Meri followed them out to the street, bossing everyone around and promising to check on her tonight. Henry and I were left with a slightly wrecked café while the bewildered staff peeked out from the kitchen.

Henry turned to me, his eyes wild and his lips parted. "I just delivered a baby," he said, stepping closer. "I delivered a *baby.*"

I didn't think twice about opening my arms to him and I didn't stop him when he gathered me up and swept me off my feet like I weighed nothing. I just hugged him back. "Amazing, isn't it?"

"So fucking much." He pressed his lips to my neck and I knew I was in over my head here, but I couldn't bring myself to care. Just like I couldn't bring myself to leave his arms. "I can't believe that just happened."

"I'd like to say it's a first, but Meri delivers a lot of babies. She hates it."

Henry held me tighter, his hands spanning my rib cage and his mouth at the crook of my shoulder, and I knew our time was running out. Meri would walk in any second and the staff would want their café back and everything else in our worlds would intrude, but I wanted every ounce of this moment. I wanted everything I could wring out of it.

He growled into my skin like he was thinking the same thing. Then, "I miss you."

"I know," I breathed. *I miss you too.*

Meri returned, clearing her throat and loudly sanding her hands together as she approached. "At least it was quick." She watched as Henry and I broke apart, her forehead crinkled. "And uncomplicated. For real though, I need to start carrying a delivery kit with me. I really hate when I have to bubblegum-and-duct-tape my way through these things. Or better yet, people could stop going into labor around me. Just one time, I'd like to see you do some work, Whit."

"The next time someone needs a heart transplant in the middle of a restaurant, I'll be sure to take the lead on that."

"You're just so funny." She turned to Henry, saying, "I went into fetal and neonatal because I liked the babies but not the birthing. You know what that got me? A lifetime of catching babies in random places. The universe enjoys saying, 'Nice try but nope.'"

I wagged a finger at her. "At least the sweater survived."

"Perhaps in principle, but it's clearly cursed," she said.

"She does this," I said to Henry. "Every time she has to deliver a baby in the wild, she decides the clothes or the place or the song playing when it went and it's all off-limits. There's a really beautiful inn near Big Sur that we can never go back to because of Meri and her mysticism."

As Henry laughed, Meri swept a glance between us. "Don't we have to get Hazlette back to Dr. Salas?"

"Oh, shit," he said under his breath. He picked his way through all the chairs and tables that'd been pushed aside and rushed toward the counter. "I forgot about lunch."

"You were a little busy," I said. "I think it will be okay."

"I'll give her a call and let her know what happened," Meri said, "but I'd hurry on back if I were you."

"Thanks for teaching me today, Dr. Mercer," Henry said as he made his way to the door. He exhaled when his gaze settled on me. I shuddered like that breath could knock me over. "I'm sure I'll see you around, Dr. Aldritch."

When he was gone, Meri nudged me, saying, "You're welcome."

"What?"

"For sending Hazlette on his way and saving you from yourself," she said. *"Again."*

"Oh." I followed her back to our table as the café crew surveyed the damage. I gathered my things and checked my phone. Took a quick sip of my drink. "Right."

As we headed back to the hospital, she asked, "That's what you wanted, isn't it? To get rid of the best man?"

We walked in silence for several minutes, which was long enough for her question to fade away. When the hospital complex came into sight, I asked, "Are you going to tell me what happened with your thing that wasn't a thing?"

She was quiet all the way to the main doors, her hands in her pockets and her gaze on the ground. I eyed her as we waited for the elevator, but she didn't say anything until we stepped inside. "I don't think either of us is ready to talk about our things that aren't things. Let's just leave it at that until we learn how to be brave."

"We're brave," I said, a touch defensive. I was really fucking brave.

The elevator dinged at her floor. "That's what I thought too."

I was fully aware that what I was doing was dangerous. Ill-advised. The kind of thing I'd talk someone out of if I had the chance.

Dangerous...but not indefensible. And that was the important part.

I'd figured out what to say while walking home from work and then rehearsed it in my head for an hour while Brie painted her nails and complained about one of her clients. I spent another hour tidying everything I could get my hands on, as if that would make any of this better, and then finally got so tired of my bullshit that I grabbed my phone and closed my bedroom door behind me.

My heart rate was an absolute commotion as I dialed the number.

I almost ended the call on the second ring, but he answered before the third. "Dr. Hazlette," I said, all business as I barreled right past his *hello*. "This is Dr. Aldritch. Do you have a minute to speak?"

He was silent for a moment, just long enough for me to seesaw between doubting my entire plan and remembering that he was one of my residents which meant he damn well had a minute for me.

Henry let out a soft laugh that sounded breathless and startled, and he said, "Of course, Dr. Aldritch. All the time in the world for you."

"Excellent," I said. "I wanted to acknowledge your quick thinking today in the café. Not everyone would've been able to stay as calm and focused as you did in that position."

"Yeah. Of course. I mean, thank you."

"I also observed this afternoon's procedure with Dr. Salas from the gallery and I have some notes for you."

"Some...notes," he said.

"Yes. I've highlighted several areas for improvement, specifically in your time in motion and instrument handling."

"Oh, really?"

He laughed again, but it wasn't startled. It sounded as though he knew I'd searched high and low for a reason to call him. While part of that was true since I had gone into that gallery looking for a reason to talk to him, I hadn't expected to notice such tentative instrument handling from someone with his experience. He needed to hurry the hell up and that wasn't my fascination with him talking.

"I'm very interested in hearing your feedback," he said.

"There's quite a lot to go over and I'd like to address certain technique issues," I said. "Why don't you come to my place on

Sunday evening? I'll walk you through some simulation practice. I'm not too far from the hospital. Thirty-two Temple Street."

Again, he paused, and I could imagine a slow smile touching the corners of his lips and brightening his dark eyes. They were a shade of midnight blue that leaned toward black. If I hadn't seen them up close enough times to know, I would've guessed them to be a rich chestnut brown, just like his hair.

"That would be very helpful. Thank you for offering, Dr. Aldritch. I'll be there."

"As you may know, Dr. Acevedo frequently hosts residents at his home in Cambridge for journal discussions and skills work," I added. "So you should expect more of these small group sessions when you get to your peds surgery rotation."

"I've heard that about Dr. Acevedo. And a few others too."

It was then that I realized I hadn't planned my exit from this conversation. I knew I was going to get down to business and keep it absurdly professional, but I hadn't thought past the loud and clear caveat that lots of attendings invited residents to their homes and this wasn't unusual. That'd been my only real priority aside from making a case for seeing him outside of our usual confines. I wasn't sure where to go from here.

We were quiet for a long, heavy moment. It reminded me of all the other moments we'd shared, the ones where we would've talked all night at the beer garden or lingered in the elevator or today in the café, if there hadn't been someone or something to cut us off.

Just as I said, "Have you ever focused in on your economy of motion in a procedure? Do that the rest of this week. I mean, really pay attention to how many moves you're making," Henry asked, "Just how many times have you and Dr. Mercer delivered babies outside of delivery rooms?"

We laughed for a second and it felt like permission to walk away from the stiff, crisp words I'd rehearsed. I leaned back against the pillows, folding my legs in front of me. "Today is probably the fifth or sixth time I've been there, but Meri's delivered at least twenty babies. Probably more. She's stopped keeping track."

"Does it ever get old?"

"I don't think so, but I'm not usually the one doing all the work," I said. "Already reconsidering your future in trauma surgery?"

"Not necessarily," he said, though the hesitation in his voice was so charming. I loved everything about it.

"You should figure that out sooner than later. Obstetrics is a whole different specialty program."

"I know, but it was—it was fun, right? Or is that what everyone says their first time?"

I dropped my head back against the headboard. I finally felt like I could breathe again. "Either they hate it and want nothing to do with OB ever again or they are blown away by the fact they helped a new human arrive into the world. There's not much in between."

"Yeah, that's it," he said softly. "I *was* blown away."

"More so than all those mountainside rescues? The ones with the helicopters and avalanches and people impaled on their own ski poles?"

"Would you believe I only ran one avalanche rescue in all those years?"

"It's still more than most people." I pushed some hair away from my forehead and took a breath. "Thank you for the pens. And the coffee. And the cupcake."

A raspy sound came through the line and I knew immediately that he was running his knuckles over the beard scruff on his jaw. My whole body clenched. I could crack a nut between my thighs right about now.

It was ridiculous.

I didn't want it to stop.

"I was beginning to wonder if you'd noticed," he said.

"And I was trying to figure out how you pulled it off."

"You have your tricks, I have mine."

"That's not an answer," I said. "At least tell me how you got my coffee order right."

He cleared his throat. "Fine. I snapped a pic of your cup during rounds a few weeks ago and then I showed it to the barista."

"I can't decide if I'm impressed or concerned that you have enough time on your hands during rounds that you can take photos without me noticing."

"Be impressed," he said. "It works out better for me that way."

"Hmm. I'll think about it." After a moment of comfortable silence, I asked, "What do you want to talk about, Henry?"

He didn't hesitate to say, "Everything, Whit."

Twelve

Henry

Transplant Surgery Rotation:
Day 7, Week 4

We talked for hours that night and talked about *everything*—except work. Neither of us had to say it, but we both knew where the line was and went nowhere near it. That was not a problem because there was so much more to discuss than the hospital and all the ways our positions complicated things.

And then we did it again the next night.

Like clockwork, Whit would call around nine thirty or ten, make it sound like she had one quick, important thing to tell me that wasn't important at all, and we'd listen to each other breathe for a minute before the rest of the conversation started. From there, it didn't stop until one of us yawned too many times to ignore. If sleep hadn't been a factor, we'd have gone for days without stopping. There was never a shortage of material. Hell, we'd spent *all* of

Friday night on the varied styles of pizza around the country and which toppings were acceptable in which cities.

Maybe it didn't sound like much, but it wasn't just pizza. It was pizza and a story about Whit and Dr. Mercer getting lost on Long Island. It was pizza and my stunningly bad med school interviews in San Francisco. Pizza and Whit's sister sending a Chicago deep dish back because she thought they'd forgotten the cheese. Pizza and all these little pieces of ourselves.

I was probably being irresponsible with myself for this, but I was starting to see some possibility on the horizon. If we could do this, if we could talk for hours about pizza and everything else, maybe there was a chance we could pull it off after this rotation ended.

Whit asked me to come over around six tonight to work on my surgical technique, which I interpreted as an easy cover for spending time together without eyes and ears around every corner. That meant I devoted most of the afternoon to debating whether to bring flowers or wine—or both—before deferring to the only right answer when it came to Whit, which was cupcakes.

With a dozen mini cupcakes in hand, I hiked the cobblestone streets toward Whit's place. I knew her younger sister, who I'd learned was visiting her for a bit, was supposed to be out tonight but she had a tendency to be unpredictable and I should be prepared for anything.

I'd responded to that with some comment about my last gig equipping me pretty well for such things. She said I hadn't met Brie yet.

My phone buzzed in my pocket and I was relieved to find it wasn't Whit canceling our skills session. But then I was confused as hell that Mason was calling. "Aren't you supposed to be leading an expedition today?"

"Hello to you too," he grumbled.

"Don't tell me there's snow already."

"No snow," he said. "Just didn't take my usual three-day trek this week."

"Why not?" I stopped on the corner of Pinckney and Joy Streets. Such a cool, old neighborhood. I really had to explore more of this city, not just the hospital and a couple of random breweries. "What's up?"

He was in his truck, the wind whistling through the window and some tunes playing in the background. If I had to guess, I'd say he was somewhere on the 80 near Truckee, just driving around. He always did that when he was in a mood—which wasn't often. Mason Ballicanta wasn't a moody guy.

"Nothin'," he said eventually. "Just in my head."

"Okay." I glanced down at the cupcakes in my hand and then around the narrow intersection. "How's it going, then?"

"Not bad, not bad. How's that fancy East Coast prep school treating you?"

"Would you believe they're letting me operate on people? I helped attach a new set of lungs this week."

"They must not know you very well if they're letting you near real patients."

"Obviously not."

He laughed, but sobered quickly. "How'd you know it was time for a change?"

"You mean, going to med school?"

"Yeah," he said hesitantly.

"It was the year we got like twenty feet of snow in two weeks."

"Don't tell me the snow did you in." He sounded infinitely disappointed in me. "Come on, now."

"Not the snow. The storms are what made that year memorable because everything else blurred together," I said. "After a while, it was the same rescues over and over. The same overly ambitious and underprepared people out in terrible conditions where they couldn't see the hand in front of their face, but that didn't stop them from going off the trails and flying straight into a tree. I realized after one rescue that I'd zoned out while prepping double tibial compound fractures for evac and that was a fucking problem."

"Only you would get bored doing that."

"You're probably right," I conceded. "But that was how I knew."

After a moment, he said, "I guess Flor thought I was going to take a break from leading wilderness expeditions after we got married."

Threading the needle between supportive friend and *yeah, I fucking told you that would happen* was next to impossible. "Hmm."

"Take a break," he said, "or maybe do something else altogether. Like working for her dad."

Considering I'd repeatedly warned him that this precise thing would occur, I was left with no other response than, "Yeah."

"Not really an office kinda guy," he went on. "But she's upset that I'm gone for three or four nights every week."

"What are you thinking?"

"Don't know yet," he said. "It's all kind of taken me by surprise."

The only surprise was that it hadn't happened sooner. "I know you'll do what's right for you."

"Yeah, but it's not just about me anymore."

I started walking toward Whit's street again. "I hear you. I'm just saying you'll know what's right."

"I hope so." He cleared his throat. "What are you doin' tonight? Or do you have to get into bed early because it's a school night?"

"I'm on my way to work on surgical skill stuff."

I loved Mason like a brother, but there was no way in hell I was breathing a word about Whit to him or anyone else at this point. I wasn't superstitious but I also wasn't stupid.

"That does not sound like a whole lot of fun, my man," he said. "Better you than me."

"Hit me up if you want to talk through any of this stuff," I said as casually as possible. "You know where to find me. Even if I can't answer right away, you know I've got you. Right?"

"No doubt."

We ended the call and I rounded the corner from Joy to Derne Street, and then down to Temple. Whit lived on one of those Beacon Hill streets that didn't look like it was meant for this century. It was only a few blocks away from my place, but it felt like a slightly different world. Brownstone homes lined the narrow street and the brick sidewalks were topsy-turvy from decades of tree roots jabbing up from below. Even a few hitching posts along the way.

I climbed the steep, winding stairs to the third floor. I knocked, reminded myself not to fuck this up, and waited.

And waited.

I glanced around to make sure I was in the right place and checked my watch, and I was on my way to texting her to confirm we were still on when the door swung open. Whit held up a finger as she waved me inside, her phone pressed to her ear. *Just a sec*, she mouthed.

I nodded as she continued with her call—it sounded like a possible donor organ match and that was important—and seized the opportunity to get a look at Whit's place. It was exactly what I'd expected. Cool, sophisticated, and comfortable. It felt like her in here. Real furniture, nice artwork, fresh flowers on the kitchen island. Something was simmering away on the stove and a pair of her heels were kicked off by the door.

She turned to face me as the call ended, motioning between us with the phone still clutched in her hand. She was in jeans and a sweater and flat shoes that reminded me she was just a pint-sized little thing. She was strong in a compact kind of way. Short and sturdy though I wasn't sure she'd take that as a compliment. "Sorry about that. I might get called in."

"I get it." I held out the box of cupcakes. "For you."

Her hazel eyes widened as she said, "Oooh. I love this bakery." She shot me a grin that zipped straight down my spine. "Once again, excellent taste, Dr. Hazlette."

"It's the least I can do," I said.

That seemed to remind her of the stated purpose of this visit. "You'll be able to do a few more things better before the end of the night and, with any luck, do them a hell of a lot faster than you have been," she said, producing a box of nitrile gloves and surgical kits from a cabinet. "Glove up."

"Yes, ma'am." I rolled up my sleeves and pulled on gloves as she grabbed a whole chicken from the fridge. When she set it in front of me on the island, I blinked down at it for a second. "What...am I doing with this?"

"Start with a clamshell incision," she said. "I'm sure you've observed plenty of that in Dr. Salas's OR."

"With a chicken," I said.

"It's better practice than you think," she said from the stove. "I hope you like Hatch chile stew."

I shot her a glance as I set the surgical instruments on the countertop. Goddamn, she was pretty. There were times when my chest hurt just from looking at her. "I'm sure I will. That's a New Mexico thing, right? The chiles?"

She bobbed her head as she moved a spoon around the pot. "Yeah. I didn't really appreciate chile season while I lived there, but there are times now when I miss it."

"Did you like growing up there?"

Whit moved to the other side of the island, watching while I examined my patient.

"We lived with my grandmother, mostly, when my mother was deployed. She was in the Air Force." She arched a brow when I picked up the scalpel. "Reach for instruments like you know what you're doing."

"This is my first avian procedure," I said. "I have several questions about whether I know what I'm doing."

She grabbed the scissors and pointed to the breast, indicating where to cut. "The last thing anyone wants in the OR is you wasting their time. Make your incision."

I thought I had this under control, but I'd also thought technique practice was just the cover story. I hadn't realized she thought I actually needed practice and I did *not* want to fuck up in front of this woman. "But you liked New Mexico?"

"Yeah, mostly. My grandmother was great." She circled the island to stand beside me, her focus on the bird. She tapped the inside of my elbow and turned my wrist, saying, "You can hold your tools like that if you want, but you'll have to work twice as hard and your patient will suffer for it. Not to mention your colleagues will hate you."

"So no big deal, then," I murmured.

"Here. Like this." She stood behind me, shifting my posture and guiding my hands like I was a marionette. I could do this all night. All week. For the rest of my damn life. "Do you see? Fewer steps. Less work, less downtime. More focus."

"Yeah," I said, though it sounded like the word was clogged in my throat. Having her this close to me, *touching* me, was too much. I could barely think. "You're right."

She pulled her hands away from me and stepped back to the island to observe. Still didn't look thrilled with my work. I had no problem with her being the powerhouse in this room, but I wasn't used to being found lacking. All through med school, I'd had the advantage of my paramedic training plus years of experience, and I'd rarely struggled.

"Keep going," she said. "Pacing is critical. Know what your plan is from the start and maintain the flow of operation throughout. You'll always have to adapt, but if you have a clear vision, you won't slow down progress unnecessarily and give up time you'll need when things go haywire."

"Understood." I nodded and kept focus on her directions.

I worked for another twenty minutes while Whit berated me. I was slow and awkward with my tools. I wasn't thinking far enough ahead with my steps. I didn't conserve energy in the right ways and I lost the proper posture multiple times, although that one had a lot to do with wanting her hands on me again.

It was the kind of humbling I hadn't experienced in quite some time, but when I let go of trying to impress her, I was able to listen and learn. And that was awesome. Whit was awesome. She was an excellent teacher. Better than anyone I'd encountered here, even better than Dr. Salas.

"You know," she started, leaning against my forearm, "it looks like you learned to suture with a hotel sewing kit in a dark room."

"Thank you for noticing." How I managed to say anything

while her breasts were on my arm was a mystery. "Where I'm from, that's called the MacGyver technique."

"Here, we call it an inability to maintain appropriate tension." She breathed out a laugh as she circled back to the stove. "Where is it you're from, MacGyver?"

"California, just northwest of Tahoe."

"It sounds like you miss it," she said.

"I do, but I'm happy I'm here."

"Start closing up." She opened the fridge and retrieved a bottle of sparkling water. I was fucking elated that it wasn't another chicken. As she popped the top, she asked, "Any siblings?"

"A younger sister. She lives in northern Nevada and teaches English at a community college. She likes to say higher ed is grueling and soul-sucking, and insists our worlds have nothing in common."

"Stop it. Surgery isn't soul-sucking. That would require surgeons to have a soul to start with." She edged closer and covered my left hand with hers, adjusting my fingers and wiggling my wrist until she was satisfied with my position. It took everything to stay focused and not drop the tools and scoop her up right then. "You know, if you go any slower, you won't need to throw any more stitches because this wound will heal on its own."

"Are you this mean to everyone or is it special just for me?"

"Please don't tell me you think this is special."

I caught her eye and shot a meaningful glance between the cadaver chicken and the stew pot. "I wouldn't dare."

She held my gaze for a second, staring at me like she'd find something in my eyes if she just looked hard enough. Whatever it was, I wanted her to have it. Take anything she needed, anything she wanted. But then she looked away, reaching for the scissors and tapping my sutures. "Too much tension here, not enough over there. Do it again."

I watched her moving around the kitchen while I started over. She checked her phone, rustled in the fridge, pulled bowls from a cabinet. I knew this move. She did it whenever she wanted to pretend I wasn't infinitely aware of everything she did.

Or she wanted to ignore me.

"This English professor sister of yours," she said after a minute tending to the stew. "Married? Kids?" She grinned over her shoulder. "I ask because you give strong Cool Uncle vibes."

A rueful laugh curled up my throat. "I'm going to take that as a compliment, but no, last I heard, Hailey doesn't see herself married or with kids. She keeps herself fed on the lingering fury from our parents' divorce."

"Messy?"

"Yeah, but not even for good reasons. They both strayed to some degree, but there was no epic betrayal or anything high-stakes like that. And we know that because they never stopped rehashing their versions of the events to us. They just realized they didn't care about each other enough to stay together and spent years tearing the shit out of each other, using me and Hail as mediators and pawns."

"I'm sorry to hear that." Her voice was quiet as she shifted toward the stove. She stayed there, stirring and testing and seasoning.

"My sister spends all her time reading," I said after a few minutes. "She sees books as the solution to all of her problems."

Her back to me, she said, "I've heard of worse coping mechanisms."

"Yeah, I probably blew through all of them until I ended up in therapy after my ex told me I had major attachment issues and needed to sort out my shit."

She laughed, returning the lid to the pot, but she didn't turn around. "How'd that work out for you?"

"According to Miah, I'm not a complete jackass anymore, so that's something." I waited for some agreement on those grounds, but it never came. "And I learned how to experience emotions like I hadn't grown up in the middle of a cliché."

"Surgeons don't know how to deal with their feelings," she said. "That's why they're surgeons and not physicians." She surveyed my progress and gave it a tolerant smile like *good job, little buddy*. I had a lot of work to do if I was going to meet her standards. "Wait. Your ex is *Miah*, as in Miah the maid of honor? Is that how Mason met Florrie? Or is that how you met her?"

I blew out a breath as I organized the instruments. "I take the blame for Mason and Florrie, but I'm not going to say another word on that topic because you're a friend of the family and I don't have anything nice to say."

Whit opened her mouth to speak but stopped herself, tapping a finger to her lips as she studied me.

"But speaking of therapy," I went on, "it wouldn't hurt them to go. Chances are good they'll get there one way or another."

She leaned back against the countertops, crossing her arms. "Does that mean your issue is with the couple and not marriage in general? You weren't just being an ass at their wedding?"

I couldn't help but smile. It was good to talk to her. Even about my less than impressive moments. "I've been told by many, many people that I was an ass. No need to debate it."

She peered at me like she'd never seen me before. "Okay."

I pulled off my gloves. I wanted to know what *okay* meant and why it looked like there was a whole world spinning out in her head. I wanted to hear everything she was thinking, even if it was that there was no way we could pull this off. I wanted to touch her and I wanted her to touch me without the pretense of surgical skills. I wanted to put my hands in her hair and I wanted her to know that I couldn't get her out of my head and I'd *tried*. I'd really fucking tried.

Instead of saying any of that, I asked, "Which direction is post-op?"

She opened a cabinet to reveal the trash bin. Once I'd sent my patient on its way and I'd washed my hands, she pointed to the round dining table near the windows and told me to sit down. She filled two bowls with stew and set them down alongside warm flour tortillas and two bottles of beer.

We were quiet while we ate, forever eyeing each other and pretending there weren't a million questions pressing in around us. We stayed at the table long after second helpings, after another round of beers. We leaned toward each other as we talked about our sisters and the city and every other little thing that came up. At first it was just our elbows bumping each other, but it didn't take long for it to be arms, fingers, knees.

"I'm going to send you some readings," she said, watching as I traced the veins on the inside of her wrist. "I know you don't have loads of time for more readings but—"

"You'd be surprised," I said, staring at her pale skin and debating whether we could have this conversation with her in my lap. "Salas's bathroom and snack breaks really add up. I find if I keep the texts open on my phone, I can get through a lot of reading."

"Then you've realized reporting to her isn't the worst thing in the world?"

Our eyes met as I lifted her wrist to my lips. "If I say yes, will you let me come back from exile?"

She snapped her hand back and started to gather the dishes. "Can't you see that it's better for everyone if you stay where you are?"

"Sit down. I've got this." I stood, scooping the bowls out of her hands and heading toward the sink.

Predictably, she didn't sit down. She followed right behind me, making it all the harder to think past the desire I felt for her. It wasn't even sexual. I mean, there was *plenty* of sex happening in my head, but more than that, I wanted us to hide out in that space where it was just us and none of the dead ends and roadblocks.

Whit emptied the remaining stew into a glass container while I washed the dishes. When that was finished, I dried while she collected the forgotten beer bottles. We didn't say a word to each other.

Without looking at me, she said, "I'm going to send you some notes on your instrument handling too, but the best way to improve is to practice."

I watched her straighten a few items on the island. She gave the cupcake box a glance filled with longing. I thought about asking her opinion on the flavors I'd chosen, but I wasn't sure I could take it if she didn't want to go another round with me. I'd walked in here with hope, with so much goddamn optimism, and I wanted to leave with just as much. But I was teetering on the edge.

"Thanks. I'll do that." I motioned to the table. "And thank you for dinner. It was great. It was really good to talk to you. Like always."

Her teeth sank into her bottom lip as she glanced away. I couldn't begin to guess what she was thinking, but I wanted to believe she was right there on that edge with me, driving a knuckle into the same fucking bruise and wondering if it would keep on hurting.

She trailed me to the door, but stopped me with a hand on my forearm. We stared at each other for a second, her lip still snared between her teeth and the walls closing in around us. She squeezed my arm. I heard her swallow.

I wasn't sure who made the first move. It was possible we moved at the same time and it was possible that such details weren't relevant when shoving a woman up against a door and kissing her the way I'd been thinking about for months. Really, the only thing that mattered was the way she immediately sighed my name against my lips.

I scooped her up, bringing her legs around my waist and not caring whether we broke down the fucking door in the process because I was not about to let her go. Not now. Not yet.

I rocked between her legs and we cried out together. Here we were, right at the edge. Maybe a little too close. *"Whitney."*

She slipped her hand into my shirt, sliding along my shoulders and settling at the back of my neck. "Don't stop yet. Just one more minute. Okay?"

I kissed my way down her jaw and back to her lips. "You can have all the minutes you want."

She locked her legs tighter around me. "We can't."

"Why the fuck not? It's just you and me, Whit."

"You have no idea the amount of pressure I'm under right now," she whispered against my cheek.

"Then tell me," I said between kisses.

"My whole life is about professional standards and ethics." She raked a hand through my hair as she said this. "And I can't be the attending sleeping with a resident. I can't. I *won't*."

"Then we won't sleep. Easy fix."

"We can't do this," she breathed. "Not yet. Four more weeks. It's just twenty-eight days."

I leaned back just far enough to catch her eyes. "I'm really fucking pleased I'm not the only one counting down to the end of this rotation." She blinked at me, saying nothing. And that was when I knew I wouldn't shake her. I couldn't. And while a good part of me admired her for it, another part of me cared only about making sure her neighbors knew my name before the end of the night. My hips still rocking against her, I said, "Then we'll get through these four weeks and then figure it out. Together. Can you let me do that?"

She pulled her hand from my shirt and waved toward the kitchen. "What do you think I'm doing? What do you think all of this is?"

"I don't know," I cried. "You don't tell me what you're thinking too often."

"I invited you to my home on a Sunday night, Henry. *Alone*," she snapped. "What the hell does that sound like to you?"

"I thought I knew what it was and then you handed me a chicken to crack open!"

"Because you need the practice," she replied.

"Message received." I brought a hand to her face and tucked her hair over her ears. I brushed my lips over hers one more time. "We'll figure it out. Okay? Trust me on this."

I would've set her down then. Disentangled our limbs, pried ourselves apart, and thought about sewing up a chicken until my jeans fit a little more easily. But Whit held me tight, tugging me closer until I had no choice but to get lost kissing her.

It felt like the elevator all over again. Back in Tahoe. That first kiss when all I could think about was consuming every inch of her until I knew her better than I knew myself. When I'd forced myself to shove past all reminders that I was moving to Boston the next day and that my life was a train lurching from station to station though never quite stopping long enough to grab hold of anything permanent. When I wanted her to rip me to shreds just so I could do the same to her.

I took a tentative step away from the door. We'd continue this conversation on the couch. Same principles, softer surfaces.

"Henry," she whispered.

"Shhh. We're just talking."

I felt her smile against my lips, and for a second I had a lot more hope than I walked in here with.

But then her phone rang and she dropped her forehead to my shoulder with an angry groan. "*Fuck.* That's the hospital."

Thirteen

Whitney

Rule Number Twenty-Five:
Always be prepared to make a swift exit.

I stared at Henry as I pressed the phone to my ear. "This is Dr. Aldritch."

He dropped his hands to his hips, a fingertip tapping rhythmically against his belt as he gazed at the floor. Though I had the kitchen island between us, it was like I was still there, up against the door with his hands all over me. I couldn't get it out of my head.

And that was a problem because I'd heard about two percent of this call. "I'm sorry. I didn't catch that. Could you start over?"

"It's Ciarra down in Emergency, Dr. Aldritch," she said. "Your sister's been brought in."

"My—what? My sister's in the ED? My sister *Brie*?"

Henry jerked his head toward me, blinking for a moment before striding across the room. He settled a hand on my back. I leaned into him. I didn't even think about it.

"Rescue brought her in about fifteen minutes ago. They're working on her now. Looks like she collapsed and has some minor injuries from that, and her ostomy bag was filled with blood."

"I'll be there in ten minutes." I pressed a hand to my forehead. *Goddammit, Brie. Not again.* "Thanks for the call, Ciarra."

"Anytime, Dr. A," she said.

"I have to go," I said to Henry, shoving the phone in my back pocket and grabbing my hospital ID. "My sister passed out somewhere and she seems to have some intestinal bleeding, which could be a sign of any number of serious problems, once again."

"Yeah," he replied, following close behind me. "I'm going with you."

"That's unnecessary." I pulled the door shut with more force than required. The staircase was steep and winding, and I couldn't focus on my steps *and* argue with Henry at the same time. Not tonight. "I don't need any help with this, but thanks. You should go home."

When we reached the sidewalk, he said, "I'm still going with you."

"I don't really need another complication on my hands right now, Hazlette. My sister is more than enough." I gave a bitter shake of my head as we walked down Temple Street. "It always goes like this too. Every few years, she forgets to take care of herself and then something catastrophic happens. She'll end up sick for months and require lots of care, and then promise she'll do it right this time until she ultimately starts killing herself all over again."

Henry didn't say anything as we crossed Cambridge Street though I could feel the gentle scrape of his glances on the side of my face. With every step down the craggy brick sidewalk, those glances pressed deeper, like he was pushing through all the layers separating me from the outside world. Like he was seeing the person underneath it all.

And the trouble with that was I rarely let anyone see through those layers. When I did—and Meri was the only real case study for this—it was only the result of growing a whole tree trunk of trust and faith in that person.

All I could do was wonder how *Henry* came to be one of those people.

And *when* had that happened?

Honestly, I barely knew the man. We were relative strangers if we weren't counting that night in Tahoe. And talking until all hours this past week. And the fact I'd just fed him my grandmother's Hatch chile stew and I was stupidly sentimental about that recipe.

Acquaintances. Nothing more.

"How long has it been?" he asked. "That your sister has been dealing with this condition?"

"Most of her life. Diagnosed with Crohn's disease before kindergarten. Constant hospitalizations. On and off feeding tubes for years. Then an ostomy after high school when it just progressed too far. That helped, it put more time between the serious flares, but she forgets to play the maintenance game."

"And you've always been the one taking care of her."

I didn't say anything. It wasn't a question, and while he wasn't wrong, this was far from the time to dump the details of my oldest-daughter complex on him. He didn't need to hear about me managing my sister's medical conditions long before earning my MD or how I'd do it again in a heartbeat, always, no question about it, but I wouldn't mind a little acknowledgment from her. That I didn't know how to live without worrying about what would go wrong with her now. That I never hesitated to help her move and get her out of leases when she grew tired of a certain city because I knew the upheaval would do a number on her body. That my home would always be her home, but hers was never mine. That it killed me a little bit every time she went a whole month without refilling her meds, or drank coffee—one of her biggest triggers—or stuck to a heavy rotation of everything bagels as if she'd ever had any hope of digesting seeds. That I didn't keep score, but I lived with a lot of deep, dark questions about whether she'd crack her life wide open to save me if I ever needed it. That all of it hurt in sharp, stinging ways that I'd taught myself to ignore.

As we closed in on the back side of the hospital complex, Henry reached for my arm, stopping us under an overhang. I twisted my lanyard around my palm with my free hand. His gaze rolled over me like a storm cloud.

"Breathe for a minute," he said. "I know you want to barrel on in there, but I need you to breathe for me before you do that. I need you to understand that I am going to hang out for a bit. I'm not going to crowd you while you do your thing, but I'm also not leaving you alone right now."

I cinched the lanyard a little tighter. "Why are you doing this?"

He pushed some hair off my forehead and tucked it over my ear. "Because I want to keep an eye on you."

"I don't need you to do that."

"You don't," he said simply. "But I want you to let me do it anyway."

He settled his palm on the back of my neck. I glanced around. We couldn't do this here. It was such a bad idea, all of it. And yet I didn't step away. My voice was pathetically small when I asked the one question I hadn't been able to get out of my head since he promised we could get through this. "Why?"

He stared at me for a second, his dark gaze sweeping over my face, down to the chains around my neck and to the fingers I drummed against my thigh. He didn't smile or laugh or offer any of his usual charm, all of which made it clear that I'd created a terribly vulnerable position for myself. Not only did I want him to provide an emotional bibliography for his claims, but I'd kicked open the secret compartment where I kept my self-worth issues for him to see, all with one word. All while my sister was passed out in Emergency.

I was nothing if not efficient.

He drew his thumb over my cheek and down the line of my jaw. "Because I like you, Whitney Aldritch. You'll just have to deal with it."

My lips parted as the most desperate of survival instincts told me to shut this down, push it away, reject reject reject. Because I knew I was hard to like and harder to love, and if I let this continue, I'd be forced to look those truths in the eye all over again.

Somehow, I said, "I'll try."

He swept a hand down my back, ending with a swift slap to my ass. "Yeah, you will."

I couldn't help it. I pressed my forehead to his shoulder and laughed. "I need to get in there and—" My phone buzzed again. I sighed as I read the message. "Looks like I'm transplanting a heart tonight too. Awesome. Perfect timing. Not like I have anywhere else to be."

Nodding, Henry led me to the door. He unwrapped the lanyard from my hand and gave me a look like *these crazy things you do* as he swiped my badge. "Then put me to work. What do you want me to do? I can prep your patient, I can scrub in, I can—"

"I can't let you scrub in with me." We cut through the back corridors of the hospital, quiet and dim in the slowdown of Sunday night. "I know you don't see it the same way but—"

"I do see it," he interrupted. "And I see that these boundaries are important to you. If that means I don't scrub in with you once in this rotation, I can live with it."

As we closed in on the Emergency Department, I glanced over at him. "You should, considering you had a private lesson tonight. Don't mention that to your cohort until I figure out how to do the same for the rest of them."

"I'd really prefer if it's not the *exact* same for them," he murmured.

I swatted his thick bicep. "We don't talk about that here."

"Yes, ma'am." He held the door open for me. "I'm going upstairs to change. Text me when you decide how you want to use me."

"I—um." I blinked up at him, my cheeks suddenly hot. "What?"

A dark cloud blew over his features. "I'm not going to say anything because we don't talk about that here and"—his brow quirked up as he leaned in just enough to tell me a secret—"you should know by now that I don't require much direction."

Again, all I could manage was, "What?"

A cheeky smile pulled at his lips as he pointed down the hallway. "Go. We'll talk about it later."

Since I didn't have time to waste and this conversation was headed down a thorny path, I followed those orders and headed straight for the Emergency Department. I only glanced back at Henry when waiting for the automatic double doors to open enough for me to slip inside. Gaze steady and arms crossed over his chest, he gave me a quick nod.

He could've meant any number of things or nothing at all with that gesture, but to me it said *I want to keep an eye on you*.

Warmth filled my chest like a gulp of too-hot coffee. I looked away. I had an hour or two before the donor organ arrived and that was hardly enough to get Brie's situation under control.

Dr. Chaudhry gave me a full update while walking me to the room where they were treating Brie. She had a raging infection that they'd classified as "five minutes away from sepsis," a mild concussion from hitting her head when passing out, and the still unexplained bleeding. There were more tests to run and procedures to schedule, but the antibiotics and pain meds were flowing and her vitals were stronger than when she'd arrived.

I glanced at my sister. Dark smudges circled her eyes and her lashes fanned out over her cheeks as she rested. The side of her face was pale and lightly scraped from the tumble she took down the stairs. I wanted to believe this infection blew up out of nowhere even though I knew that wasn't how it worked with her. It was always a slow, steady build. "Page me directly if anything comes up."

"You're not staying with her?"

"I'll be here all night," I said, already tired. My phone started buzzing again. I ignored it. "But I was just called into a procedure and I need to get upstairs. My circulator will have my phone."

They regarded me for a moment. Eventually, they said, "Your ethics program is a pain in my ass. One of my residents thinks he's being mistreated every time he doesn't get the exact cases and procedures he wants and I've had to sit through three so-called productive dialogue sessions with him because of it." They glared at me for a heavy second and it seemed like tonight was descending even further into battle mode. I felt the sigh start somewhere in my toes. "It is annoying and cumbersome. But it helps. It does what it's supposed to do for the people who need it."

Battle averted. For once. "Then that's all that matters."

They bobbed their head as they edged around the curtain. "You're right."

I studied the monitor while Shoshanna, one of the best nurses on the floor, checked Brie's lines. She had the longest hair I'd ever seen on anyone and it was better maintained than anything in my life. To her, I said, "When she wakes up, will you let her know I was here? And I'll be back when I'm finished?"

She hummed as she scanned another bag of fluids. "Of course."

"Thanks. And thank you for taking care of her."

"You don't have to thank me for that, Dr. Aldritch."

"Tough shit, because I just did."

She glanced up. "I should've expected that."

I patted Brie's arm as my phone buzzed in my pocket. "Yeah. Probably." I pulled it out, finding an avalanche of pages. "I have to head upstairs, but I—I might send a resident down to check in while I'm in the OR."

"I promise I won't put them to work unless you want me to," she said.

I laughed. Henry would probably enjoy that. "I'll leave that up to you."

I made my way out of the Emergency Department and toward the elevators that would take me closest to my office. When the doors opened, I found Henry leaning against the wall, his arms folded and ankles crossed in front of him. He'd changed into scrubs and a fleece jacket.

He must've replaced the one he'd given to me.

I stepped inside and pressed the button for my floor. "Quite the timing you have, Dr. Hazlette."

"I could say the same to you, Dr. Aldritch," he said as the doors closed. "How's your sister?"

I tucked myself against the opposite wall, mirroring his stance.

"Bacterial infection severe enough to impress the attending, and unknown gastric bleeding. Hopefully she doesn't need another bowel resection."

He ran a gaze over me, a slow study that went everywhere at once. My chest was full of that scalding coffee again. "Then I'll hang out downstairs while you have your hands full upstairs."

The elevator climbed quickly and I decided that was the reason for the drop in my stomach. Not because him being here, *staying* here, meant something. Because I wasn't ready for it to mean something. Even though I was suddenly becoming aware that this was so much more complicated than I'd ever imagined. This wasn't a one-night stand come back to haunt me anymore. It wasn't even a suffocating amount of sexual tension anymore.

It was more. Just...*more.* And I didn't know whether I should run as far and fast as I could or if I should stay here too.

FOURTEEN
HENRY

Transplant Surgery Rotation:
Day 5, Week 7

WHIT WAS STILL IN THE OR WHEN IT WAS TIME FOR Monday morning's rounds. Dr. Salas took over and insisted on rearranging the order of the cases we rounded on for "geographical efficiency." In other words, she wasn't willing to walk any more than necessary and wanted easy access to break rooms and nurses' stations to scavenge for snacks. I already knew this about Salas though Copeland and the rest of my cohort didn't, and it was amusing to watch them scrambling to adapt.

Reza was tasked with holding her water that morning and he did it like a pro. I was proud of him.

I spent that week bouncing between Salas and Hirano, and then another week paddling the same boat to nowhere. I barely saw Whit at all. We talked at night a few times, but she was wiped out from juggling both her sister, who was recovering at home after a long stay, and her cases.

I was starved for more. Anything, any little bit I could get.

I wanted to go to her place and cook dinner while she decompressed from her day. I wanted to tell her about crazy rescues to get her mind off of everything. I wanted to rub her shoulders and hands after long surgeries and just fucking *be* with her because even when we were apart she was always with me. I wanted to take off all her clothes and spend the night reacquainting myself with her body.

And I wanted to know what it was like for her to exist somewhere other than my mind. She was the beginning and end of every damn thought I'd had for months and there were moments when I questioned whether I was on her mind at all.

But I'd agreed to this. I knew I couldn't have any of the things I wanted, not yet.

And I was the one who'd promised we'd get through this. I was the one with all the faith, and here I was, falling the fuck apart two weeks later. I couldn't even believe myself right now. Crumbling under the weight of—what?—the fact that I couldn't have everything I wanted the precise second I wanted it? Who the hell was I with this bullshit? Never in my life had I ever let myself get turned inside out like this and I didn't know how to function anymore.

I knew what I signed up for and I accepted it, and yet I was pointlessly irritable after getting a message from Whit late Thursday afternoon saying she was headed into a procedure and wouldn't be finished until after midnight. That irritation spread like an ugly, itchy rash as Friday wore on and I still hadn't heard or seen her and it chafed in all the spots where this thing between us was fragile and undefined, the places where she held me at a distance.

I wanted the right to Whit's time and attention. I wanted the right to ask her medical assistant what her schedule looked like today and I wanted to leave pens and muffins on her desk without first developing a cover story in case someone caught me in the act. I wanted her to come home to me at the end of a long day and I wanted to wake up beside her in the morning.

I wanted her to belong to me and that irritated me the most of all because it was like a vague, distant dream. I knew we'd make it out of this rotation, but what then? I knew what I wanted and I also knew it scared the shit out of me because I'd never, *ever* entertained those possibilities for myself.

On the one hand, I had a fuck-ton of fear and a serious shortage of healthy relationships to build on. On the other, I had the realization that Whitney might have no interest in belonging to me or anyone else. Not that we'd ever talked about it. No, any conversation we had about our relationship centered around the aggressively hierarchical structure of teaching hospitals and all the things we couldn't do until we'd put enough distance between us and the professional radioactivity of falling for your boss.

I trudged through a procedure with Dr. Hirano, my pissy mood multiplying with every hour spent holding a retractor while he whistled along to a short playlist of old-school country tunes that he ran on an infinite loop. By the end, I'd worked up a good head of steam over everything and nothing and many other things I couldn't change. It only intensified when I checked my phone and found no new messages from Whit.

I knew she was busy. Her sister was a significant weight on her shoulders. Her schedule was packed. Heart transplants only happened when organs became available and she had no way of planning for that. I knew all of this and still I couldn't shake this irritable mood.

When I made it to the residents' lounge, I flopped down on a bench and folded my arms over my face. My shoulders burned from retractor duty and the rest of me was drained from two weeks of orbiting Whit. I hadn't had a decent night's sleep in forever and I'd adopted the practice of sticking around the hospital later than usual on the off chance of catching her in the elevators or on her way out. Add to that the fact that when we did talk, neither of us gave a damn how late we stayed up.

Though I didn't regret any of it, I was really fucking tired.

The door banged open and I heard Tori's voice. "She's going on twenty-four hours straight! What a fucking machine. Goddamn, I want to be her when I grow up."

I groaned into my forearm for no other reason than it gave me something to do with all the bitterness I'd gathered up for myself this week.

"It is impressive." That was Reza. "Have you practiced the stitches she modeled on Tuesday?"

"Every chance I get." Cami. "I think I'm working up to better efficiency too."

"I didn't realize how much extra work I was doing until she pointed it out," Tori said.

I sensed people surrounding me and I grunted when someone kicked my running shoe. "What the fuck?" I grumbled, glaring up at Cami.

"What's wrong with you this week?" she asked.

"Tired." That was more than enough explanation for any resident's bad mood. We were all exhausted, all the time. Mostly from holding retractors for seven hours while the attending hummed off-key with the same Hank Williams song you've heard sixteen times. Or worse yet, spending seven hours staring at the back of a surgeon's head because you were only allowed to observe, which loosely translated to standing wherever the circulating nurse told you to, even if that meant seeing all of nothing.

"You don't get tired." Tori approached, dropping her lab coat and stethoscope onto my chest before opening her locker. "And you don't get into funks like this. What's going on?"

Before I could formulate a response, Cami asked, "Do I have time to observe from the gallery? I need to go home and change before the softball game, but I really want to watch Dr. Aldritch. I can't believe she's still going."

I sat up, Tori's coat falling to my lap in the process. "What's Dr. Aldritch doing?"

"You haven't heard?" Cami was aghast. You'd think I'd insulted her entire family with one question. "How are you so far out of the loop?"

"I've been in the OR all day." I motioned to my scrubs and the cap I hadn't bothered taking off. "The only thing I've heard is Hirano's version of 'Jolene' and—"

"Christ, the whistling." Tori groaned as she buttoned her shirt. "It's like water torture after an hour or two."

"I am inclined to agree," Reza said.

"Easy there, Ansari," I said to him. "You're going to knock us over with these strong opinions."

"Anyway," Cami said, "Aldritch is on her *fourth* transplant since Wednesday night."

"She—what?" I *hated* that I didn't know this.

"Yep," Cami said, holding up a finger. "First one came in after hours on Wednesday, then another on Thursday, one this morning that was a patient of Galbraith's but he has a stomach virus. Vomited all over the scrub sink, told everyone he was fine, and then vomited *on his resident* while they were walking into the OR. It was a whole messy thing. They called in Aldritch to cover, and while she was working on Galbraith's patient, the call came in from the organ center about a match for one of her patients."

I stood, shoving Tori's things toward her. "She's been in the OR since last night?"

"Yeah, they said she walked out of Galbraith's case, ate a protein bar, took a thirty-minute nap, and then went back into the OR," Tori said. "That's how you get shit done."

And here I was, marinating in my own pointless feelings because it had been days since putting eyes on her, as if she needed another selfish asshole in her life. I couldn't believe I'd managed to wind myself up over this—to get myself to the point of wondering if she ever thought about me—when she'd spent the past three days hooking up new hearts.

I didn't know what the hell was wrong with me. I really didn't.

But I needed to fix it.

"And the case she's working on is really interesting," Cami added. "I wanted to scrub in, but I'm already over my max hours for the week and Copeland told me there was no chance in hell she'd ignore that since I was over last week too."

"Such a hard-ass," Tori murmured. "She probably wanted that case for herself."

"She's over her hours too. I think every resident on transplant is over," Cami replied. "I heard Hartshorn scrubbed in to assist. He pulled a few fifth-years off cardio-thoracic too."

I was going to have to screw my head on straight real fast. I could not spend all my time swimming around in my feelings when Whit was busy grinding through surgeries.

"He did and she's eating them alive."

I shifted to face Reza. "I don't know what to do with the evil amusement in your tone, Ansari. It's freaking me the fuck out."

Cami rolled her brown eyes. "He got another cat and it's

changed his whole personality. See? These are the things you miss when you're off being Salas's special project."

"And he's hooked on spicy jelly beans," Tori said, motioning to Reza. "It's got him all pepped up this afternoon which is great because we're going to need some pep to win the game tonight."

Reza gave a slight nod in response.

"Right. Okay." I shrugged into my fleece jacket and headed toward the door. I had more important places to be. "I gotta go."

"You'll be at the game, right?" Tori called.

I didn't answer.

I WATCHED FROM THE GALLERY WHILE WHIT transplanted a new heart into a nineteen-year-old woman who'd been waiting for this day for nearly three years. Donor lists could be unpredictable, but that was a long time and I had to imagine those had been hard years for her. No one lived on the list. They survived.

If I didn't know Whit had been working virtually nonstop for three days, I wouldn't have guessed from watching her. She was as sharp and focused as always and had no patience for these fifth-years on loan from cardio-thoracic. It came as a slight relief to me that I wasn't the only one too slow for Whit's liking. The only times I saw the strain was when she stepped away from the table to roll her shoulders or get a sip of water. She chatted with Hartshorn about his kids and wife, who was some kind of big-deal sports publicist, and their plans to visit his parents in Oregon for the holidays. I didn't know how she managed it, but she didn't even sound tired.

The procedure was tedious and complicated, but that new heart didn't waste a second getting to work. It was almost ten o'clock when Whit and Hartshorn walked out of the OR to speak to the patient's family. I intercepted her a few minutes later and I knew from her glazed eyes and unsteady steps that I'd made the right call.

One of the crazy things about the human body was the ability to push through intense situations for longer than logical. Whit could stand at the operating table for days on end with minutes of rest and she could do it with incredible skill—but the second her body knew the work was over, she'd crash. *Hard*.

"This way," I said, guiding her into the elevator.

She rested her head on the wall and closed her eyes as the car climbed to her floor. After a moment, she said, "You were in the gallery for hours."

I bobbed my head. "Yeah."

"Why?"

She had her hair in two French braids that'd seen better days. There were purple circles around her eyes and deep, red grooves on her face from her mask and surgical glasses. She was perfect and all I could give her was complete honesty. "I wanted to see you."

She slow-blinked like she wasn't sure she believed me.

When the doors opened, I said, "Let's grab your things and get you home."

She stepped out and headed toward her office. "No, I'll just crash here."

"The fuck you will."

Whit stopped in the middle of the hall, her hands on her hips. "What was that, Hazlette?"

She was working hard at giving me her most serious glare

though the effect landed closer to loopy and cross-eyed. Loved it so much. "I said, the fuck you will. You're not staying here tonight."

"At the rate I'm going, I'll get paged before midnight."

I urged her forward with a hand on her lower back. "Probably not. I don't think there's anyone left on the transplant list after this week. You cleared it."

She didn't bother turning on the lights in her office, instead grabbing her bag and coat from inside a small closet. I helped her into the coat when she kept missing the arm, taking advantage of the dark and smoothing my hands over her shoulders and along the curve of her waist. With one hand still settled low on her back, I unclipped her ID badge and dropped it into her bag. "I'm taking you home now."

In a remarkable turn of events, Whit didn't argue with me. Didn't make any noises about sleeping in on-call rooms or on the sofa in her office. She allowed me to lead her to the elevator and out of the hospital without a word.

I knew she was tired when she didn't have it in her to remind me of all the reasons we couldn't be together like this yet.

"Wasn't there a softball game tonight?"

I nodded. "There was."

"You didn't go."

I shifted her bag to my other hand. "Nope."

"Why not?"

I watched her for a moment because I couldn't believe she was asking this again. If I didn't know Whit better, I'd think it was some kind of pick-me act, but that wasn't her style and she was in no state for playing those kinds of games. "You really don't get it, do you?"

She was too tired to keep her reactions in check, and her sour, scowly face had me choking back a laugh. "Get what, Hazlette?"

"That I like you, you gorgeous grump, and I like being with you. I'll skip every softball game in the world if it means I get to see you."

"But you like softball."

I rolled my eyes. "Not more than you."

"Seems unlikely."

"I mean, it's your fault. You're the one who seduced me this summer."

"I did *not* seduce you," she said. "You're the one who seduced me. You worked hard on that dance floor, my friend."

"To be fair, I believe the dessert table seduced you first."

She snorted. It was fucking adorable. I mean, come the fuck on. How was I supposed to do anything other than fall for this girl? As if there was any other option.

"That's true. It was an excellent dessert table. I hope next summer's weddings go hard with the dessert tables."

"A lot of weddings on your calendar?"

"Like you wouldn't believe."

We were about five minutes from her place when the exhaustion overtook her and she started wobbling like she was six margaritas deep. "If you think I won't throw you over my shoulder and carry you the rest of the way, you are mistaken."

"You wouldn't dare," she said, and she *sounded* like she was six margaritas deep. "It's not like I'm a light package."

"First of all, I'd dare. You know I would." I tried to meet her eyes, but she was barely awake. This was as close to sleepwalking as it came. "And second, you're just right for me. Don't forget I used to carry huge guys in full mountain gear to rescue transport." I ran a gaze over her knee-length coat, blue scrubs, and navy clogs. I wrapped an arm around her waist. For safety purposes. "Just right."

I had to dig through her bag to find the keys because she was dead on her feet. Once we were inside, I locked my hands on her hips and guided her up the stairs. I didn't trust her to make it on her own.

Also, I fucking loved her hips. I had very fond memories of holding her exactly like this.

"Brie should be asleep," Whit said when we reached the landing. I couldn't bring myself to let go of her. Again, safety purposes. "That doesn't mean she will be."

"Understood." I held her close as I opened the door, her head on my chest. The house was dark and still, with no sign of Brie. "Looks like she's in bed."

"Small miracles."

I peeled off her coat before she wandered away from me.

I followed her.

I'd always follow.

And that was how I found myself standing in the middle of Whitney's bedroom.

She went to sit on the edge of the bed but missed it by a mile and ended up on the floor before I could reach her. Laughing, she hugged her knees to her chest. "Okay. No more obstacles for me. Imma sleep here," she drawled.

"No, you're not." I pried off her clogs and then went to work on her knee socks. They were pink and printed with ice cream cones. "Cute."

"If you're gonna wear compression socks, might as well make 'em cute."

I hooked my hands under her arms, pulling her up from the floor. She wrapped herself around me, arms, legs, everything. I sighed into her shoulder. Being with her like this, exactly as I'd pissed and moaned about all day, was what I needed. It was all I'd ever need.

Once she was seated on the bed, I reached for her shirt. "Arms up, baby."

With the most adorable huff in the world, she complied. "My socks are cute," she said, her words coming in lazy bursts. "But my bra is not."

"You're cute." I tossed her top to the other side of the room, toward a door I guessed was the closet. The bra was of the athletic variety and getting it over her head was like wrestling a dolphin. Too difficult for me to take any pleasure in the affair.

I had about three seconds of her sitting there, topless and delirious with exhaustion, before she flopped backward and wiggled out of her scrub bottoms. She kicked them right over my head, which was honestly impressive. Phenomenal aim. But this left her in a little pair of panties and not a single thing else.

I swallowed. Shoved both hands through my hair. Stared at the ceiling while I reminded myself of her boundaries.

"Let's get you something to sleep in, sweetheart."

"Nope." She reached behind a pillow and pulled out something that looked like a big sweater. "I'm good."

As she shoved her arms through the sleeves, I realized it wasn't a sweater. It was *my* fleece jacket. The one I gave her that day in the auditorium.

All this time, I figured she'd tossed it in the lost and found bin or stuck it in the back of a closet. I figured it hadn't mattered to her.

But—

She'd kept it.

She tucked it behind her pillow.

She wore it to *bed*.

I took a step back as the truth settled down around me like I was sitting in the bottom of the hourglass, sand falling until I was buried in it.

Whit nestled into the pillows and tucked her knees into the fleece. She held out a hand. It just about broke me. "Don't go."

She didn't mean that. I picked up her phone from the floor and plugged it in. I ran my hand over her forehead. "Get some rest, Whit."

"Please?" She closed her hand around my forearm. "I'll be good."

"I'd expect nothing less," I said. "I seem to recall you being a *very* good girl when you want to be."

A silly grin split her face and I could feel the better judgment exiting my body. "Why are you so nice to me?" she asked.

"Because you deserve it."

With her free hand, she patted the mattress beside her. The other hand yanked on my arm. "Stay."

She was swimming in that fleece, half her face hidden under the collar, and I loved it. "You wouldn't want that if you weren't out of your mind tired."

"I want it," she mumbled, her eyes closing, "all the time. But I'm bad at making things work with people because no one stays. For me, they don't stay. Everyone leaves me in the end."

Maybe we'd regret this in the morning, but she'd asked me twice and that was more than enough. Even if she was barely conscious. Even if I knew better. I didn't want to be one of the people who didn't stay for her.

So, I toed off my shoes and deposited my phone and hospital lanyard on her bedside table. "I'm not going anywhere, Whit."

"'kay." She kicked up the blankets and burrowed beneath them. "I wish I had an ice cream sandwich."

"Then you admit it, you do like ice cream."

She yawned so wide, I knew she'd had her tonsils out at some point. "Yep."

"I'll check the freezer."

"We don't have any," she mumbled through another yawn. "I don't buy them because I'll eat them."

"I'm sure that makes sense to you." I skimmed my hand over her cheek. Her skin was dry, her lips chapped. Spending all day in the ultra-filtered air of the OR and surviving on the smallest amount of fluids possible so you didn't have to break scrub protocol to use the bathroom would do that to you. "I'm going to grab some water for you," I said, still stroking her face. "I'll be right back."

She grumbled out some response while I headed toward the kitchen. I did my best to stay quiet, but it wasn't quiet enough because I turned around and found myself staring at Brie. It was like these sisters were different editions of the same book, one fair and light, the other olive-toned and dark.

"Who the hell are you?" she asked.

"Henry." I motioned toward the bedroom. "I'm here with Whit."

"I figured as much. Burglars don't usually stay long enough to pour themselves a glass of water." She gave me an up-and-down glance. "What's your story, Henry?"

"My...my story? I don't really have a story. No story here."

She folded her arms over her chest. "You have a story."

I pointed toward Whit's room again. "Not after the week your sister's had, I don't. Her story is the only one that matters tonight."

"Interesting," she said, mostly to herself.

"Are you all right?" I couldn't assess much in the dark or with her drowning in a hoodie and fleece pajamas, but I had to ask. "Any fever, nausea or vomiting, changes in—"

"Of course you're a doctor." She said it like a sigh. "Why am I not surprised?"

"Any inflammation or bleeding at your incision site?" I gestured to where the bag was hidden under her clothes. "Can I take a quick look?"

"Definitely not, but thank you for making it weird." She rubbed her temples. "Should I assume you're one of the docs who treated me in the past two weeks? That you've seen the inside of my intestines and know how much I pee in a day? Or are you the one who cut my clothes off me in the ER?"

"None of the above. I just know Whit would've asked if she wasn't bone-tired."

"She works too much."

I shrugged. Maybe that was true, but I didn't know many surgeons who had a handle on balancing work and everything else. It wasn't in our nature. Certainly not in Whit's. "There's no predicting when a heart will open up."

Somehow, that earned me another up-and-down glance. "Henry, is it? You really are an interesting one."

I watched her stroll down the hall and close the door behind her before I returned to Whit's room. She was out like a light, and as I lay down beside her, she curled into me, tucking her head up against my chest.

She mumbled out an order to take the patient off bypass, then another calling for internal paddles. I ran my hand over her hair, gently pulling the ties from her braids and raking my fingers through the strands as her rambles turned into quiet murmurs and sighs.

I didn't grow up in a family that centered religion. Mason did, and I acquired enough from hanging out with his family over the years to know the ropes, but I'd never been able to wrap my hands around a reason to believe in anything beyond myself and this world.

Fast forward twenty-five-ish years from Mrs. Ballicanta's kitchen table catechism to finally falling asleep beside Whitney, and I could see now that I was wrong. That was all it took to believe in everything beyond this world.

I knew I was pinning a lot of this belief on the shaky agreement of a woman with an extensive history of walking away from me. I was aware of that danger, but I couldn't bring myself to care. Not when I had newfound faith on my side. And, according to Mason's mother, faith never failed.

Even if I had all my usual emotionless detachment, all those years of avoiding real connection with people on the other side. Even if the shadowy truth was that I had no idea what I was doing with Whitney, that I was making promises to her I only wished I could deliver on. It all seemed to gather around me and press in from every angle until it felt too strong to overcome. Even if, in the back of my mind, these shadows were morphing into screaming high rock faces of doubt that this wouldn't last because *nothing* lasted.

Somehow I went on believing it wouldn't be like that.

Fifteen

Whitney

Rule Number Twenty-Nine:
Don't oversleep. The early bird gets out before it's awkward.

My entire body hurt. Everything felt tight and overtaxed, like I'd finished a triathlon and then tried my hand at oil wrestling. And I was on the verge of turning into jerky because there was hardly a drop of water left in my body.

I blindly reached to my bedside table, fumbling for a cup or bottle of water. When I found one, I guzzled without concern for the noises I made or the water that missed my mouth and ran down my chin. Pretty wasn't the point after making it through nearly thirty-six hours of nonstop surgery.

Setting the empty glass down, I grabbed my phone and discovered it was nearly two in the afternoon. I'd slept for—I wasn't even sure how long. I couldn't remember when I got home. But, more importantly, my phone was blessedly free of missed calls or urgent pages. Aside from Meri's stream of consciousness texts and one from Hartshorn telling me to call him to assist if I got paged this weekend, I had just one other message and it was from Henry.

In one painful breath, last night came rushing back to me. Henry buttoning my coat in my dark office. Henry walking me home while I rambled like an idiot. Henry putting me to bed while I begged him to stay. I whipped my head toward the other side of the bed, half expecting to find him there. But the blankets were smooth and crisp, just like every other morning.

And that was crazy because I remembered him here. I remembered his arms around me and his fingers in my hair. I couldn't imagine that. I knew because I'd been trying to imagine it for weeks.

I tapped open his message.

> **Henry**
> If you really must panic, at least have a muffin first. They're in the kitchen. Coffee too but don't hit that until you've had some water. Then call me.

I pressed the phone to my chest and let the warmth of his words run through my veins. I smiled up at the ceiling even though a voice in the back of my head was tsking my choices and ranting about professional boundaries. This morning—err, afternoon—I just didn't care. I knew this wasn't technically aboveboard, but it also wasn't an abuse of power. Anyone could see the difference.

I dragged myself into the bathroom, downing another glass of water while I waited for the shower to heat up.

It wasn't often that I got slammed like this past week, with organs coming in faster than I could transplant them and all the other heart specialists out of the office or busy contaminating scrub rooms with their stomach flu. It was a throwback to my residency and fellowship days, and I didn't like it.

But I *loved* that Henry took me home last night. He came here with me and he spent the night, which was commendable since my hair was gross and I smelled like the OR, and chances were good I'd been a pain in the ass after surgery. All these decidedly unsexy things, and he stayed.

Once I was thoroughly washed and dressed, I went in search of those muffins.

I found Brie sitting at the island with her laptop, her lips curled into a knowing grin and her brow arched all the way into her hairline as she stared at me.

"I have a lot of questions for you, but I've been instructed to make sure you eat." She pushed a bakery box toward me and then two cups. "Gaston's body double brought hot and iced coffees, but at this point they're both cold so best of luck with that."

I reached for the iced coffee. "Gaston's body double?"

"The boy is the size of a barge."

"Not really." Okay, a bit, but I wouldn't run around telling people that.

She closed her laptop and folded her arms over the lid. "So, what's the story?"

I fetched a plate before attacking the muffins. I liked to cut them into perfect little quarters and make a variety muffin with the different flavors. Same strategy worked beautifully for cupcakes and donuts. "No story."

"Funny. He said the same thing."

I worked hard at swallowing my reaction. "Did he?"

"Yep." She drummed her nails on the laptop lid. "I didn't buy it from him and I'm not buying it from you. There's a story. *You* brought a guy home last night."

I went to work dissecting my muffins, extremely pleased with the flavors Henry selected. "Not much to say."

I tried very hard to sound casual and Brie picked up on it immediately. "You never bring guys home."

"I do," I lied.

"Not that I've ever seen."

I jerked up a shoulder. "Doesn't mean it doesn't happen when you're not here."

"What's the deal with him? He's a doctor, obviously, but where'd you meet, how long has it been, does he have a brother, so on and et cetera."

"Why *obviously*?"

She sighed like I was causing her real pain. "Because he asked on two separate and unnecessary occasions if I was having any fevers or vomiting and then asked to check my incision."

I tore my gaze away from the muffins. The warmth was back. It spread down to my fingers and burned my cheeks and buzzed in my head like the moment a sleeping pill started to kick in. "He-he did?"

She studied her nails. "Yes. Very thorough. Last night and this morning. One might call that thoroughly unnecessary."

"We're going to need a few more weeks between your last hospital stay and emergency bowel resection before we can call it unnecessary." I broke off a chunk of pistachio muffin and popped it in my mouth. "What do you have going on today?"

"We can't talk about Henry?"

I shook my head. "Not yet, no."

She pulled the clip out of her hair and ran her fingers through the strands. "I'm a great listener."

That part was true. She was a great listener—when she wanted to be. There were times when Brie was my best friend and most trusted confidant. And then there were times when she didn't return my calls or texts for a full month.

"Yeah, I know. It's just not something I want to talk about yet."

Undeterred, Brie pressed on. "Does it help that you see each other at work? Because you have so much in common? Or do you get tired of each other and the medical stuff?"

I grabbed a quarter of a blueberry muffin, eating it in two bites. "We haven't gotten tired of each other yet."

"I'd totally get bored. I don't want to talk to anyone about work after hours. I don't even want to talk about work during work."

I went for the cranberry orange muffin, murmuring along as if I agreed. I understood her point, but our work worlds were very different. She coordinated travel accommodations for executives. She could work anywhere, any time. Arranging travel wasn't the cornerstone of her identity the way surgery was for me—and most of the docs I knew.

She tapped the clip on the countertop. "Have you given any thought to meeting up with Dad next month?"

And that was when I choked on my muffin.

I coughed and sputtered for a minute, and then gulped enough coffee to wash it all away. Once I recovered, Brie said, "I take that as a no."

"No, I haven't thought about it," I said, my voice raspy. "I'd rather not think about it."

She clasped her hands in front of her. "I know you have strong feelings about him and how everything went when we were kids, but—"

"It's not like he missed a few holidays and birthdays, Brie. He's refused to see us since we were born. He refused to acknowledge that we existed."

"The entire situation has been fucked up from the start, Whit. You know that."

"I do, and that's why I don't really understand why he wants to meet us now."

"Don't you think we've been through enough? Don't you think we deserve to put some of the pieces of our life back together? I mean, seriously, Whit, don't you ever stop and think about everything we went through back then? How horrible it was?"

"Believe me, I know more about that than you ever will. I got to watch Mom fall the fuck apart when he wouldn't visit after you were born because he didn't believe you were his kid. I got to watch her cry all day long for weeks because he showed her who he was once again. I got to call Gram and tell her we needed help because there was no food in the house, no diapers, no formula, and Mom couldn't get out of bed. I was barely seven years old! So, tell me why I have to be the one to acknowledge *him* after all this time. Why do I have to accept him when he never once did that for me? And while you're at it, can you tell me why *you* want him in your life?"

"It's as much her fault as it is his," Brie yelled. "Mom knew what she was doing the first time around. She knew he was married. She knew he wouldn't leave his family. Just like she knew he was her commanding officer and it would screw up her career. None of it stopped her. She probably got pregnant on purpose. And then she did it all over again."

I gripped the edge of the countertop. I couldn't even feel the cold of the stone under my hands. "I never said she was blameless. But she was there and he wasn't."

"Mom was *there*? I can count the school years we lived with her on one hand and I won't need all my fingers. She got the hell out every opportunity she could."

And don't you do the same?

"She was deployed," I cried.

"She reenlisted right after you were born. Right after I was born. And then over and over again. She left us every chance she got." Brie crossed her arms over her chest like she had to protect herself from my betrayal. Like I was the enemy here. "She chose to leave just as much as Dad did."

I felt like my world was tearing down the middle and I was ripping right along with it. "How can you even call him that? He's a sperm donor at best, a cruel bastard at worst."

Tears spilled down her cheeks. "Because he's the only father we're ever going to get. Gram's gone. Mom's too obsessed with her new spirituality and whatever the hell else she's doing to remember she has kids. He's all we have left." She sniffled. "Him and our half siblings."

I took a big step backward and then another. It wasn't enough. I didn't think I'd ever be able to put enough distance between me and those words. "I don't have half siblings and, as far as I'm concerned, I don't have a father. Those people are not mine and I really can't believe you think they're yours."

The silence that settled between us pulsed like a slap to the face.

Brie brushed away her tears, saying, "What if he's not the bad guy here? What if Mom—"

"What if both of them fucked up? Why can't you consider that possibility?"

"Even more reason to meet him," she shouted back. "If they're both to blame, why not give him a chance?"

"Because he's had his chances. He's had so many of them and never once has he chosen us. But Mom did. She wasn't perfect, but she chose us when no one else did."

"She chose *you*," Brie said, a fresh wave of tears brimming in her brown eyes, "but she never chose me. I had Gram and that neighbor lady from the base who stayed with me when I was home sick. That's it. That's all I had."

And me. You had me. *You've always had me.*

"It's still more than anything he ever gave you. You're right, Mom wasn't there much, but it was a whole hell of a lot more than the nothing we got from him and I just don't understand why you can't see the difference." I patted my pockets for my phone. I had to get out of this conversation. I pointed to the notifications on my screen as proof. They were mostly from a real estate app, alerting me to price changes on homes I'd never buy in cities I'd never move to. "I have to go."

"Would it really kill you to talk about this?"

Would it kill you to notice that you're repeatedly stabbing me in the back?

I stepped into shoes and pulled on the first coat I could find. I didn't even know if I needed a coat today. It didn't matter. I'd just take everything I could carry and figure it out later. "I'm pretty sure we just talked about it. What else is there to say?"

After a moment, she asked, "Does this mean you won't come with me to meet him?"

I dropped my forehead against the door. "Does this mean you still think he deserves a place in your life?"

"I just need to try," she said softly. "Even if it ends badly, I need to try."

With a nod, I opened the door and sprinted down the stairs to Temple Street. When I hit the sidewalk, I grabbed my phone to call Meri. But I stopped before I could tap her number. I knew she'd give me exactly what I needed right now. She'd patch me up and tell me Brie was intentionally pushing my buttons because that was how she coped with her insecurities and feelings of abandonment. She'd take me somewhere for appetizers and wine, lots of wine, and she'd make it not so bad. I loved this about her. I loved *everything* about her.

And I called Henry.

"Hey," I said when he answered. "Want to go for a walk somewhere? Hartshorn told me about a trail not too far from here. Said it's his favorite spot in Boston."

"We aren't panicking today?"

"I don't know, Hazlette. Did I do anything last night that would be grounds for panicking? Say anything? I need to know—did I talk in my sleep?"

"You did talk in your sleep, but it was mostly berating residents for being too slow. Just a regular day for me. Nothing new there."

Warmth wormed its way back into my chest and it didn't seem like my world was irrevocably fractured. For once, I didn't feel devastatingly alone. "Then we're good."

He laughed. "Are we?"

I stopped at the top of the street and turned in a slow circle, lifting my face to the sun. "Yeah. We are."

"Tell me where to meet you."

I GAZED OUT OVER THE SHIMMERING SURFACE OF Jamaica Pond, my hands shoved deep in the pockets of my thin zip-up. It was peaceful here. I could see why Hartshorn liked it for his weekday morning runs. Autumn leaves blazed red, gold, and orange. It was crisp and sunny, which was the best combination. Days like today always forced me out of a bad mood. It was harder to feel like I was clinging to the tattered fringes of a family when the air was clear and the sun warmed my face.

I glanced over my shoulder when I heard footsteps approaching. I couldn't have wiped the smile off my face at the sight of Henry if I'd tried. I couldn't even believe myself with this silly grin.

"You found me," I said, as if it wasn't obvious.

"I always will." He held out a small, paper-wrapped package. When I didn't take it, he said, "Ice cream sandwich."

"Why did you bring an ice—*oh my god.*" I clapped a hand to my face. "I can't believe I did that."

He curled his fingers around my wrist, tugging the hand away from my face. "I can believe it. You had ice cream cones on your socks. And I know how you feel about dessert buffets."

I stared down at the ground as I tried to get comfortable with all the vulnerability he'd witnessed while I was in zombie mode. It was like the vulnerable floodgates had opened over the last twenty-four hours. Under different circumstances, I'd ask Brie what the moon was doing this week. It was so great to blame the moon. "Thanks for taking me home last night."

"Believe me when I say I'll put you to bed anytime." He tore off the top half of the paper and handed me the ice cream sandwich. "You don't even have to grind through thirty hours of surgery either. I'll do it again tonight. Tomorrow. Any day, Whit. No charge."

I took a huge bite of the sandwich to stop myself from immediately accepting that offer. I couldn't imagine going home and seeing my sister again without something—or someone—to prevent us from picking up where we left off. Because we would. That was how we argued. One big fight followed by a painful series of smaller, increasingly hostile conversations before devolving into simmering silence.

"Hey." He tipped his head to the side as he studied me, his lips flattening into a line. "What's wrong?"

I shook my head as I devoured the ice cream sandwich. *No train wreck to see here.* Though Henry kept looking, assessing me like he'd find an answer regardless of whether I gave him direction or not.

"If I'd known you were going to use ice cream to avoid me, I wouldn't have brought any." When I lifted my thumb to my lips to lick away the chocolate crumbs, Henry took hold of my wrist again, saying, "Oh no you don't."

He leaned in and drew my thumb into his mouth, scraping his teeth over my skin and sucking away the last of the crumbs and ice cream. When he was finished, he kissed my palm, the inside of my wrist, my knuckles.

My knees damn near buckled. I didn't think anyone had ever done that to me—any part of it. I was a wreck. A light breeze could've knocked me over.

"Now, tell me," he said, his palms on my jaw and his fingertips rubbing the base of my skull. "What's wrong?"

"It's nothing. Really. I'm fine."

His features tightened as if he was on high alert, a muscle in his scruffy jaw ticking as he stared at me. "Is it because I left this morning? I wanted you to get some rest and I knew you didn't want me to watch you sleep."

"Good call on that, yeah," I said. "I didn't expect you to stick around. Thank you for the muffins and coffee though. And checking on Brie." I met his gaze for a second. "How'd that go?"

He laughed and looped his arm around my shoulders. "I think I should be asking you how it went."

I stepped out of his hold. I wanted it, but I also had too many contradictory emotions inside me right now. I wanted to scream and cry and smash things just to hear them shatter. I'd sink into Henry if he opened his arms to me and I'd feel whole again, if only for a few minutes. And I wanted to laugh and bask in the sun and just not be so fucking broken anymore.

But I needed to be the one to put me back together. I needed to feel whole on my own. I knew in a theoretical sense that relying on others in that way wasn't bad. It wasn't wrong. But it wasn't something I did. I'd never learned how.

I motioned to the trail. "We should walk."

Henry fell in step beside me as we started around the pond. "That bad, huh?"

"She asked if you had a brother and whether we get tired of seeing each other because we work together."

"No. On both counts."

"How do you know *I* don't get tired of seeing *you*?"

"Because I know your faces," he said easily. "You're not tired of me."

He brushed his hand against mine, and at first I thought it was just the rhythm of us walking. But then his fingertips slipped between mine and I realized he was asking permission. He was giving me the space to decide what I wanted.

I drew in a deep breath and pressed my lips together to fight off the tears prickling my eyes. I was not going to cry over this or anything else today.

"How often do you get slammed like you did this week?" He glanced over as we rounded a hooked portion of the trail that jutted out into the pond. "When Copeland said transplant was more unpredictable than any other service, I believed it, but I didn't dream that looked anything like the past few days."

"It's a blue moon sort of thing." I let my fingers trail over his knuckles and the back of his hand. Two could play this game. "Probably once every year, year and a half."

"Hartshorn was right." Henry gazed at the pond as we came up to another bend. "This place is nice."

"Why do you sound surprised?"

He shrugged, his elbow bumping into mine as we walked. "I don't know the guy. I don't know if I can trust his recommendations."

"You should trust him," I said, a laugh ringing in my words as I let our fingers tangle together for a second. "Did I take you away from other plans today?"

"Nope. I met with my cohort this morning for some journal and conference review. We divide up the conferences each week and present notes to each other."

"That's smart." Feeling bold, I grazed my knuckles along the outside of his thigh. His stride faltered. He cleared his throat. I decided I liked this game. "Which conference did you have?"

"Melanoma research." He dragged a hand from the back of my neck along my jaw. "Please tell me you're wearing sunscreen."

"Every day," I said with a laugh. Goddamn, it felt good to laugh. And it felt good to be with Henry. "Are they looking forward to pediatric surgery?"

"I have no fucking clue." He gave me a manic grin that had me laughing again. "You want to know why? Because you are the only thing that exists in my mind when I think about this time next week. All I want, all I can think about is finishing this rotation. I don't care if I'm operating on rotisserie chickens for the next month. None of it matters as long as you aren't my boss and this bullshit isn't our problem anymore."

Our problem.

I slipped my hand into his and squeezed. We stopped walking. "We can't be obvious. We'll need to keep it quiet for a few months."

With his free hand, he reached for the zipper on my jacket, dragging it down enough to expose my neck. He leaned in, brushing his lips over my cheeks and along the column of my throat. "Can we have more sleepovers?"

"Not until you're off my service."

"Next weekend, then."

He slipped a hand under my shirt and drew circles on my lower back. I couldn't believe how much it turned me on. At this point, with all the tension crackling between us, he could probably elbow me in the ribs and I'd be aroused.

"Next weekend," I echoed. He kissed his way up my neck and along my jaw while I locked my arms around his broad shoulders. "You'll have to stay away from me until then. Far away. No elevators. No hanging out in my gallery. Not even a cupcake. Just—just don't make it any harder than it has to be."

He held me closer and I felt his shaft, thick and long against my torso. "Really don't think it could get much harder."

I dropped my head to his chest. "Do you remember the elevator? After the wedding?"

"You ask that like I haven't been thinking about it nonstop for months." It was cute how he exaggerated. We were closing in on two months since the start of this rotation and there was no way he'd spent any time obsessing over a wedding hookup before then. Please. "If Lulu hadn't barged in, I would've been on my knees with my head under that dress."

I smiled into his shirt. "No, you wouldn't."

"I would've. I thought about kicking her out." After a moment, he asked, "You're sure about the sleepovers?"

"You'd think there'd be an exception for that, but no."

Henry brushed a sweet kiss over my lips and shifted his hands to my elbows. He leaned back and I immediately missed being close to him. "Understood."

I tipped my head toward the trail. "We should keep going."

We walked in silence for several minutes, our hands bumping and tangling with every step.

He glanced over at me as we crossed the halfway point. "Why don't you stop fucking around now and tell me what you're upset about."

"I didn't realize I was fucking around."

"I didn't realize it was so hard for you to share what's on your mind."

"Nothing is on my mind," I snapped, flailing my hands in a way that made my words much less convincing. "It's fine. Really. I just had a little thing with Brie this morning."

"Because I checked in on her?"

"No, it had nothing to do with you. Just...family stuff."

Henry stayed quiet for a minute as we continued around the trail. Eventually, he said, "You could tell me about it."

"I promise, it wouldn't interest you."

He pointed to the water, saying, "Back to the pond with you. Go."

"What?"

"If you're going to be a silly goose, you belong in the pond."

I did my best to respond, but all I managed was a loud, bleating snort that had too much in common with the honk of a goose. With both hands covering my face, I bent at the waist, laughing so hard that tears streamed down my cheeks. Henry looped an arm around my waist as he laughed with me.

"You called me a silly goose," I managed through wheezes and hiccups.

"And I'll do it again," he said, tucking my head under his chin and holding me to his chest. "I've told you my ugly stories. You can tell me yours."

We stayed there for a moment, locked tight together while serious runners and moms with jogging strollers breezed past. I really didn't want to let him go though I was certain that had more to do with the emotional devastation of fighting with my sister about our fucked-up family than anything else. I was fragile and empty right now. Of course I didn't want to let go. I needed someone to keep me from floating away into nothing.

"I know I can," I said, though the truth was that I didn't know how to trust anyone aside from Meri with my stories. And the only reason I trusted Meri was because she'd trusted me with a whole lot of secrets first. "But it's really not a big deal."

Henry shook his head and pressed his thumb to the space between my brows. "When you're upset about something, your forehead crinkles right here. It's different from when you're focused or annoyed. I see that over here." He tapped a finger to the corner of my mouth. "You pop a sweet little dimple when you're trying to set someone on fire with your eyes."

"What you're saying is it's time for Botox."

"Don't interrupt me when I'm talking about your bloodlust." He traced my lips, adding, "You don't have to tell me a damn thing. But you can. All right?"

I pressed my lips together as I sucked in a breath in another desperate, thrashing attempt at keeping my emotions contained. I stared at the pond as my nose tingled and tears threatened to spill from the corners of my eyes.

We continued down the path while I pulled myself together and, when I was certain my voice wouldn't crack, I reached for Henry's hand—all the way, not just half measure bumping and brushing against each other, but a true, proper grip, palm to palm.

"Yeah," I said. "All right."

Sixteen

Henry

Transplant Surgery Rotation:
Day 3, Week 8

"And I don't know, man, I just started thinkin' about when we were younger and everything was, well, fuck, it was simple. I probably sound like a dumb old tool who woke up some morning and realized the good old days were in the rearview. I don't know. We used to have some fun times, didn't we? We had a whole lotta fun. Back when we thought we were all grown up. We didn't know a damn thing, did we? Not that I know much more these days."

I pulled the phone away from my ear to see how much longer remained on this voicemail from Mason. Looked like I had another two minutes to go. He'd left it while I was in the OR with Dr. Hirano this morning, fixing a blood flow issue on a kidney we transplanted last week. Based on the timing, Mason had probably called on the drive home from his typical weekend trip, yet those outings usually gassed up his energy and optimism. I couldn't remember him ever coming off an expedition and sounding so down.

"Hazlette." Fingers snapped in my direction and I jerked my head up from my lunch. Dr. Salas stood in the doorway to the resident work room, hands on her hips. "Let's go."

With regret, I abandoned the tacos al pastor, courtesy of Cami, and followed Salas down the hall. She leaned against the wall near the elevators, her focus on her phone.

She didn't say anything while we traveled up several floors, still busy with her phone, which opened the door for me to wonder what the hell was wrong with Mason these days. I hadn't heard anything more on Florrie's request that he leave the wilderness expedition gig behind for something with a traditional schedule. With the time difference and both of us working all hours, we hadn't touched base beyond a few basic texts every few days confirming we were alive.

Was I allowed to say, *Hey, is this marriage sucking out your soul? Because you know you can end it, right?*

I was probably *allowed* to say it though that didn't mean I should. There was honesty and then there was the kind of brutal, emotionally decapitating honesty that ended a lifelong friendship.

I really didn't want to fall on the side of decapitation.

I followed Salas off the elevator, still longing for those tacos and debating how to talk to Mason about his strange, dark moods, and realized a second too late that we were heading into Whit's office. My body dumped adrenaline into my system as I tried to read Salas's expression.

Did Salas know about us? Did she figure it out? Was this the situation Whit had been warning me about all along, the one where everything went to hell in a sterile basket?

"Hey, I need your help," Salas announced, plopping down on Whit's sofa. She pulled a bag of walnuts from her pocket and went to town. "I'll owe you big-time."

Whit swung a glance from Salas to where I stood near the door, my arms crossed. Her brow quirked up. I gave a quick shake of my head. I had no fucking clue what was happening here and neither did my heart rate.

She rolled a pen between her hands, her gaze on Salas. She didn't look as sad and haunted as she had on Saturday, but there was something weary about her, as if she was exhausted from much more than a marathon string of surgeries.

But goddamn did she look good. I loved it when she wore those blouses that I knew cost a fortune and had to be the softest, silkiest fabric in the world. Those trousers always killed me. Something about them made her legs look much longer than they were and I had to fight off the urge to grab her ass with both hands. And the heels didn't help that. If anything, they'd launched a whole series of fantasies. I felt depraved whenever I watched her walk down a hallway. Just fucking feral.

"What can I do for you?" Whit asked.

"I need you to go to Vermont," Salas said, and if you'd given me fifty guesses, I wouldn't have come up with that.

"Vermont," Whit repeated, shooting another glance in my direction.

I lifted my shoulders like *the fuck if I know.*

Salas clasped her hands around the bag of walnuts. "There's a match for one of my patients, but the donor sustained major injuries in a snowmobile accident. The hospital hasn't been able to give me a thorough overview of these injuries other than to say they don't see any issues with the lungs."

"But you don't believe that," Whit said.

"Hell no, I don't," Salas replied. "I believe they're doing the best they can, but I have trust issues when it comes to organs from these kinds of injuries. I need you to go up and harvest the lungs for me." She rubbed her belly. "I'm too far along to fly."

Whit leaned back in her chair, drumming her fingers on her armrest. "Remind me again why you were in such a rush to go and get yourself pregnant."

"Because the rate of idiopathic infertility among physicians and surgeons is ridiculously high and we wanted to start early in case we had problems," she said.

I stared at the ceiling. Seemed like the most appropriate thing to do.

"We didn't expect to light up the scoreboard on the first try, but you know my husband. Very goal-oriented. You should think about it too," Salas continued. "If you want a baby, you need to get going."

My gaze snapped to Whitney as the adrenaline floodgates opened up again. She cut a quick glance in my direction and tucked her hair over her ear.

What the fuck did that mean?

"You need to choose where you're sending me today," Whit said, amusement thick in her tone. "Vermont or the fertility clinic, but it can't be both."

"Vermont," Salas said, wagging two fingers at Whit, "but tick-tock on the fertility stuff. The best eggs of your life are already behind you."

Whit propped her chin on her fist. "I love our chats. They always leave me feeling so hopeful."

"Yeah, it's one of my many talents." Salas struggled to her feet. "Oh, and you're taking Hazlette."

As I said, "What's happening now?" Whit stood, asking, "Take Hazlette where?"

Traveling to Vermont with Whit was not the way to keep my distance this week and we both knew it.

"He's an old pro at retrieving organs," Salas said. "You'll need another pair of hands and he knows how I like my lungs for transplant."

I didn't have a chance to enjoy those compliments because Whit turned a stricken stare in my direction.

"Okay, sure, that's great," Whit stammered. "But what about Copeland? She's excellent and—"

"I need Copeland to prep the patient." Salas made a gesture over her head that I didn't understand. "It's the young woman from Europe. I believe I've mentioned this one. High profile."

"The Crown Princess?" Whit whispered.

"Same one." Salas nodded slowly. "The family has made a private jet available to us for the trip to Vermont and would like to provide ground transportation on both ends by way of their security detail. They're waiting downstairs now."

Whit paced behind her desk. She muttered something to herself and shook her head, and there was a second where it seemed like she'd refuse. But then she reached into her closet and pulled out a pair of running shoes. "All right. I need to change. Forward me everything I need to know about the patient." She motioned to Salas's belly. "You're naming this kid Whitney."

"My husband is sold on a family name, but I'll see what he has to say." She glanced between us. "I've already told your medical assistant to rearrange your day and there's a retrieval kit on its way up if it isn't waiting for us already. Like I said, I'll owe you one."

Whit pulled Salas into a quick hug before heading for the door. "Hazlette," she called over her shoulder. Her tone was all business.

Not that I'd expect anything else. "Get the kit and meet me downstairs in five minutes."

We boarded the small private jet, empty save for the crew and the two men making up the security detail. They'd stationed themselves in a pair of seats at the back and cued up something to watch on a tablet.

Whit settled into a foursome of seats with a shiny wood table anchored between them and she set the ice chest beside her. The subtext was clear. I was allowed to sit with her, but not beside her. Got it.

"I understand the ground rules." I motioned to the table. "I have no intention of crossing any lines."

"That's all very good to know," she said. "Since I'm working very hard at doing the same."

I leaned back and folded my arms over my chest. "You say this like there's any question that you'd ever do anything other than follow rules."

A shy smile brightened her face. "You might be surprised."

"Then surprise me."

She stared down at her hands for a moment and I wanted to touch her more than anything. Just hold her hand and promise all over again that we'd figure this out, even if I didn't know what I was doing.

"There was a teacher in sixth grade who required a parent's signature on an assignment every week. If we didn't get it signed, we had lunch detention." She made a face that said *such bullshit*. "My grandmother had some issues with authority. She had zero interest in putting her name on anything official, ever, so I'd signed my own papers all along. I helped a few other people out when they forgot."

"Hold on a second." I held up a hand. "Little Miss *I Won't Fuck You Until You're Not My Resident* ran a middle school forgery ring? What's next, you're going to tell me you managed a back alley chop shop too? Is that why you're a transplant surgeon? You've been fencing high-value items since before the training wheels came off?"

"I never had training wheels."

"Of course you didn't. Did you cut your own umbilical cord too?"

She rolled her hazel eyes. I had to grip the armrests to keep myself from throwing myself at her. "I handle the problems presented to me. That's all."

"And sometimes you bend the rules."

"More than you might think, Hazlette, but only when the rules have enough flexibility to bend without breaking." She tapped her index finger on the table between us. She removed her ring, the thin gold one with the little blue stone, and threaded it onto her necklace. Probably so she didn't misplace it going into surgery. "Now, talk me through this procedure. Who does what and when do they do it, which instruments are we using, and what are we looking for when we get in there?"

While the pilot and flight attendants prepared the jet for takeoff, I went over our portion of the retrieval with Whit. She asked a lot of questions. Pushed for more specificity on everything. Made me start over twice.

When we were up in the air and she was satisfied with my understanding of the work, she spent the first ten minutes of this quick flight—less than an hour door to door—scanning the recipient and donor charts on her tablet, occasionally narrating some of the evidence she found noteworthy or quizzing me on the implications of the donor's history.

Once that was done, she alternated between responding to emails and staring out the window. She was doing an excellent job of directing her attention to anything but me and I didn't blame her. This was the first time we'd been alone since everything that'd happened over the weekend, and the end was so close I could barely stand it. I was jumping out of my skin, and if I knew anything about the panic she'd shown in her office, I knew it was the same for her.

Which brought me to a question I'd had on my mind for weeks. "Can I ask why the ethics initiative is so important to you? Beyond the obvious need for these standards, why is it so personal that these rules can't bend?"

She didn't meet my gaze as she closed her tablet and clasped her hands. A shadow passed over her face and her expression tightened like something inside her had tugged and twisted the softness from her features.

After a quiet moment, she said, "My first year in Boston, there was a resident who wasn't particularly strong, but she worked hard and developed from each rotation. She wasn't interested in transplant, but she asked me to mentor her. I didn't have much capacity at the time, especially not for someone who needed help selecting a specialty, and I encouraged her to find someone with a broader understanding of the surgical wing and everyone in it. But she kept coming back to me, asking to meet for coffee or talk more about transplant and my fellowship experiences." Whit blew out a breath. "I've never liked turning away women in surgery. It's so hard to find a mentor who understands the challenges and doesn't immediately suggest you go into derm or OB if you express any concerns with the demands or the workload. God forbid you take issue with attendings who think residency should be played like the Hunger Games. So, I kept meeting with her."

I didn't love the direction this was going.

"Her third year was really rough. She struggled. Word got around that she wasn't meeting expectations and"—Whit dropped her head back against the seat, another huge breath gusting out of her—"it seemed that there were a few attendings who took that as an invitation to run her through the gauntlet. Every time we met, I saw less and less of her. It was like she was becoming a ghost right in front of me. I told her about all the horrible, sadistic attendings I'd met along the way. The ones who didn't teach, who screamed, who threw instruments, who degraded and humiliated. Told her she could get through it. We all got through it. She would too."

Really didn't love the direction of this.

Whit pursed her lips, shook her head. After a pause, she said, "She ended her life before finishing the year."

I wanted to launch myself over the table between us, gather her in my arms, and squeeze until I'd put her back together again. "Fuck, I...I'm sorry."

"I sat there and I watched it happen. Instead of fixing the problem, I told her how to fix herself. As if being able to dissociate from abuse is an essential surgical skill." She gave a slow, tired nod. "So, it *is* personal. The absolute least I can do is take this seriously."

I reached over and covered her clasped hands with mine. She didn't pull away.

The regional hospital in St. Johnsbury was smaller than one of our parking garages back in Boston. When the driver pulled up at the front entrance, Whit leaned forward, saying, "Is there a side door? A staff entrance? Somewhere around back, maybe?"

While the driver spoke to the people on the other end of his earbud, I asked, "What's wrong with this?"

She waved a finger at the hospital logos on our jackets and the bright red ice chest stamped with *human organs* on both sides. "The last thing this donor's family needs to see is us walking in right after they've said goodbye."

That...was not a lesson I'd learned yet. I knew most of these transplants were the result of a donor at the end of their life, but until now I hadn't drawn a straight line between these points.

"There's a side door," the driver said.

"Thank you," Whit said. To me, she added, "If there's one thing you do today, let it be extending the greatest amount of grace to the family. If they need more time, give it. If they need to hear about the recipients, tell them as much as privacy will allow. If they want to know that we'll care for the donor like they're family, promise them that. And then do it."

I studied Whit as we filed into the staff entrance and up to the surgical floor. I'd always known her to be serious. Even at the wedding, she was fun, but she was *serious* fun. She committed to it, she played hard. Here, at work, she was seriously skilled. Competent in ways that knocked me back a few steps and made me want to stop people in the halls, saying, *Have you seen this badass woman?*

And she felt everything in deep, serious ways.

It was easy to miss if you weren't looking for it. I knew I'd missed it a few times. I'd also filed it away as stubbornness, avoidance, even apathy. But I knew better now. I knew there was a great big emotional world right under her surface yet she barely let it show. Almost like she was afraid to get caught feeling too much.

We scrubbed in and lined up in the OR in the order that the organs would be retrieved. I'd done this several times with Salas and Hirano. I thought I knew what to expect. I was wrong.

Whitney wasted no time telling the team retrieving the donor heart how to do it more efficiently. She stepped right up and showed them, critiqued their work, and then waved me over to learn along with everyone else.

The heart cupped in the palm of her hands as she examined it, Whit said, "This is a good one. It has many more years left in it. Take care of it."

I stared at her across the table as she moved along to retrieving the lungs, knowing I loved her and that I'd never recover from it.

THE PROCEDURE WRAPPED UP QUICKLY AND WE WERE out the door, heading for the airport. When we boarded the jet, I sat down beside her. She didn't object.

"You know," I said as we taxied the runway, "you're *really* fast. Have you considered the possibility that not everyone can be as quick as you?"

"Please don't tell me you're not up to the challenge."

"You know that's not the case." I nudged her with my elbow. "You just walked in there and took the fuck over. Even the attending was like, *Let me get out of your way.* That team from Buffalo is going to talk about that for years. It's going to come up at someone's retirement party decades down the road. Those guys from Cornell were taking notes. Is there anything you can't do?"

"Oh, yeah. For sure. So many things."

"Name them. I'm making a list."

She held out her hands and let them fall to her lap. "I'm terrible at diagnosing rashes. It's all atopic dermatitis to me."

"No. Not nearly enough. I need you to be actually bad at something other than rashes and softball."

"Wow, you just had to bring up softball, didn't you?"

"The scales needed balancing." I shrugged. "Had to be done."

"Well, I guess I'm actually bad at relationships."

It got real like the music going out at the club and the lights coming on. "Okay," I managed. "That's better than rashes."

"I don't have a lot of experience," she continued. "Things never really worked out and then I stopped looking." She glanced at me. "And here I am."

"Here we are."

"I don't know what happens next. I don't know how it will feel when I'm not hanging on by a thread anymore because you're my resident, and the last thing I want to do is cross that line." She smoothed her hands up and down her legs several times like she needed that repetition to put the words in order. "What if we spend a night together and realize it's not the same as it was at the wedding? Or we get it out of our system? What happens when the pressure of this situation is gone? What if all this tension dissolves and there's nothing left?"

I was *this* close to telling her all of those questions were bullshit. Instead, I said, "I don't think it works that way."

"How do you know?"

"Are you asking for evidence? For hard facts and proof? I don't have any of that, Whit, but I did sleep next to you on Friday night

—fully dressed, I might add—and all I could think about was how much I wanted to do it again. Even if it meant sleeping in jeans."

Whit didn't say anything and I knew she wasn't convinced. I didn't know what I could do to fix that. We just had to wait.

THE FLIGHT WAS QUICK AND THE DRIVER WHO MET US AT the airport managed to navigate rush hour like a pro, delivering us to the hospital earlier than expected. That was pretty much a miracle where Boston traffic was concerned.

When we reached the surgical wing, we found Cami, Tori, and Reza waiting outside the OR with Dr. Copeland.

"Salas wants y'all to scrub in with her," Cami said to us, her gaze locked on the ice chest.

"You're not allowed to be disappointed," Tori said to her. "There will be another princess."

"Really? How many princesses come through here each year?" Cami replied.

"More than you'd think," Whit said. "Go on up to the gallery. This is one to watch."

Once we joined Salas in the OR, she said, "Right on time. How are my lungs looking?"

"Beautiful," Whit said. "Though the team retrieving the heart tried my patience."

Even though my job was to shut up and stay out of the way, I said, "Dr. Aldritch retrieved the heart for them."

"That's why we send her," Salas replied. "She knows how to kick all the right asses."

"I was very nice," Whit said.

"I'm sure you were, honey. Just like I'm sure they're questioning their entire careers right now." Salas beamed. "Let's get started."

IT WAS AFTER MIDNIGHT WHEN WE FINISHED THE procedure. I didn't say it, but it was understood that I was walking Whit home.

"It was nice operating with you today," I said as we crossed the street.

"It was nice," she agreed. And then— "I'd like you to work on thinking through the entire series of moves you're making before you make them. If you're doing that, you won't have to stop and orient yourself as often. You'll be—"

"More efficient. Yep. Already on it."

I felt her staring at me as we walked toward Temple Street. "Does it bother you? When I give you these notes?"

"Not at all. It impresses the hell out of me that you're so fucking good. You're an excellent surgeon and an excellent teacher, and most of the surgeons I've met aren't both. But you can spot these small, specific issues from the other side of the OR, as we saw in Vermont, and you know exactly how to fix them. The only thing that bothers me is that I'm not improving fast enough."

"You're improving," she said, though it sounded a little reluctant. "I saw it today. You're better than you were with the chicken."

"Thanks for letting me work with you. I know Salas didn't give you much of a choice—"

"I had a choice," she said. "I could've insisted on Copeland. Salas would've gone along with that if I pushed."

"Then I guess I should thank you for letting me come along. First and last time operating with you."

"I like the sound of that. Especially the part about it being the last time."

She reached for my hand as we turned onto Temple. Something cracked wide open in my chest and I couldn't hide my smile. It felt like a giant billboard with bright, gleaming lights proclaiming, *This woman. This one right here.*

At her door, she said, "I'd invite you up, but I think we both know what would happen."

I leaned into her. "Just for the sake of clarity, why don't you tell me what that is."

She whacked my arm. I slapped her ass. And then, through no fault of ours, we were plastered up against the door, kissing the breath out of each other.

"Two more days," she said against my lips.

It took everything in me to kiss her one last time and step back. "Two more days." I pointed to the door. "I'm not leaving until you're inside. Get in there. Don't make me yank off your socks again and tuck you into bed."

"Don't threaten me with a good time."

I couldn't help it. I wrapped her up in my arms and held her tight. "Good night, Whit."

She pushed up on her toes and kissed me. "Good night, Henry."

This one right here.

Seventeen

Whitney

Rule Number Twelve:
Be a good time without being the center of attention.

"And then she says to me, 'Oh, I didn't realize you were a doctor. I thought you were *just* a nurse. You were so efficient and you knew your way around so well. You seemed like a nurse.' And I'm looking at her like, *Do you have any idea how ridiculous you sound?*" Meri made a disgusted noise. "Because she's going on and on about how she's seen me in the NICU every day this week and she doesn't come out and say it, but the gist is that she ignored me because she always ignores nurses. Aside from the fact that's a major miscalculation, my ID badge is right there and I've introduced myself to several parents as Dr. Mercer."

I twisted a finger around my necklace. We were waiting for our ORs to open up. Friday mornings always moved more slowly than the rest of the week. "And she thought it was a good idea to say all of this to you? My god. Does she not have any survival skills?"

"That's what I'm asking," Meri continued. "Aren't these residents supposed to know who they're reporting to? Didn't we compulsively research all our attendings when we were residents?" Not waiting for a response, she barreled on. "Needless to say, that resident will not be scrubbing in with me until she grows some situational awareness."

"I don't say this often, but you might want to get a little tougher with these residents. They need to be appropriately afraid of you."

"Um, hi. I might be able to help."

We glanced over to find two of my residents lurking near the nurses' station. "Help with what, Dr. Cortes-Dixon? Dr. Tran?"

Tori and Cami whisper-yelled and nudged each other until Tori stepped forward, saying, "If you need people to be afraid of you, Dr. Mercer, you're welcome to yell at me in front of a bunch of residents any day. I can cry, if you want."

"Yeah, that's not going to happen," Meri said. "Generous offer, but no."

"Okay, well, maybe y'all could join us tonight to celebrate the end of this rotation," Cami said.

"We have this whole ritual," Tori added. Her bow tie was printed with tiny frogs sitting on lily pads. "We go to the same place, order the same drinks, and we all get up and sing the same karaoke song."

"I have to know what that song is," Meri said.

"'TiK ToK' by Kesha," Tori said.

Meri nodded. "I'm not sure I want the answer to this but why? Just...why?"

"It's Hazlette's CPR song," Tori replied with a laugh. "We were all having trouble with our timing during orientation so he played this song until we got it right because we were such an embarrassment. Then we had it stuck in our heads for a full week." She laced her hands together in CPR position. "Whenever we're having a bad day, someone drops a few lyrics and we bust out our best compression dance moves."

"Just so you know, Hazlette has the best moves," Cami added.

Yeah, I knew all about that.

"Of course he does," Meri said. "It sounds like Dr. Hazlette is talented in many special and unexpected ways."

"Watch it," I said under my breath. When she gave me an evil grin, I decided it was time to change course. "Did you do things like that with your first-year cohort?"

"Nah," she said. "My cohort was me and three guys with anger management problems."

"We're dressing up for Halloween too," Cami said. "Everyone's going as twisted takes on different specialties."

"Explain that to me like I'm five," Meri said as she scrolled through her phone.

"I'm going as orthopedics so I'm wearing a flannel with cut-off sleeves, a hard hat, and a tool belt," Tori said. "I also have all of those at my apartment, so it seemed like a good fit."

"And I'm going as pediatrics," Cami said. "I have the cutest set of teddy bear footie pajamas and I'm drawing little freckles on my cheeks. Reza is nephrology and we found a t-shirt for him with *salty* across the chest. That's the maximum amount of dressing up he'll do."

"Hazlette is supposed to be a hematology vampire, but we hardly ever see him so I'm not sure if he remembered," Tori said.

He remembered. He told me about it when we talked last night.

"It would be so cool if you joined us for a drink. It's a really good time," Tori added.

"We'll be there," I said.

But some of us won't be staying long.

I didn't know what was going to happen tonight and it was better when I didn't obsess over the specifics, but I'd showered like I expected someone to see me naked very soon.

"Are we now?" Meri asked.

"Yeah," I said, ignoring the surprise in her tone. I still didn't know how to juggle my relationships with Henry and Meri, but like everything else with Henry, I hoped to make sense of it all soon. "We'll drop in to say hello."

"I'm not wearing a costume," Meri said. "I haven't dressed up for Halloween since I was five and I wanted to be a Cabbage Patch Kid, but all my parents heard was cabbage."

"It's true." I tipped my head toward Meri. "I've seen the photos. She was an actual cabbage."

"I'd pay money for more details on that," Tori said.

"Even if you don't dress up, we'd love to see you tonight," Cami said, handing me a note with the location. "This has been such an amazing rotation. We're excited for pediatrics, but we all hate that it has to end."

Not all *of your cohort.*

I smothered a laugh with a weird cough that had Meri eyeing me. She knew exactly where my mind was and there was no chance of getting this one past her. "I'm happy to hear that."

"Don't misunderstand this as an invasive comment on your body," Meri said, circling a hand at Cami, "but you smell really nice and that's going to be a big problem for some of the respiratory patients you're going to meet next week in pediatrics. Whatever it is—and it really is nice—get rid of it."

"Okay. Got it." She blinked at Meri, her dark eyes wide. "Not that you asked but I am a little afraid of you, Dr. Mercer."

"See? I'm fine. I just have a random resident who doesn't know how to act." Meri glanced over with a shrug. "I suppose you know all about the best ways to handle your residents—and the ones who used to be your residents. Isn't that right?"

I choked down a laugh.

My phone buzzed again as I headed toward the elevator. I was already behind schedule for the afternoon and did not want to spend the rest of the day fighting to catch up. To make matters worse, I had to cancel the time Jenelle had reserved on my calendar. Which would've been fine if I hadn't canceled on her during the transplant marathon a few weeks ago and again for my trip to Vermont the other day. Instead of another scheduling issue, I found a message from my sister.

"Going up?"

I startled to a stop. Henry stood outside the elevator, his hand holding the doors open. He wore dark trousers and a crisp white shirt with the sleeves rolled up to his elbows, his thick forearms on display for the whole world to see. *Obscene.* A stethoscope peeked out of his pocket and his tie was slightly askew.

In my mind, I grabbed that shirt and ripped it open, sending buttons flying everywhere.

In reality, I offered him a polite smile and stepped onto the elevator.

We settled along the back wall, standing close enough that our elbows bumped. Returning to my messages, I asked, "Conferences this morning?"

"Yeah, endocrine surgery," he said. "Cami tripped and spilled coffee all over my coat."

I shot a glance at his forearms. "What a shame."

"There are times when you're about as readable as a stone wall and other times when I can see straight into your filthy mind, Dr. Aldritch." He ran a hand up my arm. "Not that I'm complaining."

Smiling to myself, I opened the text from Brie.

Brie: Hi! Ok! So! Everything is fine! I am going on a little journey to the Berkshires with some friends to recharge and reset. Don't sweat it if you don't hear from me because everyone says the cell service is terrible out there. I'll be back in a few days and I promise I won't lift anything heavy or eat/drink anything I shouldn't! Have a gorgeous weekend!

There was no point in pretending this wasn't an enormous relief. Brie and I needed a break from each other and from the looming storm cloud of our father's visit.

I handed the phone to Henry. He nodded slowly as he scanned the message. Then, he leaned around me, one hand planted on the wall beside my head, and reached under my white coat to slip the phone into my trouser pocket.

And this was why we had to stay away from each other. Because he wouldn't stop doing things like that and I had the resistance of an over-ripe banana.

He leaned in, his lips grazing my ear. "Your place, then."

I managed a nod as he stared down at me. "Cami told me all about your costume for tonight."

"*Fuck.* I forgot about that." He trailed a finger down the side of my neck. "Do you think I can take a bite out of you in the spirit of Halloween?"

"You can, but questions will be asked if you don't bite everyone."

"I guess I'm scrapping that plan because you're the only one I want to bite." He returned to his position beside me, his fingers brushing against mine. "I might be a little late. I have a procedure with Hirano in an hour."

The elevator bounced as we arrived at our stop. I stepped forward. My whole body tingled from the heat of his stare.

"Enjoy it," I said. "It's the last time you'll ever scrub in on transplant."

The doors opened. "You're damn right it is."

"I forgot how feral residency is," Meri said over the music when we arrived at the vintage arcade. "It's all a little savage, no?"

I was prepared to disagree with her until I spotted Cami bounding toward us in her teddy bear onesie, a tray of shots clutched between both paws. Reza followed in a white sequined baseball cap and his *salty* shirt that I knew many nephrologists would love.

"You're here!" she yelled.

Beside her, Reza nodded in greeting. I barely recognized him without a bow tie. "Good evening."

Cami held out the tray, saying, "You have to try this. We call it Life Support."

Meri, never one to run from danger, reached for a glass. "Because that's where you'll end up? Or that's how it feels?"

"We've never figured that out," Cami said, bouncing on her toes. "It's vodka, dark rum, triple sec, and orange and pineapple juices. Hazlette came up with it."

Of course he did.

Meri knocked back the shot. "Whew. All right. There's some fire power in there." She dug her phone out of her bag and handed it to me. "Take this before I write page-long texts to people who can't be bothered to respond in the first place and just don't deserve my time."

I pocketed the phone. "And who might that be?"

She held up a hand like we could hide from Cami and Reza. "Not in front of the children."

"Hazlette's finishing up a procedure and Tori is playing on her phone and being antisocial," Cami said, "but we've reserved that booth over there. The pinball games are super fun and we're all signing up for karaoke, which you definitely should do—"

"And we definitely will," Meri said, selecting another shot.

"The best part," Cami went on, "is that there's a tarot reader here tonight! I was so happy when I saw her setting up. We haven't been able to get up to Salem yet so this makes my witchy heart happy."

Meri set the empty glass on Cami's tray. "Love it. Point me toward her. Maybe it's time for some mystical direction in my life. Hell, any direction would be nice at this point."

With Meri it could be hard to tease out her real thoughts and feelings from the occasionally outrageous things she said. She liked to disarm people with her boldness. She could be brash and bawdy, but she talked so fast and smiled so bright that most people didn't catch everything she said. Even when they did, it seemed to me that they dismissed anything that didn't make sense. Which was most of her comments.

I knew better and I knew when she was being outrageous just because it suited her mood.

Yet I couldn't tell whether any of this—the phone, the shots, the sprint to the tarot reader's table—were all a product of her digging deep into a mood or her being raw and honest and telling me exactly how she felt.

Or both.

It had been a long time since it'd been both. A long time since I'd dragged her to a therapist and stayed with her through the first grueling session. Since I'd promised to see a therapist to sort out my own shit so long as she kept up with hers. We were nothing without our pacts.

When I caught up to her at the table tucked around the corner and behind a strip of game machines, she was already seated, staring down at the cards as the tarot reader placed them in front of her. Rather than listening, I leaned against an old-school pinball machine and tried to estimate how much longer Henry would be at the hospital. Assuming the procedure went well, they should've finished an hour or two ago. I was sure Hirano had Henry monitoring the patient in post-op, but that couldn't take much longer and the fourth- and fifth-year residents covering that service overnight usually barked at anyone who intruded on their territory. He'd be here soon and then—

I sensed someone approach from behind, but before I could turn, hands settled on the pinball machine, strong arms caging me in. "Do you know how to play?"

It took everything in me to keep from melting into him. "Yeah."

I knew nothing about this game.

Henry ran a hand up the outside of my thigh and inserted some coins into the machine near my hip. The lights blinked to life and a ball dropped to the starting position. Mechanical music echoed under glass.

"People are watching," I whispered.

"People are drunk. People are not paying attention to us." Henry placed my hands on the control buttons, covering them with his. He pressed his hips forward, trapping me between him and the game. I was suddenly aware of my bra and the way my nipples tightened against the fabric. "People will believe me if I tell them I was teaching you how to play."

We tapped the buttons, our fingers intertwined, and sent the ball flying across the board. When it went somewhere we didn't like, Henry rocked against me, forcing the ball in a different direction and making me reevaluate my whole stance on exhibitionism because all I needed was one more good thrust and it would be game over for me.

"Another round?" he asked when our score flashed across the screen and the ball went back into its hiding place.

"Even the drunk people will start to notice if we keep this up."

He groaned into my shoulder. "Let's get out of here."

"Not yet. Meri's in a mood and Cami has a checklist you need to complete before going anywhere."

He squeezed my hips. His fingertips seemed to burn through my clothes, marking me. "Thirty minutes."

I put some space between us before we forgot where we were. "Love the enthusiasm, but it will probably be longer than that." I perked up as Meri rounded the wicker screen separating the tarot reader's table from the games. "How'd it go?"

She slumped onto the pinball machine, burying her face in her hands. "Something about the Five of Swords and me banging my head against the wall. I don't know. Apparently I try too hard and wring the life out of everything? Energetically, or whatever." Trapping Henry with a hard stare, she asked, "Where did you come from?"

"Northern California," he replied. "A little city in Nevada

County, just north of Tahoe. Lived around that area until med school in San Francisco. Or did you mean, where did I come from right now? I was in a procedure with Hirano. Kidney transplant. Got a little hectic at the end, but all good."

Pointing at Henry, she said to me, "Have you not taught your resident to present the most pertinent details first?"

Henry grinned down at the floor. "I notice you don't have a drink, Dr. Mercer. Can I fix that problem?"

"Now you're interesting to me," she said. "I want a beer that tastes like dark chocolate. Can you do that?"

"Consider it done," he replied.

When he was out of earshot, she asked, "Do you think I wring the life out of things?"

I eyed her carefully. Yep, this was a mood, and from the sound of it, a dark one. "I know for a fact that you don't."

"What if that's my problem?" she continued as if I hadn't spoken. "What if I'm just too much?"

"There is no such thing as too much. Just people who don't have the strength to embrace all of you." A moment passed while she went on scowling at the pinball machine. "What's making you think this—and don't tell me it was the reading."

Meri started to respond but then lit up when Henry came around the corner with a pint of nearly black beer. "Nice and snappy, Hazlette. I like that about you." She took a sip, bobbing her head as she sampled the beer. "Well done." She glanced between us. "I'm going to mingle with the kiddos. See if I can lure any of them into the neonatal cult."

"Start with Tori," he said as Meri backed away. "She loves ridiculously difficult things." She winked and shot him a finger gun that was definitely a product of the shots. "Are we going to have to get her home tonight?"

"No, she'll order a car and become the driver's biggest cheerleader within eight minutes. She actually really enjoys it."

"Well, hello there! Who's next? Oh, you two look like a lot of fun."

We glanced over to find the tarot reader coming around the wicker screen, a deck of well-loved cards in hand. She wore a silvery shawl over dark jeans and a dark shirt and had her pale lavender hair twisted up into a magnificent beehive. She had a dozen piercings in each ear, all filled with silver pieces, and if I had to guess, I'd say she wasn't a day over thirty.

"Oh, no, we're just—"

She stepped forward as I tried to decline, but the toe of her boot snagged on a taped-down extension cord and she tripped, pitching toward one of the pinball machines. She broke her fall on the machine and righted herself quickly as Henry rushed forward to help.

"Are you okay?" he asked.

She held up a finger as she stared down at the floor. She'd dropped her cards somewhere along the way and a few of them fanned out between us, faceup. "Well, that's interesting," she drawled. "I would've guessed some of these though probably not all."

"As long as you're all right," I said, "we should get back to—"

"Seeing The Lovers crossed with The Ace of Cups always makes me happy," she said, her gaze on the floor. "It's a king tide of overflowing emotion and new beginnings. It's like the universe is saying, 'This is happening to you right now and it's time to ride this wave.' But it's also saying you need to make a choice. This isn't a small decision. Emotions are messy. Beginnings are scary. And the only answer is the one in your heart."

There was a time when I explained to people that the heart

beating behind your sternum was not the organ involved in thoughts and feelings. I stopped doing that when Meri told me it was the medical equivalent of correcting someone's grammar in conversation and that I wouldn't make many friends or be invited out often if I kept it up.

So, I pinched my lips together and forced a tight smile. Beside me, Henry seemed to do the same.

"And then we have The World," she went on, "alongside The Fool. How fun is that? The universe is saying you're in for a transformation. Even more new beginnings! One of the things I love about these cards in combination is that they're telling us that you've found harmony, found balance. That you've reached the end of a cycle, you're at a point of equilibrium, and you're ready to trust the universe to send you on a wild new journey."

Henry and I glanced at each other. He had his hands at his waist, a finger tapping against his belt. Did he remember the cards falling out of Aunt Luisa's deck in the elevator last summer? Did he realize that these were nearly the same cards? I couldn't read his expression, but I also didn't know if this mattered. How could it? These were just some cards that meant something to certain people. Coincidences aside, they didn't have to mean anything to me.

Even if they landed a little too close to home.

"Good stuff. Thanks." Henry motioned over his shoulder. "We should get back to our group. Watch out for that cord there."

As we made our way through the arcade, I asked, "Was that—"

"Really fucking weird? Yes," he said.

At least I wasn't the only one thinking it.

"We're not mentioning this to Lulu," he added. "It'll go right to her head."

The group was gathered in a circular booth with Meri and

Cami on the inside and Jenelle, Reza, and Tori flanking them. Henry and I settled on opposite sides of the table and did a respectable job of folding into the ongoing conversations as if we weren't coming down from multiple intense experiences and counting the minutes until we could leave.

This worked well enough until Cami shuffled out for the bathroom, forcing one side of the booth to shuffle with her. I ended up between Tori and Reza for a bit until Tori decided to visit the bar and Jenelle followed, sending everyone out of the booth and then back in. Later, Henry and his team exited for their version of "TiK ToK," which was astounding primarily because Reza assumed the role of lead singer and was *exceptional* at it.

It went on like this, the whole group migrating in and out until Henry and I ended up in the back of the booth, his knee pressed to my thigh under the table. He talked to Reza about the idiosyncrasies of the public transit system in Boston and then to Meri about the pediatrics rotation. She assured him that first-year residents wouldn't be going anywhere near her NICU. When he leaned forward to grab some nachos off a plate in the middle of the table, he dropped his hand on my knee and kept it there.

I could've stayed here, just like this, for hours. Longer, even. I never wanted this to stop.

Then, fracturing all my daydreams and bliss, Meri appeared with a tray full of drinks and jabbed a finger at me once she set it down. "You," she said, "you're coming with me."

"But not for long, right?" Henry asked under his breath. He gave my leg a meaningful squeeze.

"Probably not. We'll see."

Meri dragged me toward the karaoke stage and started flipping the pages of the songbook while someone chewed their way through a Britney Spears tune.

"You don't have to do this thing with me anymore," she said. "I never should've forced you to keep that single-girl pact going for so long. It was never meant to last forever. At first, it was a life preserver. But then it evolved into my whole personality."

I tried to find threads of hurt in her voice, some indication that she was struggling with this decision. I couldn't find any, which only made me more suspicious. I couldn't imagine her washing her hands of the most defining piece of herself. And maybe that wasn't what she was saying at all. Maybe she was simply cutting me out of it. "That seems like a slight exaggeration."

She kept turning the pages. "I'm ending the pact. It's over. It's done. No pact, no reason you can't go home with Hazlette tonight. And before you deny it, just don't. You think I didn't notice you two being profane over pinball? Please."

"What brought this on?"

Meri shrugged away the question but I knew there was more to the story. With Meri, there was always more.

"Do you have any intention of telling me about the thing that wasn't a thing from a few weeks ago? Or are we going to pretend that never happened?"

"I was hoping we'd ignore it. Your budding romance with Hazlette seemed like a fine diversion." She slapped her hand to the page. "This is it. This is our song."

I knew a change of subject when I saw one. "We have a song?"

"We do tonight." She handed over the book and tapped the page. "Come on. We're singing this."

"'Total Eclipse of the Heart'?" I shook my head. "You've got to be kidding."

"What? No! It's a great song. It's cool and nostalgic. It's retro."

"This is a really strange way to get out of a conversation," I said as she steered me onto the stage. "I don't really sing!"

"That's what makes it fun," she said as the first chords started. "I'm on backup. This one's all you, my love."

The spotlight was blinding though I could still make out the circular table and group gathered there. Cami noticed us first, waving and calling out as I stationed myself in front of the microphone. Tori sat up on her knees and clapped her hands over her head, yelling something I couldn't make out. Henry stared at me, his drink frozen halfway to his mouth.

I wasn't lying about not being able to sing. I was *not* good at this. But I had a stone-cold poker face and never backed down when it was time to play the part, so I sang like this song owed me money and I was coming to collect. I belted it out—*badly*—and the residents went totally nuts in the process. They were on their feet, singing along with every word. They couldn't have known why Meri chose it, why she knew these lyrics would hit the bull's-eye straight on, but they sang their hearts out just the same. When it was over, they rushed the stage, cheering like I was some kind of small-town hero.

Henry leaned in close, saying, "Thank god you're so damn good at surgery because you are terrible at this."

"I was told that made it more fun."

"Whoever said that is lying to you," he replied, and that was all the reminder I needed to keep Meri from sneaking away from me tonight.

I pulled her into the bathroom and propped my hands on my hips. "No more games. What's going on with you?"

She leaned back against the sink and gestured to the door. "I'm not playing games. You're not confined to our crazy single-girl deal and Hazlette isn't your resident anymore, and it's time for you to get out of here. I fully endorse whatever it is you choose to do to him in your free time."

I stared at her for a long moment. I wasn't ready to accept any of this at face value. "You're not allowed to say all of this and be sad and lonely at home. You're not allowed to cry alone, remember?"

"I do remember, even though I try to forget."

"I need you to know that I will always choose you. There is no man who will ever come between us. We're the ones who are going to grow old together, we're the ones who will always be there when our families fall apart and guys disappear, we're the ones who will pull the plug when the time comes. Always."

A bit of her bravado crumbled as her shoulders sagged and she rubbed her eyes. "I know, but you have a guy now and—"

"And if he doesn't accept and eagerly embrace the fact that you are the best person in my life, then he isn't who I thought he was. I don't care whether we have a pact or not. Nothing happens in my life without you. I'm not going anywhere and you can't make me."

Meri pushed off the sink and flew into my arms, which stunned the hell out of me because the extent of her affection was usually a genuine smile. "He's exactly who you think he is," she said. "And I want you to go home and let that big barge of man wreck you so hard you have to sit on a pillow next week."

"Only if you promise you won't go home and cry alone."

"No crying." She stepped back, pushing her hands through her hair. "I think it's time for this change. For both of us."

"Maybe. But nothing will change *us*. Deal?"

"Ugh, yes, fine. Let's invent a new pact if we must." She spun away from me and turned on the water. "Where did all these feelings come from? Goddamn. I thought I was supposed to outgrow this shit."

"I think we tried that," I said, scrolling back on all our years of escaping ourselves for a few weeks each summer. I handed over her phone. "I guess we have to deal with them now."

Eighteen
Henry

Transplant Surgery Rotation:
Day 5, Week 8

Whitney
My place. 15 minutes.

I pretty much ran to Beacon Hill.

She'd barely opened the door before I pushed my way in like a brute, taking her face in my hands and kissing her with everything I had. She tasted minty, as if she'd just brushed her teeth. I loved it. Loved everything.

"You," I said against Whit's lips, "are stunningly bad at karaoke. I mean, it's actually impressive how bad you are."

Her laugh bubbled up between us. "Meri made me do it."

"How is it possible that you are"—I kicked the door shut

behind me and gestured down the length of her luscious body and back up—"all these glorious things and more, and yet you get lost on the way to second base and can't sing your way out of a shower?"

She glared up at me, all rosy-cheeked and defiant. Fucking *loved* it. "I didn't get *lost* on the way to second base."

"Okay, honey, we'll go with your version." I locked my arms around her torso, holding her like I wanted to cram her inside my chest and keep her there forever. As if she wasn't already there. "I might be completely out of hand here, but there's nothing in the world I want more than to rip this shirt off you."

"I happen to like this shirt very much and would be disappointed if it didn't survive the night."

I might not survive the night.

"Then I'll carefully unbutton it like the fucking gentleman I am," I said. "But then"—I dragged a hand up from her thigh to the full curve of her ass and grabbed like I was trying to take a bite out of her—"all bets are off."

Whit stared at me, her lips parted just a breath and her eyes wide, and she shocked the shit out of me by sliding her hand between us and giving my cock one good, firm pump through my trousers. Yeah, I'd be dead by morning. No doubt. I was going to burn the fuck out on this woman and I'd have not a single regret.

That hand still teasing my erection, Whit said, "I think you know where the bedroom is."

I turned her around and pointed her in that direction, my hands glued to her plush hips. "Have I ever mentioned how much I love your efficiency? Because I do."

"Do you also love regular screenings for STIs and other issues?"

"I do. I love them as much as anyone can love a six-inch swab coming at them." A lamp illuminated her room and it wasn't obvious though I knew she'd tidied up, which gave me a weird jolt of pleasure. "All clear on this side and you are the only person I've been with this year."

I waited for her to do something with that. Anything. If she gave me the opening, I'd take it.

She reached for my belt and had it flying across the room in three seconds flat. "I have an IUD. We can skip the condoms if you're comfortable with that."

"Sexiest goddamn sentence I've ever heard." I worked hard at keeping her shirt in one piece, but these buttons were small and slippery and my fingers were designed for neither of those things. "Fuck, I want you naked."

She had my trousers open and her hand in my boxers within an eye blink. I couldn't think with her fisting my cock like that. I could barely stand. "Then get me naked."

"Believe me, honey, I'm trying." I cleared the final pair of buttons and immediately buried my face between her lace-covered breasts. She was heavenly everywhere, but this—*this* was the place that'd occupied my dreams for months. The only reason I made it through July was because every time I closed my eyes, I thought about her bouncing on my cock while I sucked her nipples. "Hello again, my lovelies."

Whit went to work on my shirt and had it hanging open in record time. I shook out of it while she unfastened her pants, and then I was finished being polite. I kicked off my pants and wrapped her in my arms, groaning at the feel of her silky skin under my hands as I stripped her of everything else.

She sat on the edge of the bed in nothing but those delicate necklaces around her throat, and the look she gave me could've set the whole city on fire. I cupped her jaw and ran my thumb over her lips. "Careful there, beautiful. You have no idea how long you've had me on edge."

Leaning back on her elbows, she said, "Maybe you should show me."

I did the one thing available to me. I dropped to the floor, shoved those creamy thighs wide open, and prayed at the only altar I'd ever need. She cried out when my tongue met her flesh and her fingers were tugging at my hair a second later. Her clit was the sweetest little berry in the world. Exactly as I'd remembered.

I leaned back as I teased at the wet waiting for me. She was gorgeous. Just devastating. "Mine," I said, pressing a kiss to her clit. "You're all mine, Whitney."

She glanced down at me, her eyes hazy and her nipples hard. It required serious restraint to keep from coming all over myself right then. "Am I?"

"Yeah." I pushed two fingers inside her as I drew circles around her clit. Tremors moved down her belly and I knew she was close. "Don't forget it."

"What if I do?"

I looked up to find her pulling at her nipples and I handled that by pressing my face to her inner thigh and biting until I felt her inner muscles clench around my fingers. "I'll remind you."

She rocked against me, serving up every inch of herself for my use as she said, "Henry. *Please.*"

I almost laughed because didn't she know by now? Didn't she see? There was no need to beg when the only thing I wanted to give her was everything. "Tell me what you need, baby."

"More."

"Not a problem." I returned to her clit, sucking and circling until her knees came up and my hand was soaked down to my wrist. "That's it. That's my girl. Give it to me. Fuck, Whit, you feel amazing."

She closed her fingers around my hair and yanked. "If you don't get up here and fuck me—"

I was inside her before those words could pass over her lips.

"Such a bossy little thing," I said.

Her body was incredible, all lush curves and smooth skin, but it was more than that. It was the sounds she made and the way she met my thrusts with her own that drove me wild. It was the way she watched me rubbing her clit, occasionally grabbing my hand and showing me how she liked it. The way she breathed my name and the way she'd turn her head and yell *oh, fuuuuck* into the pillows.

I pinned her wrists over her head. It was all I could do to keep a grip on my control, but she was quick to say, "I want my hands back." Her words were all pout. "I don't like this."

"If I give you your hands," I said, pulling all the way out and then slamming back in, "I get you on top of me."

I loved the lazy nod she gave me. It was like we'd tripped and stumbled out of the tension of the past eight weeks and into the kind of well-worn comfort I'd never thought I'd know. I released her wrists and slapped her thigh, and though it felt like the last thing I'd ever want to do, I pulled out. "Get up here, gorgeous."

I settled back against the pillows as Whit climbed into my lap. My hands instinctively went to her waist as she sank down. I gripped her hard and held her body as still as possible until I talked myself out of exploding on the spot.

"Oh my god." Her hands flexed on my shoulders, her short nails pressing into my skin. "This is—"

"Better than you remembered?" I dropped my head to her chest, my mouth on her breast while I debated if there was any true downside to coming this soon. Aside from the fact it was very complimentary to her, it wasn't as though I'd roll over and fall asleep. Fuck, no. I'd dust myself off and get back to work. "I know, Whit. *I know.*"

I eased up on my grip, finally letting her rock against me, and I filled my hands with her breasts to distract from the incredible heat and clench of her pussy. As if that was even possible.

"No one has ever liked my tits as much as you do."

"Let's keep it that way." I brushed my lips over her nipple. "These are mine."

"Is that how it is? All of me is yours now?"

I nodded as I licked her. "That's right."

"And what do I get?"

I didn't know how she was capable of speaking. I was having a tough time with breathing. Still, I managed, "Everything. Anything you want, it's yours."

Whit ground into me hard and I bucked up into her, wanting this to last forever and wishing it could end now so we could start all over in a few minutes. Her hands were everywhere, pulling at my hair, scratching my shoulders, clawing at my wrists when I pinned her nipple between my teeth.

"I love the way you feel," she said, her eyes closing and head dropping back. "It's like—"

"Like this is the way it's supposed to be. Like it's finally *right.*"

Those admissions seemed to unleash something in us because we went a little crazy then. I rolled her to her back and pounded into her like I was trying to leave a mark inside her. She dug her heels into my ass so hard I knew I'd feel it for a week. I flipped us over again and watched her ride me until I was on the verge of saying things neither of us were prepared to hear.

When her hums turned to shrieks and her pussy was all but

strangling my cock, I put her on her back one last time. With two fingers tracing her clit, I said, "You know what I want."

Somehow, she found it in her to give me a devious smile. If she only knew what she did to me. "Do I?"

I hitched her knee to my hip and stared between us, watching her stretch around me. "Come the fuck on, honey. Can't you see I'm dying here?"

I didn't expect a serious answer to that. Or any answer. But then she asked, "Are you staying tonight?"

And I said, "I'm staying always."

The rest was a sweaty blur of limbs and mouths and *fuuuuck*, and she came so intensely, so thoroughly that my body had no choice but to follow. When I collapsed beside her, my chest heaving and my head dizzy, I pulled her into my arms and dragged sloppy kisses over her collarbones and up her neck.

A moment later, she patted my chest and slipped away to the bathroom. By the time she returned, I'd done a mediocre job of straightening the sheets and blankets, and fetched most of the pillows she'd thrown. It thrilled me to no end that she didn't waste time on pajamas or anything like that because I would rip it right off. After all this time, I wasn't here to play around in pajamas.

We tangled ourselves together under the sheets, my thigh between her legs, her arm around my neck, my hand on her ass. I went back to her neck, running a finger along the delicate chain there. She hadn't worn it at the wedding. I wanted to know if it was new. If it had been a gift or she'd picked it out for herself. She'd probably picked it out. It was elegant and sophisticated, and I didn't get the sense she let anyone choose things for her.

"So," she said, drumming her fingers against my chest. "Do you think you've gotten it out of your system yet?"

"That's not how it works. That's not how it's ever worked for anyone." If anything, she was deeper into my system now. She was my system.

"What if we had sex again?" Whit asked. "We might shake it loose."

"Whit, honey, there is nothing I'd rather do than fuck you until I shook something loose and I'm open to testing that hypothesis of yours day and night until you finally succeed in stopping my heart—"

"You know that's very unlikely."

"—but I can promise you that you're in my system and you're not going anywhere."

Whit hummed like she was thinking this over and I let her do that because I needed the time to recover and there was no talking her out of anything. Instead, I asked, "What was the deal with those tarot cards?"

I felt her shrug. Her words were stiff as she said, "Pretty random, huh?"

"How...I mean, how could that happen? That we ended up with most of the same cards? Statistically, it's—"

"Yeah. I know."

I ran a hand over the gentle curve of her belly. Another spot I loved. If she held perfectly still and didn't giggle at all, it was a fine spot for drinking whiskey. She'd giggled. Back in Tahoe, she'd giggled the second the liquor landed on her skin and we'd made a whole damn mess. But fuck we'd had so much fun. I hadn't known sex could be that fun and silly, hot and intimate. I hadn't known.

But now I knew it wasn't a one-time thing. I knew this was how it was with us and that realization made it hard to breathe because she was real. I'd imagined nothing. Exaggerated nothing. Whitney was real and we were electric and I could never go back to not knowing.

So, I kissed her forehead and shoved down all the things I wanted to say. It was too soon and this was too delicate and I was too much of a mess to get it right. Instead, I said what I'd wanted to say since the start of my transplant rotation. "I've missed you so fucking much."

After a long exhale, she said, "I've missed you too."

Never. I could never go back to not knowing.

Nineteen

Whitney

Rule Number Ten:
Don't even think about going to the newlywed brunch, no matter how good the buffet looks.

I woke up when the sun slanted in through my windows. Henry was sprawled on his stomach beside me, one arm curled around his pillow and the other across my torso. I studied the long sweep of his lashes, the mountaintop tattoo on his bicep, the way he was still tan even though he spent sixteen hours a day indoors. It was like summer lived inside him and refused to let go.

I was beginning to understand the feeling.

I managed to sneak away to the bathroom and did a quick job of tidying myself up. Nothing major, no makeup, just a fresh face and clean teeth. Still, this was mostly uncharted territory. I hadn't woken up with a man—not on purpose—in a terribly long time. If it was possible, I was more nervous about this, about today and everything after, than I'd been about last night.

I snagged Henry's button-down shirt from the floor on my way back to bed. It brushed my thighs and smelled like him, and there was nothing better.

When I slipped between the sheets, his arm shot out, circling my waist and dragging me across the bed as I yelped and laughed. "Right here," he growled into my neck. "This is where you're allowed to be. Nowhere else. First and last warning. Don't test me, young lady."

I was about seven months older than Henry. That didn't figure into his use of *young lady*. I acted like I didn't mind. It secretly tickled me to no end.

"That sounds extreme," I said as I burrowed into his big, warm body.

"It's not." Another growl. I couldn't believe how much I loved that sound. Even more when it was delivered directly to my skin. "What's this? I didn't tell you to put clothes on." He pushed up on an elbow to inspect me, his midnight eyes bleary and his hair a wild mess. "Never take this off. Ever."

"That was a pretty quick change of heart, don't you think?"

"I reevaluated the situation based on emerging data," he said through a yawn. "The data being you're hot as fuck in my shirt."

He thumbed open the buttons, kissing his way down my torso as he went. It was like a tiny path of fire, and by the time he reached my belly button I could barely hold still. I wanted to pull him over me to feel his weight pinning me down, to drag my fingers through his hair when I couldn't take it anymore, to whisper and beg for all the things he already knew I wanted.

He shifted away from the pillow, running both hands over my breasts and down, down between my legs. Parting my thighs as he bent over me, he said, "Now, be quiet. I have work to do."

The first swipe of his tongue was nearly enough to do me in.

That was appalling on multiple levels and I almost told him to stop so I could get a hold of myself, but then he did it again and the thoughts poured right out of my mind.

He ran his fingers down my seam as he licked me and it was a gentle, almost absentminded touch. It was like he was aware of the heat and the wet, and he was in no rush to attend to either when he could suck on my clit until I lost my entire vocabulary.

Leaning back, he stared between my legs as he stroked me. "Aren't you pretty?"

A noise came out of me then, a sigh garbled around a plea for more and a murmur of *oh my god*. Henry must've understood this noise because he bowed his head with a chuckle. The next passes of his tongue were more determined than anything that'd come before. He was working for it now, chasing me down one lick after another like he could burn out all memory of previous tongues in this territory if he put everything into it.

And the problem was that I wanted him to burn out those memories. I wanted to remember the scrape of his beard on the inside of my thigh and the way I could feel his jaw working me over. I wanted this, and I wanted it so much I could barely bring myself to form those words.

Rather than doing anything dangerous like letting myself imagine that we could be more than a few wild nights, I slapped a hand across my mouth while I shook and convulsed.

When I was wrung out and panting, and Henry was certain he'd melted every bone in my body, he settled between my legs and pushed inside me with one long, fluid thrust. "Do you know," he started, moving in me like we had all the time in the world, "how long I've wanted to do this? To wake up with you? To roll over and find you there, just warm and sleepy and waiting for me to fuck you?"

I locked my arms around his neck, ran my hands over his shoulders, urged him down to meet my lips, *closer closer closer*. "No," I whispered. "How long?"

He hooked an arm behind my knee as he sank deeper. A rough, perfect rumble sounded in his throat when my inner muscles started pulsing around his cock. He rocked into me hard, like he had a mind to plow me straight through this bed, through the floor, through the earth itself.

"Always," he said.

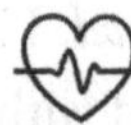

WE WENT TO BREAKFAST AT A SMALL CAFÉ NEAR BOSTON Common and sat outside, soaking up the best of the bright October sun. When I had coffee in hand, Henry scooped up my legs and set them on his lap with a smile that said *this is how we do things now*.

I didn't have any problem with that.

With a hand locked around my ankle, he asked, "So, how long until you completely panic?"

"I am *not* going to panic."

I dropped my gaze to his fingers which quickly led me to his forearms, bare and rippling thanks to a t-shirt with *Sunnyside Tahoe* across the front. I was suddenly very resentful that winter would inevitably arrive and I wouldn't get to ogle those arms unless he rolled up his sleeves. Or when he was in scrubs. Or when he was naked. Naked was...it was great.

"Yeah, that's not the face I associate with panic." He stroked his fingers up my leggings, over the back of my calf, and I almost purred. Out loud. "It's good seeing you like this. When you're not so stressed and serious."

No more purring for me. "Even though I was very unserious when you met me, I'm a serious person. That's not about to change. If you don't like it, you need to walk away right now."

He leaned forward, his hand on the back of my knee. "I'm not going anywhere, Whit."

"Well, in that case," I said, "we should set some new ground rules. Assuming you haven't gotten this out of your system yet."

"I've told you, that's not how it works." He laughed, shaking his head like I was a real piece of work as he reached for his coffee. "Let's hear it. Give me these ground rules."

"Even if you're not reporting to me anymore, we still work together. I think we should agree to be mature and civil when we decide to end things."

"When we—no. That's not happening." He arched a brow and gave me the same arrogant look that he'd had this morning when he braced my hands on the bathroom sink and took me from behind. "What else do you have?"

"What do you mean, *not happening*?"

"I mean, I finally found you. I'm not letting go."

I was profoundly aware of each of his fingers as they traced my calf down to my ankle, though more than that, I felt his gaze like the sunlight. There was no hiding from it. "That's very sweet, but I'm trying to be practical."

"Practical like those heels you wear to the hospital?"

"I happen to like my heels," I said.

"Fuck, I'd hope so. I don't want you wearing them just to feed my fantasies." Henry tightened his grip on my leg like he was mentally scrolling through those fantasies right now. I almost asked him to take me home and narrate. I wanted to know *everything*. "What other rules do you have cooked up?"

"We've survived enough secrets and I don't want to do that again, but I think it would be good if we kept this—whatever it is —quiet around the hospital. It would be best for both of us."

"*Whatever it is*," he repeated to himself. "Allow me to be clear since it seems like we're not. I'm not seeing anyone else and I'm sure as hell not sleeping with anyone. Maybe it's presumptuous of me, but I want you all to myself. I'd find a way to survive if I couldn't have that but I'll be a hell of a lot happier knowing you're all mine. That's what *this* is."

I put the coffee down so I didn't spill it. I didn't know if Henry could feel the tremors rippling through my body. I wanted him to know that he'd shaken me right down to the marrow and my entire body was too busy processing those words to do anything as complicated as speaking.

And I wanted him to tell me what he truly meant because no one wanted me all to themselves, no one promised to never let go. That wasn't real. It wasn't *my* real. It couldn't be. Just like he hadn't been waiting for me all this time. At best, he'd waited since crashing into my life at the start of his rotation.

He propped his chin on his fist as he swept an unhurried gaze along the flare of my hips and up to my breasts. Rarely did I concern myself with how others viewed my body, but there was something in the way he stared at me, his lips slightly parted and his granite jaw pulsing, that made me wonder what he saw.

"I'm not interested in sleeping with anyone else," I said.

That lazy gaze stayed fixed on my breasts for another moment, moving like the kind of caress that started tender and ended with a rude pinch. "Any other ground rules?"

And now my nipples joined the party. The only proportional

response was to stare at his forearms. I tapped my coffee cup to his, saying, "Hands off at the hospital."

"That's not a new rule, honey. Give me something harder. I need a real challenge."

In truth, I was out of rules. I was too busy taking *I'm not letting you go* and holding it up against all the peace I'd made with staying single. All the soft spots and dark corners where I hid away the bitterness of never being chosen by the ones who were supposed to want me. All the doubt that this would last beyond a few more feverish moments.

So, I said, "I want to get some pumpkins."

"Pumpkins. Sure." He glanced around Mt. Vernon Street. "Nearby? Or are we leaving the city and finding ourselves a farm?"

My god, he'd be adorable in a pumpkin patch. Thinking about it was like a sugar rush. My teeth hurt. "There's a farmers market not too far from here. We could walk."

He set my feet on the ground and ran both hands up my thighs, his thumbs pressed to the tender insides. His palm spanned the thickest part of my leg and I watched as he pressed each fingertip into me like he wanted me to feel every one of them. "Then let's get you some pumpkins."

I discovered rather quickly that Henry knew little of Boston. He had a sketchy understanding of the public transit system and his points of reference included the hospital campus, one grocery store, and several bars. To be fair, that covered the breadth and depth of a resident's life, but I took it as an opportunity to show him some of my favorite spots.

We wandered through the city, our fingers twined together and the sun beating down on our shoulders, and it was like it'd always been this way. Like *we'd* always been this way. There were moments when I glanced at Henry and I was certain I was looking at one of our million lazy weekend memories.

I caught myself wanting it to be one of our million.

We shared a soft pretzel as we strolled around the farmers market. Whenever Henry wanted a bite, he'd take hold of my wrist and eat right out of my hand. My entire torso broke out in goose bumps over that move. I didn't think I'd ever recover.

We let our bellies lead us around the market, sampling everything and buying anything that sounded good. It was all *Do you like this cheese?* and *What do you think about blackberry thyme jam?* and *How about some apples?* and *That bread smells phenomenal.*

I spent an unacceptably long time surveying the pumpkins. It made no sense seeing as I was only putting them on my stoop and the squirrels of Beacon Hill would surely disembowel them within days. Still, I wanted the right pumpkins, and every time I said to Henry, "I'm almost there. Just another minute," he was quick to reply with, "Take your time, sweetheart. I'm not goin' anywhere."

He didn't hurry me. He never zoned out with his phone. He didn't even look bored. Whenever I talked to myself about one having a wobbly bottom or another looking a little too flat, he'd respond, telling me he agreed or to check out the one to my left. And when I finally made my selections, he said, "I've got them," and tucked two huge pumpkins under his arms like they weighed nothing at all.

Once again, I enjoyed the gifts granted to me by this man's t-shirt collection.

I repeatedly offered to take one of the pumpkins as we walked back to my place. He always refused, laughing to himself as he swept his gaze over me like there was something very amusing about that request. "Let me do this," he said.

We talked about the hot, not-especially-autumnal weather we were having and how this city wasn't what either of us had expected. He told me about his sister's research into the Brontës' impact on modern feminist literature, I told him about Meri's inability to find a resident she could mentor into a neonatal surgery fellow. We complained about how there was a lot less sky out here compared to where we'd grown up.

When we reached my doorstep, Henry indulged my need to get the pumpkins just right on the stoop. I'd never decorated for Halloween before so I didn't know what qualified as *just right*, but we debated every possible arrangement until after the sun went down.

Again, I was struck by the sense that we'd done this for years and years. That he'd always lugged our pumpkins home and then watched while I fussed over them forever. That we'd stood in the inky evening darkness, staring at the stoop from across the street with our arms locked around each other, admiring our handiwork.

And yet, when we went inside, I didn't know what to do with Henry—or myself. I didn't know if I was supposed to drag him into the bedroom or cook some miraculous meal from the cheese and apples we'd bought or do some other amazing thing that I didn't know about because I hadn't dated in ages.

In the end, I leaned into the best and worst thing we had in common. "Do you like doctor games?"

He arched a brow as he failed to fight off a dirty grin. "Do they involve you getting naked and waiting for me to come into your bedroom to check you out? Because yes. Definitely yes."

I tossed a dishtowel at him. "Not that kind of game."

He rounded the kitchen island, his hands open like this was an idea fit for juggling. "Then I get naked and wait for you?"

I yelped as he pulled me into his arms and off my feet. "No, no one gets naked."

"Tell me about this game," he said against my neck. I loved it when he talked to my skin. And that beard? *Gahhh.* Goose bumps forever. "I'll decide if it would be better naked."

Laughing, I said, "It's a game Meri and I play where we watch movies and diagnose the injuries."

"Is the objective to diagnose quickly? Or diagnose the most injuries?"

"Both," I said, "although we usually play this while drinking wine and we forget about the rules after the first hour."

Henry set me down and backed me against the island, his arms caging me in. There weren't many times when I felt small. Short, yes, but rarely small. Though being here with him looming over me, hips pinning me in place and those tree-branch biceps at eye level, I got a taste of it. There was a primitive appeal to his size, his strength. If I closed my eyes right now, I could let myself believe that everything would be all right as long as I had my big, strong mountain man to protect me from—from everything.

Naturally, he said, "Even more reason to do this naked."

"We'll start fully dressed," I said, "and see where it goes from there."

"Ahhh. Now that's the kind of challenge I can get my hands around."

"Don't be so sure of yourself. I have quite the win record."

He shoved his hands into my back pockets and gave my ass the kind of squeeze that said he intended to win by any means necessary. "Does Meri usually do this while you're playing?"

I slipped a hand between us, cupping his shaft over his jeans. "No, but I don't usually do this either."

He grinned down at me, his eyes dark and filled with promises I really wanted him to keep. "Such a scrappy little fighter you are. Love that about you."

All over again, I was inside a memory.

"EARDRUM!" HENRY SHOT TO HIS FEET, JABBING A finger at the screen. "Ruptured eardrum. Bilateral. Concussion and —and clavicle fracture!"

"Are you kidding me?" I muted the movie as the battle scene faded to black. The good guys won. "I'll give you the eardrums but that clavicle is fine."

"He slammed into a boulder." He jabbed that finger at the screen again. "The dude was thrown into a giant fucking rock, Whitney. It's either a busted clavicle or many cracked ribs. Or both! And then there's the possibility of a collapsed lung."

I tipped my chin up as the final scene started. "And yet here he is, walking around with nothing more than a few appropriately masculine scratches on his cheek. Breathing, too."

Henry stared down at me where I'd cozied into the corner of the sofa. With his hands on his hips and looking fully perturbed with my comments, he said, "Just because you can't see the vestibular injuries doesn't mean they're not real."

He took this game far more seriously than Meri and I did and it was adorable. Thoroughly charming. Especially the part where he took all of my responses seriously. I'd realized early on that he intended to diagnose every single injury he could. The only thing to do was argue with him about all of them. There was absolutely no fun in letting him be right. What kind of game was that?

Henry pressed a hand to his chest. "It's a good thing you found your way to transplant surgery but—and I say this with love—you'd lose more than a few trauma patients."

"Would I?" I took a sip of wine, feigning a whole lot of shock. "Because I'm pretty sure I spotted a cracked pelvis, two liver lacerations, and multiple catastrophic knee and ankle injuries that you didn't mention."

"I...what?" He glanced to the screen as the credits rolled. "Have you—for fuck's sake, Whit, you've been playing me this whole time?"

I held out my hands, shrugging. "I can't possibly know. I'm just a transplant surgeon."

He stared at me for a moment, shaking his head like he just couldn't believe that I had it in me to be that devious. "Enough," he said under his breath. "More than enough out of you for tonight." Then he scooped me up, taking hold of me as if I weighed hardly more than a throw pillow, and marched toward my bedroom.

"Enough meaning...what? Enough diagnoses? Enough superhero movies? Enough—"

I didn't get to say anything else because he dropped me to the bed in a heap and forced me to watch while he took all the time in the world to unbuckle his belt. He whipped it off and let it fall to the floor. "Enough," he said, as if that explained everything. "Get that sweatshirt off."

I'd changed into lounge pants and a big hoodie before starting the movies. Since it was my policy to never wear a bra around the house save for extraordinary circumstances, following through on this request meant I'd be sitting here topless. I didn't mind that. I mean, we'd known each other naked before we knew much else.

But there was something deeply ordinary about this moment. We weren't fumbling around each other, trying to figure out how it was going to be and who we were in this revised version of us. Trying to figure out if we had enough for more than one night.

"Dr. Aldritch, I told you to remove the sweatshirt and I don't like to be kept waiting." Henry pulled off his t-shirt and then pushed his jeans down. They fell to the floor along with my jaw. I'd never heard such a commanding tone from him. "Show me you're up to the task."

My body responded to that tone with such an immediate rush of arousal that my inner muscles ached. I couldn't decide if I wanted to figure out why those rough words had me springing to attention or if I'd be happier not tracing the roots of this one.

I decided to pull off the sweatshirt.

"Much better." He folded his arms over his bare chest. His cock strained the soft fabric of his boxers, jutting out toward me. "And the pants too. Promptly, this time."

Still too dazed from the sudden onslaught of need buzzing inside me, I wriggled out of the pants without protest. As if there was anything to protest here. If anything, this reminded me of that night in Tahoe when we hadn't been able to get enough of each other.

It was the same now—except we knew it wouldn't end with the morning.

I stayed there, flat on the bed and stripped down to my skin, while Henry stared down at me. His jaw flexed as he looked me over. Because I knew he'd say something about it, I fought the urge to drape an arm over my belly or curl myself around a pillow.

He opened the top drawer of my nightstand and sifted through the contents. I had a good idea what he was looking for and my cheeks burned at the thought of it. When he took my wrist and placed a long, thick vibrator in my palm, my entire body flushed.

"Demonstrate the correct usage."

I blinked up at him. My core clenched so hard it hurt. My nipples were pulled so tight they felt sunburned. I couldn't think beyond those aches. "Um. What?"

"I expect you to come prepared." His grip on my wrist tightened as he guided my hand between my thighs. "Now, pay attention. I won't repeat myself."

The blunt head of the toy pressed against my seam and a startled noise slipped out of me. Henry paused, studying me for a moment as he ran his thumb over my knuckles. "Stop?"

I shook my head. "I'm okay."

His expression tightened as he nudged the vibe forward. There was no resistance, even for the size of this toy, because I was making my own personal monsoon tonight. "Are you holding your tools properly?" He arched a brow. "You'll end up doing more work if you don't."

Is that how I sound when I give him orders? And does it have this *effect on him?*

I shifted my hold on the base. "I think so."

He let out an impatient sigh that destroyed any resistance I might've had to this man. It was just gone. "For your sake, let's hope so." He rolled his eyes and the only thing I wanted was a hint of approval. Just a tiny flicker of approval from this cool, authoritative version of him. "The pussy is"—he cleared his throat—"it's very wet."

"Is that good?"

"It's perfect." Another throat clearing. *Argh.* I loved it. "Check for yourself. Do you feel that?"

Henry reached for my free hand and brought my fingers to my clit. My legs fell wide open, giving up any pretense of modesty. He teased me with small, steady circles that made it hard to keep my eyes open. "Yeah. Yes. I-I do."

"Good. Don't move." He shifted my other hand, guiding the toy inside me. "We'll start off easy and see how much of this we can take." He said this conversationally, as if I wasn't already shaking and throbbing and fighting for my life here. Glancing up at me, he added, "It's important to have a plan in place before you begin." He turned the vibrator on. "It's more efficient."

My god. This man was going to destroy me and he was going to do it using my own instructional feedback. How was that even possible?

"You'll notice," he continued, rocking the toy inside me at a lazy pace, "that the right timing is critical. Too slow and we don't make enough progress."

He went on teasing me for a leisurely minute. It was enough to keep me on edge. Hell, he could've *stared* at me extra hard and I would've been hanging on by my fingertips over here.

But then Henry said, "Too fast and—"

He held my hand tight as he increased the vibrations and drove the toy into me. "Oh god. Oh fuck," I gasped. "I-I can't—"

"Too fast and we rush to the end." His gaze moved up my torso to settle on my breasts. If it was even possible, my nipples tightened even more at his attention. A breath stuttered out of him. "Now, show me the right way to finish this. Show me that you've been listening."

He trailed his fingers around my wrist, along my arm, and up the line of my belly. He closed his hand into a fist at my breasts and lingered there. I couldn't look away. I didn't know what he was going to do but I knew I wanted it—*needed* it.

Another rough, ragged breath. Then— "I gave you an order."

For reasons I refused to examine, there was nothing more important to me than proving that I'd listened to every damn word. Lucky for me, I'd spent a lot of time with this particular toy over the past two months.

As I eased into a rhythm, Henry dragged his knuckles over my breasts. He made a point of ignoring my nipples with every pass. It almost killed me but I knew from the way he squeezed the erection straining against his boxers that it was killing him too.

Between the fingers on my clit and the toy thrumming inside me, I knew I couldn't hold out much longer. But I was obsessed with his growly commands and the harsh, impatient way he stared at me. If I could make this last all night, I would.

"Have you noticed the condition of these nipples?" he asked.

The only response I could manage was a gasping cry.

"Hard." He drew a fingertip around one tender nipple and I felt myself fraying at the seams. He blew out a breath. "Remarkably hard."

Then he slapped my nipple with just enough force to make everything pulse and sting in the most torturous way. "Oh my god," I said, the words flying out in a wheeze.

He slapped the other side and murmured to himself. "Sensitive," he mused. "Observe the response when I—"

He closed his fingers around both nipples. My eyes were damp. My fingers were flying over my clit. Everything inside of me contracted. "Oh my god."

He released me only long enough to deliver another round of light slaps. I would've screamed if I could've. The best I could do was more gasping and slurred curses. "You're doing so good."

That was all I needed. That plus everything else but my body took those words and put them to work unfurling a long, thrashing orgasm that forced me to consider the possibility that my bones no longer existed. That didn't seem likely as far as my knowledge of the human body went but this was fairly extraordinary.

"Well done." His voice was raw like he'd bitten the words off piece by piece. I couldn't hold back a blissed-out grin. "But we're not finished."

He plucked the vibe from my hand, tossed it to the floor—which was no way to treat toys but we'd address that later—and shoved down his boxers. He crawled over me, swiped his tongue over my nipples, and pushed inside me with one perfect thrust.

"You are un-fucking-believable." He hitched my knee to his hip as he hammered into me. "Though you still have more to learn. I'll expect you back here tomorrow and maybe then"—he groaned into the space between my breasts—"you'll be prepared for me."

I slipped my hands into his hair, over his shoulders, as far down his back as I could reach. I just wanted to touch, to hold him as close to me as possible. Even with him buried inside me and his mouth on my breast and his growls stamped on my skin, I wanted more. Deeper. Tighter. *Always*. I wanted him to mark me in a way that only we knew and I wanted to go back and press that spot over and over.

Loose tremors gathered inside me. I didn't think I could come again, not after the bone-melting of the first one, but this one was shaping up to be different. It was mild, almost mellow. The kind of fizzy orgasm that just wanted to keep the fun going.

Henry surged into me with a low roar. He was almost there. I knew it. I could feel it in the tension of his muscles and the erratic snap of his hips. The press of his teeth against my shoulder, the bruising hold he had on my thigh. The way his hips nailed me to the mattress and refused to let go. "Look how good you're doing. Look how good you are for me."

He sealed his lips to mine as he came and then his lips were on my cheeks, my jaw, my neck. Panting, he said, "I know you can give me a little more."

All at once, he pulled out and settled between my legs. He sucked at my clit for less than a minute before I felt that mellow orgasm curling and tensing inside of me. I cried out when it broke free, melting my muscles and electrifying my skin in a warm, hazy pulse.

I pulled at Henry's shoulders until he returned to my side and gathered me in his arms. I breathed out a sigh and let my eyes drift shut. "What the hell was that?"

"You have your doctor games, I have mine." He dropped a kiss onto my temple. "Too much?"

I shook my head. "No, it was good. It was *great*. I just—I don't know."

After a moment, he said, "Everyone always looks to you for direction. You're always in charge. I figure you could use a break from that."

I pushed some hair out of my face and rubbed my eyebrows. Anything to give myself a minute to process those words without dissolving into an emotional puddle. *Goddamn*. Why did he have to say things that just sliced me open and went in search of my softest, my most vulnerable places? Was this what it meant to feel safe with someone? To feel protected?

Because I did and I didn't know if I should trust any of it.

"What happens now?" He traced the line of my clavicle. I could tell he was still the tiniest bit salty about the game. He'd get me next time, I was sure of it. "When do I get to see you this week?"

"You're not going to have time for me. You'll be busy."

"Trust me. I've never had a problem finding time for you."

There was something so certain, so definite in his tone that I shifted to face him, thinking I'd find something more in his expression. I found his sleepy eyes and warm smile. "Then come find me when you get some downtime."

He pulled me tight to his chest. "Don't think I won't."

On the other side of the room, the vibrator continued buzzing. "We'll see how it goes. Okay? We'll see how this rotation goes and then—"

"Don't finish that sentence."

"Why not?"

"Because I'm not interested in hearing your strategic exit plan," he said. "I'm going to finish this rotation and then I'm going to start another one. You'll tell me all the ways it's going to kick my ass. You'll probably be right but I'm gonna hope for the best anyway. I'll finish that one, tell you that you were right, and then start another. We'll repeat this cycle many times. We'll make it work. I promise."

"How do you know we'll make it work?"

He ran his fingers through the ends of my hair, pulling the slightest bit. I never wanted him to stop. "Because I love my challenges, Whit."

Twenty

Henry

Pediatric Surgery Rotation:
Day 4, Week 4

My cohort's introduction to residency was burn surgery which, to put it mildly, was really fucking intense. There were a lot of great attendings on that service though the one we reported to, Dr. Pecklewithe, was what I could only describe as a miserable bastard. Teaching was the least of his concern. He lived to shame and belittle at every turn. It was awful. I doubted whether I'd make it through residency if every rotation was like that one.

After the burn unit, we were shipped off to a satellite campus for our community general surgery rotation where Dr. Bass proved it was possible to be more of a miserable bastard than Pecklewithe. The guy seemed to think residency was one big cockfight and his only purpose was to pit us against each other.

With those horror shows behind us, we assumed transplant was a high point though not the norm. Imagine our surprise when we rolled up to pediatrics and discovered that Dr. Acevedo didn't bother with shaming or cockfighting. If anything, he seemed intent on getting to know us as people and inviting us to his house for dinner.

I was stunned to learn that I loved pediatric surgery.

I wasn't especially great at operating on kids and I wouldn't be choosing peds as an elective anytime soon, but the cases were nothing like I'd ever seen before, my entire cohort was rocking this rotation, and Dr. Acevedo was an incredible teacher. No cockfighting, no ritualistic shaming, not even a water bottle to hold in the OR.

Best of all, Whit wasn't my boss anymore. There were still times when she made me practice techniques on raw chicken, but there was no limit on the sleepovers. We spent as many nights together as we could, and with that, a new fear burrowed into the back of my brain: what if I fucked it all up? What if this fell apart and I couldn't fix it? If this ever ended, I was sure I'd wander into the woods and never return to society. I didn't want to function without her.

There were times when all I could think about were the months that I'd wanted her, *needed* her, and how I'd survived only on the thin hope that everything would be better when I figured out how to make this work. What would I do if I didn't even have that hope? And what would I do if I did fuck it all up yet had to see her every day at the hospital? I had another four and a half years of residency left. I'd never make it.

It *would* be my fault. I didn't know how or why, but I was positive it would be me. I knew all of Whit's soft spots and dark corners and I knew she'd only turn away from me if I gave her a reason, because she wanted this as much as I did. She wanted me to keep on showing up and proving that I'd stay for her, I'd *always* stay, and I intended to do that.

Until I fucked it up.

DR. ACEVEDO AND HIS WIFE INVITED THE *ENTIRE* residency program and a bunch of attendings to their house for Thanksgiving. They started serving food around eleven in the morning since many residents were stuck on overnights. They didn't stop until eleven tonight because most of us couldn't get away much earlier as the hospital was already running lean for the holiday.

Pediatrics got lucky today. Not a single procedure on the board, just post-op patients to look after. I spent most of my day learning how to knit from Reza while Tori and Cami planned vacations they couldn't afford.

I was meeting Whit at Dr. Acevedo's Cambridge home although the official story was that we weren't there together. In all honesty, it didn't bother me. As long as it gave Whit what she needed to not stress every time she thought about the ethical stuff, I didn't care. We'd leave together—discreetly, of course—and that was the only thing that mattered to me.

The street was lined with cars and every light was on in the grand old Victorian. It took all of a minute before Acevedo met me at the door and introduced me to his wife Erin, a short redhead who seemed ridiculously happy to see me.

My own family had never been this happy to see me.

They showed me to the dining room where the long table was loaded with all the traditional Thanksgiving dishes plus curries, koftas, enchiladas, and many other items I didn't recognize. They'd planned for everything—and everyone.

People were scattered throughout their home, mostly gathered in small groups with overflowing plates in hand, though the real party was in the open-plan family room and kitchen. The island was covered end to end with pies.

Whitney was nestled on a sofa between Dr. Mercer, who I still couldn't think of as *Meri*, and Dr. Shapiro, one of the few burn surgeons who didn't believe in eating the young. She glanced over when I walked in but that was the only recognition she offered.

I kinda loved it.

There was nothing better than being in on a secret.

Acevedo clapped me on the back, saying, "I told O'Rourke and Stremmel about your rescue experience and they want to talk to you. They think we can juggle a few of your second-year rotations to get you more time in trauma and emergency."

I'd promised myself I'd see the year through before making any decisions about specialties. Elective rotations weren't even offered until the third year so it hardly mattered whether I chose a direction before then but I'd be lying if I said I wasn't ready to dive into trauma surgery.

"That would be incredible," I said.

"Stremmel is going to want you to commit to staying here for your fellowship but—"

"I don't mind," I said quickly. I missed the West Coast like crazy and I wouldn't say I adored this town, but I wasn't going anywhere. Not while Whit was here. "Actually, I'd love it."

"Don't show your hand too fast," Acevedo said with a laugh. "Let them work for it. Come on, we'll get you a beer on the way."

And that was how I found myself grazing on pie and beer while Stremmel and O'Rourke, two of trauma surgery's biggest power hitters, argued over how they'd convince the residency director to swap out my second-year breast surgery rotation for an extra spin through trauma.

I was a big fan of that idea. No shade to breast surgery, but one less rotation spent learning procedures that I'd never use as a trauma surgeon made all the difference. Except that meant breaking away from my cohort. They'd all go on to breast surgery while I hooked up with a new team in trauma.

I knew we'd split up sooner or later. Obviously. Tori didn't have a specialty in mind yet but Reza walked through the door knowing he was headed for surgical oncology, and Cami had always leaned toward general but our time in pediatrics had her waffling. Even if we stayed together this year and next, the rest of our residencies would be a mix of required rotations and electives.

And it wasn't like we'd never see each other. If all else failed, Cami would still herd our asses up for weekend journal sessions.

But they were like family to me now. I didn't want to be the one to break us up.

Watching the trauma guys was amusing as hell. They were like a black and white film era comedy duo where Stremmel was the curmudgeon who only spoke in glares while O'Rourke was the Jack Russell terrier talking in stream of consciousness circles.

"Here's how the rest of your year is going to go," O'Rourke said around a mouthful of cashews. He held the bowl of nuts in the crook of his arm like he was running to the end zone. "Four months on general, which is gonna be great. Do you know Emmerling? Emmerling's awesome. She'll kick your ass, but you'll thank her for it."

Stremmel nodded. "Accurate."

"Then you're on general night float which is a bitch and it's gonna fuck up your life but everyone has to do it."

Another nod from Stremmel. "Mmmhmm."

"Then you're playing in our sandbox," O'Rourke continued, knocking back another handful of cashews. "Two months in trauma and emergency surgery, one on trauma night float."

"Is that going to fuck up my life too?" I asked.

"You won't even notice it at that point," O'Rourke said. "But that gives you three straight months with us this year and then you'll roll right into your Emergency Department rotation which you'll love. You're gonna be a pro at that on day one."

I didn't know about that but I appreciated the vote of confidence.

O'Rourke dropped a hand to my shoulder. I was pretty sure it was the cashew hand and that I now had salt and nut dust on my shirt. Of all the things that ended up on me in a given day it wasn't the worst, though I had learned a lot about him tonight.

"We're doing this thing. We've got a plan for you, young man." My best estimate put O'Rourke a couple years younger than me, though he seemed like the kind of guy who called everyone he liked *young man*. "But if we do this and then you fuck off to Penn or U-Mich or UC fucking San Diego for your fellowship, I will dedicate the rest of my career to trolling you. Do you understand?"

"O'Rourke." Stremmel sighed. "Could you spare us the drama? Please?"

"I'm not going to San Diego." My gaze traveled across the room to where Whit sat, her back to me as she and Dr. Mercer told a story that had the group rolling with laughter. "There's a lot keeping me in Boston."

"Good to know," O'Rourke said.

Dr. Shapiro circled the island, her eyes darting to the mostly devoured pies before stopping beside Stremmel. He looped his arm around her shoulders and tugged her close. I forced myself to look away because neither one of them wanted me staring, but how had I made it this far without knowing Shapiro and Stremmel were together?

I almost had myself convinced that it was new when I noticed a platinum band around his fourth finger—and a daintier one around hers.

Huh. Would not have guessed that.

"I'm done," she said quietly.

It made me wonder when Whit would be done. Brie was off somewhere with friends tonight which meant we could break out the toys and be as loud as we wanted. Whit didn't love making a lot of noise when Brie was around.

"Then I'm taking you home," Stremmel replied. To O'Rourke, he said, "Find a way to not be obnoxious."

"I haven't a clue what you mean," O'Rourke said.

Shaking his head, Stremmel led Shapiro to the hall. "Hang in there, Hazlette," he called. "And you know exactly what I mean, O'Rourke. Behave yourself."

Watching them leave was like looking into the future. I could see me and Whit walking out of here after talking sense into some hyper residents over thirteen types of pie. We'd have the wedding bands too though they didn't have to match. Whit's style was too precise for that. Maybe we'd go home to a babysitter looking after our kid. Or a beagle. I'd be good either way. Brie would have her own room, preferably one far away from ours and with a private entrance for the ungodly hours she kept, and Dr. Mercer would have her own house keys, a dedicated seat at our table, and a steady supply of her preferred bottle of wine.

Whatever it was, I'd give it to Whit. I'd give her everything I could.

O'Rourke glanced at his watch. "Time for my next act. I gotta shoot my shot with Aldritch tonight."

I almost choked on my beer. "You fucking what?"

He rooted around the nut bowl. "I hit her up about once a month though I haven't gotten any traction. I don't think she's sold on the whole workplace romance thing but I can change her mind."

There was fire in my chest. Burning straight through tendon and bone. I could barely see past the flames. "You won't but I'd like to see you try."

His gaze gradually lifted from the nuts to me. I watched him replaying my words in his head while he studied me, and I knew it was a mistake. I knew I should've choked on the beer and the fire and shoved down every territorial urge rather than walk my way into this kind of quicksand.

But it was out there now and there was no missing what I'd meant.

He shook some nuts around his palm, his brows gathered tight. "At least now I know why I've struck out."

Because I couldn't help myself, I said, "Stop swinging."

He stared at me for an endless moment that twisted my gut into a knot. "Okay, Hazlette. All right. Good thing we straightened that out." He held out the nut hand. "How about I promise to keep it cordial with Dr. A and we never speak of this again? That way you won't have to glare at me like you're thinking of gagging me with my own ball sack?"

I shook his hand harder than necessary. He attempted the same but I had at least thirty pounds of muscle on him and he was smart enough to know it. He made a solid attempt at staring me down but it didn't work. There was nothing in the world more important than Whitney and I didn't care who knew it.

This was new for me. I'd never reacted this way before. Never sensed that I'd actually explode into a ball of fire if I had to watch someone trying to pick up the person I was with. Never wanted to make it as clear as the fucking dawn that someone *belonged* to me. Never felt so much for someone that I was willing to risk everything, including a sweetheart setup in trauma surgery.

Right here, right now, it didn't matter to me if I'd blown it with O'Rourke. It was stupid and irresponsible but I couldn't bring myself to care.

"Good talking to you, then," O'Rourke said, finally pulling away. "We're all right, yeah? I didn't know and"—he tipped his head to the side, his face scrunched like he was trying very hard to hear something—"I don't think it's common knowledge."

"It's not and I'd prefer if you kept it that way." It sounded like a threat.

He scooped the last of the cashews into his hand and tossed them into his mouth. "Yeah. No sweat. So, we're good? You're gonna be my guy. I won't be able to sleep tonight if we're not settled."

My jaw flexed. It was for the best that I hadn't burned this bridge. "We're good."

"Then I'm gonna go find someone else to play doctor with tonight." He bobbed his head as he scanned the kitchen. "See you later, man."

After a fascinating conversation with Acevedo about all the docs who'd lived in my apartment building in recent years, he, Stremmel, and Shapiro included, I realized Whit and Dr. Mercer had left the family room. As I made a pass through the other rooms stuffed with sleep-deprived residents in search of Whit, my phone buzzed.

Whitney

I'm outside. A few doors down, closer to the top of the street. Ordered a car. It'll be here in 10.

Henry

Has anyone ever told you that you're very efficient? It's one of the things I love about you.

Whitney

I hope you're not looking for me to love your lack of efficiency.

Henry

I'm hoping you find other things to love.

To this point, I was always the one who dropped that word first and we only used it with a heavy pour of humor. We were never truly talking about big, serious love. Rather, we were horsing around with the semi-sarcastic things we loved about each other. It was safer that way. Less official.

And I had no problem with this. So far, it was working exactly as intended. The fact that Whit even played along meant I was doing something right. It also felt like I'd ingested a liter of Pop Rocks, which was an experience that split the difference between fun and fucking terrifying.

I said my goodbyes, declined repeated offers to take some leftovers, and got myself up the street. When I approached, I beckoned to her, saying, "Get over here."

She walked into my open arms with a laugh. "What's this all about?"

I tugged on her scarf as I brushed my lips over hers. "I had to listen to O'Rourke talking about how he's been hitting on you for months."

I felt her smile. "And that's my fault?"

"Of course it's not," I said. "I'd just like to get you home and remind you that you're unavailable."

"Oh, am I?"

She was teasing. I knew she was teasing. I still nipped at her bottom lip and slapped her round ass. She yelped and wiggled in my arms, and I held her tighter as I kissed her neck and jaw and that ticklish spot behind her ear that made her crazy.

I looped my arms around her shoulders. "Why didn't you ever tell me about this?"

"Because it didn't matter?" She shook her head, a puzzled expression pulling at her features. "Why would I bother telling you?"

"I can't believe I didn't pick up on it before now," I said. "I knew there was something weird about the way he hugged you at the softball game."

"I believe *I* hugged *him* because he brought an extra shirt for me after I'd left mine at the office."

"And his obsession only grew from there." An impatient noise rose from my throat. "How many people do you have chasing after you? Who else is there? Names, Whitney. Give me the names. I want a list."

"There's no need for another one of your lists." She brought her palms to my face, holding me steady as she stared up at me with bright, wild eyes and our breath mingled into tiny clouds in the cold air. "There is no one else, Henry. After everything we've been through, you know there's no one else."

I backed her up against an SUV parked on the side of the street, one arm locked around her waist while I slipped a hand into her hair and crushed my lips to hers. She tasted the same as she had that very first night, sharp and sweet and unforgettable, and I knew without a stitch of doubt that I loved her.

I loved her the way the dark of night loved the dawn, and just as one always chased the other, I didn't think I'd ever stop chasing her.

A horn honked nearby and I tipped my forehead to hers. "I'm still going to remind you that you're unavailable when we get home. Many, many times."

"I mean, if you have to." She rolled her eyes like this was a major inconvenience to her. Goddamn, I loved this girl. "I guess I can deal with that."

"Good, because—"

Headlights flipped on from the car behind us. I held up a hand to see over the glare and found Tori sitting in the driver seat, Reza beside her and Cami leaning forward from the back. Cami lifted both hands to her face, covering her mouth. Reza blinked furiously. I watched Tori's lips form the words *what the fuck?*

Before I could react, Tori pulled away from the curb and down the street. I stared after her taillights for a moment, not sure what had just happened.

What the fuck was right.

"Henry," Whit said, tugging at my coat. "Come on. Our car's here."

Though I remembered none of it, I was aware that she'd directed me into the car at some point and we were now cruising over the Longfellow Bridge toward Boston.

Whit closed my hand between both of hers, rubbing them together as she said, "They were just surprised. That's all."

I wanted to respond. To agree with her. To believe that I hadn't screwed things up with my team.

"Do you want to call them? It's not too late." She kept rubbing my hand. "Invite them over. You can talk and everything will be—I'm sure it will be fine."

It took a minute to blink away the sand of this shock. "Can we stop at my place?"

"Yeah. Of course."

She dropped a hand to my thigh as she leaned forward to speak with the driver while their reactions played on a loop in my head.

Was it really *that* bad? All this time, it'd never crossed my mind that I should tell them about my relationship with Whit. Especially not during the transplant rotation. And the past month, everything was new and fragile. Even if I'd wanted to, I wasn't sure how to explain this. Did "I met her at my best friend's wedding and then it turned out she was my attending which meant I couldn't touch her and now I don't know how to exist without her" sum it up? Was that an adequate explanation of the past few months?

They'd understand. I knew they would.

Except—

Tori was like a dog with a bone when it came to anything she considered a betrayal. There was a page in her notebook where she kept a list of people who'd crossed her which included the coffee cart guy because he'd once given her oat milk instead of almond.

There'd been a week during the community general rotation when Cami barely spoke to me when she found out I hadn't eaten the curry egg salad she'd made after I let her believe it was great. Egg salad just wasn't my thing. The texture didn't work for me. I couldn't help it.

I didn't know what to think about Reza. Short of insulting one of his cats, I couldn't imagine him having any reaction whatsoever to my personal life, even if it did involve one of our supervisors. But he'd looked stricken. As if I'd gone so far as to suggest dogs were the superior animal.

When we arrived at my building, I led Whit up the front steps and into the vestibule, still sorting this all out in my head. I knew she was watching me closely. I could feel her gaze on the side of my face and I wanted to reassure her but the words stuck in my throat.

I just needed a minute to think and then everything would be fine. A minute to talk some sense into Tori and Cami, and to assure Reza that cats were wonderful. They'd understand because that was what they did. We accepted all the weird, illogical things about each other. Embraced them, even.

If I asked them to accept and embrace my relationship with Whit, they would. Even if they bitched about being the last to know. Even if they asked questions I wasn't ready to answer, like what I'd do if I didn't get a fellowship here or what would happen when Whit was inevitably recruited away to another hospital.

"They'll understand," I said, mostly to myself.

"Yeah, they will."

We climbed the stairs to my third-floor apartment, vaguely aware of music and laughter coming from the other two units. As we rounded the second floor and started up the last leg, I noticed a figure up ahead.

I stopped a few steps from the landing, a hand on Whit's hip. Slumped on the floor with a bottle of liquor tucked between his long legs sat a man who was a very long way from home.

"There you are," Mason drawled, lifting his arm in a sloppy approximation of a wave. "How the hell are ya?"

"I could ask you the same." My stomach sank as the pieces fell into place and I was suddenly aware that, if he was here and diving deep into a bottle of bourbon, we now had much bigger problems than whether I'd pissed off my team tonight.

"Not great, man." Mason pulled himself to his feet as we

approached, still holding the liquor close by. "My marriage is over. Just like you said it would be."

Twenty-One

Henry

Pediatric Surgery Rotation:
Day 6, Week 4

I'd always known Mason's marriage would fall apart.

I'd known when they got engaged and I'd known the first time I showed him the evidence of her infidelity.

I'd known it back when they started dating and Mason swore she was the one because her sister, the woman who handed my attachment issues to me on a platter and dared me to fix them, often let slide Florrie's conflicts with monogamy and how she'd never, ever be content within its confines.

But I hadn't planned on Mason flying all the way to Boston, getting drunk on my doorstep, and telling Whit that I'd flake out on her one of these days because I didn't fuck with relationships.

Thankfully, Mason fell asleep after raiding my cabinets and slept all the way through the next day. When he did wake up, he split his time between sharing uncomfortably sentimental memes on social media, bingeing a few television action series, and ordering an obscene amount of food, even for him. I returned home to find him on the couch, wing sauce all over his face, and Jack Ryan shooting up the bad guys.

By some gift of scheduling and karma, I barely saw my team on Friday. Cami and Tori were both paged to the hospital early to scrub in for procedures, Reza was assigned to babysit a touchy case, and I was shipped off to the ER to work with the peds attending down there.

Save for Reza, who cut me off with "It's not my business and I wish to leave it at that" when I tried to talk to him about what happened outside Acevedo's house, I didn't even get a second with the others. Everyone left for the weekend before I finished in the ER, and when I texted to ask if they were okay, I got a smattering of responses that included a pic of Cami and her husband sharing a donut, a question about next week's conference schedule, and a bunch of random emojis.

I didn't know how to interpret any of that and I didn't have time to worry one way or another because Mason demanded we hit the bars Friday night.

Not a great idea.

I spent the whole night preventing a guy who was roughly the size of a grizzly bear from picking fights with every other drunken fool in Boston because he was full of feelings and didn't know what to do with them.

We were escorted out of three bars, left before management got involved at two others, and narrowly avoided a chat with the cops at another two. Mason made it back to my building with only a few busted knuckles and a bloodied but not broken nose that would result in some gross bruising.

The stairs, however, presented many problems to him.

We sat on the floor in the foyer for an hour while the nausea and dizziness passed. Mason told me about some of his recent expeditions and the state of the snowpack in the Sierras. It was shaping up to be a heavy year.

When we finally arrived at my apartment, he flopped down on the couch and didn't move again until this morning. He was hungover as hell and both eyes were bagged and bruised, but he didn't complain about coming with me to meet Whit for breakfast.

"It would be really cool if you didn't say anything weird to Whitney about how I'm trash at relationships," I said as we walked toward the café. "I'd consider it a pretty big favor."

"When did you start chasing women?" he asked, his voice still rough from last night.

"When I found one worth chasing."

"But you're the president and founder of the Love Isn't Worth It club. What the hell happened?"

"People change," I said. "I've changed."

"Didn't mention any changes to me."

"I've had a lot going on," I said, hoping that was adequate. I rounded on him, holding up a hand before we crossed the street. "I would really appreciate it if you didn't tell Whitney that I'm probably going to fuck it all up one of these days and ruin everything. Okay? Just keep those details to yourself for now."

He threw his arms around me and swallowed me up in a bear hug. "What are you talkin' about? You're not gonna fuck anything up. That fancy girl likes you a whole damn lot."

I wanted to believe all of that.

We found Whit and Brie seated at a table inside the café, both staring at their phones. Brie looked like she'd been chewing on something bitter all morning and Whit looked like she'd had to hear about it.

Spending time with Whit meant I'd learned pretty quickly that Brie controlled the weather. For the most part, Brie did her own thing and paid little attention to her sister, but when the winds changed, everyone knew it.

Whit startled when I trailed my fingers across her shoulder blades, then pulled me down for a hug. "I've missed you," she whispered.

God, I loved this fancy girl.

I pressed a quick kiss to her lips. "Missed you too."

Mason lingered behind me, taking in the black and white décor and eyeing the locals like he didn't recognize this species. He liked everyone and everywhere, but if presented with a choice, he'd never choose city living. If I asked him what he thought of this place, he'd probably tell me it was too damn loud. As if his favorite taverns and sports bars back home were library quiet.

"You've met Whitney," I reminded him as I dropped a hand on her shoulder. "And this is Brie."

Mason cupped his ear as he held out his hand to her. "Sorry, didn't catch that. It's loud in here, right? Did he say Ree? Or Tree?"

She pushed out of her seat to reach his hand. "Brie," she said, tapping her chest. "Like the cheese."

"I'm Mason," he said, still clutching her hand. "Like...the jar."

Brie blinked up at him. "And quite a tall jar you are."

"I'm—what?" Mason stared at her. There was a good chance he hadn't heard her. The espresso machines were pretty noisy. He dropped into the chair across from her. "Have you always lived here?"

"I don't even live here now," she replied. "I'm still deciding where I want to be."

I settled across from Whit while Brie and Mason launched into a conversation about neither of them enjoying this city much. It was a good thing, seeing as he was no longer welcome at many of Boston's bars.

"How did it go yesterday?" Whit asked.

I gathered her hands in mine as I shook my head. "I didn't really see anyone."

"I told you that would happen." She grinned. She loved being right. It was hard for me to find fault because she made gloating look good. "Do you feel better?"

"Maybe? I don't know. Everything feels off." I passed her my phone to read through the text exchange. "Does that make any sense to you?"

"If either of them was upset or had something to say to you," she said, scrolling back and forth through the messages, "they would've done that. Those two don't bite their tongues."

"But then why did they look so upset the other night? And why did Tori speed off like that?"

She shrugged. "I don't know, but isn't it possible they're over it now?"

"Hey, we're going to order," Brie said as she and Mason stood up. "What do you guys want?"

"I want the muesli bowl," Whit said, "and Henry wants two breakfast sandwiches with extra bacon."

Yeah, I *really* loved this girl, and one of these days she'd be ready to hear those words from me.

As they left, Whit caught my hand and brushed her thumb over a bruise on my knuckles. "What happened here?"

"That's where I stopped Mason from taking a header into a bar last night."

"Which bar did you go to?"

"All of them," I said. "And I'm not allowed back at a few." When she frowned, I shifted gears. She didn't need the gory details. "I talked to Stremmel and O'Rourke the other night. They're working on adding an extra trauma rotation to my schedule for next year."

She laced our fingers together, her delicate rings sliding against my skin. "You're one of them now."

"Why do you sound disappointed about that? You want me back on transplant?"

"Not for a single minute, no." The hard flash of her hazel eyes made me laugh. "Though I'll be seeing plenty of you over there. Your patients have a way of becoming donors for my patients."

I sucked in a breath. "We're going straight into the dark humor this morning?"

"No reason not to."

I glanced down at our joined hands. I'd spent all night thinking about her. *Missing* her. The only reason my hand was bruised was because I'd drifted away into my own world of *What if I just asked her to marry me right now?* and had overlooked Mason getting into it with some dude over college basketball, of all things. The entire time we'd been sitting in the foyer, my mind was busy constructing a world where she knew I'd never leave her, where she knew I'd always stay for her.

On the other side of the café, a coffee bean grinder kicked into high gear and a baby started howling. I blinked in that direction, unseeing.

What if I asked right now? What if we stopped wasting time and took the plunge without looking back? If Stremmel and

Shapiro could pull it off, surely we could too. And then what would happen? Who would we be when it was just the two of us and none of the tension we'd carried in one shape or another for months?

Maybe I'd still fuck it up. Every step was a fumble in the dark. Maybe I just wanted to hide out in the quiet peace of her arms forever and avoid all the problems pressing in around me. Maybe—

"Let's get out of here."

"What? And abandon our charges?"

I glanced at Mason and Brie as they waited. They seemed to be debating something about the menu. Or whatever else they'd stumbled onto.

"I never told him about going to therapy." I wasn't sure why I said that but it was out before I could think better of it. "I didn't say anything about it when I started because I wanted to be able to quit without anyone giving me shit about it." I turned her wrist over and rubbed her palm. "So, yeah, he knows the version of me that treated relationships like minefields. He doesn't know that I put work into fixing that shit."

Whit was quiet for a long moment. I went on working her abductor muscle. All that surgical efficiency made her hands tight.

She nodded like she accepted this. Like it all made sense even when it didn't make sense to me. "I talked to my mom after I left your place. She told me I couldn't trust anyone except myself."

"You can trust me."

She twisted a finger around her necklaces as a shy smile bloomed on her face. It made me feel like gravity had given out and I was about to fly off into space, and that would be fine because I could exist for lifetimes on the warmth of one smile.

"Change of plans." Brie dropped a tray to the table, sending coffee sloshing out of cups and breakfast sandwiches toppling. "I'm going to meet some people at a lawn bowling tournament in Somerville. I told Mason he can come if he wants."

And now Whit's warm smile was gone.

"You're—what?" Whit glanced between Mason and Brie where they stood beside the table, apparently united in their newborn plan. "Did you say lawn...*bowling*?"

"Yeah, it's just a few stops on the Green Line, and don't worry, I'm not asking you to come along." Brie grabbed a paper bag from the tray and fished out a scone. Pointing to it, she said, "Before you get yourself all worked up, these are chocolate chips. Not raisins or blueberries. Totally safe for me."

Whit looked like she wanted to strangle her sister with that scone. "Fantastic."

Before I could remind him to stay away from alcohol and social media, Mason said, "Don't worry, man. I'll behave."

"Bold stance for a guy with two black eyes," I said.

"Gotta start somewhere. First day of the rest of my life or something like that." Mason raised his coffee cup in salute. "Catch you later."

We watched them weave through the busy café and out onto the sidewalk, neither of us speaking for a moment.

Whit cleared her throat. "That's probably fine. Right? They're fine."

Was I going to disagree with her now, when I was starved for her undivided attention? Not for a fucking minute. "Yeah," I said, all confidence. "Of course. What's the worst that could happen?"

She grimaced and gave me *I can't deal with that* hands. "Let's not open the door to those kinds of questions."

"Yes, ma'am." I reached for her coffee and mopped up the spill down one side. I wiped off the lid's opening and set it in front of her before reassembling the sandwiches.

"You always do that," she said, almost to herself. "Don't you?" She pointed to the cup. "Whenever you leave coffee on my desk, it's tidy like that. Not even a drop on the lid. I didn't think about it until now."

The back of my neck heated. I stared down at the sandwich. "If I'm bringing you coffee, I'm not leaving a mess on your desk."

Whit leaned in, her arms folded in front of her. "What do you say we take this to go?"

"I'd say you have excellent ideas." I met her gaze. "Love that about you."

Twenty-Two

Whitney

Rule Number Two:
Gift generously.

"Not that this isn't great," Henry said, gesturing to the smooth surface of Jamaica Pond with his coffee cup, "but I thought you had something a little more private in mind. Your bedroom, for example."

"The weather is ridiculously good." I scraped the last of my yogurt from the bowl. "And I need to work out some tension."

"I can relieve your tension. Trust me on that."

Two boulder-sized balls of stress had parked themselves on my chest, and while I knew sex would shake them off for a time, they'd be right there waiting for me when it was over.

"Let's take a walk." I gathered up the remains of our breakfast. "Then we can get into bedroom activities."

We started around the trail with an unseasonably warm sun shining down on us and our hands clasped together. We were quiet for the first few minutes and that silence let me breathe deeply for the first time all morning.

Brie had started the day with another appeal for me to join the meeting she'd planned with our father. He'd be in town late next week. She insisted that leaving her to do this alone would be a betrayal. That she'd never do anything like that to me.

"This would be a perfect time," Henry started, "for you to tell me what's bothering you today."

Another minute or two passed before deciding that I could share this with Henry and a few more before I figured out where to start. "My father has never been in the picture. Not even for a minute. But Brie got a hold of him, don't ask me how, and she wants me to come with her to meet him. Next week."

"What do you want?"

I laughed loud enough to startle a few birds into flight. Did it even matter what I wanted? Not to Brie. That was obvious. "I'm not interested in meeting him, but Brie has asked for my support."

He chuckled, running his thumb over my knuckles. "How is it that you scare the shit out of the entire surgical wing on a daily basis but you let your little sister hold you emotionally hostage?"

"Wow. Okay." A breath whooshed out of me. "That was direct."

We neared the bend where the trail followed a small peninsula into the pond. "You don't have to go, Whit."

I nodded. I knew this. I knew I had a choice even if Brie refused to see it that way. "I know."

"But you're going to."

"Probably," I said miserably. "The thing is, Henry, I don't want her to do this alone. I wouldn't want anyone to do it alone. But I don't want to sit through what will inevitably be an all-around train wreck of toxicity."

"I'll go with you."

"No, you have better things to worry about than the live-action performance of my family's ongoing paternity drama. You're going into general surgery starting on Monday and I'd bet anything that Emmerling has the week packed top to bottom." He had the audacity to look at me like I was exaggerating. As if I didn't know exactly how hard Alexandra Emmerling worked her residents. "Trust me on this. She's going to kick your ass."

"I'm sure I can handle it. I did survive your service, you know, and there was no shortage of ass-kickings there."

"You're going to be busier than you think."

"Then I'll wear my running shoes," he said. "But promise me one thing. If you do meet your father, call me when it's over. I'll come get you. You're not allowed to go home alone."

That sounded so much like the promise Meri and I made to each other to never cry alone. My chest pinched. "I promise."

"That's all I need."

We walked a few more minutes in comfortable silence. It was easier now that I only had one boulder weighing me down. "So, now that your cohort knows—"

"I don't think they'll mention it to anyone," he said quickly. "But that is one of the things I want to talk to them about. It's weird, right? We've lived in each other's pockets since July, but the only response I get is some emojis and a donut photo."

"And the question about the hepatobiliary conference."

"Can't forget that," he muttered. "And we didn't even celebrate the end of the peds rotation. It's weird."

"I'd agree with you if it wasn't a holiday weekend." I chose my next words carefully. "No elevators for us this week."

"We're going back to avoidance?"

I couldn't miss the bitterness in his words. In all fairness, I was just as bitter. I was tired of calculating the exact minute when I could safely reach for his hand when we left the hospital every night. I was tired of going to Acevedo's Thanksgiving party and acting like we weren't going home together. I was tired of constantly crafting and revising a version of myself that was suitable for the consumption of everyone else but failed to meet my basic needs.

"Just for a bit," I managed. "We can stay away from each other until things settle down."

Henry stopped walking and pulled me into his arms. His lips found my neck as I twined my arms around his broad shoulders. He really was a whole mountain range. "But what if you got lost?"

"If I got *lost*?"

"Yeah. What if you wandered into those woods over there and got lost? What if I happened to find you? I am highly skilled in wilderness rescue. Would I still have to stay away?"

"I guess not." I ran my fingers through his hair and I was hit with a memory of the night we spent together in Tahoe. I hadn't been able to keep my hands out of his hair. It was soft and wavy, and every time I pulled, his eyes would darken and he'd get even more wild. "It's not like I meant to get lost."

"Of course you didn't." He held me tight, groaning into my skin. Then he slapped my backside and said, "All right then. On your way. Pay no attention to the trail, and if a wolf tries to eat you, well, I can promise it will work out very well for you."

A giggle slipped over my lips as he smacked me again, pointing to the trees beyond the paved walking path. I had no idea what was happening. "Wait. What are we doing?"

"You have five minutes to get lost. Three if I remember that I haven't woken up with your ass in my lap for days."

I flattened my palms on his chest. "That sounds a little"—I swallowed an entire stress boulder—"risky."

He brought his hands to his waist as he stared down at me, tapping his fingers against his belt the way he always did when he needed a minute to think. I liked that I knew his mannerisms now, his quirks. Like the way his brows arched and his lips curled and all his different smiles. The way his scruffy jaw tightened and clenched and the way it felt under my palm. The way his entire expression could shift from light to dark, and all the things that meant.

"If you don't want to get lost in the woods, Whit, you shouldn't go in there."

I took a step back when his words sank in. I nodded, shoving my hands in my jacket pockets. "You're right."

He understood my boundaries. He respected my limits. He heard me when I spoke. He cared about the things that were important to me. And that was why I walked right off the trail and into the woods.

It was a damn good thing I'd chosen running shoes this morning because I never would've made it in booties or anything with a heel. A real wilderness rescue would've been required within a minute.

It was darker in here, the canopy letting in fingers of light where the trees had given up their leaves. And it was quiet, the hum of the city fading away even more than on the trail.

I didn't have a lot of experience with outdoorsy things, especially of the walking-in-woods variety, but I kept going. We were in the middle of Boston after all. There had to be a street on the other side of this.

While I was busy wondering where I'd end up if I did wander all the way through these woods, I failed to notice my wolf sneaking up behind me.

His arms came around my waist, pressing my back into his chest while I let loose a startled shriek. A hand covered my mouth and he leaned down to speak into my ear. "Can you be quiet for me?"

My pulse was hammering in my throat. I nodded. I didn't know what I was agreeing to with that, but I knew I was safe with Henry—and that realization hit me harder than anything else that happened today. I trusted Henry, just as he'd told me I could.

He dropped his lips to my jaw and I stopped thinking. "That's what I thought," he said, his words growled into my skin. "You're coming with me."

He led me deeper into the woods, my hand swallowed up inside his. "Is this your kink? Chasing people through a forest?"

"My kink is doing anything to get you alone," he said. "And I didn't chase you. I found you. There's a difference." He pulled me behind a huge, grand tree. The trunk was so wide, Henry wouldn't be able to get his arms halfway around. "Now, come here."

My back met the bark and I reached for him, but he was already there, gathering me up and holding me close as our lips met. It was frantic and a little violent—I nipped him twice without meaning to—but I couldn't help myself. I couldn't stop it. I couldn't stop this any more than I could stop the final leaves of autumn from fluttering down around us.

"I've missed you," he said into the corner of my mouth.

"I've missed you too." I shoved my hand down the back of his shirt, trailing my palm over the muscles bunched and coiled there.

He scraped his teeth over my bottom lip as he rocked into me, his shaft thick and hard against my belly. He reached under my jacket and sweater, tracing the waistband of my leggings. "Missed talking to you," he said between kisses. "Missed seeing you when I wake up. Didn't even see you in the elevators this week."

"Those elevators. They're going to get us in trouble one of these days."

"That won't happen."

"You're going to start taking the stairs?"

He shook his head against my shoulder. "I won't touch you there. You've worked too hard and everyone respects you too much. I'm not going to fuck it up like that."

"That's the hottest thing anyone has ever said to me."

"Haven't you noticed? Everyone admires the hell out of you."

"Not everyone," I murmured, running a hand down his torso.

"Because they're intimidated. You get that, right? I'll explain it if I have to but I'd rather do disrespectful things to you."

I knew I had to tell him about the weddings today though there was no reason the cringey confession couldn't wait until after the disrespectful things.

He dipped his fingers beneath my leggings and his lips wobbled into a half smile as he said, "Um, excuse me, ma'am, but where the hell are your undies?"

"Must've forgotten them at home."

The words had barely left my tongue before his lips were on mine, kissing me like he wanted to make this the only kiss I remembered for a long, long time. He moved his hand to my hip and then between my legs, his fingers closing over me but not moving. Waiting for me to be ready.

"Whit...*please.*" He dragged a finger along my seam and he had to swallow my moan with another bruising kiss. "Your pussy is dripping all over my hand."

"Do you say that to all your attendings?"

He squeezed me hard enough that I couldn't stop myself from rocking into his hand. It was all I could do to relieve the ache gathered low inside me. "The inappropriate humor is another thing I love about you."

"That, plus all the chicken surgeries and inside info on how to survive your rotations."

"We both know that the only way I'd ever get preferential treatment from you was if I needed a new heart."

As he drew lazy, maddening circles around my clit, I gripped his hair tight, my lips never more than a breath from his. "I like your heart. Don't make me find you a new one."

"Shh. I'm rescuing you. Let me do this."

He pulled my knee to his hip and pushed two fingers inside me, his thumb still teasing the life out of my clit, and it was just about enough. I was right there, teetering on the edge, and if I allowed it, this would be over within a minute or two.

"I don't need to be rescued." I said this while gasping and clinging to him like I wanted to tie myself to him in a way that would never break.

He covered my lips with his as he went hunting for my orgasm. "You don't need it," he said, his thumb tormenting me in the best way, "but I want it. Let me do this."

I didn't know why that snapped my restraint in half, but I couldn't hold back anymore. Couldn't stop the swell of sensation inside me any more than I could stop the gravity that had me falling and falling and falling for this man. That was it. This was what it felt like to fall. I could see every moment all the way back to the first time his gaze fell on mine, but I didn't know what would come next or where I'd land.

I didn't know how that was possible. I didn't believe in this kind of love. I didn't believe in *falling*.

A sob broke free from my chest as my body shuddered, all this tension finally breaking free, but Henry didn't let up. He stroked me through the hardest pulses and, when I'd caught my breath again, he pressed a slow kiss to my lips and dropped to his knees.

I grabbed his shoulders. "What? No. *Wait.* You don't—"

"Shut up, Whit."

He edged my leggings down just enough to swipe his tongue over my clit. I cried out in a way that must've sent some kind of signal to the wildlife because it seemed like all the birds started chirping at once.

My grip on his shoulders was brutal but I didn't dare let go. I was certain I'd fall over—in the woods, with my ass hanging out, while the birds were talking about me—but more importantly, he had me on the edge once again. A little more pressure was all I needed.

A little more pressure and—and *I could feel his cock on my leg.* My god. Why did that turn me on so much? I shifted my leg, giving him the soft inside of my thigh. He rocked into me and groaned against my clit. It struck me like a wave of tiny, pin-prick orgasms.

He kept one arm locked around my waist because he was well aware that he made it difficult to stand, and brought his free hand between my thighs. His fingers coasted over me, gentle at first and then spearing inside me as he thrust hard against my leg. When my back bowed and I was bent over him, convulsing and crying out and tearing at his shirt, I wondered for one fleeting moment how this had happened.

How had I ended up in a *forest* with my *former resident* and my *ass* out? And more importantly, how had this gone from a one-night stand to a cautionary tale to a story that sounded impossible to my ears and absolutely right to my heart?

I pulled at Henry's shoulders when my vision cleared, dragging him to where I wanted him with unsteady hands. He stumbled up to me, his lips shiny with my arousal, his hands everywhere at once, his hips rocking into my belly.

"What do you need, gorgeous?" he rumbled, his arms closing tight around me and his mouth on my neck. "I'll give you anything."

All at once, I knew that was the truth and it would never change.

So, I did the only reasonable thing and stuck my hand down his jeans. He was hot and just as thick as always, and his breath caught in his throat as I stroked him.

"Wait, wait, wait," he said, taking hold of my wrist. "Whitney. Slow down, baby."

"It's your turn," I said, fumbling with the buckle on his belt and loosening his button-fly. I *loved* his button-fly jeans. There was no logic to it, no reason, but the filthy little sex monster I kept tucked away in my mind didn't care about those things.

"It's not about turns—oh, *fuuuuck.*" His grip on my wrist relaxed just a touch. "You don't have to do this."

I loved the weight of him in my palm, the hungry jerk of his hips. I loved the way he growled every time I twisted my hand up to his cockhead and shoved it down to the base. I never thought I'd like that, the growling, but I loved it. "I know. I want to."

"If you keep that up, this is going to be over real fast."

"Sounds fair," I said. "Considering."

His laugh turned into a starved groan and he covered my hand with his. I listened as his breathing turned ragged, his chest rising and falling against my shoulder, and I watched as we stroked him together. He dropped his other hand to the back of my neck, squeezing as we stroked down.

"I love this about you," he said, his words strained. "I love—"

Before I could do anything with those words, he buried his face in my shoulder and shifted his hips away just enough so I didn't end up wearing his orgasm.

"The birds are going to talk about this," I said.

"What...what did you say?"

I decided to keep that one to myself. "Nothing. It's fine."

"I haven't said this in at least twenty years," he rasped, his lips pressed to the tender spot below my ear, "but that was an incredible hand job."

I dug in my pocket to find something to help him clean up. I found a pair of nitrile gloves and some gauze. "Here." I unfolded the gauze. "This might help."

He glanced at me, his brows pinched. "Do you keep gauze in all of your pockets?"

"You don't? It comes in handy." I motioned between us. "Right now, for instance."

Henry accepted the gauze while I straightened my leggings. He stared at me as he buttoned his jeans and fastened his belt, and something in that stare poured over me like liquid heat, warming everything it touched.

"It's a good thing I finally found you," he said.

I bobbed my head. "Yeah. It is."

"I always will."

If ever there was a sign that the time for keeping slightly awkward secrets was over, that was it. I'd done the math on all the different ways this could go down and I felt confident that we'd be okay in the end but it'd be a strange ride getting there.

With frantic, flappy hands, I motioned between us. "Yeah, so, can I tell you something weird?"

A laugh shook out of him. His cheeks were flushed and he still looked a little dazed. God, he was so sweet. "You can tell me anything you want, Whit."

"About the wedding," I said carefully. "I don't know Florrie's family. We weren't actually supposed to be there."

He pushed a hand through his hair. "What does that mean?"

"Meri and I, we—well, the thing is, we plan vacations every summer and go to a bunch of weddings as uninvited guests."

Henry stared at me, tapping his fingers on his belt and blinking not even once. "You crash weddings?"

I clasped my hands in front of me. "Yes."

"You weren't on the guest list. Because you weren't invited." He said this mostly to himself as he brought his palm to the back of his neck. He was silent for longer than I could withstand and then, shaking his head like he really couldn't believe I'd do something like that, he asked, "Why?"

"Uh, well, it's amusing. There's that. Good parties, good times. And cake, as you're aware. And we, um"—I rolled my hand between us in a gesture that I hoped he interpreted as *girls just wanna have fun*—"often make new friends by the end of the night."

His jaw fell to the forest floor. "You go on vacation to crash weddings and have sex?"

"That is a highly distilled way to phrase it but yes."

"Wait a minute. You crashed a wedding and had sex with me!"

I bobbed my head at least five hundred times. "Yeah, that's what occurred that night."

He ran his knuckles along his scruffy jaw and turned in a circle. "And Dr. Mercer is in on this? She was there too?"

"It's her ball game. She plans the whole thing. She finds the weddings, stalks the websites and social accounts, and—"

He whirled around to face me. "Did you target me? For sex?"

"Oh my god! No!" I jabbed a finger at him. "*You* were the one who came over to talk to *me*."

He dropped his fists to his waist. "Sweetheart, please. You had me eating out of the palm of your hand long before I cornered you at the cupcake table."

"I didn't target you," I said, still bristling about that. "I was supposed to stay far away from you because the bridal party is always off-limits. We have rules, you know. We adhere to a code."

"Of course you do." He stared down at the ground. "That's why you left? That morning? Because you had other weddings to crash?"

"Mason's was our last wedding. We went to a resort outside of Wine Country and hung out by the pool for a few days before flying home. We always end our trips with just the two of us together."

A grumble sounded in his throat. "So, you were *really* surprised to see me again."

"Oh, yeah. My entire life flashed before my eyes that day. I practically hyperventilated in Meri's office."

He bent at the waist, dropping his hands to his knees. "Is there anything else I should know? Any other secret lives you haven't mentioned?"

"That's the only one."

Henry pushed to his full height and stared at me long enough that I started to wonder whether I'd miscalculated. Perhaps this bridge, the one I'd crossed for years and years without question, was too far for him. Perhaps I was asking him to rewrite too much history or ignore the gray areas. And perhaps he saw me in a new, unflattering light that turned all the trust and faith we had into ash.

If that was the case, if this really was our breaking point, then I'd have to accept it because I couldn't change these things and—

Henry scooped me up and backed me against the tree. My legs went around his waist as his lips found mine. "I can't decide if I'm more confused or impressed by this revelation but I do know that you're the best thing to come out of Mason's wedding." He dragged my bottom lip between his teeth. "But I need two more promises from you."

"That seems fair."

He arched a brow. "Wait until you hear them first." His hips pressing between my legs like a promise all of its own, he said, "One, we're not mentioning this to Mason just yet. He'll find it funny as hell in six months. Maybe a year. This, right now, is not the moment to drop that news. And two, if you're crashing weddings this summer, I want to be the only one you target for sex."

We hadn't stopped to assign labels to this or define where we were going. Who had the time? And why would we bother when there was a possibility we'd get it out of our systems anyway? Not that Henry cared much for that theory but it'd lingered in my mind until—well, until very recently, now that I thought about it.

I couldn't decide whether it was the empty space where my reaction to Henry's cohort catching us should've been or the realization that, despite everything, I was falling for this man, but now I knew there was no getting this out of my system.

So, it brought me no pain to say, "I promise."

Twenty-Three

Henry

General Surgery Rotation:
Day 3, Week 1

I refused to admit this to Whit for another week or two but Alex Emmerling ran her service like it was a battle-ready brigade. I wouldn't be surprised to learn she was descended from Julius Caesar. Or whoever it was from the Roman Empire that did the most conquering.

The woman was nonstop though the thing that set her apart from other attendings was that nothing was sacred in general surgery. Cohorts, for example. First thing on day one, she divided us up and shipped us off to work with groups of more senior residents. Under this regime, I barely saw Tori, Reza, or Cami outside of rounds and I hadn't yet managed to talk to any of them about what happened last week. I went to work every day with a plan to get a few minutes with them and every day, I succeeded at nothing.

Another thing about Emmerling: she was one tough cookie.

Tori would whip me with her stethoscope for referring to our attending as a cookie but I'd stand behind that assessment. Emmerling invited us to join her for lunch on Thursdays, schedules permitting. She was warm and friendly, and seemed genuinely engaged in helping us learn. And she threw me out of her OR on Monday for not being able to answer a highly specific and arguably unknowable question. She kicked residents off cases for making her wait too long for info during rounds. She provided feedback that was clear and specific but there was so much of it that my pen ran out of ink yesterday while trying to write it all down. And it was a fairly new pen.

Even if I was standing in the back of an OR, Emmerling never stopped tossing out questions or posing scenarios. There were no slow moments, no downtime. Whit said I fell asleep the second my head hit the pillow last night.

She recounted that with an *I told you so* gleam in her eye this morning. I promised a better showing tonight and I intended to make good on that even though we both knew the odds of me showing up on her door dog-tired and mentally zapped were high.

That was why I made some questionable decisions with espresso shots at the coffee cart this afternoon. Smart? Probably not. Effective? I fucking hoped so. I wasn't about to be that guy who passed out on her night after night. I wouldn't keep going to her place after work if I couldn't stay awake long enough to at least give her some attention. It didn't have to be sex. I was happy hearing about her procedures and her weekly lunch date with Dr. Mercer. I could listen while she complained about Brie's plan to meet their father. I'd listen to any random thing that crossed her mind. I wanted to be with her and I wanted her to feel like being with me was worth her time.

And I liked the way she always nestled up next to me in the

night. I woke up with her wrapped around me or tucked into my lap every morning. I couldn't get enough of it.

I also wanted to give Mason as much space as possible. He was doing all right, far better than his first few drunken and disastrous days here. He had a lot of decisions on his hands and he'd made it clear he needed to process those on his own. I'd discovered this when I asked about his day and he told me that he had enough problems without me hovering.

So. That was where we were with that.

Over the weekend, Whit pushed me to get Mason in touch with an attorney. She passed along a name, someone who was a vascular surgeon's wife and willing to carve out some time as a favor to Whit. Mason got some good advice and a referral to a lawyer who could help him back home, and that was handy seeing as Florrie let him know that she filed for divorce.

I assumed it was her father who'd moved that process along. He never liked Mason. He wanted more for Florrie—whatever *more* was to him.

Regardless of the family drama and the mess of this whole thing, I still couldn't comprehend how simple it was to end a marriage. Maybe it was naïve of me but it seemed like it should take more than a few signatures to end something that was supposed to last a lifetime.

For all that it was worth, Florrie apologized when she called to tell him about starting the divorce proceedings. Apparently, she regretted the way it all happened and she said she didn't mean to hurt him. She mentioned nothing about all the lying she'd done previously but I had to give her credit for being honest now. Mostly because Mason appreciated the call. He believed she was sorry. He told me she sounded genuine.

I decided to let that be. I'd never managed to change his opinions on Florrie anyway.

Henry
Just finished here. Is it too late?

Whitney
No. Come over.

Henry
You should be in bed, young lady.

Whitney
I am in bed.

Henry
Say no more. I'm on my way.

Whitney
Let yourself in.

Henry
Believe me, I will.

I FOUND WHIT PROPPED UP AGAINST HER PILLOWS, A book resting on her legs and my fleece zipped up to her throat. Her face was shiny from the nighttime oils and creams she used and her hair was tucked over her ears. She looked warm and sleepy and wonderful. I loved everything about it but more than that, I loved coming home to her at the end of the day.

I pulled my shirt over my head and dropped it to the floor. "You didn't have to wait up for me."

She lifted a shoulder. "Mmm. I wanted to." Her gaze dipped to my waist as I unbuckled my belt. I nearly choked when she ran the tip of her tongue along her upper lip. "Salas came in today with her baby. Did you see them?"

"Yep." I kicked off my pants. Her brows lifted. "Salas made me hold the kid while she went to the bathroom. Some things never change."

She laughed. "Did you notice how the baby isn't named Whitney? Not even the middle name either."

"Hate to break it to you, honey, but you were never going to win that one." I set her book on the nightstand and I brought my hands to her face, cupping her jaw and sliding my fingers into her hair. I bent down to kiss her. "Hi."

Her eyes brightened with a smile. "Hi."

"Where's Brie?"

"Out somewhere. A pop-up thing with some friends. Did you find time to talk to Cami and Tori?"

"I didn't even see them today. It's like we're on different planets."

"If they had a problem, they'd tell you. I think it's going to be all right."

"You're right." I wanted to believe she was right. I tugged at the zipper on the fleece. "Get this out of my way." A moment passed where we stared at each other before she pulled the zipper down. She was bare underneath. Loved it. "Much better."

"It would be better if you got under the covers with me."

I pressed a kiss to her forehead and the tops of both breasts. "Tell me what I'm going to do to you under those covers."

Laughing, she said, "I don't have a plan. I just want—"

"No plan? How inefficient." I plugged in her phone and then mine. Switched off the lamp. Checked my alarm. Took off my watch. Rounded the bed. As soon as I slipped between the sheets, I yanked her across the bed and into my arms. "I expect more from you, Dr. Aldritch."

She reached for me, palming my cock over my boxers. "I'll do better next time."

I drew circles around her nipples while I kissed the line of her shoulder. "You're so soft right here." I gave her a light pinch. "Love that about you."

Whit pushed my boxers down and pulled me on top of her. She settled her hands on my sides as she opened her legs. "I missed you today. Last night too."

I rocked against her. She was hot and wet, and once again, I was *stunned* that I'd found her. That this woman existed in my life against the most ridiculous of odds was almost unbelievable. There were moments when I just didn't believe that I could keep her. "I missed you too. Sorry about last night."

"You're not allowed to apologize for that. It's residency."

"I'm gonna do it anyway." I pushed inside her with a groan they must've heard down the street. "*Fuck*, Whit. Don't kill me all at once, honey."

She let out a sleepy laugh as I gripped the soft flare of her hip. "I love when you're all over me like this. When you—when you just hold me down and all I can do is take it."

I answered that with a slow, heavy thrust that had her back bowing off the bed. "Do you want to get married?"

She blinked up at me. "Do I—what?"

"Someday," I added, although today would work too. "Do you want to get married someday?"

Another blink. "Maybe. I don't know. Do you?"

We stared at each other as I drove into her. As she cried out. As her nails sank into my biceps. "I think so."

She curled a hand around the back of my neck and pulled me down for a kiss. "Someday," she whispered.

I leaned down to tease her nipples for a minute. It was that or asking her to marry me right now. I didn't want to ask until I was positive she'd say yes.

I ran a hand from her jaw down around her neck, over her breasts, and along the line of her torso to her belly. I lingered there a moment before sliding over her clit. "Do you want to have kids? Someday?"

She rocked up against me as I thrummed her clit. "I haven't really thought about it."

On a gasp, she broke apart and all I could do was follow. I growled into her neck as my body coiled tight and heat blasted through me. "Killing me here, honey."

Whit murmured some sleepy, sated response as I collapsed on top of her. We stayed like that for a few minutes while my heart banged around in my chest. She held me tight, her hands mapping my back and shoulders. Eventually, she escaped to the bathroom. It took everything in me to stay awake until she returned.

When she did, she curled up beside me with her head tucked under my chin. A few minutes passed before she asked, "Do *you* want kids? Someday?"

I could've given her an oblique answer. I could've made it sound like I wasn't talking about our life a few years from now. But I didn't want to do that anymore. "I want what you want."

"Was it Salas's baby? Is that what made you think of this?"

"No, Whitney. It wasn't."

"Then—"

"Shh." I kissed her temple. Another word out of her and I was going to throw myself on the floor, naked and half dazed from that orgasm, and beg her to marry me. "Someday."

Twenty-Four

Whitney

Rule Number Seventeen:
Be kind to everyone. You'll get away with more.

"This is a nice place, don't you think?" Brie bounced her knee under the table. The ice in my drink clattered against the glass from the force. "It's nice but still casual. I wanted something casual. There are too many uptight, stuffy places in this city."

I glanced around the hotel bar. It was newer; everything in the Seaport District was newer. And I couldn't comment on whether it was any better than other hotel bars. I'd stayed in one hotel in Boston, which was an old jail of all things and that was when I flew in to interview for my job.

I forced a smile. "It's great." I desired as little information on the subject as possible, but I still asked, "Is he staying here?"

She never stopped scanning the room, her fingers twisting and tangling together. "I don't know. He didn't mention it."

I leaned back and crossed my legs. We were a few minutes early, and though I knew next to nothing about this man, I fully expected him to show up late. What was ten minutes when he was already thirty-five years late?

I plowed through emails while we waited. There was a year-end staff survey coming up and it had a couple of questions about the professional standards. I was bracing for the worst. I knew the board of directors wouldn't walk back this initiative, but it wouldn't help anything if it was widely panned.

When I closed out of my email app, I realized our sperm donor was almost fifteen minutes late. Brie was still simmering in her seat. I opened my texts rather than commenting on either situation. Everyone was trying to coordinate holiday gatherings and I was at least thirty messages behind in the group chats.

When I set my phone down again, Brie hadn't touched her drink and he was now fifty-three minutes late. She'd gnawed off her lip color and started twisting her necklace hard enough to leave red welts around her throat.

I knew it wasn't a smart idea to rattle this cage, but I said, "Do you think we should—"

"Where's Henry tonight?" she asked.

As predicted, general surgery was kicking his ass. It was fun to watch. "He's finishing up a procedure and then he'll be in post-op for a bit."

I was thankful his schedule had worked out this way. I loved that I could lean on him for crazy, messy things like this, but I also wanted to be able to process it on my own first. I needed a minute to figure it all out and put the pieces away in an order that I could manage before I could even consider reaching out for him.

"Do you think you guys will move in together? You basically live together already. Or you have for the past month. No, it's been longer, hasn't it? Maybe six weeks? Seven? I can't keep track of your life but it's been a while. Are you thinking about getting a new place or staying where you are? It's a cute spot but it's small and he's a big guy. Hmmm. Are you going to get married? I feel like you'd be into more of a nontraditional wedding. Would you even wear white? No veil, obviously. Have you thought about any of it?"

Brie rambled on, her words flying out so fast that I couldn't possibly keep up—and that was the point. The more she spoke, the less room there was for us to acknowledge that our father was more than fashionably late.

I nodded while she explained all the reasons why an oatmeal-colored wedding dress would be "divine" with my coloring. I'd never thought about going to my own wedding. Even with all of my summer trips with Meri, I never let myself wonder how I'd plan my day. And I wasn't wondering about it now, not beyond a passing curiosity about oatmeal dresses, but I did wonder what I was supposed to do now that I knew I was falling for Henry.

Or was it fallen?

I didn't know. I was unfamiliar with the levels and stages of all this. I was still talking myself into believing that it was real and not a product of feel-good hormones, familiarity, and believing in fairy tales.

I didn't want the fairy tale. That kind of perfection, where everything ended up tied in a pretty little bow, didn't interest me. No one lived that way, not even the people who were honest-to-god happy like Acevedo and his wife or Emmerling and her husband.

If I was being honest, happy endings and pretty little bows scared me. They were always too good to be true and they didn't last.

So, no, I wasn't planning a wedding or thinking about finding a new house or doing anything other than taking each day as it came because I didn't know when I'd be able to explain to Henry that the feelings I had for him had grown into something big and overwhelming yet strangely permanent, and I didn't know what to do about it.

There was a weak, rusty spot inside me that wanted more than anything to hear that I wasn't alone in this, that Henry was falling for me too, and maybe we could be overwhelmed about it together. I didn't need to hear those words from him though as the days slipped past and he came to occupy every corner of my life, I had to admit that I wanted them.

"Though you should grow this out," Brie said, a shaky hand brushing at my hair. "You can't do much with it being that length. A couple more inches will do the trick."

Again, I couldn't help it. "The trick for what?"

"Your wedding," she said loudly.

"Right, well, I like my hair better when it falls somewhere between my chin and shoulder. It's easier to tie back in braids too."

"You look like a child when you do that. Especially when you wear those tragic little clogs."

I made a pointed glance at my watch that sent her swiveling in her chair again. "Has he tried to call you? Sent a text? Any sign of life?" She shot me a glare that would've shut me up on a different day but I was coasting on a thick layer of not giving a fuck. "I'm just saying, maybe he's delayed. Traffic or whatever. Did he mention why he's in Boston?"

Brie pulled her phone out of her purse, shaking her head as she said, "We didn't get into that." She set her phone on the table, face-down. "Let's get some more drinks."

I picked up her untouched martini. "Same thing?"

She murmured in agreement as she gripped the edge of the table hard enough to turn her knuckles white. For her sake, I was hoping it was a matter of terrible traffic and other explainable delays.

While I waited at the bar, I texted Meri. She lived around the corner from here and had offered-slash-threatened to pull on a disguise, camp out at a nearby table, and support, intervene, or cause calamity as she saw fit.

Whitney

No sign of the sperm donor.

Meri

Should I take off the wig?

Whitney

I can't make that decision for you, honey.

Meri

How much longer do you think you'll wait?

Whitney

I'm pretty sure Brie would wait a week.

Meri

Yeah, I was hoping for something more in the range of 10 to 15 minutes.

Whitney

Me too.

Meri

You're closing in on 90 minutes past the planned time now. That's not an accident. It sucks. I'm sorry. Come to my place when it's over. We'll have cheese.

Whitney

I'll keep you posted.

When I returned with Brie's martini and my vodka soda, I knew she was unraveling. Her cheeks were flushed, her breathing shallow, and her brown eyes rimmed with red. I didn't want to make this worse but Meri was right. Ninety minutes late without getting in touch meant something—and not what Brie wanted to hear.

"What about giving him a call?" I asked as gently as possible. "Just to check in?"

She sank her teeth into her bottom lip. "Okay. Yeah." She blinked down at her phone as tears filled her eyes. "I'll call him."

As she lifted the phone to her ear, the dam broke and those tears came rushing out with hiccupping sobs. As much as I didn't want to be here and I didn't want to meet this selfish jackass, I wasn't about to allow him the pleasure of hearing the child he'd rejected cry over his absence. He didn't deserve it.

I plucked the phone from her fingers and walked into the lobby. The line rang for a few seconds before Colonel Joseph Conklin answered with a rough, irritable, "Yes?"

"Joseph," I said like he was a med student who didn't know how to keep the field sterile. "Hi. Whitney Aldritch. You were due to meet my sister Brie an hour and a half ago."

A nasally sound came across the line that placed him squarely in the category of gross, rude man. "About that," he said. "Plans changed."

"Then you are not in Boston," I said, every single word sharper than a scalpel.

"No." I could almost see the arrogant shake of his head. "We'll do it some other time."

"And you didn't find it necessary to mention that to her?" When his only response involved more sinus production, I continued. "Allow me to make one thing clear and two things certain, Joseph. There will not be another time. This was your chance—your *last* chance—and your choices tonight have foreclosed the possibility of any future contact with Brie. Do not call her. Do not propose future visits. Do not send others to contact her. Should you find yourself in need of a kidney, the lobe of a liver, some bone marrow, I suggest you look elsewhere. She's finished with you. Understood?"

Another nasally inhale and then the jackass hung up on me.

I scowled at the phone. "Lazy son of a bitch." Behind me, I heard a watery sniffle. I turned around to find Brie with tears streaming down her face and both hands filled with crumpled napkins. My stomach flopped down to my feet. "I know you wanted to build a relationship with him but if you heard what he—"

She barreled toward me, her arms wrapping around me. Her hard head connected with my sternum with enough force to steal my breath and make me drop her phone. "Thank you," she whispered. "I know I couldn't have done that."

She sobbed into my shoulder for several minutes while everyone in the bar and lobby shot awkward glances at us. A very kind bellhop picked up her phone, dusted it off with a handkerchief, and handed it back to me with the kind of gracious smile that everyone else could've learned something from.

Then, when she was out of tears to cry, she pressed her palms to her eyes and said, "I need to get out of here. I want to buy something pretty that I don't need and then scream at some TVs in a sports bar or something."

I could only blink at her. I understood the retail therapy but she lost me at the sports bar. I didn't like sports bars. Not my vibe. And I'd never known them to be her vibe either. But— "Sure."

She held out her hands like she was forcing away the negativity of this night. "Don't take this the wrong way or anything, but I really want to be alone now."

With that, she marched through the lobby and onto the sidewalk, instantly fading into the evening foot traffic. Still, I stared after her for a minute. I didn't want to stay here any longer, but I just felt like I needed to exist inside this moment, this awful fucking moment, before I could do anything else. I had to feel the disappointment and the abandonment and the unfortunate vindication since I'd been right about this from the start.

But then I realized Brie had left her coat here, and the only emotion I could wrap my hands around was frustration. It was an especially cold December night and if the temperatures hadn't already dipped below freezing, they would soon.

I fired off a text letting Brie know I had her coat and I'd be at Meri's place for a bit if she wanted to pick it up. I waited a few minutes, staring at the vodka soda I hadn't touched. I didn't remember why I'd ordered it. Probably to have something to do with my hands or my mouth when our father made his appearance.

It was funny that I'd never thought beyond that moment. Hadn't scripted out a conversation in my head. Hadn't practiced any disinterested stares or planned an exit.

It was almost like I'd known he wouldn't come.

When she didn't respond—and I didn't blame her for that even if I was perturbed about the coat—I rounded the corner to the new-construction high-rise where Meri lived. She liked crisp, open, and new, whereas I leaned toward small, cozy, and old.

"I was about to send out a search party," she said, holding open her front door.

I held up the coat. "Brie left in a slight whirlwind."

"Much like a Tasmanian devil," she murmured. "Come on.

Get in here. Have some of this cheese before I eat it all. Wine? The answer is yes, you need wine."

I let her fuss over me, pulling off my coat and leading me to the best corner of her sectional, pouring an overfull glass of wine and fixing me the perfect plate. With my heels kicked off and a gorgeous blanket tucked around my lap, I said, "This might make me a terrible person, but I think it was for the best that he didn't come."

Meri propped her feet on the ottoman. "You're not a terrible person," she said, holding up her glass for a clink, "and I happen to agree with you."

"It's not that I'm happy she had to go through this or I didn't want her to have a relationship with him."

"You just knew it would never end up the way Brie imagined it," Meri said. "You have a different perspective on this than she does. She has glimmers of hope while you have—"

"An unrelenting awareness of all the ways life will invariably disappoint you."

Meri drew in a breath. "Sure, let's go all the way into those deep, dark pits. I might need something stronger than malbec for that, but let's do it."

I waved her off with a laugh, saying, "Nope, I'm done with the deep, dark pits for tonight. I don't want to spend any more time in the pits."

She snagged a slice of cheddar from my plate. "Then can I ask if you've taken my advice with your best man? Is he blowing out your back day and night?"

I dragged a cracker through some fruity jam. "Don't you think day and night is a bit excessive?"

"You have to build up to it," she said, fully exasperated. "Have I taught you nothing?"

"Apparently not." I gave her an indulgent smile. "It's good, but he's had his hands full trying to put the groom back together again."

"I really thought those kids were going to make it." Her wistful sigh said it all. "I guess that goes to show I don't know what the hell I'm talking about."

"Wedding days aren't a great barometer. Unless one of them is over-the-top awful—and I'm talking aggressive cake smashing, tanking the vows, getting into fistfights on the dance floor—we're not going to get a real read on their relationship."

She arched a brow. "It sounds like you're rewriting our belief system."

"Maybe I am." I gulped my wine before I could blurt out any of the things I'd thought about while dissociating earlier tonight. None of that was fit for sharing, not even with Meri. Not yet. "I just think weddings are the first day of residency when your coat is clean and pressed and you know you're going to be the best doctor in the world. But real life and real medicine are nothing like that. It's exhausting and messy and it's filled with stupid, bureaucratic bullshit created by people who couldn't tell you what DNA stands for."

Meri was quiet and we gazed out her floor-to-ceiling windows for a few minutes. The lights of Boston Harbor winked back at us in the darkness. It was cold out there. The wind blowing in off the water sounded like snow and ice. It was different from the wind in northern New Mexico when snow was on its way. It'd been during my first winter here that I realized not everyone listened for snow.

"I take it he's in the OR this evening," Meri said. She stuck her feet under my blanket. "Or shepherding the groom around town on his grief tour."

"He texted me on my way over here. Just finished a hot gallbladder." I went back for another cracker. "And the groom hasn't required too much shepherding recently. Not that Henry's had the time for it. Emmerling has kept him running."

"I've always liked that about her." She nudged my thigh with her foot. "How about a movie? Or are you heading out since he's wrapped up the gallbladder?"

Though we never spoke of it, there was something of a custody arrangement in place these days. Meri had me for weekday lunches while Henry had me for weeknights. Weekends were split between lazy mornings in bed with Henry and shopping, pedicures, and drinks with Meri. This worked well, but there were some hazy gray spots. Like right now.

"Movie, for sure," I said. No need to mention that Henry had another hour or two in post-op. The custody agreement functioned best when we didn't acknowledge it. "Something we can pick apart. I want to rip open all the plot holes the writers hoped we wouldn't notice. Bonus points for characters sustaining major, life-threatening injuries and unrealistically getting up to save the day."

"I believe you're talking about *Jurassic World*." She flicked on the television and went to her streaming apps. "And I love when we pick apart fictional things. So much less stressful than dissecting our own problems."

I glanced at her. "We could pick apart your real problems. That would require you to share them with me, but you've done that before. You survived."

"Mmm. Nope. Not tonight." She gave her signature *We're not talking about this* headshake. "Not when we have *Jurassic World*."

Two hours, one torn-to-tatters movie, and another bottle of wine later, Meri bundled me into a cab as small, frosty snowflakes started falling. It'd all been a wonderful distraction from the slow creep of the realization I'd spoken to my father for the first time in my life and he'd proven himself to be a lousy dick.

I'd never imagined him as much more than a lousy dick, but now I couldn't even allow for the possibility that my parents were good people who'd tangled themselves up in a bad situation. He hadn't bothered to apologize. He could've lied and we both would've known it was a lie, but at least there would've been some effort. But he'd turned his back on us all over again—and he didn't bother to care.

Instead of staring at that straight on, I watched the snowflakes land on the cab's window and immediately dissolve. They just kept coming, one fleck after another. I didn't look away until the cab jerked to a stop at the bottom of Temple Street.

"Thanks," I called to the driver as I climbed out.

I knew Henry was on his way from the hospital and that I didn't want to go home alone, so I lingered on the corner while snow fell in fine, erratic patches. I'd given him the quickest of highlights and I hoped that would be enough.

"What are you doing out here?"

I glanced up from a study of the snow accumulating around my shoes to find Henry crossing the street. He was in trousers and a fleece jacket as if he was immune to this weather. A St. Bernard of a man.

"You said you were coming," I said. It wasn't much of an explanation. It was the best I could pull together.

"That didn't mean you needed to wait outside." When he reached me, he looped his arm around my waist and led me up the narrow brick sidewalk. "I guess I'm going to have to heat you up and I'm going to have to do it quickly."

"Is there any other way?"

"Not that I've found," he said, all solemn silliness. "I'll warn you right now that I'm very hot. It might be uncomfortable for you. You might find yourself yelling, screaming, swearing. Even begging for a reprieve. But you'll thank me when it's over."

I peered up at him, willing him to understand that I didn't want to talk about my night, I didn't want to talk about anything. If we could play this game, the one where I was cold and he was hot and the world beyond my bedroom door couldn't bother us, nothing else would matter. I wouldn't let it matter. "If that's how it has to be."

He spared me a glance as he reached into my bag to retrieve my keys. "It has to be that way." I ducked under his arm as he held the door open for me. "It may seem extreme, but it might be safer if I tie you down."

I started up the stairs and Henry followed, his hands low on my hips. I wanted to rip off my coat because I could barely feel him through the thick wool, but we were almost home and then we could rip off everything. "That does sound extreme."

"All in the name of safety, I assure you." He scooped me into a hug when we hit the first landing, his arms lashed around me while he kissed my cheeks, my forehead, my lips. "Just think of me giving you all that heat," he whispered. "It's going to be intense. Overwhelming, even. Wouldn't want you to hurt yourself while you're taking it all."

My fingers in his thick, dark hair, I pulled him down for a kiss that said all the things I was too scared to say out loud. And then, "What if I promise to be very, very good?"

"*Fuck,*" he groaned against my lips. "That's it. I can't play anymore. I'm throwing you over my shoulder. Don't say another word until we're in your room."

I didn't let him carry me, though we did scramble up the stairs, laughing and clawing at each other the whole way. Something inside me—though not my heart because that was not where love lived—flipped and flopped as he backed me up against the wall, dragged his fingers up my neck and into my hair, and kissed me like he had scary things to say too.

"Straight to bed with you, young lady," he said as he unlocked the door.

With my cheeks pink and a smile filling my face, I stepped inside—and into complete mayhem.

Right there, in the middle of my living room, was Mason, stark naked and banging my sister over the arm of my beautiful, custom upholstered sofa.

"Oh my god," I said, paralyzed in place and incapable of looking away.

Behind me, I heard, "What's wr—*oh, shit.*"

"Oh my god!" Brie cried when she saw us. "Mason! Fuck! Oh my god, oh my god, oh my god."

Then, somehow, it got worse.

Another beat passed before Mason appeared to recognize that they had company and everyone was screaming, and when he did, he plucked Brie off the arm of the sofa and tucked her behind him. But there was a small ottoman behind him, which she tripped over, leaving her sprawled on the floor, legs sticking up like the back alley of a mannequin factory.

Mason, still naked and exceptionally aroused, went to help her, but with his jeans and underwear tangled around his ankles, there was no hope. He pitched backward as he tried to find his footing, and went flying onto the sofa.

I watched, too stunned to form words beyond quiet shrieks, as he twisted and rolled on my sofa, kicking at his jeans and flailing to find his way out. By the time it was over, there were several stains I didn't want explained and not a single inch of upholstery unacquainted with his genitals.

Brie, who'd pulled on Mason's shirt while on the floor, wrapped him in a throw blanket when he was finished fighting my furniture. We'd be burning the blanket later. The sofa too.

"I'm really sorry," Brie said. "It wasn't supposed to happen like this."

"How was it supposed to happen?" I asked. "Were you confused about this being the middle of my living room?"

Brie brought her fingers to her temples. "Could you just do me a favor and skip the lecture? In case you haven't noticed, I don't need any more shit tonight."

"Dude," Henry said to Mason, a whole bunch of words packed into that one. *"What the fuck?"*

"*You* don't need any shit tonight?" I repeated. "I had the same night you did, in case you forgot that part. Do you think *I* needed to walk into *this*?"

"I think I might've messed up a nut," Mason said, cupping himself over my blanket.

"That's not what I'm fucking talking about," Henry replied. "What the hell is wrong with you? You've been separated for two weeks and—and *this* is what you're doing?"

"*This* is a beautiful, intelligent woman who deserves your respect," Mason replied.

"Don't stand there and pretend you're sad about anything that happened," Brie shouted. "It went exactly the way you wanted."

"That is *not* fair," I shouted back.

"What am I supposed to be doing?" Mason asked, holding up

his left hand and pointing to his empty ring finger. "I'm free. No reason to sit around. Florrie sure as hell isn't doing that."

"You're fucked up is what you are," Henry replied.

"Forgive me for processing my emotions," Brie said. "You should give it a try sometime."

"Do you really think that hooking up with a guy you barely know five minutes after your absentee father affirms once again that he's too busy being an asshole to take part in your life is a good way to process emotions? Because if you truly believe that, there's not much more for me to say."

"Then, for once in your life, don't say anything else," Brie cried, flinging her arms out wide. She jostled Mason's grip on the blanket in the process and it hit the floor, giving us yet another visit with his anatomy.

"That's enough," Henry yelled, one hand on his waist while the other gripped his forehead. "*Enough.* Time out. Whit and I are going to"—he glanced toward the hall leading to my room, but the abandoned clothes and the sofa of ill-repute all blocked the path—"we're going to step outside for a few minutes. You two put some clothes on. Everyone slow down and catch your breath."

I let Henry lead me back to the landing and I plopped down onto the first step, my elbows on my legs and my head clasped between my hands. I didn't have to stay here, did I? It was my house, this perfect little slice of a perfect little brownstone with a view of the horizon and a spider that kept on spinning despite all the reasons to give up, but I could leave that behind. It would be better this way. It would be better for me to leave my home than stay here and watch while Brie continued to leave me.

"It's probably nothing," Henry said, pacing behind me. "There's no reason to panic. Don't build this into one of your catastrophes."

I could go to Meri's place. She had an extra room. But I couldn't go home. Not after all of this. I couldn't pretend that we could keep doing this to each other and live to tell about it.

"Let's not make a big deal out of this," he went on. "So, they got together. It happens. They're both going through difficult times. It'll probably fizzle out if it even lasts beyond tonight."

I didn't want to be the one to go, but after being left so many times, I knew I couldn't endure it again.

"I don't want you to worst-case scenario your way through it," he said. "All those terrible outcomes that you have spinning through your head right now, shut them down. No catastrophes."

It took a minute, but his words finally seeped in. I shifted on the step to face him. "What is it you don't want me to do?"

"I'm telling you not to take this too seriously."

I didn't know why that wounded me, why I felt those words like an accusation. I felt a rush of anger inside me, unruly and made of thorns, and I couldn't shove it down. I couldn't shove anything down.

"Why not? I'm just wondering, Henry, why it's so bad for me to take things seriously. If I don't, who will?"

"Because we don't have to care about them hooking up." He set his hands on his waist. "It's probably a one-time thing."

"And if it's not? You said it yourself, he's fucked up. She's acting out some destructive daddy issues. Why shouldn't I care? And before you tell me it's not my problem, it ends up being my problem sooner or later. Don't you get that yet?"

"Okay, then it's just a new challenge to tackle. Nothing we can't do."

I shoved to my feet. I felt heat climbing up my neck, over my cheeks. "That's all it is to you," I said softly. "It's just one challenge after another, isn't it?"

He drummed his index fingers on his belt. "Yeah. We'll get through it."

I stared ahead at the wall, not wanting to see his face when he heard the question that came from a hollow, fractured place inside me that ached even more after this fight with Brie. "Is that what I am? A challenge?"

"Is that—what?" He jogged down the steps to meet me at eye level and shifted me to face him. "Explain yourself."

I jerked up a shoulder, trying to dislodge him, but it was no use. "I'm just wondering," I said, the words coming out with a harsh, frosty edge, "if it's always been about the challenge for you. I mean, isn't that what you do? You went to med school because the hardest possible rescue assignment wasn't interesting enough anymore. Why wouldn't you then go after someone who is completely off-limits? And won't you get bored soon enough now that the stakes are lowered?"

He dragged his fingers along my neck, pressing and kneading the muscles as he stared at me. "No."

"That's it? Just *no*?"

"It's the answer."

He leaned in to kiss me, but I turned my head. I didn't want that right now. I didn't think I could bear it. I felt as though I was minutes away from crumbling—or exploding.

With a sigh, he said, "You weren't off-limits at the wedding."

I shrugged out of his hold, stomping down a few more stairs. "That was different. We both knew it was just one night."

"Maybe you did."

"You knew it was one night," I argued. "You gave me the whole speech about how you never did things like that and—"

"I didn't until you."

"—and now I'm one of your many challenges," I said. "Is that how it happened? I left without explanation and then, months later, I'm your supervisor, so what choice did you have? It's not like you could've listened when I told you this wasn't an option."

"You wanted this as much as I did," he roared.

I stared at him, his dark-of-night eyes wide and wild, his broad chest heaving with his breath. "Because you run headfirst into challenges. The harder, the better. Isn't that how it goes?"

"That is not what you are and you damn well know it, Whitney."

"Then tell me why I'm wrong," I said.

He held up his hands. "You've had a really rough night, honey. Let's just—"

"Why do you want this? Answer me that, Henry. One reason to believe I'm not your newest obstacle course. That's all I'm asking."

He dropped his gaze to the stairs and his shoulders sagged. "You know how I feel about you."

"Do I? Because it sounds to me like I'm telling you that I need some reassurance, some proof, and instead of giving me any of that, you're saying I should simply know your feelings. What is it you want me to know, Henry?"

He blinked at me. Silence stretched between us until it pulled at the seams. Eventually, he said, "I—I don't know."

We went on staring at each other. Brie and Mason's muffled voices filtered through the wall. The building creaked and hummed. City noises rose around us.

Then my phone rang. I knew right away it was the hospital. My brain shifted into autopilot while I took the call, my gaze never breaking from Henry's.

I'd pushed because I believed he'd give me an answer. Never did I imagine he'd turn up empty. This was Henry, the guy who had a solution for everything. The person who made me promise over and over to let him get us through the tough spots. The one who'd figured out my coffee order and sneaked cupcakes into my office.

And he didn't know why he wanted a relationship with me.

When the call ended, I said, "I have a heart coming in. I need to go."

Henry zipped up his jacket. "I'll go with you."

"No. You're not my resident anymore and, in case you weren't aware, heart transplants are serious business." I pointed to my door. "Take Mason home and remind him that he has an entire divorce to get through. Oh, and have a talk with him about condoms while you're at it."

"Whitney, stop. You have at least an hour before you need to go anywhere and we are not finished here."

"Yes, we are." He reached for my wrist, but I shook him off and started down the stairs. "Don't call me until you figure out why you want to."

It was still snowing when I stepped outside. Tiny flakes hit my cheeks, burning up on impact. When I arrived at the hospital, it didn't look like I'd been crying. Just out in the cold.

Twenty-Five

Henry

General Surgery Rotation:
Day 5, Week 2

"You're scaring me."

I cut a glance at my best friend as he walked down Myrtle Street toward my apartment. It was dark between the streetlights, the old cobblestone sidewalks slick with a dusting of fine, icy snow. Clouds pressed down into the city like they were trying to touch the ground and I had no idea what the hell had happened in the past hour. "You should be scared."

"I can admit that mistakes were made," he said with a laugh. "But I think you're blowing it out of proportion. It's not like you flopped around naked in front of a bunch of people. I really do think I messed up a nut. It feels weird."

I pointed to the right. "ER's that direction."

"Come on, Hazlette." He smacked my shoulder, but I kept my head down. "What's the point of being a doctor if you can't tell me if I'm gonna lose a ball? I don't think I have the personality to be the guy with one ball."

There was no way in hell I could have this conversation right now. Everything inside me wanted to go to the hospital and wait outside Whit's OR. I wouldn't even piss her off by parking myself in the gallery. I'd just wait for her in the hall and then—well, fuck, I didn't know what I'd do. But I had to do something.

Whit thought she was a challenge of mine. She didn't even know the half of it. Yeah, she was an obstacle through and through. Maximum difficulty. Triple black diamond. She was *the* challenge.

And somehow that was a problem.

I didn't understand. I didn't know where this was coming from—aside from her useless father and her emotionally stabby sister—or how to handle any of it. All this time, I'd put so much energy into worrying about screwing this up and never once did I consider what happened when I finally did it.

The only thing that made sense was trying to talk to her again. Trying to explain that—that I needed her. And I was pretty sure she needed me too. Even if she didn't admit it often.

I shook some snow off my jacket as I climbed the front steps to my building. "You're fine. You'd know if you'd twisted the spermatic cord or torn the appendix testicle."

"Yeah, but I *know* something feels weird so—"

"The fact you can walk and talk tells me you're good. Now, please, shut the fuck up."

We made it up the stairs and into my apartment without further discussion of his balls. But then Mason strolled straight into the bedroom, stripped off his jeans, and propped a foot on the edge of the bed to examine himself in the closet mirror. "Everything looks okay," he murmured.

"Because it is," I said, glaring up at the ceiling. "Listen, I have to go. I need to head back to the hospital."

"You said you were off for the rest of the night."

I heard the closet shut and then the rustle of clothes. "Something came up."

Mason emerged from the bedroom in joggers, his hands perched on his hips. "I've never seen you so wound up about anything. When did you turn into the kind of person who gets bent out of shape so hard?"

"This city is filled with women. Have you noticed that? The women are fantastic and they're everywhere. If you stood on the sidewalk for half an hour, even now, at eleven-the-fuck-thirty at night, in a goddamn snowstorm, and asked every woman who passed if she wanted to get some hot fucking chocolate with you, you'd be booked up through the end of the month." I fisted my fingers in my hair. "Did you really have to pick my girlfriend's little sister for your rebound?"

"Number one," he said, holding up a finger, "I happen to like this girl. Not that anyone's bothered to ask, but I do. And second, why the hell does it matter if she's your girlfriend's sister?"

"It matters because you were with Florrie for years and you are still married to her. You haven't even started untangling your life from hers." I pressed my fists to my head when he only shrugged as if this fact was irrelevant. "You, right now, are not the person anyone would want for their little sister."

Mason was quiet for a moment. Then, "I still like her. I would've done things differently if I'd known everyone was going to walk in, but I care about her."

"Great. I don't even know how it's possible for you to bounce from one woman who you planned on being with for the rest of your life to another you met like two weeks ago, but that's awesome. Cheers."

"Things change real fast when you walk in on your wife in bed with someone else."

"And don't you think you need a minute to deal with all the shitty things that come with having your trust in someone shattered? Or are you expecting Brie to hang around while you do that?"

He shot me an impatient glare. "It sounds like you're the one having a hard time dealing."

"Yeah, I am," I shouted, slapping a hand to my chest. "All I wanted was to take Whit home and help her forget about her asshole father. Instead, I had to deal with you forgetting what bedrooms were made for, another Whit and Brie blowup, and then whatever the fuck I did wrong in the hall."

Mason dropped down on the sofa, careful to mind his balls, and blew out a ragged huff. "We should've gone to her room. I'll give you that. But the rest? I'm not the one you need to blame there, brother."

He scrolled through sports news channels while I scowled at the possibility that he was right.

I spent the night waiting outside Whit's OR, and when she stepped into the hall, she gave me one look and said, "No. Not now."

I'd expected that, which was why I said, "Then tell me when."

She glanced over as I fell in step with her and I knew she was trying hard to kill me with those hazel eyes, but it wasn't working. "I'm tired and starving and—"

"Coffee and muffins are waiting in your office."

I knew she wanted to argue, but she took a breath and said, "Thank you. I appreciate it and I also need you to accept that I want some space right now. That probably sounds really selfish considering you brought me breakfast and you've been here all night, if my circulator can be trusted, but that's what I need. Too damn many things happened yesterday and I don't"—she brought her fingers to her temples as she shook her head—"I can't even distinguish one explosion from another."

We stopped in front of the elevators. I stared down at her clogs. Emerald green. I didn't imagine she'd want me to ask about her socks. "I understand."

"I need some time to breathe before I can go through it all again." She glanced away from me. "And it would really help if you figure things out on your side too."

The elevator opened and she stepped into the car. I didn't know what it was I needed to figure out. This was the part I didn't get. "But, Whit, I'm—"

"No." She held up a hand, cutting me off. "Give me a chance to breathe."

I stood there, watching as the doors closed between us.

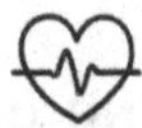

ONE OF THE PERKS OF BEING A FIRST-YEAR SURGICAL resident was that no one gave a damn about me. Sure, I had to be in certain places at certain times and there was always work to be done, but I could spend eight hours of my day in an OR and do nothing other than hold a retractor. Questions might get lobbed my way. The team could involve me in their chatter. Or I could stand there, staring into someone's abdominal cavity while replaying conversations in my head until words lost all meaning.

That was how my day went. *Retract. Replay. Retract. Replay.*

When it was over, all I knew was that I'd succeeded in breaking something. I wasn't quite clear on what or how, aside from the parts about her not wanting to be the newest challenge I'd set my sights on and some sensitivity about me telling her not to be too serious.

Maybe that was enough? I wasn't sure, and there weren't a lot of people for me to ask. Mason was not a resource on intimate relationships at the moment. I loved my cohort—even if they were currently avoidant pains in my ass—but Whit would go off like a bundle of illegal fireworks if she knew I'd shared our issues with them.

It seemed like I had to figure this out on my own.

With that sobering realization in mind, I decided it was time to get my hands around the one problem I could solve and went in search of my cohort. I plucked Tori out of post-op, grabbed Cami outside the surgical ICU, and found Reza hunched over a computer in the residents' work room.

"Family meeting," I announced, towing them into a small conference room.

"I need to get back to post-op," Tori said, her arms crossed over her chest.

"And I should be in the SICU," Cami said, mirroring Tori's pose as she stared down at the floor.

Reza didn't say anything.

"I don't know what the hell is going on here, but we're getting to the bottom of it now. We've been through too much together to throw it away on silent treatments and cold shoulders. I'm sorry I didn't tell you what was going on sooner, but Whit and I were trying to do the right thing." A breath stuttered out of me as it hit me that we'd survived all that stress and struggle, and where we were now? Goddamn, I needed to fix this. To fix everything. "It wasn't about keeping secrets or shutting anyone out, but—"

"Sorry to cut you off, Hazlette," Tori said, "but what the fuck are you talking about?"

"I'm talking about the three of you blowing me off since that night at Acevedo's house," I cried.

"We don't care what you're doing with Dr. Aldritch," Cami said, her gaze still on the floor.

Reza shook his head. "We do not."

"I think we all understand the, uh, logistical issues at hand," Tori said. "If any of us were in that position, I'm positive we would've handled it the same way you did."

"I mean, maybe not making out on the street after a party with colleagues," Cami said. "If there was one thing any of us would've done differently, it might've been that."

I swept a gaze around the group, confused as hell. "If you haven't been icing me out because of my relationship with Whitney, then why does it seem like you're avoiding me?"

Tori clasped her hands behind her back. "Someone is going to have to tell him."

"Tell me what?" I asked.

"We swore we'd never speak of it again," Cami said, her tone lethal. "Do *not* break that vow."

"Tell me what?" I repeated, louder this time.

"There was an incident at Dr. Acevedo's home," Reza said.

I waited, expecting him to elaborate, but it seemed like I had to be the one to beat answers out of everyone these days. "What kind of incident?"

"Reza broke a rock," Cami yelled, pointing at him.

"You peed your pants," Tori shouted, pointing at Cami.

"No, I didn't," Cami whisper-shrieked. "Your small intestine was making really loud cartoon noises."

"Have you returned the hand towels you *borrowed* from Dr. Acevedo's powder room?" Reza asked, tipping his head toward Cami.

I leaned back against the door, even more confused than I was about how I'd hurt Whit's feelings. "What—and I cannot stress this enough—the actual fuck is going on here?"

After a moment where it seemed like no one would ever speak to each other again, Tori said, "It was the pumpkin cheesecake." She strolled toward the window, giving us her back. "I thought it was vegan. The OB fellow told me it was." She shook her head. "Dairy protein destroys my gut. I can tolerate a small amount, but that night—"

"She wolfed down three slices and was eyeing a fourth," Cami said.

Tori hung her head. "Soon enough, I realized my mistake. I knew what was in store for me. That's when I tried to round everyone up."

Reza stepped forward. "I was looking at some of the rock specimens on display in Dr. Acevedo's living room. His wife is a volcanologist. Her collection is exquisite. Back in my university days, I took some geology courses. I found myself intrigued." He folded his arms across his torso. "I picked up one of the specimens. In hindsight, I know it wasn't wise, but I was so curious. Just as I turned it over, a great, thundering noise came from behind me."

"It was Tori," Cami shouted, her entire body vibrating to the point that even her headband was falling off. "The thundering noise was her intestines revolting against dairy protein."

"CCD, I realize how dangerous it is for me to say this, but you need to calm down," I said.

"It startled me," Reza went on with a shrug. "I dropped the specimen to the floor. It broke on impact."

"There was nothing we could do," Tori said. "It was in too many pieces and I didn't have the time to stop and explain everything to the Acevedos."

"What happened to the rock?" I asked.

Tori groaned. "Reza stuck it all in his pockets."

He bowed his head. "It still brings me shame as I imagine they consider it stolen."

I turned back to Cami. "And what is your role in all of this?"

"She was drunk," Tori said.

Cami propped her hands on her hips and lifted her chin. "I was drunk," she admitted. "It was my first big holiday away from my husband and my family, and I didn't handle it well."

"After everything that happened with the rock," Tori said, "we just needed to get the hell out of there. So, I picked her up and—"

"You *picked her up*?" I glanced around the group. "When was this? How did I miss it?"

"I have to assume it's rather simple to miss these things when your entire focus is trained on one person," Reza said.

I couldn't help but grin. So, he'd noticed that. I motioned to Tori. "Keep going."

"I picked her up and everything was fine until we hit that hallway area near the front door," Tori said.

"Hazlette, you have to believe me when I say her gut sounded like a roller coaster. I thought there were people trapped in there. It was so loud and I was so hammered that I couldn't stop laughing. The giggles started and then—"

"She peed her pants," Tori said.

"I did not pee my pants," Cami yelled. "A little bit of pee came out and—"

"She had to wrap herself in towels from Acevedo's bathroom," Tori said. "At this point, we've broken some priceless geological artifact, stolen some very nice towels, and probably left a small puddle on the floor. The only thing we could do was run for it."

I ran a hand down my face. "Oh my god."

"It gets worse," Cami said.

"How? How is that remotely possible?" I asked.

"We make it to my car and my body is surrendering to the dairy. The fight is over. It sounds like there's a rockslide plowing through my intestines. I'm cold-sweating. Cramps like a sinking ship. My hands are shaking. I'm not sure I can do anything but go straight home," Tori said.

"It was tense inside the vehicle," Reza said. "I don't drive and Cami was intoxicated. We agreed it would be best to go to Tori's apartment and then find our own transportation from there."

"We turn on the headlights to leave and there you are with Dr. Aldritch," Tori said, her back still turned to us. "Honestly, I'm not sure it even registered. My only objective was minimizing the fallout."

"We drove off," Cami said, "but only made it a few blocks."

"I pulled into the first Dunkin' Donuts I saw," Tori said. "I couldn't help it. I'm strong, but the dairy was stronger."

"And this is why we're avoiding each other?" I asked. "This...is it? A broken rock, drunk girl problems, and some lower GI distress?"

"You weren't there!" Cami cried. "You don't know what it was like."

"I know we're keeping you to a two-drink max from now on," I said to Cami. "You weren't mad that I'd kept my relationship from you? Not wondering whether I'd gotten preferential treatment during the transplant rotation?"

"Don't take this as a criticism, but I don't think Aldritch is capable of preferential treatment," Cami said. "Just speaking for myself, but that's not something that crossed my mind."

"Me neither," Tori added.

Reza gave a single shake of his head.

"Okay." I tried to gulp this all down. Here I was, spending the better part of two weeks obsessing over this single event when I'd had it completely wrong. "Are we good now? Can we all stop avoiding each other?" When no one responded, I added, "Do not make me drag your asses out for make-up karaoke tonight. These things happen, am I right? Families break shit. Families get into dangerous territory with dairy. Families drink their feelings. Families steal towels and peel out of parking spots like they've got the cops hot on their tail. Families tease each other mercilessly about it all after the fact. So, let me ask you this. Are we a damn family or what?"

"We're a damn family," Tori said, finally turning away from the window.

"We're a damn family," Reza said.

All eyes turned to Cami. "I'd really just prefer it if we never referenced anything involving—"

"Too bad, so sad," Tori said. "We all had rough showings that night, CCD. Accept your part in it so we can move on."

"Fine." Cami rolled her eyes. "We're a damn family—and we're going to karaoke tonight. We've got a long road ahead of us in general surgery and I think we need this."

I pointed at her. "I'm serious about the two-drink max. I'm holding you to it."

Cami grumbled something under her breath as she straightened her headband. "Thanks for being everyone's big brother even if you have been carrying on a salacious love affair with the baddest of the badass surgeons in this place and never mentioning a word of it to us."

That badass surgeon would kill me with one efficient flick of her scalpel if I confessed an ounce more than the basic facts. "What kind of fucked-up family do you think this is? We're not sitting around talking about our salacious affairs, Cami."

"So, you admit it's salacious," she said.

At the moment, it was a pile of burning tires. "I'm not saying a word on the topic."

"And I thank you for that," Reza said.

"Do you think Dr. Aldritch will come along for karaoke?" Tori asked. "We obviously can't invite Dr. Acevedo. To anything. Ever again."

"Yeah, I'm currently rethinking my entire elective agenda because I'm afraid he'll know what I did in his house and with his towels," Cami said. "I die a little every time I see him in the halls."

"I, as well," Reza said.

"Whit probably won't make it tonight," I said with as much neutrality as possible. "Some other time, I'm sure."

"That's a bummer." Tori slipped her hands into her pockets and seemed to study her shoes for a long moment. "There's some stuff I want to talk to you guys about but not until everyone is adequately drunk. Everyone except Betsy Wetsy."

Cami stomped her foot. "I thought we agreed to stop talking about it!"

"We did not," Reza said.

"I'm going to stop feeding y'all," Cami said.

"What? You're going to magically learn how to cook a normal amount of food? I don't think so."

I shook my head with a laugh. "Come on, kids. Back to work."

As we filed out of the room, Cami stopped me with a light hand on my elbow. "Hazlette," she started, "you should know we weren't the only ones on the street that night. I couldn't tell you who was there, but I know I saw other people getting into cars and waiting for rides. Maybe it's nothing. Maybe they didn't see anything. But if anyone is talking about you and Dr. Aldritch, they didn't hear it from us."

I nodded and thanked her, promising to meet up in a few hours. And then I closed myself inside the meeting room and pressed my fists to my eyes as I muttered, "*Fuck*."

Twenty-Six

Whitney

Rule Number Eighteen:
Live in the moment. No one wants to talk about tomorrow.

"At that point," I said, stabbing at my salad, "it was a relief to get called in for a procedure. Any exit from the night of a thousand family horrors was welcome, even if it meant sleeping on the sofa in my office."

Meri stared at me, her fork hovering over her bowl. For the first time in months, we'd been able to get away on Wednesday for our Wednesday lunch. Miraculous. "Let me get this straight. Your sister took daddy dearest's latest rejection and decided the best way to soothe that wound would be hooking up with a guy who's been separated from his wife for like forty-five minutes? And who also happens to be your guy's best friend? *That* was the rebellion she chose?"

I held out my hands. "She's going through a selfish moment."

Brie and I hadn't spoken much since the night I'd walked in to find her with Mason. There was a fair amount of avoidance coming from both sides.

"They're all selfish moments, Whit." She dropped her forehead to her palm, grumbling to herself like this whole affair was really wearing her down. "How did you leave things with the best man?"

I speared a cucumber slice harder than necessary. I hadn't talked to Henry since asking him for space. I didn't want to admit it because I was remarkably stubborn, but I missed him. "I told him I didn't want to be one of his quests."

"Why not? That sounds great. I'd love to be someone's quest."

"But what happens when he realizes that a real relationship isn't that exciting?"

"Neither is medical school or residency, but he seems to be doing just fine with that." She reached for her water, giving me a side-eye glance. "And what do you know about real relationships?"

"Nothing, clearly."

"Listen." She leaned forward and motioned for me to do the same. "Maybe the best man is caught up in the thrill of the chase, but I don't think that's a bad thing. Let him chase you. Play hard to get. Be mysterious. Make it into a role-play. Dress up, dress down, whatever floats the boat. Let it get weird—and then a little strange. You might be surprised to find you like it that way."

I wagged my fork at her. "That's not—that's not the advice anyone needs right now. We need to stay focused."

"Okay, yeah, I can do that. Here we go. Brace yourself. I don't think the thing you're worried about is the thing you're actually worried about," she said. "I think you don't trust that he's chosen you. You're betting on him changing his mind and walking out on you, and you're going to hold tight to that until he has no other choice than to do it. It's the abandonment issues combo platter." She paused to glare at the men seated nearby who were obviously listening to our conversation. When they were adequately terrified, she went on. "I can sit here all day and tell you that those concerns aren't real, but you're the one who has to decide to believe it."

I pushed the remains of my salad around the bowl. "You didn't have to focus so hard."

"Sorry, I only have one setting and it's power thrust." She glanced at her phone before turning it facedown. "I wonder if it would've gone differently if you hadn't walked in on Brie and the groom."

"I mean, I wouldn't be shopping for a new sofa to replace the one that had some dude's balls all over it."

She gave me a *you know what I'm talking about* face. "It was a really rough night for you. Everything went wrong even before your sister got into some shenanigans. I think you were emotionally overtaxed and that's made it all seem so much worse."

Rather than acknowledging any of those fine points, I said, "Tell me about the thing. With the guy. That you've refused to acknowledge for months."

Her gaze shot to her phone. "There's no one."

"Why don't I believe that?"

"I don't know, babe, you're struggling to believe a lot of true things this week."

I steepled my fingers under my chin as I watched her. She was just itching to reach for her phone again. "The only reason you haven't told me is because it's not actually over. If it was, I would've heard about it." When she didn't respond, I added, "If this is something you need to keep to yourself, just say that and I won't ask again. You won't hurt my feelings."

Meri took a sip of water and glanced out at the people walking along Newbury Street. She smoothed the cloth napkin on her lap and straightened the silverware. Then, "It's not over."

"Are you going to tell me who this person is or are you hoping I'll guess?"

After a breath, she said, "Simon."

"Simon...do I know this Simon?"

She ran a finger over her brow. "The Tahoe Dance Floor guy."

"From the wedding?" I cried. "All this time, it's been Simon from the wedding?"

She nodded, her gaze on the table. "Yeah, and believe me, I've wanted to tell you but—" Her phone buzzed in a long, low pattern. She frowned at the screen and then her eyes widened like a pair of full moons. "Shit. Twenty-seven-week twins."

"Can you fill me in on the rest of the Simon story on the way back to campus or will you be jumping into a bike messenger's basket in the next thirty seconds?"

She stood, reaching for her coat as she surveyed the traffic outside. "Do you think I can find a bike messenger? That would be great." She glanced back at me. "We'll talk. I promise. In the meantime, thank you for lunch and don't give up on the best man. I'm rooting for you two."

The elevator was being cranky today. It wouldn't go to the right floors or it went up when it was supposed to go down. It made for a long ride to my office after lunch and I used that time toggling between trying to remember Simon from the wedding and wondering what to do about Henry.

I didn't have any answers when I reached my floor though I decided that was fine because—

"Aldritch!"

I skittered to a stop in the middle of the hallway. Dr. Cossapino marched in my direction, hands fisted on his hips and his mostly bald head tucked low into his neck. Wiry chest hair puffed out of the v-neck of his scrubs. His face was red and his eyes angry. He looked like a charging bull.

"What kind of double standard is it that allows you to run around here preaching about *ethics* and so-called standards of *professionalism*," he roared, drawing the attention of everyone nearby, "while you're sleeping with one of your residents?"

Ice ran down my spine while my salad flipped over in my stomach. *Fuck*. From the corner of my eye, I spotted Jenelle and several other fifth-year residents. The cohort that rotated in after Henry's was nearby. I was pretty sure I saw Cami and Tori. Others spilled into the hallway, following the noise.

Quite the audience I had for this.

I squared my shoulders and tucked my hands in my pockets. I wasn't about to let this gasbag see me fidget even for a second. "That's inaccurate, Dr. Cossapino. Allow me to correct your facts."

"You're not going to get away with this. I know what you're doing," he yelled.

"Of course you do," I said, hoping my voice was as sturdy as it sounded in my head. "Then you're aware that my relationship with this resident began before the start of the residency program, and that when he rotated to my service—which is mandatory, as you know—I recused myself from his training and assigned him exclusively to Dr. Hirano and Dr. Salas's cases." When Cossapino started to huff and sputter, I added, "As I'm sure you can see, it's not that difficult to make fair, appropriate choices. It's just a matter of shifting supervision to another attending and continuing to keep my private life private, but if you have more questions, I'm happy to explain."

A ripple of laughter moved through the crowd gathered around us.

"How convenient that you have an answer for everything," he snarled.

I shrugged and I knew it was going to irritate the hell out of him. "Sure, when it's a simple matter."

"There's nothing simple about you abusing your position," he said. "It's come to my attention that you canceled procedures last month to get your *sister* an OR."

"No, no, excuse me, I've heard enough." I glanced over to find Dr. Emmerling pushing her way through the crowd. "That was all me. You want to holler at someone about that, you'll be hollerin' at me. And before you give me the *young lady* routine, let me hand over some receipts. First off, Aldritch was in a procedure when I made that call. She had no idea it was happening. Two, my patient needed an emergency bowel resection. And finally, for fuck's sake, nothing was canceled. Moved around and rescheduled to put the right people in the right ORs? Yes. Surely you can comprehend the difference, *Marvin*." She clapped her hands together. "Now then. I'm going to invite you to apologize to Dr. Aldritch for being completely unnecessary. If you can't do that, I suggest you walk away."

Cossapino jabbed a thick finger at me. "I'll be watching you."

"Thank you. Your professional admiration means so much to me."

Another roll of laughter from the onlookers. Someone loud-whispered, "Finish him!"

"That's not what I meant and you know it." He turned and stomped off, muttering to himself as he went.

I glanced to Emmerling. "Thank you for that."

She pulled me in for a side hug. "Anytime. I would've thrown hands if he kept going."

Rather than waiting around for another outburst, I ducked past the crowd and into my office. A breath sagged out of me as I paced behind my desk. I'd always known something like that would happen though I'd never expected it to be out in the open, a modern-day duel.

The door swung open, banging into the wall and then slamming shut as Jenelle darted inside. "I need to talk to you," she panted.

"Can I just have five minutes to recover from that or—"

"Now." She bent at the waist, her hands on her knees and her braids swinging over her shoulders. "It needs to be now."

I'd known Jenelle for years. I'd seen her at her best and at her very worst, but this was new and I didn't like it. Even through the corn chowder of my present calamities, I was worried.

"Have a seat." I placed a call to my medical assistant to push back my appointments since I was already one full showdown late. When I dropped into my desk chair, I asked, "What's up?"

"I've been trying to talk to you for a couple of months now," she said, her head bowed and her hands still on her knees.

"I know, I'm sorry about that," I rushed to say. "Let me take you to dinner some night this week. We'll get away from here and I'll be able to give you my full attention so we can—"

"I've been seeing Tori Tran since halfway through her transplant rotation." When I didn't respond right away, she peeked up at me, her brown eyes brimming with tears. "I'm so sorry. It happened and then—then I couldn't stop it, even when I tried. The last thing in the world I'd ever want to do is let you down."

I sucked in a wobbly breath. "Did you give her preferential treatment while she was on the service?"

A watery laugh croaked out of her as she reached for the tissues on my desk. "No. I was probably tougher on her than the others."

"Did you ever make access to cases or OR time contingent upon sex?"

Another laugh. "Hardly. She's the dominant one in this relationship."

"Didn't need that detail, but thank you for clarifying." I pressed a fist to my lips. "You didn't let me down, Jenelle. The power dynamic around here is complicated, but you're consenting adults and it sounds to me like you made an effort to keep the boundaries clean. I'm sorry we didn't get to have this conversation sooner."

She blotted her tears and blinked at me, confused. "You're not going to kick me out of the program?"

Once again, my door banged open. This time, Cal Hartshorn, the Chief of Surgery, stepped inside. "Gonna need a minute with you," he said.

Holding up an index finger to Hartshorn, I said to Jenelle, "Absolutely not."

"I thought I was going to be the only one in my family in four generations to not make it out of residency," she said, almost to herself.

"That won't be happening. If anything, I expect to see you back here next year as a fellow. Text me with a few nights next week that would work for us to grab dinner. We need to talk about your future."

She pushed to her feet and I could almost see the tension drain from her shoulders. She snagged a few more tissues. "I can't believe it was that easy."

"I'm sorry that you thought it wouldn't be."

"Thank you for understanding, Dr. Aldritch."

I held out my hands. She'd heard everything Cossapino said. "How could I not?"

When Jenelle closed the door behind her, Hartshorn dropped into the seat she'd vacated. "Is there something you need to tell me?"

I clasped my hands in front of me. "Not really," I said, as casual as I could force myself to be. "Cossapino is up in arms because I have a personal relationship with a resident. Oh, and he thinks I canceled procedures to get my sister an OR."

"And this resident," he said, rolling his hand for me to fill in the blanks.

I pulled together all the composure I had left in me. There wasn't much in the tank. "We met before he was a resident. I didn't supervise him when he came to transplant. He's been off my service since the end of October."

"Then what the hell is Cossapino's problem?"

I cleared my throat. "He's not alone in trying to catch me breaking—as he'd call it—my own rules."

"Well, that's just bullshit," he said. "And we're going to put a stop to it."

I leaned forward, convinced I hadn't heard him. "We're—what? We're doing what?"

He laced his hands behind his head, saying, "I've tried to let this play itself out over the past year, but I'm tired of these people mouthing off to you. I'll deal with them now. If they want their preferred OR times and the surgical techs whose names they refuse to learn, they'll have to go through me to get them. Be sure to loop me in the next time someone gives you a hard time. The last chief might've allowed it, but I'm not about to put up with that."

"Thank you," I managed. "I-I appreciate it. Very much."

He waved me off. "Don't mention it. You've done the heavy

lifting on this. Now it's my turn. And I still owe you for that week of back-to-back transplants when you covered for Galbraith." He rapped his knuckles on my desk. "But allow me to offer some advice on this personal relationship with the resident. Don't show up at this year's holiday parties together and give the vultures a reason to feed on you. Give it some time. Let him get his bearings here."

"Noted," I said with a wry laugh. "And thank you for that colorful visual."

Right then, when I felt like I had a toehold on my life for the first time in a hot minute, my door burst open again and with it came Dr. O'Rourke. "It wasn't me," he cried, slapping a hand to his chest. "I didn't do it, I swear!"

While Hartshorn and I gaped at him, Stremmel walked in eating an apple. He shrugged like *my guess is as good as yours*.

"What didn't you do?" Hartshorn asked.

"I didn't tell Cossapino—or anyone else," O'Rourke said.

All eyes swiveled toward me. As if I wasn't living through this alongside them. "Well. Thank you for that."

"I wouldn't do that to you," O'Rourke went on. "Or my boy Hazlette."

"He wouldn't," Stremmel said. "He's an asshole, but not a dickhead."

O'Rourke turned a squishy grin on him. "That's the nicest thing you've ever said about me."

"Hazlette, is it?" Hartshorn eyed me. He didn't need to say it, but I could tell he was relieved I wasn't plucking one of the baby-faced twentysomethings. "If these two have already claimed him, maybe he doesn't need much time to get his bearings after all."

They showed themselves to the door while the weight of this day settled around me. On the one hand, I was relieved to have it all out in the open and have loads of support for it too. On the other, the entire surgical wing got to hear the most dreadful version of things from Cossapino. Anyone who wasn't there was going to get ugly, garbled renditions of the truth.

Although it was nice to hand Cossapino his ass and then watch Emmerling do it all over again. Hopefully that part made it into the rumor mill's accounts.

I dropped my arms to my desk and put my head down for a moment, focusing only on breathing. My heart rate evened out after a few minutes and I knew from the buzzing of my phone that I had to get back on schedule. When I lifted my head, I noticed a small box from my favorite cupcake bakery tucked beside a photo of me and Meri in Vancouver.

I pulled the box closer, revealing a folded note. I was smiling before I opened it.

CALL ME ANYTIME.

Twenty-Seven

Henry

General Surgery Rotation:
Day 3, Week 3

I could get myself to and from the hospital half asleep. I knew this because I'd stumbled home after plenty of eighteen-hour days with little more than muscle memory to lead the way. It helped that my commute was pretty much a straight shot down Charles Street and less than ten minutes on foot.

But tonight was different.

Almost thirty minutes different.

I missed the cue to cross at the light. I turned down the wrong side street and didn't realize it until I found myself in an alley I didn't recognize. I had to stop *twice* just to breathe slowly. I couldn't put my finger on what had changed, although the splitting headache cutting most of my thoughts off at the knees probably had something to do with that.

I barely drank at karaoke so I couldn't blame it on that. I was too busy being bowled over by Tori's announcement that she was dating Dr. Copeland to do anything more than nurse one beer. The whole thing came as a shock—but also a strange sort of relief. Finally, I had someone who understood the bullshit of hospital politics from this angle. Someone who knew what it was like to be with a woman who had a lot on the line.

By the time I made it up three grueling flights of stairs to my apartment, all I could do was slide down the door and sit while everything seemed to spin and strobe around me. Cold sweat ran down my back and it set off a shiver that turned and twisted my guts.

How I managed to get myself off the floor and into the bathroom before gagging up the contents of my stomach I would never know, but I was thankful it happened.

I wasn't sure how long I spent on the floor, my head resting on the edge of the tub while I tried to negotiate a peace deal with my belly, but I knew moving—even a little bit—would be the worst choice in the world.

This point was proven when Mason banged the front door shut, which seemed to rattle the building down to its foundation, and my entire being lurched forward for yet another round.

He called out, "I'm back," and I was positive I'd been hit with a sledgehammer.

Since the place wasn't huge and it sounded like I was regurgitating all of Zeus's siblings, Mason showed up in the doorway real quick.

"Oh, shit. Sorry," he murmured, closing the door behind him with enough force to make me hear my brain's heartbeat.

When it was over—this time—and I was pressed back against the wall, a towel wrapped around my shoulders and my head on the tub, I managed to check my phone. There were several texts from

Tori about how we needed to talk Whit and Jenelle into a double date even though we knew they'd hate everything about that. There were a few from the fifth-year we were reporting to in general surgery, endless "Aldritch????? For real?!?!" messages from half the residency program, and not a damn thing from Whit.

That last one didn't come as a shock.

I'd planned on grabbing some ice cream sandwiches and heading to her place tonight on the off chance she wanted to talk, especially after Cossapino reminded everyone that he was about as useful as an ingrown hair. But the last thing she needed was me vomiting on her doorstep. She'd have me expelled from the program and I wouldn't even blame her.

My hands shaking from the ravages of this miserable fucking virus, I typed out a quick message to her.

Henry

I'm sorry about what happened today and that you took the brunt of it. Are you all right?

I waited until she read the message and then put my phone down. I doubted she'd respond tonight. But then the phone buzzed across the tile.

Whitney

Thanks. I'm okay.

Henry

Do you want me to trip Cossapino on the stairs?

A minute went by and then another. After five, I accepted that Whit was maxed out for the day. At least she'd answered. That meant something.

At some point, the front door opened and I heard Mason say, "Back again."

I didn't know he'd left.

He knocked on the bathroom door. "Okay to come in?"

"Yeah?" My voice was like a pile of broken bricks. "It's probably contagious."

"Nah," he said, leaning in the open doorway. "I'm always immune to that stuff."

"So am I," I grumbled.

He dropped to the floor, folding his long legs in front of him and setting down a grocery bag. "Ginger ale, crackers, electrolyte drinks," he said, setting each item on the tile. "You probably have better doctor stuff, but I thought it might help."

I eyed his haul. I trusted my stomach with none of it. "Thanks."

He leaned back, his arms stretched out behind him. "I should probably apologize." When I only stared at him, he went on. "I think I've been a pain in the ass since I showed up at your door. That wasn't the intention, of course, but you know how these things go." He twisted open an electrolyte drink and gave me a pointed look. "You were a pain in the ass for the whole year leading up to my wedding."

"But you see where I was coming from now. Right?"

He slid a sleeve of crackers across the floor to me. "I'm not playing Justifiable Asshole with you tonight, but thanks for the *I told you so.*"

I opened the package, but left it at that. "I did tell you so."

"You know what's funny? Florrie and I had the worst first date in history. Have I ever told you about this?"

I started to shake my head, but quickly thought better of it when my stomach churned. "I don't think so, no."

"Yeah, it was after you'd split with Miah so I think I kept most of it to myself so it didn't get weird." He gave me a sheepish look that said *It ended up kinda weird, didn't it?* "We'd been texting for a few months at that point and we decided to hang out. We made plans to meet somewhere for drinks, maybe dinner, but when we got there, the whole place was locked down. Some kind of event going on. We end up parked on the side of the road, trying to figure out where to go. We make a new plan, she follows me to another spot, and I'm convinced it's gonna be great. But the restaurant is closed. Out of business. At this point, we're two and a half hours into the date and I'm ready to call it. I want to go home and order some wings."

"Fair," I said.

"Right?" He laughed. "But Florrie isn't having it. She tells me she didn't get dressed and put on her makeup just to drive around in circles. She tells me she has a plan and if I can get over these minor inconveniences, I'm welcome to follow her. Dude, she led me to the oldest, most broke-ass Dairy Queen in Nevada, and proceeded to order half the damn menu. Two Blizzards. She ate two Blizzards all by herself while telling me stories that had me cry-laughing and I—fuck." He shook his head at the ceiling. "One of her favorite songs came on and she made me get up and dance with her. We were dancing in the middle of the Dairy Queen. It was the best date of my life. I fell in love with her that night. Not all the way, but a lot."

Maybe it was the dehydration or the headache from hell, but I didn't understand why this was the story he wanted me to hear. I broke a cracker into quarters and then broke those pieces in half. I ate a bit and waited for my body to reject it.

"I was never afraid of falling for Florrie," he continued, "and I was never afraid of making a fool of myself for her. I wasn't afraid of any of it and maybe that's why I jumped in headfirst. Maybe I ignored the signs, the red flags. Maybe I should've stopped to look around before leaping, but I don't regret any of it." He rolled an electrolyte drink toward me. "I don't regret anything that I did with Florrie, not even now that it's over."

"Why not?"

"Because I loved that girl, even if it didn't last. She loved me too, even if she wasn't made for married life. I wouldn't trade any of that away."

I ate another fraction of a cracker. Paused to find out if there'd be an eruption. "Okay."

He fiddled with the cap on his drink. "And I'm dumping all this on you because I've figured out that it's worth going after the good times even if they don't last."

I rubbed my brows. I didn't know what the hell he was getting at here. "Okay."

"Some of us will have shitty endings. My marriage ended. Your parents' marriage ended—badly. But there are tons of people who get together and figure it out, and it doesn't end badly for them."

"I hear what you're saying," I said, "but weren't you drunk and hostile over finding your wife in bed with someone else not that long ago? And then checking off the rebound-sex box with *Whit's sister*? Sorry, but I'm having a hard time believing that you're suddenly cool with it all."

He stared down at his palms, laughing. "I'm not cool with it. Like you said that night, it's gonna take a little while to be anywhere close to cool with it. But I need you to know that just because this happened to me doesn't mean it will happen to you."

Was this what my patients felt like when I strolled in at five in the morning to check their incisions and ask if they'd pooped when all they wanted was to find a few minutes of peace in their post-op misery? Because I had some newfound sympathy. "I'm aware of that."

"Are you? Because it seems like you've hit one rough patch with Whitney and convinced yourself it's all going to hell."

"That's what happened." I pointed at him with half a cracker. "I don't think I convinced myself of anything."

"You had one fight."

"More like a slow-moving train wreck where I hurt her feelings in a way that I don't understand at a time when she was already in a low place, you told her I'd jump out a window to avoid commitment, and then this guy at work called her out in front a lot of people about the ethics of being with a resident when she's an attending—and she takes ethical stuff *very* seriously so I doubt she ever wants to speak to me again."

Mason grabbed some of the crackers and shoved them all in his mouth at once. "When did I say anything about you jumping out a window?"

"That was the effect. You were drunk. Very drunk."

"You had one fight," he repeated. "One rough night where everything went wrong. My wife has been sleeping with a bunch of guys while I've been away at work. Plus the ones you told me about and I'd ignored. Those things aren't the same."

"I know—"

"Then fix it. If you want this, if you want her, stop moping around and fix it." He shrugged. "If it's worth fixing."

I closed my eyes because I felt my stomach sloshing around again and the only thing I could do was concentrate on breathing evenly until it passed. A few minutes went by before I said, "It is."

There were no sick days for a surgical resident. In order for me to take a day off, I had to be the one *on* the operating table. Though I did miss pre-rounds because I was sitting on the second-floor landing in my apartment building while I repeated, "It's just a virus" for thirty solid minutes.

The walk to the hospital zapped what little energy I had and I headed straight for the elevators. As luck would have it, Whitney slipped in right before the doors closed.

Her golden brown hair was loose this morning, not tied back in those twin braids like usual for surgery. She wore a long dark coat with a little scarf around her neck. It looked silky and mostly decorative. I wanted to run it between my fingers and press it to my face to breathe her in. Her trousers were a creamy coffee color and her shoes matched, and she froze when she saw me.

"Hi," I said from my corner of the car, where the walls were holding me up.

She blinked several times. "Hello."

"You never got back to me about throwing Cossapino down some stairs."

She went on blinking. "I thought you said you'd trip him. Throwing seems less plausibly excusable."

"I'd make it look like an accident."

She took a step closer, her eyes narrowed. I loved it when she did that makeup thing with the dark line on her lids. "What's happening here? What's wrong with you?"

"Nothing," I lied. "All good."

"Why are you...green?" She pressed the inside of her wrist to my forehead. "You're cool and clammy. What's that about?"

I dropped my hand on her arm to keep her close a little longer. "Just a stomach bug."

"Lovely." She scrunched her nose. "How long has this been going on?"

"Are you diagnosing me?"

"Just trying to prevent another scrub room contamination." She pulled her phone from her pocket and tapped out a message. "Go down to the clinic after rounds. One of the nurse practitioners will get some fluids and an anti-emetic into you."

"Thanks." Her gaze didn't leave her phone. "So. Cossapino."

"Cossapino." She gave one brisk nod. "It's handled. Spoke to Hartshorn. Everything's fine."

"I'm sorry it all happened that way."

"I figured it would. That's the upside to constantly mining all these worst-case scenarios." The smile she sent me could've burned through steel. "I'm prepared when they happen."

"I didn't mean—"

"Except you did mean it."

My stomach burbled. "I really didn't. I love your worst-case scenarios. I love the way your mind works. I love—"

"Let's not do that this morning. Conserve your energy. Please. You're going to need it."

"Then tell me when I can see you."

"I need another minute. Okay?" She tucked a few honeyed strands over her ear and I realized how much I missed touching her hair. Just all of her. "I just need one more minute when I'm not in the middle of five different crises."

"Is everything all right? After what happened with your father? And Brie?"

The elevator doors opened and Whit stepped forward even though it wasn't her usual floor. "Reference my previous comments on multiple, ongoing crises."

I shuffled forward. "But are you all right?"

She stared down at her shoes for a moment and I held my hand against the door to keep it from cutting me off from her before I was ready. As if I'd ever be ready.

"I'll be fine," she said eventually. "I always am."

I wanted to rip myself open and tell her everything. Just pour it all out and hope the pieces landed in the right order because I couldn't hold them in anymore. But I wasn't going to do that to her. Not here, not now. Not after she'd endured that dickhead Cossapino running his mouth and god only knew what she'd had to deal with after him.

I could wait. I'd waited this long, I could wait until my body didn't sound like a clogged garbage disposal. Until Whit and I weren't making the rounds as the main characters of the hospital's gossip machine. Until Mason went home and things cooled down with Brie. Until she had that minute to breathe.

She shot a glance over her shoulder. "Thanks for the cupcake though. It helped."

Twenty-Eight

Whitney

Rule Number Twenty-Three:
Pack your own protection.

I stared up at the brownstone I called home with a grimace that seemed to pull at every muscle and tendon in my body until my entire being was swallowed into a twisted, snarly pout.

I didn't want to go home. I didn't want to kick off another argument simply by walking in the door and I didn't want to wade through a dense fog of cold shoulder comments until it was time to go to work again.

But it was *my* home and I didn't see why I had to be the one avoiding it any longer.

I dragged myself up the old, winding staircase and I felt the weight of this day, this whole damn week, heavy on my shoulders. The scent of cleaning products hit me first. Panicked—because why else would Brie seek out *and use* cleaning products if not for a true disaster?—my gaze darted around the living room and kitchen. I found Brie standing at the island, a bottle of wine and two glasses waiting beside a small cheese plate.

"What's wrong?" I asked. "What happened?"

She shook her head and gave me a practiced smile like she'd expected that response. "Nothing is wrong. Take a minute to put your things down. Then we'll talk."

I hung up my coat and marched into the kitchen, still looking for bloodstains or scorch marks on the walls. I stood, hands closed around the back of a chair. At a minimum, I was alarmed. "What's up?"

She uncorked the bottle and started filling one glass. "I talked to Mom today."

I reached for the glass before she was finished pouring. Wine spilled onto the counter, but I didn't care about that. I gulped it down while she stared at me, her brows arched and her mouth open.

"I see we're being dramatic tonight," she said.

I grabbed the bottle from her and refilled my glass. "How are things with Pearl?"

Brie nudged the cheese plate toward me. "Well," she said, her focus on mopping up the spilled wine and far away from any sort of eye contact, "we decided it was time for a visit to Colorado. To spend some time with her."

I stared at her dark hair for a moment, wondering what could make her think I had the time or desire or emotional capacity for another family reunion. Weren't we still fucked up from the last attempt? I sure as hell was. "And you're telling me this because you want to do it."

Brie bobbed her head. "I think it's time."

I went to put the wine down, but clipped the edge of the

cheese plate and the glass pitched over, shattering as it hit the stone countertop and taking the other glass down with it. "For fuck's sake." I gave myself a moment to groan, to kick and flail at the world, to mourn the cheese that was now drowning in wine and broken glass. "I'll take care of this," I said, carrying the plate to the trash bin. "We can talk about this idea of yours in a minute."

Brie reached for the plate, saying, "I can help."

"If that's what you want." I let her take it and went back to the rest of the broken glass on the island. "Did she call you?"

She closed the bin and turned on the faucet. "Actually, I made the call."

"You—*shit*." Blood spilled over the tip of my index finger and tears burned in my eyes. It was silly. It was a minor cut. It stung, but it didn't hurt.

"What?" Brie asked over the water.

I didn't answer. I didn't trust myself to speak without sobbing.

A moment later, she appeared at my side, wiping her hands on a dish towel. When she caught sight of the blood, she sucked in a breath. I knew she couldn't stomach it. She had to close her eyes and talk to herself or sing whenever she needed a blood draw, and had a fun habit of fainting if she saw the filled vials.

"Okay," she said, leading me to the sink. "We'll just get this cleaned up. No problem. Nothing to worry about. All good here."

"Everything is not all good here." She held my hand under the running water. "Nothing is good and there are tons of problems. How do you not see this?"

After a moment, she said, "I see it, Whit, but I can't stare too long or I won't be able to function, and I guess that's the difference between us. You see the problems and march straight toward them. I see the problems and go looking for a sunny spot where they won't bother me unless I want them to." She moved my hand away from the water, cringing as a small rush of crimson appeared along the cut. "Another minute under the water."

I stared at the side of her face, not sure I recognized her in this light.

"I thought you'd be happy about me going to visit Mom," she said. "I thought you wanted me to give her a chance. And it would get me out of your hair, which has to be a positive."

"You're talking about visiting Mom...by yourself?"

She snorted. I'd forgotten we had that in common. "Did you think I was going to drag you out there with me? No, no, no. I'm crazy, but I'm not cruel." When I could only blink at her, she added, "I'm sorry about everything that happened with Joseph. You were right about him. I should've picked up on all the red flags along the way, but I didn't, and it was awful. For both of us."

I nodded and let her examine my finger again. The bleeding had stopped. It wasn't deep enough for stitches, but would be annoying for a few days.

She wrapped a paper towel around my hand and pointed at me, saying, "Stay there while I clean this up."

I watched as she gathered the broken glass and mopped up the wine while I slumped against the sink. Exhaustion hit me all at once and I was more than ready to crawl into my bed, wrap myself in Henry's fleece jacket, and sleep until it was time to do this all over again. But we were in the middle of a conversation that felt important and I was also starving, if the rumbles from my stomach could be trusted. The bed would wait.

When Brie finished cleaning up after me, she opened the fridge and surveyed the contents, tapping a finger to her lip. "Okay, yeah, that would work," she said to herself as she gathered ingredients in the crook of her elbow.

"Have you planned when you're visiting Mom or is that to be determined?"

"I've given it some thought. It's time for a new adventure." She opened a few cabinets and pulled out some bowls. "I was thinking about heading out on a road trip after the holidays. I told Mom I was going to visit some friends and stop in some new cities, and I'd make my way out to Colorado, but that my timeline is very flexible. Not sure when I'll get there, not sure how long I'll stay."

I watched as she whisked eggs and milk in a bowl, and though I had many questions about many things, I grabbed the medical kit I kept in the bathroom, sat down at the island again, and kept it all to myself.

"She was good with that plan," Brie went on. "She said she was flexible too and we'd figure it out when I arrived." She glanced around, her brow furrowed. "Do we have vanilla? Like, the stuff that comes in the little bottle?"

I pointed to the cabinet beside the stove. "You don't have to leave," I said. "You don't have to get out of my hair."

"I think I do," she said, shooting me a glance as she resumed her whisking. "But not for the reasons you're thinking. It's not about Joseph or Mason or any of that. I think, maybe"—her shoulders lifted to her ears and she kept her gaze locked on the bowl—"maybe I've been unfair. To you. There are times when I do things that push people away. There are times I know I'm doing it and I know I should stop, but I don't because I want to know what it will take for someone to leave. To decide I'm too much trouble." She balled her sleeve around her fingers and wiped away the tears streaming down her cheeks. "But usually I don't even realize I'm doing it until I look around and notice I'm alone all over again, and that you're the only person left in the world who tolerates me. Like when I was sick. I was alone in that ambulance. No one came to see me in the hospital, not even once. I try to stop being awful to everyone, but somehow I end up doing it to you instead. I want to stop because I know it's fucked up, but every time I try, I just make it worse."

It took me a minute to find my words. "You're not making it worse."

She dropped a slice of bread into the bowl. "I'm not making it better," she said with a sour laugh. "For real though, I've been here long enough and now things are"—she waved the whisk around, sending a splattering of eggy raindrops over the counter—"messy. There's no coming back from that scene you walked in on the other night or the things I said. I'll buy you a new sofa, by the way. Or pay for that one to be reupholstered. Whatever you want."

"It's messy because *we're* messy," I said. "You're not the only one who—" I circled my paper-toweled hand between us. I didn't want to pretend like she hadn't hurt me over and over, and that it had eroded my trust in her down to nothing, but I did want us to find a way to be okay. "You're not the only one."

"Well, even if we weren't messy, it's time for me to find a new sunny spot to avoid my problems. Or finally deal with some of them, who knows." She leveled me with a flat stare. "But don't hold me to it."

"Wouldn't dream of it." I painted some wound glue on my finger and waved it around until it dried. Feeling bold and at least half convinced she wouldn't bite my head off, I asked, "Any plans to see Mason on this road trip?"

She slapped two slices of bread onto a hot pan and shrugged. "Maybe. Not sure yet. He has a lot of issues to work on and he needs to do that without me around." She glanced at me over her shoulder, a small smile pulling at her lips. "It would be cool if it worked out. I don't know if it's because he's in a tremendously fucked-up era of his life and that speaks to me as someone constantly living through fucked-up eras, but we've both seen each other at our lowest moments and that cuts through some of the bullshit. When everything went down with Joseph, my first thought—aside from wanting to crack a beer bottle over Joseph's dumb head—was that Mason would know what I needed."

I went in search of another wineglass. Seemed only fair. "Then I hope he gets those issues resolved."

"Me too and not just because I want to spend time in Tahoe and around all these mountains he hikes. He's fun and he has an *amazing* dick. Like, so good. Form and function, all in one package."

I emptied the last of the wine into my glass. "Yeah, it was hard to miss that the other night when he was wagging it all over the place."

She cringed as she pulled plates out of the cabinet. "I really am sorry about that. Just tell me when you pick out a new sofa."

"I'll keep that in mind."

I glanced at the notifications on my phone. Mostly calendar reminders and alerts about all the houses I'd never buy. Nothing from Henry. Not that I expected anything. Though I did wonder if he was feeling better.

Brie set two plates on the counter, saying, "I really hope we have syrup. It would be a bummer to make it this far and not have syrup. Should've checked on that first."

I stared at the plate in front of me. Whether it was the wine or the general bleariness of my life, I had to ask, "What is this?"

"French toast," she said, her head in the fridge. "Ah, yes! Found some."

As she settled on the seat beside me, I said, "Thanks for cooking. I probably would've taken a jar of olives to bed and called it a night."

"Yeah, about that," she murmured. "Probably should've mentioned it earlier, but this is an intervention."

I froze with the fork on its way to my mouth. "Excuse me?"

"Yep, an intervention. For you. Because Henry loves you and—"

"Henry does not—"

"He *loves* you," she said. "And if you're just going to eat olives in bed until he stops calling and leaving cupcakes at the door—he sent more cupcakes today, I forgot to mention that during the emotional purge segment—then you're no better than me, pushing everyone away just to see if they'll go."

"That's not what I'm doing," I said, stabbing at the French toast. "I told him to figure out why he wants this and—"

"How are you allowed to be a doctor if you're this much of an idiot?"

"Wow, thank you for that. So helpful." I shoved another bite in my mouth. "The thing is, he's a bit of an adrenaline junkie, always hopping from one challenge to another, and I asked him to make sense of his reasons for wanting this."

"He wants it because he loves you," she said, "and it's never been a choice for him."

I dropped my fork to the plate and dragged my fingers through my hair. "I don't know what that means or what I'm supposed to do with it."

"It means he didn't sit down and logic his way through his feelings for you. He's not going to be able to provide you a bullet point list of his reasons. He knows he loves you and he knows nothing else matters."

I wished she'd stop saying that. It felt too close, too real. If I spent too much time with those words lurking in my mind, they might stick around. Then what would I do? What would I do when this thing finally fell apart and those words had burrowed inside me like artifacts? How would I go on, knowing I could run into Henry around any corner, in any elevator, all while those words went unspoken?

"You're telling me people actually go through life like that?" I glanced over to catch her reaction. We didn't have much experience talking about these things.

"All the time." She patted my arm and gave me a smile that said I was very simple. "Think of it this way. When Henry met you, something changed for him. Like a chemical reaction or he was struck by lightning. Since that moment when you locked eyes across a crowded operating room—"

"We didn't meet at the hospital."

"Are you being serious?" She twisted in her seat to face me. "Then where did you meet?"

I cleared my throat. "At a wedding."

"Really? I don't remember you going to any weddings. Whose wedding? When was this?"

"Uh, it was actually Mason's wedding." Murkier territory I could not have stumbled into. "Last summer. June. While I was out of town with Meri."

She tipped her head to the side. "I didn't know you went to a wedding then. Or that you knew Mason."

"Yeah, it's kind of a long story."

Brie gathered the plates and carried them to the sink. "Well, we have about three dozen cupcakes and another bottle of wine. Why don't we sit down and"—her gaze snapped to the sofa and she winced—"or pile into your bed since my room is going through an identity crisis, and we'll make our way through this long story. Because I, for one, need to understand how all of this happened."

I bit back a cool, snappy reminder that we didn't do things like that. She was trying. I could try too. "You want to hear about Mason's ex," I said.

"Obviously, yes, no detail spared."

She dumped all the bowls and pans into the sink while I checked my phone again.

"Text him. Thank him for the cupcakes. Tell him you need him to create a slide deck outlining his adoration for you. Whatever. Just don't go to bed with olives."

The funny thing was, I knew Henry would create a slide deck if I asked for one. He'd get serious about it too—while also being extremely silly—and he'd make a whole event out of it. He'd do anything I asked.

Thinking about that hurt my heart.

Not the one in my chest. Not the organ I knew better than any other in the human body. No, I felt this pain in a place I couldn't examine, couldn't study. I couldn't even press a hand to that pain to alleviate the throb because it was everywhere, all over, all at once.

"I need to change out of this and take off my makeup." I headed toward my room before she noticed the tears in my eyes. "Give me a few minutes, okay?"

Hands in the soapy water, she said, "Call him. I swear I won't listen at the door, but you should know the walls in here are very thin."

True to my word, I stripped off the day's clothes and wiped away my makeup. Then, I pulled Henry's fleece out from between my pillows and stared at it for longer than made sense. Eventually, I tugged it on and sat on my bed, staring at my phone.

Whitney
Thanks for the cupcakes.

Henry
Anytime.

Whitney
Are you feeling better?

Henry
Yeah. Last night was the worst of it. I'm just wiped out now. But thanks for sending me down to the clinic this morning. That helped.

Whitney
You should get some sleep now.

Henry
I'll see you tomorrow.

Whitney
Okay.

I waited, wondering if he'd say anything else. After a minute or two, I set the phone down and buried my face in the collar of his jacket. It smelled like him and that brought the pain roaring to life all over again.

Twenty-Nine

Whitney

Rule Number Eight:
Stay out of the photos.

"So," I said after the server delivered our wine, "this thing with Dr. Tran sounds pretty serious."

Jenelle winced with her entire body.

"I know, I know, I'm sorry," I rushed to say. "You are under no obligation to share anything with me. However, it is Friday night. Neither of us are on call. It's been a disgustingly long week and we've both aired some painfully personal business. If there's anyone who can empathize with you, it's me."

After a moment, she pushed her glasses up her nose and said, "I didn't have serious relationships on the agenda until after my first fellowship year, but she's a pain in the ass like that. And I knew she was trouble right from the start. Just the most infuriating, adorable, know-it-all trouble. God, I love her." She picked up her glass but only stared at the wine. "She figured out that I'm @That-HenriettaLacks."

"How?" I knew Jenelle's social media account and I knew it was as anonymous as possible. She was never on camera. If she spoke, she used voice modulators. The cases she discussed were thoroughly redacted, and never recent ones at that. "Don't tell me she's a hacker on the side."

"Not a hacker, but her brain is faster than any machine." Jenelle pulled out her phone and swiped to a video she'd posted last summer. "I made a mistake of mentioning that case in rounds at the beginning of Tori's transplant rotation," she said. "A few days later, she starts asking questions that all have details from other videos. *Have I ever seen something like this? What would I do in a situation like that?* At first, I tell myself it's nothing. Has to be a coincidence, you know? But then she focuses in. Brings up more precise presentations, asks how I'd address issues of bias in diagnosing."

I handed back her phone. "You must've loved that."

"She spent a lot of time glaring at the back of my head in the OR." A smile filled Jenelle's face. "She started engaging with my posts. Asking questions, requesting follow-ups, fighting with idiots in the comments. I knew it was her from the profile pic, but her handle is @DrThuyToriTran so I couldn't even delude myself. I realized she'd been following me for *years*. Within a week or two, we were messaging constantly and then—then, it wasn't just online. And here we are now."

I dropped my head onto my hand with a sigh. "I love that."

"Me too," she admitted. "Even if she destroyed all of my nice, tidy plans."

"They always do."

She watched me as she sipped her wine. "Is this thing with Hazlette serious?"

It was my turn to cringe. Henry and I hadn't crossed paths in the past two days save for some quick text messages the last few nights. He was recovering from his stomach bug and I was recovering from my—well, I was recovering from my life.

I didn't like the way he'd called out my catastrophizing and I still had a lot of questions about how everything was a challenge to him, but I was embarrassed that I'd taken those things and thrown all my stress and hurt and fear back at him. I'd never wanted to send him away. If anything, I'd wanted him to hold me even tighter. That night, I'd needed it more than anything. I still needed it.

"Perhaps." I hoped I could sneak by with that after prying into her personal life. "More importantly, let's talk fellowships and figure out your next few years."

"I hope you know you're one of the good ones, Dr. A."

I pulled together the pieces of a smile. "Thank you. That means a lot to me."

I remembered with such searing clarity the morning I crept out of Henry's hotel room, thinking the exact same thing about him.

I walked home after dinner with Jenelle, bustling through Boston Common and around the State House in the cold. I would've ordered a car, but I got it in my head that I needed to walk and think, and now I had to deal with the consequences.

As I started down Temple Street, my heels hammering against the ancient brick sidewalk and my nose running from the freezing temps, I ripped off one glove and sent a text.

Whitney
Is it too late to talk?

Further down the street, I saw someone step out of a doorway, a phone illuminated in their hand. My pocket vibrated.

Henry
Never.

When I looked up from the screen, he was right in front of me. As if I'd summoned him.

"Hi," he said. "There's something I need to show you."

"Oh. Okay." That didn't sound ominous at all.

I fumbled in my bag for the keys. When I started muttering about it being too damn dark to find anything, Henry reached right in and snagged them for me on the first go.

"Thanks." I pointed to my door because I'd recently decided to be awkward. "I don't think Brie will be there."

He shook his head. "She and Mason are at my place. He's heading home tomorrow."

"Yeah. She mentioned that." I stepped onto the stoop. He followed. It wasn't a large space and he was *right there*, the frosty white of his breath mingling with mine. I did my best to get the key in the lock and somehow failed repeatedly. "Just a second."

Henry came up behind me, the broad expanse of his chest at my back, and covered my hand with his. I felt his words move over my skin when he said, "Let me."

Without any difficulty, he unlocked the door and held it open for me. He kept a polite distance while we climbed the stairs, never once brushing my hand on the banister or crowding into my space on the landings. I hated polite Henry. I wanted him to yell or tease or slap my ass. Anything but this stiff, withdrawn formality.

Once we were inside, coats shucked and heels discarded, I charged into the kitchen, intent on getting us glasses of water though mostly needing a project so I didn't melt down. "It's very dry right now," I said over my shoulder. "Do you have a humidifier?"

He set a laptop on the island. I hadn't even noticed he was carrying his messenger bag. "I don't."

"You should look into it." I stared into the refrigerator. It was packed with cupcakes. Boxes upon boxes. "I love you, but you have to cool it on the cupcakes. We have enough. More than enough. Which probably sounds crazy coming from me but—oh. *Oh.*"

What the hell did I just do?

Henry took a step toward me, his hand closed around the back of a chair and his scruffy jaw flexed. "That's going to make what happens next a whole hell of a lot easier because I love you too. I've loved you longer than you'll ever believe."

I expected him to rush over and sweep me off my feet, clutching me to him as he spun us around the kitchen and said it over and over.

But he didn't move and neither did I. We stared at each other, frozen, because there was something he needed to show me before we could fix this.

I closed the refrigerator. Not knowing what to say, I asked, "Is there anything else I can get you?"

He clicked a few times, pulling something up on the screen. "No. All I need is for you to hear me out."

He was never solemn like this. Even at work, there was always a lightness to him, a buoyancy that I hadn't noticed until it was gone. He didn't say anything else until I sat down in front of the laptop.

"Last week, I was—" He leaned a hip against the island, crossed his arms. It seemed like I could hear his jaw at work. "I love that you're serious and that you're smarter than everyone so you come up with forty different outcomes for every problem before the rest of us have figured out what the problem is. What I said last week—I was wrong. Everything went wrong that night and I said things that weren't fair."

"I did the same thing," I said. "I'm sorry. It wasn't just you. I—I can't believe I shut down like that."

"It was rough on everyone," he said gently. "If you let me stick around after this, I'll tell you how Mason complained about—and openly examined—his scrotum that whole night."

"No, you actually don't need to explain that. I'm more than content with just that bit of info, thanks." A laugh shook his shoulders and we shifted at the same time, looking toward the sofa. "I'm having it picked up for reupholstery next week."

"That's good. That's...a really good idea."

"I am sorry," I said. "I'm sorry about the way I latched on to your challenges and—"

"About that," he said carefully. "You were right. You are a challenge." He tapped the keypad, waking up the screen. "And you have been for a really long time. Last week—when I said that I didn't know—I meant that I didn't know how to explain that I want this because there hasn't been a minute since meeting you that I didn't want it."

He motioned to the screen. I didn't understand any of it. "Okay. What am I looking at?"

"It's a folder I created in June." He pointed to the date and then the name of the folder. *Wedding Whitney*. "You asked me for evidence. This is the best answer I can give you."

I blinked at the screen. The back of my neck heated. "Am I supposed to know what any of this means?"

He pointed to the files. There were *hundreds*. "Open the first one."

I clicked on the name, simply labeled *1*. It was a distant photo of the bridal party while the photographer was staging them.

"There you are," he said, a hand on the back of my chair as he leaned forward to point at the screen.

I zoomed in and found a blurry bit of me glancing over my shoulder. "How did you even catch that? And where is this from because the photographer is actually in the photo."

"One of Mason's cousins' social media." His knuckles grazed my spine. "Open the next one."

The second image was a wide shot of the tent during dinner and, once Henry told me where to look, I found what appeared to be the back of my head. The detailing on my dress was the only real giveaway. I opened another five files, all photos with the vaguest of glimpses of me. Eventually, still in the dark over here, I said, "I'm not sure what this is."

He pointed to the date stamps beside the file names. June, July, August of this year. "I searched for you," he said. "I looked *everywhere*."

I didn't know what to say. I clicked through several more files.

"When I woke up the morning after the wedding," he continued, "I turned the hotel upside down. I interrogated the front desk staff for information about you until they called security, and then I asked security to pull up surveillance footage from earlier in the day. I talked to all the bridesmaids, though it wasn't without its costs. Due to that legendary toast, half of them slapped me before I could say a word and the other half tossed their mimosas at me. I almost missed my flight to come here. I was ready to skip orientation and you know that's as good as throwing away my spot in this program."

I nodded, still staring at the screen.

"I watched Mason and Florrie's god-awful wedding video dozens of times for a glimpse of you. I went through thousands of photos to find you. Literally thousands. These are just ones that seemed like a lead. And for *months*, this"—he motioned to the blurry images—"was the best proof I had that you were real and not a gorgeous goddamn dream who turned my life upside down."

He'd searched for me and then he'd waited—and then he waited again while I made sense of myself. All this time. I brought a hand to my chest, tangling a finger in my necklace as my heart raced and the images flew past.

With a stiff laugh, he said, "I've been calling this my psychopath wall since the summer. Though that might not help my case." He pulled a stack of papers from his bag and set them on the counter. The top sheet was covered in numbers and notes. "From there, I started matching the photos to people on the guest list. It didn't occur to me that you weren't on the list. Obviously my first mistake, given your flexible relationship with invitations."

I opened more files. Most featured Florrie, Mason, and their families or the bridal party. As I scrolled through, Henry offered brief footnotes like *I thought that was your arm* and *I wasn't sure if that was us on the dance floor* and *Nothing useful in that one.*

"The guest list led nowhere, but then I figured I'd focus on your table. Someone had to know who you were and all I had to do was compare the seating chart to the photos. That logic held water until the end of July when I realized most of the people at your table weren't sitting where they were assigned."

He dropped another stack of papers on the island. The seating chart, complete with thumbnail photos of people positioned around the table. It was a little messy, a bit haphazard. I could see what he meant about the psychopath wall now. Throw in some red yarn and we'd be in business.

"Apparently, no one sat where they were assigned," he said, his outrage obvious. "I don't know what I'm doing wrong in life, but it's never occurred to me to disregard my assigned seat at a wedding."

"That's because you're one of the good ones."

His hand settled on my shoulder, tentative at first, and then I covered it with mine. I heard him exhale though I didn't dare glance up because I knew I'd jump out of this chair and into his arms, and we had to get through this. We had to go back to the beginning so we could start again.

"August was almost over when I'd nailed down the majority of the tables, but I still couldn't get *your* table right. There was one guy I couldn't place at all and—"

I slapped my hands on the countertop. *"Was it Simon?"*

"Who the fuck is Simon?"

A snort blasted out of me and I immediately burst into giggles, dropping my head into my hands. "I don't even know why I did that."

Henry's hand still on my shoulder, he said, "You should know that I love when you snort, but I might love your reactions to it even more. So fucking precious, Whit."

Still hiding behind my hands, I said, "I'm really not."

"Trust me on this. You are." He dragged his palm up the back of my neck and kept it there. "Now, tell me who the hell this Simon is because he was *not* on the guest list."

"Simon is—well, I don't actually know anything about Simon other than his interest in the bodies lost in Lake Tahoe and his aversion to pomegranate seeds, but I promise I'll tell you everything later."

He pulled my chair away from the island and stepped between my knees, forcing me to look up at him. "There's going to be a later?"

"I hope so." Dragging a finger over the seating chart, I said, "I want to hear the rest."

"Basically, I was banging my head against the wall to understand what the hell was going on with your table. Up to that point, I hadn't mentioned any of this to Mason. Definitely not Florrie. I'd called in help to identify some folks, but kept most of this off the radar. And the only reason I had a lot of this info was because the wedding planner included me and Miah on the emails. But all this time had passed and I was no closer to finding you."

I nodded. Meri and I had worked very hard at making sure we couldn't be found.

"I was out of options and I needed you," he said simply. "I couldn't sleep. Even in those brutal first months of residency when I was dead on my feet every damn day, I'd get into bed and I—I'd miss you. And I told myself it was crazy because we'd had *one* night. Twelve hours. But I felt like I knew you and there was nothing I could do to get you out of my head."

"It wasn't crazy."

A real, true smile broke across his face. "That's good to know."

"I thought about you too," I admitted. "After."

"What did you think about?"

I raked my teeth over my bottom lip. "The horrible toast, mostly." He turned and stalked into the hallway, a hand on the back of his neck as he grumbled about never living that one down. "I wanted to know why you couldn't stay in character during the ceremony and whether you liked the job you were married to and how many Taylor Swift songs you knew by heart." I ran my hands down my legs and forced myself to say, "And I wondered whether you remembered me."

"I couldn't forget." He returned to the kitchen, pointing to the piles of papers. "I talked to Mason that morning, before the start of the transplant rotation. I was trying to get more photos and"—he tapped his fingers against his belt—"and if I hadn't been running late for pre-rounds, I would've confessed this whole scheme to him because I knew I couldn't survive September without an answer."

"Funny how things work out sometimes," I said.

Henry closed the laptop and shot a quick glance at me. Somehow, after all this, he looked nervous, his gaze falling to the floor and his finger still wearing a divot in his belt. Then, "Whitney." He said my name like a sigh. "I need you to know that I didn't spend three months of my life deep-diving into the identities of six hundred wedding guests at the slim hope of finding you because I wanted to change a single thing about you. I love you exactly the way you are and I want this because you cleaved my life into two parts that night. There's before and there's after, and even when I had hardly any hope of finding you, I still wanted the after."

I wasn't sure when I'd started crying, but I was, and I couldn't seem to stop. All this time and all this energy I'd put into holding myself together but I couldn't do that anymore.

"When you blew my whole fucking world up by walking down the hallway that morning," he continued, "I knew I'd wait as long as it took. The rotation, the year, the whole damn residency. I didn't care. I still don't."

"A whole damn residency is a very long time," I said, still sobbing my face off.

"I don't think you understand how mad I went looking for you." Henry ducked into the bathroom and returned with a box of tissues. "I would've waited. At least I knew where you were. Hell, I finally knew *who* you were."

I blotted my eyes and cheeks. There was a hot, simmering pressure building in my chest and I didn't know if I was about to laugh or scream or watch while my internal organs shot out from behind my rib cage and flopped on the floor at his feet.

"This is the last piece of evidence I have for you," Henry said, pulling his phone from his back pocket. He tapped the screen a few times before turning it to face me. "Do you see the date that I made this?"

I scanned the playlist and glanced up at him. "Two days after the wedding."

"Because I couldn't get any of this out of my head." He ran a thumb over my cheek. "It was the only thing I could do to focus on orientation—and the truth is, I only survived because Cami, Reza, and Tori wouldn't let me blow it. That week was complete hell. I wanted to fly back to Tahoe and find you. I had to talk myself into staying every day."

"It's a good thing you did."

"You are the challenge, Whit. You're the only one that has ever truly mattered."

Henry reached for my hand and pressed play on his phone. The first chords of "Into the Mystic" filled the kitchen. I went into his arms, my head tucked under his chin and my arms around his waist, and we swayed with the music. It wasn't so much dancing as holding each other while the world went on spinning, while some hearts stopped and others started all over again for the first time, and I finally knew what it meant to fall in love.

"I guess that means I have a challenge of my own," I said, my head resting on his chest.

He locked both arms around my shoulders and I could feel the tension I'd held there all week starting to unwind. "What's that, honey?"

"I think I have to learn how"—I couldn't even get half the words out before I was crying again—"to let you love me now."

"Finally," he said. "Something I can teach you."

Epilogue

Whitney

Rule Number One:
Never outshine the brides.

June

"There's nothing I love more than a sunset ceremony."

I glanced across the suite and found Meri gazing out the balcony doors, her hair still in rollers and the breeze blowing her bathrobe around her legs. "I don't think sunset is until eight tonight and this ceremony is at five, so don't get your heart set on anything," I said. "Also, you need to get dressed, missy."

"That is a massive amount of flowers," she went on, ignoring me completely. "Look at this. Get over here, Whit, you need to see this. I think they're bringing in—my god, they're bringing in entire trees. *Trees!*"

Since my head was busy with a curling iron at the moment, I asked, "What kind of trees?"

"I want to say cherry blossom," she said, leaning over the railing. "But you know I'm better with orchids than I am trees."

Any minute now, the wind off the Pacific would kick up and she'd flash everyone preparing for the wedding down below. I wouldn't say she wanted that to happen, but she wouldn't be too broken up if it did. "You definitely know your dendrobium from your cattleya."

"It's going to be a big party," she added. "I'm guessing three-fifty, four hundred. They've got a lot of chairs."

"And if you'd like your ass to be in one of them, I'm gonna need you to get dressed." I inspected a curl in the mirror before glancing back to Meri. "We have less than ninety minutes until game time and we both know you're going to change your mind about whatever you're doing with that hair before we leave the room. Why don't we get moving, hmm?"

She flopped down on the bed, two rollers sliding out of her silky hair and onto the floor. "How soon are we leaving for Carmel? Because I want to be in a situation where the only thing I'm responsible for is marinating in mud for approximately six hours and none of this *get moving* business."

We were six days into this summer's vacation. Our plan was to follow the California coast from San Diego to St. Helena, with selected stops along the way. "Not until Monday. You'll have to endure two more nights of me keeping you on schedule until you can sit in dirt."

She lifted her head, sending the rest of the rollers flying. "We sent the gift. Right?"

I laughed at my reflection. We'd only devoted two whole Wednesday lunches to poring over the registry. "We sent the gift."

"This is a nice spot," she said, flipping onto her belly. "I'd get married here."

I shot her a pointed glance. The kind that said *oh, really?* and *tell me more.* When she acknowledged none of it, I went back to my hair. "On the lawn? Or the beach? Ooh, what about the ballroom?"

"Beach ceremony, ballroom reception. Only right answer when you're getting married at the Hotel Del Coronado." She scooped up her stray rollers, asking, "And what about you?"

Again and always, I burned the back of my earlobe. I swore under my breath as I fanned my ear. "Haven't really thought about it."

"That's not true," she sang as she crossed the room and took the iron from me. "Everyone has ideas. Especially people who've been to hundreds of weddings."

I watched while she finished curling the last few sections for me. "I don't know." I waved a hand at the balcony. "You're probably right about the beach and the ballroom."

"No, you'd want the lawn. You'd hate walking down a sandy aisle."

I caught her eyes in the mirror. That seemed oddly specific. "Okay."

"And you'd want something smaller than the ballroom. More intimate. You're not inviting the whole world after all."

"What a relief," I murmured. "Anything else I should know about my fictional wedding? Aside from the fact it'll be held in San Diego, of all the random places?"

"San Diego is delightful. You'd be lucky to get married in this town."

"Yeah, of course, sure." I took the curling iron from her because this conversation was getting a little chippy and one accidental burn was enough for today. "Fantastic on all fronts. Hate to mention this, but there's a slight hiccup in the plans because I'm not getting married."

"Not yet, but if you think your best man is going to wait much longer, you're nuttier than I am."

I reached for my makeup bag and started setting out my products and brushes in the order that I'd use them. I needed a bit of structure. "One thing at a time."

"You've been living together for months," she said, still making no progress on her hair or face. "The fact that he's moving in when we get back from this trip is more of a formality than anything."

I started with the concealer, leaning close to the mirror as I worked around my eyes. She was right about the move. By the time Brie headed out to wander the country in January, Henry and I had stopped dancing around whether we'd be spending the night together. The default assumption was yes and it didn't matter whether one of us was on-call or in surgery until three in the morning. Before the end of February, I'd made space for him in my closet and the fridge was filled with his protein shakes.

But it felt like more than a formality. We weren't just sleeping together, just hanging out, just dating, just seeing where it went. Adding someone's name to the utility bills wasn't sexy, but it was a statement. We were doing this and there weren't any questions about it.

Not that I had questions. I didn't. But I did feel like I was holding my breath a bit. Waiting, perhaps, for something to go wrong. I was working hard at not catastrophizing—and I didn't really have any reason to look for worst-case scenarios—though I'd been aware of a slight and growing tension between us for the past few weeks.

I assumed it was the pressure of his first year coming to an end and grappling with all the things that would change when the second year started next week. Add to that exams and final presentations and everything else, and of course he was stressed. It had nothing to do with me.

"I'm not talking to you until you're dressed," I said. "We're not going to be late to this one."

"I am never late," she drawled as she swept into the bathroom. "Everyone else is just too damn early."

MERI GRABBED MY ARM, DIGGING HER LITTLE TALONS into my skin as she said, "They're just so beautiful and I'm so happy for them."

We watched as Tori and Jenelle exchanged rings in front of their families, friends, and most of the surgical residents in the hospital. "Me too." I edged forward to get a better view of Jenelle's dress. "I love that she went for a full, badass ball gown. She looks gorgeous."

"That suit could kill." She tipped her chin toward Tori. "Absolute perfection, though I do hope she's wearing some boob tape because it's breezy here and that blazer is cut down to her belly button."

"Not that far," I said, though I did support boob tape since she'd skipped the shirt. Sequins and crystals ran the length of Tori's trousers and along her lapels, and she had a small boutonniere and blood-red bow tie pinned there. "They're going to make it. I know they will."

Meri nodded. "I think so."

I covered her hand with mine. "We're going to make it too. You know that, right?"

"I really hope that we do." It took a moment for her smile to come together. "I was expecting your best man to catch another case of the giggles, but he's keeping it together today."

Henry stood between Cami and Reza on Tori's side of the altar, looking woodsy and wonderful as always in his tux. Even better, he'd only laughed at the appropriate moments and there hadn't been a snort all day. I'd worried when Tori's old family dog decided to wander between the brides during one of the readings and then proceeded to scratch like he'd rolled in fire ants while Reza read an Adrienne Rich poem, but Henry had made it through with a hand to his face and a stern elbow to the ribs from Cami. "I don't think he has a problem with this union."

"Who would? Those two are obsessed with each other. I can actually see the pheromones wafting off them." She smoothed the skirt of her dark green dress. It made her eyes look incredible, like huge, mossy moons. "Who knew transplant surgery had such a hot hookup scene?"

"I wouldn't need another gift as long as I lived if we stopped referring to my service as a hookup scene."

The hospital gossip channels feasted on me and Henry for some time and there was a bit of snarky chatter about the ethics of all, though I invited myself into plenty of conversations to correct those assumptions. It kicked into high gear all over again when Tori and Jenelle went public with their relationship. That they got engaged only a month later kept it going even longer and gave me a few more opportunities to set everyone straight.

As Henry liked to say, it provided me with a chance to practice lighting people on fire with my eyes. Even if Hartshorn had stepped in as the heavyweight, I didn't mind going a few rounds.

"Does it feel weird to you that we actually know this couple?" Meri watched while her favorite new fetal-neonatal resident dipped my favorite new transplant fellow for a scorching kiss. "I can't decide if it's weird."

"It is weird," I said, thinking back on all the weddings that came before this one. All the couples we'd celebrated, the families we'd wedged our way into. The vows and first kisses, the toasts and the first dances. "But I think I like it even more this way."

"Do you think they'll change for the reception?" Meri asked as we stood to cheer Tori and Jenelle on their way up the aisle. "I know it would be incredible, but I kind of want to obsess over these fits a little longer."

Henry winked as he filed past, Cami on his arm. I pressed a hand to my chest because, even though love didn't live there, it was where I felt it right now. "Me too."

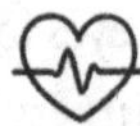

LONG AFTER SUNSET AND LONG AFTER THE COSTUME changes, the toasts, and the cakes—one for each bride—Henry pried me away from Meri with some grumbles about this being his week and her getting me next week, and he led me to a far corner of the dance floor. The band was playing something loud and fast that had everyone bouncing along, but we fell into each other, swaying like always.

"I'm going to miss the hell out of you next week," he said, his lips on my temple and a hand low on my back.

"I'll miss you too." His jacket was long gone and the bow tie loose at his collar, and if I ignored the warm, humid San Diego air, I could almost convince myself no time had passed at all. "But you'll be too busy in the ER with the trauma bros to even notice I'm gone."

"Now, that's just silly. I'd notice when I reached over in the middle of the night and didn't find anything warm and soft waiting for me."

"Like a hot water bottle?"

He sighed like it was a real hassle to put up with me these days. I loved it. "What a little wiseass you are."

I rested my head against his chest and smiled. I loved *him*. "I'll be back before you know it."

"Remember what I told you," he said, his tone turning stern. "I don't want to hear about you two staying up all night, raising hell, and drinking tequila. And, god help me, if you find yourself at a wedding—"

"I'm only crashing for the cake these days," I said with a laugh. "As you're well aware."

"Well fucking aware, honey." He smacked my ass like that sealed the deal. "You might not be the innocent angel you've convinced everyone that you are, but I'm more concerned with Meri." A strangled noise rumbled in his throat. "And Brie."

I wasn't sure which of them the strangled noise was for, but I understood the overall sentiment. The next two weeks were full of variables. An algebraic equation of vacations.

This summer's getaway, while similar on the surface to all our previous trips, came with several new features. We hadn't completely foreclosed the possibility of stumbling into a wedding or two, though like I said, I was only in it for good times and dessert buffets. No bedfellows for me this year.

I had my hands full with the bedfellow I'd found last summer.

Another switch-up was that we were visiting people. Historically, we'd gone to great—often ludicrous—lengths to avoid running into anyone we knew on these trips. We'd wanted those vacations to be complete and total departures from our real lives. We'd *needed* it.

And now, for a grab bag of reasons, we'd carved out time to pop-in on Meri's parents in Orange County and visit Brie in Sonoma. My sister made her way to Colorado sometime in April and spent several weeks there. She hadn't shared many details. Most of what I'd learned about that visit had come from my mother, but I could live with that. It wasn't my job to know everything about my sister anymore. She could do that for herself now.

After Colorado, she'd gone straight to Lake Tahoe and Mason, who was fresh off his divorce and riding high after getting his hands around a whole lot of big feelings. This, Brie was happy to share with me. There was no shortage of updates on Mason's rerelease into the wild or Brie's breathless, sometimes grudging acknowledgment that Florrie had made serious efforts at taking apart their married life with kindness and generosity. She'd insisted Mason get the house even though her family had paid the entire down payment and her father had lobbied hard for her to keep it. In the end, they sold it and split the proceeds.

Brie hung out with Mason for a month or so before heading out to Wine Country where she was housesitting a massive hillside estate for the next six months. Mason visited on his weeks off and between leading mountain expeditions. They'd decided to see where it went, neither in a rush to put too fine a point on anything.

My sister and I were in a better place these days. Still tentative, still slightly distant, but it was like a great storm had blown through and swept the set pieces of our little family drama out to sea and now we had only each other to deal with, not our histories.

"I can't make any promises to you about tequila because it tends to be an essential part of our summers—"

"You say that as if I haven't heard enough stories from you two," he grumbled.

"—but I know how to keep a handle on Meri. As for Brie, well, I think it's going to be all right." I gave him the same shrug I had every time this topic had come up for the past month. "If it's not, Meri has been waiting *years* to step in and I think you know she'd make for a dirty ref."

"That sounds about right."

"I'll be okay," I said, my hands skimming down his sides.

"I'm expecting souvenirs," he said, a little mulish. It was cute.

Next summer, he'd have more time off before the start of his third year. We wouldn't have to cram everything into one week before shipping him back to Boston. "The best souvenirs," I promised.

As we swayed in our corner, we watched the happy couple dancing and soaking up all the love around them. They were going to make it. I could feel it.

Cami and her husband—everyone just called him Dixon—floated over, all smiles. "You're going to be next," she said, wagging a finger in my direction.

"I'm what?" I asked, not sure I'd heard her over the throb of the music.

"Don't listen to her," Henry said. "She gets mouthy when she's drunk."

"I do *nothing* of the sort," Cami replied, all indignance.

"You do, babe," her husband said lightly. "Y'all wouldn't believe the trouble she gets into sometimes."

"Never would've guessed," Henry mused. "We're on our way out. We'll see you two in the morning, yeah?"

Dixon studied his wife with a fond smile. They were going to make it too. "I can't make any promises."

They drifted away, and I asked, "We're on our way out?"

His hands landed on my hips and he held me, his grip tight like he was thinking about plucking me right off the floor. "Have you not tortured me long enough with this dress?"

I glanced down at the peachy-pink dress with the flowers climbing over my shoulders. Where else would I wear it but to a fabulous, over-the-top June wedding? I had yet to find a use for it back home. "It's not torture if you're having fun."

He leaned in, his lips on my cheek, my jaw, my lips. "I'll have fun when this dress is on the floor."

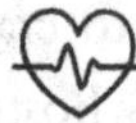

HENRY

WE MADE OUR WAY THROUGH THE OLD VICTORIAN hotel, to the elevators that would return us to our suite. This week had been a magnificent reminder of how incredible it was to be with Whitney away from work. All the weight fell away and there she was all over again, the woman I'd met a year ago.

The second we stepped into the elevator, I had her up against the wall. Hands everywhere, mouth everywhere. I wanted to consume her and I wanted to keep her.

When the doors closed behind us, I trailed my fingers down her arms to her hands until we tangled together. I stared at her, wondering how I'd traveled the circumference of this year and come out on the other side an entirely new person. The things I wanted with this woman, the future envisioned—it would've sent the version of me from last year running for cover.

And yet here we were, in an elevator about to forever change our lives one more time.

"I've been thinking about doing this all night," I said, dropping to my knees.

"No, you haven't," she cried, slapping her hands over her skirt. "It's only a few floors. There's no time."

I ran a hand along the thick of her thigh, around her knee, down to her ankle. "I like where you're going with that," I said, laughing, "but no. I'll save it for when we're in our room."

She blinked down at me, the confusion written across her brow. "Then—"

I pulled the ring box from my pocket. The box I'd been clutching and hiding and hyperventilating over for weeks. "I'm going to need you to marry me, Whitney."

"Ohmygod." She brought both hands to her face as her lips parted, her eyes wide and shocked. The tears came when I opened the box, revealing the ring Meri had helped me pick out. "Oh...my god."

"I didn't think I'd ever be here," I said, tipping a hand toward the floor. "I didn't think I'd want this or—or that I'd trust in something to the point that getting married felt like the simplest choice in the world. Like it was a privilege offered to me rather than the ticking time bomb I'd convinced myself it was." I drew in a breath, not at all surprised to find it shaky. "But I'm here now and I know—I think I've known, at least in some small way, from that first minute—you're the only one for me. And I'll wait. You know I'll wait as long as you want and—"

"No," she said.

My heart stopped. I knew Whit would argue otherwise, but hearing *no* when down on your knees with a ring in hand was a fast way to fuck up normal cardiac rhythms. "Oh." I shut the box with a sickening snap. "Then—"

"I meant," she started, reaching for my lapels and yanking me up, "no, you don't have to wait."

The elevator door opened, hung there, gaping, and then closed again. I staggered to my feet, her fingers still curled around the front of my jacket. Then— "What?"

"I don't want to wait." It rolled off her tongue the way a question would, high and lilting at the end. She took my hand, loosened my grip on the box. She swept her thumb over the velvet lid before meeting my gaze. "I didn't think I'd be here either. I didn't think this was real or that I'd want to give up a single piece of myself in order to make room for someone else, but now I know the truth."

The elevator started descending. I laced my fingers with hers, both of us holding the box now. "And what's that?"

"It is real." Again, the words fell together like she'd only now reached this realization. "And I don't have to give up anything. I can share myself with you and I can know—I can *trust*—that you won't break the things I give you."

"I won't." I shook my head and thumbed the tears off her cheek. "I'd break myself before I ever broke you."

"I'd rather you didn't do that," she said with a sniffly laugh. "Let's just promise to not break each other. I think that's all we need."

"Is that—does that mean—"

The doors opened again as she said, "It means yes, of course. Always, yes."

My lips connected with hers, instinct rather than thought, and I held her as close as I could with that ring box clutched between us. And then a raucous cheer went up and we discovered we had an audience. Tori, Jenelle, Reza, Meri, Cami, and Dixon—they were gathered in the lobby along with another dozen people from the hospital, all shouting and clapping and holding their phones up to memorialize the moment.

I slipped the ring onto her finger. It was elegant and understated, just like Whit, but as Meri put it, also really fucking spectacular. "We're really doing this?" I asked, drying the rest of her tears.

She beamed up at me. "Consider it our next challenge."

Thank you for reading *Change of Heart*! If you need more from Henry and Whit, I have a special chapter for you here (https://geni.us/conepi)

If you need Meri's story, I can promise it's coming! Sign up for my mailing list and you'll be the first to know!

If you need more from Dr. Stremmel and Dr. Shapiro, you'll find them in *The Worst Guy*.

For Dr. Hartshorn and his wife Stella, you'll want *Before Girl*.

For Dr. Acevedo and his wife Erin, check out *The Spire*.

For Dr. Emmerling and her husband Riley, they appear in *Preservation*.

If you're looking for Dr. O'Rourke, I promise his moment will arrive soon!

Author's Note

Organ donation and surgery are personal to me.

The first time transplant surgery touched my family was a living donor kidney transplant. Both the donor and recipient are close family members. Even all these years later, I remember with outrageous, searing clarity the phone call that came after the procedure to let us know everyone had come through and was doing well. It was a crisp, sunny day just before Thanksgiving and I remember my sister and I sobbing in a busy grocery store.

The second time was when my brother died suddenly at thirty-two. There are few things quite so stunning as that kind of loss. Knowing that his organs and tissues have provided others with a more time doesn't erase the fact that we had so little time with him though it makes it more bearable.

Please consider your organ donation status. In many places, it's as easy as checking a box when renewing your driver's license. In the US, www.organdonor.gov and https://donatelife.net are excellent resources. While it's no one's favorite topic, please tell your loved ones of your wishes.

I want to acknowledge (again, always) that while tons of work goes into portraying hospital life in a realistic manner, some of those details do get smoothed down and shaved off along the way. Certain elements are implied and others are glossed over entirely to avoid presenting information that veers off from the true core of the love story. Schedules and timelines are adjusted to give our love interests (and their friends) the most time together. The true portrait of the many staff members involved in surgeries and healthcare as a whole is minimized as not to bog readers down with a massive cast of characters. The realities of malpractice insurance are set aside for café births. All of this is done because the most technically correct book about surgeons and hospitals isn't always the most readable or enjoyable. To those of you who know the healthcare life intimately, I apologize for spots that stick out to you.

With that in mind, I want to touch on Brie's chronic conditions and how her story is not meant to be representative of all people living with Crohn's, repeated bowel surgeries, or permanent ostomies. Brie's experiences with these conditions are simply a snapshot of one woman's life.

Acknowledgments

There are a bunch of people who've been with me throughout the somewhat long, winding journey of this book that started more than two years ago. Thank you so much to Jess, Becca Mysoor, and Erica Russikoff for thinking through this couple (and another one) and then helping me bring it to life. Thank you to my family for listening to me talk about this book for actual years and cheering me/ignoring my dramatic outbursts through it all.

Thank you to Julia Ganis for loving this couple and for always being on my side with this one. I'll never truly be able to express how much I needed that. To Debra Akins, thank you for allowing me to be a hater when I needed it, for experiencing Zoom calls in wide-eyed wonder with me, and for not even batting an eye when I threw out the plan and started over. Thank you to Isabella for your beautifully thorough proofreading eyes.

I was reminded recently (thank you, Sweetgrass and Southern Belle Events) that I have been blessed with some of the best readers in the book world. So many people who've been with me from the very start—which is a long damn time in this world!—and baptized me into Romacelandia. So many people who've found their best friends because they connected over these books. So many people I've known long enough to watch their babies grow up over the years of sharing book recommendations and bringing my new work to you, always a little shocked and amazed that y'all still love it.

I consider y'all part of my bookish family. Thank you for allowing me to be part of yours.

Thank you to the creators, bloggers, and bookish folks who've loved my books. It has always been the readers who make all of this possible and I couldn't do it without you. Thank you for being there for me.

And finally, I want to thank me. Yes, me. My intuition knew what was right for me with this book and it sat there with me for months, if not years, waiting for me to listen. It's altogether too easy to ignore intuition—especially when it's fond of catastrophizing—but I didn't and that has made all the difference.

Also By Kate Canterbary

Vital Signs

Before Girl — Cal Hartshorn and Stella Allesandro

The Worst Guy — Sebastian Stremmel and Sara Shapiro

Friendship, Rhode Island

In a Jam — Shay Zucconi and Noah Barden

Shucked — Beckett Loew and Sunny DuJardin

The Walsh Series

Underneath It All – Matt Walsh and Lauren Halsted

The Space Between – Patrick Walsh and Andy Asani

Necessary Restorations – Sam Walsh and Tiel Desai

The Cornerstone – Shannon Walsh and Will Halsted

Restored — Sam Walsh and Tiel Desai

The Spire — Erin Walsh and Nick Acevedo

Preservation — Riley Walsh and Alexandra Emmerling

Thresholds — The Walsh Family

Foundations — Matt Walsh and Lauren Halsted

The Santillian Triplets

The Magnolia Chronicles — Magnolia Santillian

Boss in the Bedsheets — Ash Santillian and Zelda Besh

The Belle and the Beard — Linden Santillian and Jasper-Anne Cleary

Talbott's Cove

Fresh Catch — Owen and Cole

Hard Pressed — Jackson and Annette

Far Cry — Brooke and JJ

Rough Sketch — Gus and Neera

Benchmarks Series

Professional Development — Drew and Tara

Orientation — Jory and Max

Brothers In Arms

Missing In Action — Wes and Tom

Coastal Elite — Jordan and April

Get exclusive sneak previews of upcoming releases through Kate's newsletter and private reader group, The Canterbary Tales, on Facebook.

About Kate

USA Today Bestseller Kate Canterbary writes smart, steamy contemporary romances loaded with heat, heart, and happy ever afters. Kate lives on the New England coast with her husband and daughter.

You can find Kate at www.katecanterbary.com

"Unless you want to hand-select this boy to scrub in on your procedures, you'll primarily see him during rounds. Do you think you can keep your hands off each other for an hour or two each week? Or will you need eight condoms for that too?"

"He's going to know I'm avoiding him," I said.

She threw her arms out at her sides. "So what? He's just a guy. Let him suffer for a couple of months."

facebook.com/kcanterbary
instagram.com/katecanterbary
amazon.com/Kate-Canterbary
bookbub.com/authors/kate-canterbary
goodreads.com/Kate_Canterbary
pinterest.com/katecanterbary
tiktok.com/@katecanterbary

Printed in the USA
CPSIA information can be obtained
at www.ICGtesting.com
LVHW030926180624
783440LV00011B/125